GRAY DEATH RISING

A BattleTech Collection

BY JASON SCHMETZER

BATTLETECH: GRAY DEATH RISING
By Jason Schmetzer
Cover art by Marco Mazzoni
Interior art by Alan Blackwell, Eldon Cowgur, Harri Kallio, Duane Loose, Justin Nelson, Matt Plog, Anthony Scroggins, David White
Cover design by David Kerber

Printed in USA.

Published by Catalyst Game Labs,
an imprint of InMediaRes Productions, LLC
5003 Main St. #110 • Tacoma, Washington 98407

CONTENTS

FOREWORD

Working on such a huge IP like *BattleTech* leads to some very interesting thought experiments.

For example, there are several family dynasties that have spanned centuries, ruling their houses through direct heirs. Having successive generations appear to take control of a duchy—or a throne—allows for intriguing takes on how one generation rules compared to the next.

This also works for mercenary commands as well. A recent project, *No Greater Honor*, examined centuries of the Eridani Light Horse's trials and tribulations from the Star League era through the current IIClan one.

But what happens when a mercenary unit reforms from the ashes of complete destruction?

Well, you are now holding the answer to that question in your hand. *Gray Death Rising* is the collected three stories that detail the reformation of the Gray Death Legion by the heirs to Grayson Carlyle's legacy. Written by long-time *BattleTech* author Jason Schmetzer, this volume includes the short novel *Decision at Pandora*, which is appearing in print for the very first time here.

Out of all the mercenary units that have come and gone over the centuries, the Gray Death Legion, at least to me, seems to be an obvious choice for revival. The main reason we chose it is because the unit was and is a fan favorite. I've talked to so many readers who share this experience: the very first *BattleTech* book they read was William H. Keith's *Decision at Thunder Rift*, the first Gray Death Legion novel. That was the book that hooked them on the universe.

It was the same for me, all those years ago. I read that original trilogy, and all the other Gray Death Legion books, until the Legion died in the closing days of the FedCom Civil War in *The Dying Time*. And from that moment on, I felt like something was missing.

Luckily, I'm the editor of the line, which meant I could do something about it. And as it turned out, I wasn't the only one thinking that way.

First, I was fortunate enough to have worked with Bill for many years before I came to CGL, and I approached him about writing a direct sequel to *The Price of Glory*. He was amenable to the idea, and in 2021, we published *A Rock and A Hard Place*, the first new GDL novel in almost 20 years. It's an amazing read, continuing the adventures of Grayson, Lori, and the rest of the unit in the Succession Wars.

But as we moved into the new ilClan era, I also wanted to bring back the GDL in a new incarnation. And our amazing line developer, Ray Arrastia, was thinking the same thing. So we put our heads together, developed a story that would fit this new era and tapped Jason to write it.

As it turns out, there was an amazing coincidence in that decision. Because I had no idea at the time, but back when Jason was in grad school, Bill Keith had been one of his first instructors. I asked him to tell you what he told me:

> I had to get a calculator and do this math, but when I was 23 years old Bill Keith taught me how to write a book. I was a kid, cocky, and I can't imagine he even remembers me. We haven't kept in touch. But I remember the lessons.
>
> When John and Ray asked me to tackle the new Gray Death Legion, I said "Sure," because when you get offered work, you say "Sure." But inside, I was suddenly 23 years old again, sitting at a table in a library in Pennsylvania, across from a man who'd written more books than I had years of life at the time.
>
> I had a lot of brilliant teachers. But Bill stood out.
>
> If you read Bill's books, his BattleTech books or his original ones, you get certain themes: good people, making the best decisions they can. Technology in

warfighting changes, but people don't. And in the end, people come first.

I sometimes get asked what my favorite BattleTech *novels are. I can narrow it down to two: Bill's* Mercenary Star *and Victor Milan's* Hearts of Chaos. *Most people expect me to say* Wolves on the Border, *and that is a fine book that I enjoy immensely. But those two are fantastic* BattleTech *books filled with everyday people doing amazing things.*

That's what I tried to do here. I hope I did him justice with these stories.

I love it when the universe gives me exactly what I want—which doesn't happen all that often.

I think Jason's done a fantastic job in creating the new Gray Death Legion, with characters and stories we hope you'll like as much as the first generation—and I can't wait to see your reaction to *Decision at Pandora*.

But we want to hear what you think, too. Leave a review on the forums or Amazon or wherever you get your ebooks. If you all agree, I'll have Jason write more new Gray Death Legion stories.

—JOHN HELFERS
EXECUTIVE EDITOR,
CATALYST GAME LABS

THE PRICE OF DUTY

CHAPTER 1

Words seemed more real on hardcopy.

Ronan Carlyle sat on a folding camp stool at the foot of his *Gauntlet* OmniMech, holding a printout of the general's message loosely in his hand. The paper was already going limp from the moisture in the morning air. He frowned at the dirt, trying to make the words make sense in his head.

"...and because we cannot trust the Archon or the Estates General to look after the people of Arcturus, because they have failed at the basic duty we have sworn our lives to, and because the people of Arcturus and all the worlds of the old Tamar Pact still need, right now, this instant and all the days that follow, protection..."

He'd heard the address at morning formation; he'd heard the words from the speaker, and the whispers in the company behind him, and the noise in his head, but he hadn't really believed it. But there'd been hardcopy waiting in his temporary office, printed on the flimsy yellow paper Lyran clerks carried along on missions for such things. It was thin and light and didn't last long.

You didn't spend a lot of mass carrying stuff from one star system to the next things that wouldn't matter for long.

"Can you believe this?"

Ronan looked up. His sister stood nearby, in her cooling suit and holding a similar scrap of paper. Her blond hair hung loose, long enough she could part it and cover the sides of her head shaved for better contact with her neurohelmet.

"You're holding the same message I got," Ronan mumbled.

"...protection, we must accept that sacred duty ourselves. We must man the walls at night ourselves. We must look around ourselves and declare that these people are our first responsibility. The Commonwealth has failed them. The Clans who conquered them have abandoned them. But we will not..."

Isobel Carlyle frowned and stepped closer. "What does this mean?"

"It means the general is a traitor," Ronan said, letting the words that had been running through his head nonstop out into the air for the first time. "It means we need to find out how much of the rest of the RCT supports her." He crumpled his hardcopy up, frowned, and looked back down at the dirt. "Because if it's a lot..."

The Lyran Commonwealth was one of the star-spanning empires of the Inner Sphere, encompassing hundreds of worlds and billions of people. It was centuries old. It had survived the worst of the Succession Wars and the Word of Blake Jihad. Before the Blackout and the invasions of the last few years, it had remained an economic powerhouse. The planet they now stood on, Arcturus, had been one of the Commonwealth's founding worlds, all those centuries ago. And now...

"It's going to be a lot," Bel said, bringing him back. She crouched down on her heels next to him. "I heard cheering as I was coming over here. She brought the Guards back to Arcturus. And you heard the same barracks grousing as I did on Kandersteg..."

Ronan grunted. Soldiers complained; it had been that way since Sargon. The Twenty-sixth Arcturan Guards regimental combat team was a young unit in the Lyran Commonwealth Armed Forces, but it was still a *Lyran* unit...except it wasn't. It was an *Arcturan* Guard regiment. And it had just liberated Arcturus from the Jade Falcons.

"...we cannot. Because today, we declare the Tamar Pact reborn. Our history with the Lyran Commonwealth is long and *sacred, but Trillian Steiner and her government have abandoned their duty to the people of the Pact worlds. We can no longer look backward for guidance about the future. Today we must look to ourselves, and trust ourselves to build our own brightest future."*

"We swore oaths," Ronan said. "I can't believe all of our comrades will forget that."

Bel frowned, tugging at her hair with her left hand. "We all swore those oaths," she parroted, "but there a lot of people in this RCT who are *from* here. They swore oaths about that, too."

Ronan stepped into the kommandant's office and braced to attention. Kommandant Sunrise Merkel did not look up from his noteputer. Ronan, not having been released from attention, could not relax, but he chanced looking around at what he could see. The room was bare, almost spartan, but there were signs.

Merkel was a swarthy man, too dark to show a blush, with close-cropped hair. He stood just under two meters, where Ronan stood just over, and went exclusively by his last name. With a first name like Sunrise, Ronan understood why. Like Ronan, Merkel wore standard Lyran battledress. Unlike Ronan, who wore the Lyran fist flag on his shoulder, the battalion commander's shoulder was bare.

Ronan swallowed; he'd known there was a chance Merkel supported the general's treachery. When he put his outrage aside and considered it rationally, he knew General Regis would have to stack the deck with people who thought like she did. It wouldn't be much of a desertion if her XO shot her on the way to announce her treason.

"Hauptmann Carlyle," Merkel finally said, looking up. "Stand easy." As Ronan relaxed, he saw the kommandant's eyes flick to his shoulder flash and then back to the company commander's face. "Echo Company has received the general's message?"

"Yes, sir."

"And? What's the response?"

"I haven't asked them, sir," Carlyle said stiffly. He wanted to say he knew none of his MechWarriors would ever turn their back on the Commonwealth, but he couldn't. He only trusted his sister, and while Bel knew most of the troops better than he did, even she hadn't been confident. "I am not in the habit of asking them how their mail makes them feel."

"I see," Merkel said softly. He stood. "There will be another formation in an hour. Outside the hangars. Troops are to muster with personal gear packed for change of station." He paused, mouth working. "It should go without saying that attendance is mandatory."

"Where are we going, sir?"

"Hopefully nowhere," Merkel said. "But we will have to wait and see."

"What does that mean, nowhere?" Bel hissed. She stood one rank behind him, in the same file, in the Echo Company formation. Behind the twelve MechWarriors were assembled the technician and assistant technician teams assigned to Echo Company, in a similar but larger formation. It took a half-dozen technical staff to keep a BattleMech running, but only one MechWarrior. "Why have us pack and get out here if we're not moving?"

"Be quiet," Ronan said. "I've told you everything I know."

"But—" the sound of an approaching skimmer cut her off. Ronan looked to his left, toward the BattleMech hangars. A two-person skimmer skittered toward them on soft skirts; at the last moment it spun in place and flew backward, drive fan blasting to slow it down. Two people climbed out when it stopped: Kommandant Merkel, and Leutnant-Colonel Kathleen McQuade, the regimental operations officer. McQuade, short and stocky, like the tanks she used to command, openly scowled at the assembled troops.

"Company, atten-HUT!" Carlyle called. Heels clicked as the troops and techs came to attention.

Another vehicle appeared, a big civilian commuter bus. The vehicle's big fuel cell engine wheezed and moaned as it approached. Its wide rubber tires squealed as it rounded a corner to come closer.

"That's not enough for all of us," Bel said quietly.

"Be quiet," Ronan growled, his mind racing. Bel was right. That bus would hold maybe thirty troops with their personal gear. He glanced down at the duffel at his feet; maybe thirty-five, depending on the storage underneath the passenger compartment.

"Good afternoon, Echo Company!" Colonel McQuade had a carrying voice. She stepped closer as the bus creaked to a stop, Kommandant Merkel a step behind. Neither of them, Ronan saw, wore Lyran fist shoulder flashes. "Everybody got the general's announcement this morning?"

"Yes, ma'am," Ronan said loudly.

McQuade's head rotated like a tank turret to look at him. Her eyes were dead as Takashi Kurita, despite the fake, friendly smile on her face. "That's good, Hauptmann, but I asked the whole company." She looked back down the line of MechWarriors and past them, to the line of technicians. "What about it?"

"*YES, MA'AM!*" the group shouted back.

"That's good," she repeated. McQuade walked, leaving Merkel where he stood, down the line of MechWarriors. "General Regis has the best interests of the people of Arcturus at heart," she said, still in command voice. "She knows—we all know—that the Arcturan Guard will never let any of the people in the Tamar Pact be abandoned again. The Jade Falcons could come back. The Ghost Bears are still out there. The Hell's Horses are still out there." She turned and marched back up the line.

"We will not—*I* will not—let those bastards come back and threaten a single person on this world, or any other world of the Pact." McQuade all but snarled the last part. Ronan could hear the sincerity in her voice, even if he didn't want to believe it. Worse, he didn't disagree with the mission, but that was the *LCAF*'s mission.

"*That* is why we're here," McQuade said, not shouting, but still able to be heard by the astech in the last rank. "*That* is why the general said what she said. And *that* is why we are not going anywhere."

She stopped beside Merkel again. "At least, the true sons and daughters of Arcturus aren't."

Ronan stiffened. Icy sweat broke out between his shoulder blades, and his fingertips and cheeks tingled with immediate adrenaline.

"Because she has valued your service up to now, the general has decided that any of you who still harbor loyalty to the Commonwealth instead of Arcturus will be allowed to depart." McQuade's expression looked like she'd been sucking a lemon. "Personally, I can't even imagine how someone who'd come back to all of this—" she waved around her, "—could refuse it. But we have fought and sweat and bled together, and the general says that means something."

Ronan could tell from her tone that McQuade didn't really believe any of that, and it scared him.

"So here's the deal: any of you who feel a greater duty to the Commonwealth than to Arcturus, any of you who'd turn your back on the people we are sworn to protect, grab your bag and board that bus. General Regis will send you, at her expense, back to the Commonwealth." McQuade sneered. "Arcturus only wants soldiers ready to defend her."

Ronan wanted to look around, to get the tenor of his soldiers, but he knew he couldn't. He was in command. He had to set the example.

So instead, he bent, grabbed the straps of his duffel, and stood. Then he marched purposefully toward the bus, not looking back. Kommandant Merkel and Colonel McQuade watched him without comment.

The steps toward the bus were the longest of his life. He didn't doubt his choice: his father was baron of Odessa. He knew about duty. There was no other choice he could make.

That didn't mean these rebels wouldn't machine-gun the bus and bury them all in a mass grave to preserve the secret of the general's treachery. But that didn't affect the decision he'd made, because there wasn't any other choice he could make and look at himself in the mirror.

Ronan stopped at the bus' doorway, shouldered his duffel, and turned around. He expected—hoped—that he'd see all of Echo Company following him. He hadn't led the company long, but he trusted his MechWarriors...

His sister Bel was halfway to the bus, frowning at him.

None of the other MechWarriors moved.

Bel came and stood beside him. In front of them, McQuade twisted around to smirk at him. Ronan ignored her. Instead, he looked at Sims and Catawba and Minges, the other MechWarriors of his command lance. None of them would meet his eye.

A clutch of support staff, about a half-dozen astechs with a pair of tech sergeants leading them, came to stand with the Carlyles. The senior sergeant gave Carlyle a confident nod.

There was no one else.

"On the bus," McQuade called so the left-behinds could hear. "I don't want your kind on Arcturus an instant longer than necessary."

CHAPTER 2

CASTEL MILITARY SPACEPORT
GARRISON
LYRAN COMMONWEALTH
2 SEPTEMBER 3151

Hauptmann-Kommandant Jennifer Kipping stood in a shaded part of the hangar, watching the air shimmer around the just-landed DropShip. Behind her, a platoon of military police clustered around a clutch of old Blizzard hover transports. Three of the squads were in normal duty fatigues, but she heard the *clomp-scrape* of the quartet of dog-shaped Fenrir II battlesuits. She frowned at that, not for the first time, and looked at the noteputer in her hand.

These are bad orders.

They were legal orders, though, and her opinion of them didn't matter. They came direct from General Bondayehr himself. Kipping clenched the noteputer so tightly she heard the plastic creak. A discreet throat-clearing told her someone was behind her. "Speak."

"The ship is down," First Leutnant Scholz said. The military police platoon leader had kept his distance, for the most part.

"I can see that."

"The general's orders—"

"Will be carried out," Kipping said. She slapped the noteputer against her leg. "Get them aboard the vehicles. It's time."

"*Jawohl!*"

Kipping turned to follow once she heard the MP officer step away. This wouldn't be the first time she had to carry out a duty she didn't like.

"Sorry, Ronan," she whispered.

When the DropShip cracked its hatch, the outside air smelled dry and foul, tainted with ozone stripped from the atmosphere by the DropShip's thrusters and the petrol-based exhaust of the spaceport vehicles. Ronan Carlyle sneezed immediately as the ozone attacked his sinuses.

After most of three weeks crammed into a cargo hold converted to steerage passenger space with the 216 other Arcturan Guard loyalists, Garrison's air was the most amazing thing Ronan had ever smelled. He shouldered his duffel and eyed the tarmac, hoping against hope for an LCAF transport to be waiting. Or an officer. He'd gotten the DropShip captain to transmit his report the moment they came out of hyperspace, but that had been more than two weeks ago, and there'd been no response.

The rapid departure from Arcturus had been a series of shocks. First, that they'd actually been allowed to depart at all. Ronan had been amazed that they hadn't immediately been put into detention to protect the secret of Regis' treachery. Without the hyperpulse generators, it would take time for news of her desertion to reach the rest of the Commonwealth. Letting a boatload of loyalists go back to a Lyran world would definitely speed that up.

The second shock had come on the first day's transit to the jump point. Interstellar travel was accomplished via JumpShip: slender, delicate vessels that never came near a planet's surface—or its gravity. Travel between JumpShip and planet used heavy, armored DropShips, interplanetary vessels that could, and often did, fight space battles. Where there were a handful of JumpShip classes in service, there were multitudes of DropShip classes, both military and civilian.

The tramp hauler that had brought Ronan and his people to Garrison held air and had a drive, and that was about all he was prepared to admit.

My people. That had been the second shock. He and Bel had gone looking for a more senior officer in the racks of acceleration couches in the hold, but they hadn't found one. That made Ronan the highest-ranking Lyran officer in the group, which put him in command of the entire group. There had only been one other officer at all, a portly, forty-year-old leutnant named Gregor who'd been in charge of a section of quartermasters.

Gregor had been drunk; a couple admin troops near him told Ronan that was the leutnant's normal state. They figured he was going back to the Commonwealth to keep ahead of getting arrested for conduct unbecoming. Ronan had glanced at the unconscious man, sniffed the heavy scent of schnapps wafting off him, and kept his distance the rest of the journey.

Ronan had no plan beyond getting back in touch with his chain of command and reporting the general's treachery. Anything more than that was above his pay grade; he was a 'Mech company commander. Two hundred and more souls was more than he'd ever been directly responsible for before. He'd done his best to keep everyone safe and calm during the trip, but he was anxious to hand off command.

Which was what made standing here, on the lip of the DropShip's bay, with no escort waiting, so frustrating.

Bel came up beside him. "I heard an interesting rumor," she said. "It seems our esteemed captain let all the other passengers debark from different bays. And he's pulled his crew back inside the ship and sealed the hatches."

Ronan frowned. "Why would he do that?"

"I have no idea," Bel said. She looked up and met his eye. "But I had Gonzalez go try one of the hatches, and its dogged tight."

Ronan glanced backward, but he couldn't see the personnel hatch behind the sea of Arcturan Guards waiting to debark. He met a couple of pairs of eyes, nodded as confidently as he could, then turned back to face into the glare.

"It doesn't matter," he said. "We're here. Garrison is a Lyran world. We'll report in, get a debrief, and then we'll get reassigned."

Bel grunted, but before she could say anything the whining keen of lift fans cut across the tarmac. A half-dozen Blizzard hover transports in the blue-gray of the LCAF sped out of a distant hangar and arrowed for the DropShip.

Ronan felt a weight lift off his shoulders. He grinned down at Bel, then stepped down onto the ramp. "Come on!" he shouted to those behind him.

At the bottom, he stopped, dropped his duffel, and eyed the crowd. "Let's get into formation!" he shouted. A couple of the staff sergeants took up the shout. Bel followed him down, but instead of watching the troops, she shaded her eyes and looked toward the APCs.

By the time the APCs got close enough to drown at any reasonable conversation, the staff sergeants had gotten the troops into a ragged-edge square. They were enlisted troops and junior NCOs from across all the regiments of an RCT, and well over half of them were support troops. Ronan knew the staff NCOs had done well to get them to that.

The APCs spread out as they closed, forming a half-circle around the troops, nose-outward so their massive rear ramps faced the Arcturans for easy boarding. Ronan stepped to the front of the square, Bel a few steps behind. He couldn't—and didn't—fight the easy grin that lifted his cheeks. It felt good to be home.

The rear ramps of the APCs all dropped at once, a reverberating *clang* that shook the ears. Ronan frowned.

Ice-blue painted Fenrir battlesuits leaped out of four the Blizzards; the four machines were all set in the crowd-control model, with paired 12.7mm machine guns set over their backs. Battlesuits couldn't snarl, but Ronan felt like if these dog-like armor suit could, they would have.

"Ronan..." Bel said. A susurrus of concern washed across the waiting troops. Ronan's frown deepened, but he said nothing. From behind the battlesuit came several squads of military police, each of them holding a wide-mouthed Crowdbuster riot control rifle.

Any good Ronan had been feeling evaporated.

Last down the ramp was a small woman in a Lyran MechWarrior's uniform. She was slender, with short brown hair and skin the color of soot. Bright, piercing eyes glared at him. Ronan swallowed. *There's no way that's Jen Kipping...*

A moment later the Blizzards' fans cut off. The tarmac was silent.

"Ronan Carlyle," Jen Kipping said. "You're under arrest."

Kipping wanted to frown at the look of pure shock and betrayal on Ronan's face, but she didn't. Instead, she looked past him and—*Odin's balls, is that his little sister?*—pitched her voice to carry.

"You are all under temporary detention," she called. Voices erupted in protest, but she just held up her hand, waiting. Beside her, Leutnant Scholz stood with his hand on the butt of his sidearm, but said nothing.

"You will be taken to Castel Military Reservation," she continued. "Where you will be debriefed, and then released based on the outcome of that debriefing." She put her hand down and gestured at Scholz. "These policemen will now process you for transport."

She stopped, looked at Ronan, and held his gaze. "Welcome back to the Commonwealth."

As the MPs broke into motion, Ronan and his sister stepped closer. "Jen—" Ronan started, but she held up her hand.

"Leutnant Scholz. See to the processing, yes?"

"*Jawohl*," the MP officer said. He clicked his heels and stepped away.

"What the hell, Jen?" Ronan hissed.

"It's good to see you too, Ronan." Kipping nodded to the sister. "Jennifer Kipping."

"Isobel Carlyle," the young woman said. "Pleasure, Hauptmann-Kommandant." The younger Carlyle glanced back and forth between her brother and the new senior battalion commander her brother appeared to know.

"And as for you, *Hauptmann*," Kipping said, "what did you expect when you send a message like that one, accusing a whole RCT of deserting to build a bandit kingdom in Jade Falcon space?"

Ronan took hold of his emotions. She could see it in his face, in the way his mouth worked and his brow furrowed. "It's the truth," he finally ground out.

"Then that will come out in the debrief," Kipping said. She heard herself, heard the flippant tone, and hated herself for using it, but there was no other way she could act. "Shall we?"

Ronan followed Kipping toward the waiting Blizzard. He was a head or more taller than both she and Bel; his steps were longer. He used the time to twist around and make sure his people weren't being manhandled. They looked confused and scared, but they'd looked that way since they'd boarded ship on Arcturus.

"So how do you two know each other?" Bel asked him, sotto voce.

"KSK 9," Kipping chimed in. Ronan ground his teeth. *You can't say something like that to Bel—*

"KSK what?"

"*Kommando Spezialkräfte,*" Kipping said. "*Gruppe 9.*"

"Jen—"

Bel slapped his arm. "You *never* told me you were in special operations!"

"No, I didn't." Ronan glared at Kipping. "And I won't. Not can't. *Won't.* It's classified."

"Not even your sister—" Kipping lilted.

"Look, Jen—Hauptmann-Kommandant—my people don't deserve to be treated like prisoners. They showed exceptional dedication to duty in returning here. And I don't know what the general's plan is, not all the way, but she declared something called the Tamar Pact to all the gods and radar. We need to get a response together, not waste time making my people feel like criminals." Ronan didn't stop walking, but he felt his anger rising.

He didn't know what kind of homecoming he'd expected. He'd spent every waking moment since walking toward that bus and this moment worrying: worrying about what would happen, worry about his people, whether they'd survive the trip. It hadn't even entered his mind that his people might be treated like pariahs.

"Then that's what the debrief will show," Kipping said. Her tone had shifted, a little more serious than before. She stopped at the foot of the Blizzard ramp and spun. "Are you armed?"

"What? No..."

Kipping looked at Bel. "You, Leutnant?"

Bel frowned. "I'm not wearing a sidearm, if that's what you're asking."

"Was that what I asked?"

Bel glanced at Ronan. He nodded. Bel did something to her sleeve and a slender, three-edged stiletto fell into her hand. She flipped it, grabbing the tip, and offered the hilt to Kipping. "Just this."

Kipping grasped the hilt, tested the weight, and nodded. "Good blade."

"I want that back."

"I'm sure you do." With that she spun and led them up the ramp, into the cramped interior of the APC.

"Are you in command here?" Ronan asked as they sat down. He grabbed the buckles of the five-point harness and started pulling them out to their maximum length. He was taller than most infantry troopers he'd met. When Kipping shook her head, Ronan persisted. "Then who is?"

"Hauptmann-General Timofey Bondayehr," she said.

"Who?"

"Don't say that to him," she warned, then pounded the tank hull twice with her fist. The fans started right up.

Behind them, the ramp slid up with the finality of a coffin lid.

CHAPTER 3

Hauptmann-Kommandant Jennifer Kipping stood near the general's desk, trying not to scream, as the staff judge advocate general's representative came to the end of his presentation. It had been forty interminable minutes, standing here, listening to this *dummkopf* prattle on.

"—And so, this office cannot conclusively state that there are no dissenters in the ranks of the forces of the Twenty-sixth Arcturan Guards who arrived on-planet two days ago."

The palatial office's acoustics meant there was no way Kipping could tune the briefing officer's monotone voice out. The floor was marble, the walls marble, and the general's desk was a solid chunk of sand-polished granite that looked like it had once anchored a continent.

"Thank you, Kommandant," the general said. Hauptmann-General Timofey Bondayehr was a squat man, barely a meter-seven. His hair had fled the top of his head a lot of years ago, and Jen knew he was self-conscious about it by the way he combed the long, wispy strands from the sides over the top. He wore a thin mustache that he must have dyed; the hair on his head was yellow-white with age.

Bondayehr had risen to his present rank without ever having heard a shot fired in combat. Kipping knew this because she'd snuck a look at his service record. For most of his career he'd been assigned as LCAF representative to Doering Electronics on Hesperus II. It boggled the mind that there, on perhaps the most important Lyran holding after Tharkad, the capital, Bondayehr had avoided any combat. He'd been stranded here on Garrison during movement, and forced to take command when the Jade Falcon border went apeshit.

Kipping resisted rolling her eyes. If she had to design the worst possible person to put in charge of a planet's military affairs when an entire Clan had disappeared, she might have turned in something like Timofey Bondayehr.

The general tapped his finger on the noteputer. "I have the complete report here?"

"Yes, sir." The JAG officer, Kommandant Lentz, cleared his throat. "I've included an appendix of the raw recordings, if the general wishes to review any pertinent interviews himself."

"Excellent," Bondayehr said. "Context is everything." He glanced at Kipping. "What is your opinion, Hauptmann-Kommandant?"

"Case closed, sir," Kipping said. "The problem is on Arcturus, not here."

Still tapping his finger on the noteputer, Bondayehr nodded several times. His head bobbed in time with his finger. "It certainly seems so." He breathed in and then out. "What is JAG's recommendation?"

"None of our conclusions are what I'd call equivocal, sir," the lawyer hedged.

Kipping almost rolled her eyes again. "What he means, General, is that a lawyer's job isn't to make decisions, it's to advise their principals on the level of risk they're incurring." She glared side-eye at the kommandant. "Two days he's had a platoon of MPs interrogating these people. And all he can tell you is that they *appear* to be loyal soldiers in the LCAF."

"And what do you think?" Bondayehr asked.

"I served with the senior officer," Kipping said. "Hauptmann Carlyle is one of the finest MechWarriors I've ever known. The fact that he is here speaks for itself." She braced a little straighter. She'd be damned if she had to stand here and listen to these two rear-echelon bastards malign the honor of combat soldiers who'd chosen to turn their backs on friends and comrades out of duty to the Commonwealth.

"I see..." Bondayehr said. His finger started tapping again.

"Sir..." the JAG murmured. When Bondayehr looked up, Lentz cleared his throat again. From the side Kipping could see the back of his neck, above his uniform jacket collar. He was red, flushed, with a sheen of sweat. "The hauptmann-kommandant isn't wrong, sir, about our role in this matter. You asked us to gauge the risk these persons pose."

"Risk—" Kipping said, but Bondayehr held up a hand.

"Risk, as I said," Lentz went on, "is a malleable thing. The situation here on Garrison is fragile. The people are nervous about the rumors and the lack of concrete news. The rumors about the planetary militia—" Lentz stopped, swallowing. When Bondayehr didn't say anything, he took is as proof it was safe to speak.

Kipping chewed the inside of her cheek. The situation with the militia wasn't rumored. Garrison had a long and proud tradition of military service; a huge percentage of its sons, daughters, and persons volunteered to serve in the military. Veterans from the regular LCAF often returned from service in frontline regiments and entered the planetary militia regiments. And according to the current rumor mill, those veterans were *pissed*.

Word had broken that the Jade Falcon border looked empty. Across hundreds of light years of space, soldiers were hearing these rumors and thinking of worlds just across the border, some of them newly-lost to the Falcons, and some held by those invaders for centuries. Hell, the teenagers just coming into the Garrison militia had been small children when Clan Wolf had briefly held Garrison itself. Those battles were still fresh in the planetary psyche; Kipping had seen just this morning the words *Never Again* painted on walls and stuck on vehicles in sticker form.

What was missing was a response from the LCAF, liberating those lost words.

Barracks rumors six floors down in the infantry barracks of Castel itself was that the *clerk* here in the desk in front of her was afraid to take action. That's he'd finally found himself in a catbird seat, and he was afraid to risk upsetting anything that might push him off it. Soldiers talk shit about their COs; that was a fact of life. But from what Kipping had heard, the grousing was getting *dangerously* serious. She'd heard people openly using the nickname "Fat Timmy" in the hallway.

"The risk here on Garrison is that word will spread that Lyran soldiers were able to lay down their arms and carve an ancient and historic world of the Commonwealth out for themselves."

"I don't follow," Bondayehr said.

"The Twenty-Sixth Arcturan Guards is in rebellion against the Archon," Lentz said simply. "And not only that, but they did so while in the course of pursuing the action that our own soldiers are grousing we're afraid to undertake."

Bondayehr swiped the air with his hand. "Fear has nothing to do with it," he spat. He stabbed his finger down onto the noteputer. "Nothing!"

Real convincing, Kipping thought.

"And now, we have a contingent of Lyran soldiers who appear to have come back. They're reporting treachery. The rank and file—" it was Lentz's turn to side-eye Kipping, "—will see them as heroes, because they went to liberate the worlds the Jade Falcons have abandoned. And doubly heroes, because they came back."

"I fail to see the risk," Bondayehr said. For once, Kipping agreed with him. "And remember, Kommandant, there is as of yet no proof the Jade Falcons have abandoned their occupation zone." *Except that Sarah Regis just successfully took Arcturus back*, Kipping didn't say. *And declared a whole new star nation there.*

"The risk is this, General: what if our interrogators are wrong?"

Kipping frowned. So did the general.

Lentz grinned, the first confident emotion he'd shown in the whole interview. It twisted his face into a shape that unsettled Kipping in a way she couldn't quite define.

"What if these 216 heroes are allowed to spread throughout the local LCAF? What if they're able to share their stories of heroism on Arcturus, their bravery in returning, but their secret agenda is to suborn additional LCAF forces to their general's cause?"

That's the most paranoid thing I've ever heard, Kipping didn't say. "Your own interrogators found no evidence to support that assertion," she said instead.

"Rot is contagious," Lentz argued. "And if you'll recall, what my investigators said was they can't prove there aren't traitors in that batch."

"Rot," Kipping repeated. "And of course, you can't prove a negative, no one can!"

Lentz ignored her. He knew where the decision would be made. "This is the risk, sir: can you risk exposing soldiers already unsettled by the lack of news to this new influence? What will it do to your career—your reputation—if they talk a battalion of the Garrison militia into deserting?"

"There's *no evidence*—" Kipping repeated, but Bondayehr held up a hand.

"We don't make decisions based on what we want to be true," Bondayehr said. "If I learned anything in my years at Doering, it was that. I can't tell you how many prototypes we had such high hopes for, just to discard when they failed testing."

Kipping opened her mouth to argue, but Bondayehr's hand never wavered. "We can only act on what we know, and what we can measure." He looked at Lentz. "What do you suggest?"

"Cashier them."

Kipping blinked. "What?"

"Dismiss them with other than honorable discharges. No charges will be placed, but separate them from the LCAF. That will send a clear message to the other units on Garrison, and around the Commonwealth: disloyalty will not be tolerated."

"How is it disloyal to refuse to commit treason?" Kipping demanded. She stepped forward, putting her shoulder in front of Lentz. "Sir. You cannot simply throw away the service and honor these people have shown the Commonwealth. They acted in the best traditions of the LCAF."

"Their general didn't," Lentz put in. "Their colonel didn't, even their kommandants didn't. Your man Carlyle is the only company grade officer to have returned."

Kipping bit back her retort. She knew where the decision would be made as well. "Sir. General. This is madness."

Bondayehr shifted his hand to tapping his upper lip. He glanced between Kipping and Lentz. Finally, he tapped and pressed his lip down. "I want it done today," he said to Lentz.

"*Sir!*" Kipping shouted.

"I'm sorry, Hauptmann-Kommandant, but he's right. When a batch of circuit boards is defective, you pull and replace the whole lot. It's the only way to be sure." Bondayehr lowered his hands into his lap. "It may be that you're right, and I'm doing these soldiers a disservice. But I can't take that risk. Their whole RCT went over to the other side."

Kipping spun on Lentz. "What are you playing at? These are your *comrades*."

"My comrades don't consort with traitors."

"They *left* those traitors. They came *back*, here, to rejoin the LCAF and the Commonwealth and *warn* us."

"It's my decision," General Bondayehr put in. "Carry out my orders, Kommandant."

Kipping stood. Her throat was tight. She felt the flush in her face, the tingles in her fingertips. Her pulse was fast enough that she could feel it where her uniform sleeve pressed against her wrist. She looked back and forth between the general and the JAG kommandant. Lentz, with an air of smugness Kipping couldn't stand, clicked his heels and about-faced.

"You can't imagine the mistake you're making," she whispered.

"What's that?" Bondayehr asked. He'd already keyed the noteputer open, ignoring her. "If there's nothing else, Hauptmann-Kommandant, you're dismissed."

Kipping opened and closed her mouth. "Thank you, sir," she made herself say.

Ronan Carlyle actually shuddered in fury when he heard the key rattle in the door to his cell. For two days they'd been locked up like criminals, being questioned, then questioned again. He hadn't seen or spoken to Bel or any of the others. His hands, curled into fists, shook. He stood as the door stood open, putting his hands at his side. He wasn't surprised when Jen Kipping stepped inside.

"This has gone on long enough, Jen," he barked. He knew she didn't deserve his anger, that she was under discipline and following orders, but he couldn't help it. Ronan wasn't an angry man, not usually, but this was beyond the pale.

"It's over," she said, not meeting his eyes. Something in her voice made him angrier, not less so. Her words should have been calming.

"What do you mean?"

Now Jen looked up, and for the first time since Dustball he saw honest, naked rage in her eyes. "You don't deserve this," she told him. "None of you do."

"What?"

Jen swallowed. Ronan frowned, his anger shifting back and forth between fear and anger, which only made him angrier. He was a big man. His fight or flight reflex defaulted to *fight*.

Two MPs stepped into the cell behind her. Ronan frowned, stepped back.

"Ronan Carlyle," Jen said, her voice hollow, "you are hereby relieved of your commission and discharged from the Lyran Commonwealth Armed Forces..."

CHAPTER 4

**BASTION
GARRISON
LYRAN COMMONWEALTH
14 SEPTEMBER 3151**

"Bel," Ronan said, "I really don't have time for this."

"You do," Bel said. "You're not going to believe what Buthra's people found."

Ronan sighed and pushed back from the too-small desk. When he stood, his knees and hips cracked and popped loud enough that she looked at him and chuckled. "Getting old, big brother."

"It's not the years," he said. "It's the kilometers. And this damned desk." He knew he looked like an adult behind a kindergartener's desk. It was the only desk in the office. And he wasn't going to put precious funds toward furniture.

He waved her out of the small office in front of him, then followed. Outside, a pair of admins worked at workstations in the converted trailer-cum-office. Neither looked up as the Carlyles passed, which was fine.

It wasn't like they were soldiers.

Ronan fought down the now-familiar bite of rage. It was always there, simmering. He rubbed at his left shoulder with his right hand, where the patches used to be on his utility jacket. The fabric was darker and smoother where it'd been protected from sun and sand and wear by the patches he no longer wore.

Cashiered. It still rankled, more than a month on. It had all happened so fast. First the general on Arcturus, then the DropShip ride and the inquisition and then, finally, kicked out of the very organization they'd all risked so much to rejoin. Unceremoniously, he might add. Literally.

Once Jen had read him out of the LCAF, he'd been marched out of the building, put on a bus, and dropped outside the personnel gates of the military reservation. Across the next hour the bus had left and come back, left and come back, dumping the Arcturan Guard loyalists outside the gate with nothing more than what they carried. They hadn't even returned the soldiers' duffels.

Ronan, livid, had stood with clenched fists and glaring eyes as the MPs shoved the last of the people he'd been responsible for—was still responsible for—onto the street.

"What are we going to do?" Bel had asked.

Stepping out of the trailer, looking across the mountains of rusting metal and decrepit equipment, Ronan was again forced to chuckle darkly at the answer.

Garrison's star system was twenty-five light years from Arcturus, well within range of a JumpShip. Odessa, the world ruled by Ronan's father, Gardner, was only a little over eighteen light years away from Garrison. Though direct trade between the two worlds couldn't be called active, they were close enough that there was some. And each was a common destination when someone gathered enough capital to "find their fortune off-world."

The Arcturans had pooled what funds they had on their persons and found enough to get transport back into Castel proper. There, they'd broken up into small groups beneath NCOs—former NCOs—and found shelter, while Ronan and Bel and a couple of the senior noncoms had put their head together.

About twenty of the former Arcturan Guards disappeared during that first night. Just vanished into the mass of people in Castel and never came back. But the rest showed up or kept in touch. They were a group united by shared hardship, and none of the remainder wanted to let the others down. Those that were left were professionals who preferred the company of other professionals. In the civilian world, finding people who did their job well just because it was their job was a difficult task. In an elite military unit...not so difficult. The twenty who'd left probably wouldn't have fit with the others, anyway.

The rest continued to meet with Ronan and the others, looking for a solution. Looking for a way to reverse the travesty of justice that had been thrust upon them.

Just looking for leadership.

Bel had found the records, of course. She had a knack—almost an obsession—with digging into old archives. She'd found the investment portfolio records showing their father's ownership stake in a supply and salvage yard about fifty kilometers outside Bastion, a desert city a couple hundred kilometers from Castel. They'd gone to see the owner—rather, the late owner's wife, Siobhan.

"Take it," Siobhan had said as soon as the Carlyles told her who they were—and who their father was. "And be welcome to it. I hated this damn place all the years Tricia ran it. It's your problem now."

Ronan had stood there, dumbstruck. "Mistress, we came here for a loan, because you know you can trust my family to repay it." He'd been hoping to secure enough *kroner* to fund as many of his people's trip off-world as wanted to go. Nothing more.

Siobhan—she had to be in her eighties, with skin the color of aged mahogany and laugh lines deep enough to swim in—had cackled at him. In the few minutes he'd known her, that had been her only animated moment. "Son, you see a line of people out there?"

"No, ma'am."

"Bunch of guys and gals working the yard, doing survey and salvage?"

"No, ma'am." Ronan had noticed how deserted the yard was.

"Your old man gets copies of the books every year," Siobhan said, still chuckling. "There's a solid amount of capital out there, sure, but it ain't exactly what you'd called liquid, you see?" She waved generally toward the door. "It's all out there in the yard, like buried treasure."

Ronan had frowned. "I don't—"

"I could *maybe* loan you enough cash to get bus fare back to the city," Siobhan said flatly. "If you could pay it back by Friday next, because I got the waste removal bill."

Bel, sitting beside him, had tried and failed to cover a snort-laugh. Siobhan had looked to her and grinned until both of them were laughing. Ronan had just stared, until the third person with them, Staff Sergeant Buthra Azarri, had cleared his throat. Ronan and the two women looked at him.

"Might I have a look around?" the diminutive technician had asked.

A few hours later, covered in rust, dirt and the excrement of at least three animals, Azarri had returned and stared hard at Ronan. "Take the offer, Hauptmann."

"Come again?"

"There are hectares of equipment out there," Azarri had said. "And yes, much of it is scrap. But we can salvage it. We can rebuild it and, if we choose, sell it." Azarri, a small man of indeterminate years who wore a Sikh *dastār* and a full beard in observance of his religion, had blazing bright eyes. "It is as the mistress said, trust me. There is much here."

Siobhan had only smiled. "I'll even throw in the machine shop."

Now, looking at the mountains of decrepit equipment and scrap, Ronan allowed himself a grin as he watched teams of techs and astechs swarm across the piles. A pair of battered DiNapoli SalvageMechs worked at a mountain of tangled metal and myomer, sussing out the good from the bad. Not all of the former Arcturans had been happy to become salvage experts and yard hands, but they'd all pitched in.

Bel stood at the bottom of the short steps leading up to the HQ trailer, beside a battered, centuries-old jet sled. Ronan had never seen one outside a museum before today, but the way Bel stood with a proprietary hand on the tracked vehicle's fender made him cringe. "Oh, no."

"Oh, yes," Bel said. "It's too far to walk."

"And you couldn't get a skimmer?"

"This is more fun," she said. She hopped over the welded fender into the two-person cockpit. The vehicle looked for all the world like a toy armored personnel carrier; Bel's head and shoulders lifted above the front glacis and that was all.

Ronan high-stepped over the side and settled into the rusty, damp seat. He frowned. "This thing is disgusting."

"You mean amazing."

Ronan crossed his arms. "You're insane. They called this a jet sled, right? It's not a jet or a sled. It's a damn baby tank."

"I know. Amazing. Hold on!" Bel gripped two bars on either side of her seat, toggled the engine live, and pushed both of the bars forward. The jet sled lurched forward like a dog chasing a squirrel.

Ronan clamped both hands on the edge of the armor.

A few minutes later, spines compressed from the bumpy ride, Bel lurched to a stop near a clutch of technicians and astechs. Buthra Azarri stepped out of the center of the group, grinning. He was just a filthy as ever. "You will never believe this, Hauptmann," he said, gesturing.

"Don't call me that," Ronan said for what must have been about the thousandth time. "Bel says you found something?"

"Indeed," Azarri said. "Come. Look." He led the Carlyles through the group of techs and gestured with one arm. "Behold!"

Ronan looked where the master technician pointed. The tech and salvage teams had dug out almost twenty meters of dirt and scrap. It looked like nothing so much as it looked like a giant, opened grave. Ronan frowned, trying to see. It was a BattleMech, unquestionably, but...

"Gods of fortune and wonder..." he whispered.

It was an 80-ton, Clan-built *Gargoyle* OmniMech.

BattleMechs were 12-meter-tall walking tanks, powerfully armed with missiles, beams and cannons that made them more powerful than anything other than another 'Mech. For centuries they had been the pinnacle of warfighting technology, until the Clans, descendants of the ancient Star League, had introduced the OmniMech, 'Mechs that were even more powerfully armed with modular technology that allowed technicians to reconfigure them within hours. In the mid-31st century, when the Clans had invaded the Inner Sphere, OmniMechs and their other advanced technology had made them nearly invincible.

That had been a century ago. Clan technology was no longer the cipher it had been, but their BattleMechs were still prized. A culture predicated on a warrior ethos tended to make powerful machines. Especially when those warriors tended to do things like purge the scientist and technician castes when those powerful machines couldn't be repaired quickly.

Ronan looked at Azarri. "Is it functional?"

"It is not, at the moment," Azarri said, beaming. The incongruity of the statement and expression made Ronan wait. "But with the rest of this yard to salvage from?" The Sikh snapped his fingers. "A matter of time and effort only."

Ronan looked at Bel. "This is it."

"It?"

He pointed at the wrecked OmniMech. "That's millions of *kroner*, once it's up and running." Ronan grinned. "Hell, we can sell that to Bondayehr's people if we have to." He smiled, the first honest smile he'd felt like he'd had in months. "That's everyone's ticket home!"

Bel grinned and grabbed his elbow, turning him away. "It could be," she said, squeezing his arm. "Buthra, everyone, excellent work. Is there anything my brother or I can provide that will help you with this?"

Azarri's smile had not diminished. "A matter of time and effort only, as I said," he told her. Ronan glanced between them, confused. "Significant time and effort. And once we are done, a test pilot, perhaps?"

"Keep digging in there for a *Shadow Hawk*," Bel told him with a chuckle. She tugged on Ronan's sleeve, guiding him back to the jet sled. Ronan smiled at Azarri, still confused, but let himself be pulled.

"What the hell, Bel?" he asked, once they were out of the techs' hearing.

"We need to talk about the future," she said. "Get in."

"The future—"

"I said get in."

Ronan climbed back into the claptrap tracklayer and crossed his arms again. "I don't understand." Bel ignored him. She engaged the engine, lifted one rod and shoving the other forward; the jet sled spun in a track-steer.

She drove them a short distance away, then stopped. "It's like this," she said, letting go of the controls and twisting around to face him. "Not everyone wants to go home."

"What?"

"We've got a good thing going here," Bel said.

Ronan exploded. "A good thing? What the hell are you talking about?"

"This place. This yard. We can build something here."

"Yeah, we can. A ticket home for everyone."

Bel frowned. Her mouth wrinkled into a moue as she shook her head. "That's not what we want anymore."

CHAPTER 5

By the time Jennifer Kipping reached the operations room, someone had shut the alarm down. Garrison's alarm system must have been installed in the Stone Ages; the last syllables of the ancient *ah-whoo-ga* horns still reverberated down the hallways.

"Report!" she shouted as she came through the door.

"Unauthorized movement," the watch commander, First Leutnant Connaught, reported.

"Where?"

"Entrepot Military Reservation," the officer said, pointing to the large flatscreen mounted on the forward wall. Kipping stepped down into the small viewing area, accompanied by the leutnant. "Here's what we know, ma'am. About ten minutes ago we were copied on a warning alert from the MPs on gate guard; unauthorized movement in the vehicle bays." Connaught was a young man, maybe twenty-three standard years, but his baritone voice was firm. "They were speaking to their local CO, ma'am, but our sigint unit tracks all—"

Kipping waved his explanation away. "I'm aware, Leutnant. I was there when the orders were cut." She hadn't told General Bondayehr about those orders. She'd just had them cut after the general's last planning session with the local officers.

"Yes ma'am," Connaught said. "Three minutes later, the unit broadcast infantry APCs approaching. They haven't broadcast since."

"Local video?"

"None, ma'am. Disconnected, we think."

"What unit is based at Entrepot?"

"*Aufklärungsbataillon 29*," Connaught said.

"Kommandant Wagner."

"Yes, ma'am."

Kipping closed her eyes. Of course it was Wagner. It wasn't going to be anyone else, not after that last planning meeting. It was the worst possible time, but her mind went back to that meeting, a week earlier.

"With the greatest respect, sir, we have sat here long enough," Kommandant Liesl Wagner said. "If the reports are true, if they are even *half*-true, then there are Lyran citizens out there waiting for us to return and liberate them."

Kipping, along with the rest of the room, twisted her head to look at Hauptmann-General Bondayehr at the open hatch of the APC. Rather than call his officers into another conference room, Bondayehr had ordered the senior staff planning meeting be held outside, in the armor marshaling yard. Bondayehr, in starched battledress that looked fresh out of the wrapper, stood nearly a head shorter than almost everyone else.

Kipping had carefully schooled her expression when she'd realized that. And it hadn't taken the general more than a few minutes to realize his mistake, which was why he now stood at the top of an ancient hover armored personnel carrier's egress ramp, while the rest of the colonels and kommandants stood on the sandy ground.

"We have no idea if the reports are true," Bondayehr said. "And if they're in error, we could be walking into a Jade Falcon trap." He folded his arms behind his back. "I will not be responsible for risking your lives, the lives of your soldiers, and the irreplaceable equipment you operate on the basis of rumors."

"Sir—" Wagner began, but the general cut her off.

"Also," he said, "we do not have sufficient force on-planet to stage raids of that scale. We would have to criminally weaken Garrison's own defenses in order to release that many troops."

Kipping looked at the kommandant. Liesl Wagner was already a twenty-year veteran of the LCAF when she'd returned home to Garrison, her pension secure, to join the planetary militia. From what Kipping knew about her, she'd been a crack armor officer her entire career, and since returning, had become one of the few non-MechWarrior officers to have BattleMechs under her control.

She was also pugnacious, determined, and completely uninterested in anything except her duty. She was a fierce Lyran patriot who'd built a unit in the Garrison militia that could probably match a frontline combat battalion blow for blow.

The other thing Kipping knew about her was that she hated Fat Timmy with a *glowing* passion.

"General Bondayehr," Wagner said, her voice glacially cold, "no military unit in history has ever stepped off with complete intelligence. It doesn't exist. Gathering that intelligence, sometimes the hard way, is why units like mine exist. Respectfully, we are a tool you are wasting."

Bondayehr frowned, but didn't speak. He almost seemed to be waiting for one of the other officers to step in. When no one did, Kommandant Wagner took the opportunity in both hands.

"My Twenty-Nines can get in and out, sir. We can deliver you the direct intelligence you need. And then when you ask Tharkad for more support, you'll be giving them information they don't have."

"I appreciate your enthusiasm, Kommandant," Bondayehr finally said. "But..." his voice trailed off. "I will not weaken Garrison by sending you away. The risk is too high."

Kipping was in a position to see the shutters close behind Liesl Wagner's eyes. The kommandant made no outward sign, but something in her posture changed. Kipping's right palm suddenly tingled, like it wanted to feel the butt of a sidearm in it.

"Now," General Bondayehr continued, stepping carefully down the ramp, "let's move on to..."

All the officers followed...all except Liesl Wagner.

"All right," Jen Kipping said, turning her back on the display and stepping toward the console where enlisted soldiers manned stations, "here's what we're going to do—"

"Attention!" someone bellowed from the back of the room.

"Fat Timmy, inbound," the soldier nearest Kipping muttered as she stood. When she saw Kipping standing next to the, her eyes widened. "Ma'am—"

"Say it again and I'll have you up on charges," Kipping said, *sotto voce,* but sharp enough to cut. She glanced at Leutnant Connaught, but the leutnant was braced and watching a Lyran officer's cap come down the ramp. Kipping rolled her eyes and did the same.

"What's happening?" General Bondayehr asked as he came into view. He strode around a console, glaring at Kipping, until he realized everyone around him was still standing braced to attention. "At ease, damn you!" he growled. As the rest of the room sat down, Bondayehr flared his eyes at her.

"Sir, unauthorized movement at Entrepot Military Reservation." Kipping decided at the last minute that her duty was to report the information, nothing more. If the general needed editorializing, he could fill it in himself.

"What do you mean, unauthorized movement?" Bondayehr's frown was probably meant to look stern, but instead it just looked confused. "And where the hell is Entrepot?"

"First Leutnant Connaught will fill you in, sir," Kipping said. "Leutnant?"

"Sir. About fifteen minutes ago..."

While Connaught repeated what he knew, Kipping turned away and leaned over the console of the woman who'd spoken earlier. The soldier looked doggedly at her console, ignoring Kipping.

"Call up a topo map of the 500 kilometers around Entrepot," Kipping ordered. The console operator—the name tape on her battledress said MARE—tapped her screen until the map Kipping had asked for appeared.

"Overlay current LCAF and Garrison militia deployments," Kipping ordered. The screen didn't change. "Did you hear me, Private First Class?"

"Yes ma'am," Mare said. "There are no marked deployments within this range."

"You're joking."

Mare twisted in her seat to glare at Kipping. "All due respect, ma'am, I don't mess around with my duties." Kipping met her stare, then nodded.

"Zoom out. Where's the first significant force?"

"I can already tell you that, ma'am. It's here. Your 'Mech, and the militia regiment based in Castel."

Kipping opened her mouth, but a shout rang out across the room. "Status change!" a watch-stander called. Kipping stood and looked across the room, but all the other heads were turned toward the big flatscreen. She looked, too.

Unit in movement icons were sliding infinitesimally away from Entrepot, headed south-southwest. The icons read for a full battalion with logistical support.

"Where are they going?" Kipping called.

"Too soon to tell," First Leutnant Connaught replied from where he stood with General Bondayehr. Kipping saw the general glare at him, but he ignored him.

"Guess," Kipping ordered. Connaught had served on Garrison his entire career.

"Bad Tölz," Connaught said instantly. "There are spaceport facilities there, and it's only about 300 hundred kilometers, if you go by way of Bastion." Kipping gestured "go on" with her hand, inclining her head toward the general. Connaught took the hint and turned. "Sir, assuming they hold to a standard road march speed of forty or fifty kph, they can be there within six or seven hours."

The general looked back and forth between Kipping and Connaught. "Who can be where?"

"Sir, it's the Two-Nine Recon Battalion," Kipping said. "Kommandant Wagner." She gestured toward the flatscreen, where one of the watch-standers had helpfully projected a likely course that snaked along the ravines and dunes south-southwest, past the city of Bastion, and on to Bad Tölz, a mid-sized city with significant off-planet trade. It mostly served in-system vessels, but there was no reason interplanetary DropShips couldn't land there.

"Wagner?" Bondayehr's face worked. "I didn't order any movement. Where's she going?"

"Status change!" another watch-stander called. The flatscreen flickered, and shaky helmet-cam footage of a group of Lyran infantry in desert-pattern battledress were being released from confinement. They'd been lying face-down on the floor, hands secured behind their backs to their feet.

"I think that answers that question," Kipping said. "Sir, your orders?"

"Wh-what?"

"The Two-Nine is clearly away from base without leave," Kipping said. "They're almost certainly going off-world."

"I didn't order that!"

"No, sir," Kipping replied. Turning her head, "Someone find out what's on the tarmac at Bad Tölz, ASAP."

"Already on it, Hauptmann-Kommandant," Mare called. "According to manifests its mostly shuttles and cargo haulers, but there're at least four old military DropShips on the pad claiming to be merchantmen. Three of them have never been on Garrison before, or at least their transponders haven't."

"And the jump points?"

Mare turned in her seat. "Plenty of choices, ma'am."

Kipping nodded once, then straightened and turned back to the general. "Your orders, sir?"

"I did not order this movement," Bondayehr said, glancing back and forth between Connaught and Kipping. "You mean to tell me Kommandant Wagner is going off-planet with her whole battalion? And they're just *following*?"

"She's popular with her troops, sir," Kipping said. And didn't say *And you're not*.

"That's madness. That's *mutiny*." Bondayehr's upper lip shone with sweat. "Is this Regis? Is she running to join Tamar?" He rubbed his hands together in front of his belly, looking back and forth between Connaught and Kipping.

"There's no indication of that," Kipping said evenly.

"Then what's her plan? Go AWOL, do her damned recon mission without orders, and come back? And what, expect all to be forgiven?" Bondayehr snorted nervously. "When has that ever worked?"

Kipping kept her features still. "We can't know her plan, sir, unless she tells us. But that would be a likely scenario based on what we can guess." How Bondayehr didn't recognize that the woman who came back with news that the Jade Falcons were gone, and likely having liberated a planetfull of Lyran citizens for the Commonwealth, was more likely to be decorated for her display of "incredible initiative" and "dedication to the best traditions of the LCAF" than be court-martialed. That would only happen if she failed.

Kipping wanted to chuckle, but didn't. Liesl Wagner knew better than anyone that taking a recon battalion up against the Jade Falcons was likely not survivable. She wouldn't *be* back if she failed.

"We have to stop them," Bondayehr said. "What units are in place to block their path?"

"None, sir." Kipping didn't look back at Mare. If Fat Timmy blew up, she wanted that to splash on her, and not on the enlisted watch-stander who just happened to report the information. "Not before they can reach their likely objective."

"That's unacceptable," the general snapped.

"Reality often is, sir," Kipping said. "If you'll look at the map projection, you can see there are no Lyran units between Entrepot and Bad Tölz." She hesitated. Considered what she'd be about to say, without knowing it. Then reconsidered.

"What," Bondayehr demanded. "You have an idea?"

Kipping sighed. "An idea, yes sir. But you are not going to like it."

CHAPTER 6

BASTION
GARRISON
LYRAN COMMONWEALTH
26 OCTOBER 3151

The dust from the Ferret Light Scout Helicopter whipped at the exposed skin on Ronan Carlyle's wrist as he held his hand up to shield his eyes. That gesture was even more necessary since the Ferret's pilot had opted to set down inside the scrapyard proper, on what passed for the review field. Who knew what else was being picked up by the rotors?

He'd stopped being surprised weeks ago by what his techs and astechs were digging out of the scrap piles. A half-century of demobilization meant machines that would have been valuable salvage during the Succession Wars had been abandoned here, waiting to be picked over and salvaged now that hostilities were common enough to call even decrepit machines back into service.

The sliding door on the side of the Ferret slammed open as soon as its wheels touched down. Jen Kipping jumped down and stalked toward him, one hand shading her eyes. She walked with her head down, watching her steps, but with a sense of urgency he recognized from their KSK 9 days.

Still, the burning sense of betrayal and anger stirred inside as his eyes flicked over the LCAF badges on her battledress. He knew his fists were clenched, and he knew if Bel were here she'd tell him to relax, but this was an emotion he just couldn't put down.

"What are you doing here, Jen?" he shouted over the dwindling roar of the helicopter blades as its engine ran down. Kipping looked out from beneath her hand, half-grinned, and lowered her arm.

"Got a mission for you!" she shouted back.

"You can't give us missions anymore. You kicked us out, remember?"

Kipping's grin morphed into a wide, saccharine smile that showed white teeth, startling against her dark skin. "I brought *kroner.*"

"Get back on your chopper, Jen," Ronan said.

"It matters, Ronan. And we need to decide right now. Two hours from now will be too late."

"We're not thugs for hire."

"It could save lives. LCAF lives."

"You *put us on the street*, Jen. With *nothing*. You don't get to play that card with me anymore."

"Fine. It'll make Bondayehr look really stupid. Would that work?"

Ronan scowled, then motioned toward their temporary headquarters. "Let's go inside."

"Oh, hell no," Bel said after Kipping finished.

Ronan had brought Kipping into the yard office, where Bel waited with three others, senior tech Azarri among them. The other two were Marianne Kojima, the other MechWarrior, and Elia Sarris, the seniormost of the infantry that had come out of Arcturus with him. They'd become the effective leadership cadre of the group.

Outside, through the thin walls, with the Ferret quiet, the sounds of the working salvage yard played a background mishmash of noises. Wheezing diesel engines, high-pitched screams of metal cutting saws, the *crash* and *crunch* of scrap piles being overturned.

Ronan heard it now, as if for the first time, and marveled that he'd gotten so used to it he barely heard it anymore.

"Let me get this straight," Bel said, her flushed cheeks revealing how worked up she was. "You want us to go stop a recon battalion that's AWOL from its base, that you think is headed off-world. A *battalion*." She scoffed, spread her hands, and looked at the others in the room. "That's insane."

"Maybe not," Kipping allowed.

Ronan considered her. She'd come alone, with nothing more than the offer of money, to ask them to take up arms for the nation—for the *person*, in the body of General Bondayehr—who'd kicked them out of the LCAF. That wound was still fresh for all of them.

But Jen Kipping *had* come. Ronan had to admit he wasn't surprised. Kipping was a lot of things, but she wasn't a coward, not when it came to her duty.

"You have at least three operable BattleMechs," Kipping said, meeting Ronan's eye. "At indeterminate number of combat vehicles, and we've seen infantry drilling, both armored and unarmored. You're building a military unit here, and it's getting big enough that pretty soon we'd have to take official notice anyway."

"You're spying on us?" Bel demanded.

"We have satellites," Kipping said. She didn't shy away. "And we pay attention, yes."

"That's still three 'Mechs against a battalion," Ronan said. "Bel is right."

Kipping rolled her eyes. "Don't be silly," she told him. "You were the one always quoting Clausewitz at people."

Ronan blinked, but the reference came to him immediately. "War is fought by human beings," he quoted.

"Exactly."

Bel looked between them into the silence. "And that obvious statement means what?"

Elia Sarris chuckled. "It means our mission wouldn't be to beat them. Just to stop them. Just so, Hauptmann-Kommandant?" Sarris' voice was thick and nearly buzzed, thanks to a rebuilt larynx. The scars on her neck tanned at a different tone than the rest of her leathery skin, and stood out red when she was emotional. Like now.

"Just so," Kipping said.

"I don't understand," Bel said.

"What are they teaching on Coventry these days?" Kipping asked with a brief smile.

"You think they'll turn if they're challenged," Ronan said, bringing the conversation back on course. "You think if we go out there in the name of the Lyran government, and turn their grand act of initiative into an attack on the Lyran government, they'll return to Entrepot and accept their consequences."

"I do," Kipping said.

"And Fat Timmy is prepared to back you on that?" Ronan asked. He didn't even pretend to keep the venom out of his voice.

"I'm not asking you to adjudicate the court-martials, Ronan. Just halt them long enough that the armored battalion I have headed toward Bad Tölz can get in the way, or capture their DropShips." She spread her hands. "After that, you can get out of their way if you like." Her spread hands clenched into fists. "But regardless, you have to decide right now. If you're not on the road in an hour, you won't be able to get in front of them."

"An hour," Bel repeated.

"Maybe a few minutes less."

"And we get what for this? A chance to do our civic duty?"

Kipping brought her hands back together and rested them in her lap. "I brought credit," she said. "Isn't that your grand plan? Go mercenary? Here's your chance."

"Wait outside," Ronan told her.

"I say we let Fat Timmy burn," Bel said as soon as the door closed behind Kipping. "It's his screw-up. Let him clean it up."

"Oh, he's going to burn regardless," Sarris said. Ronan looked at her, surprised. She'd been a battalion sergeant major in the Arcturan Guards, with more than thirty years' service. She was normally taciturn, only offering advice in her specialty, but the infantry that had come with them worshipped her. "He let a battalion get off post with orders, and his best plan for stopping them is hiring a bunch of suspected fifth columnists he ran out of the LCAF. Even if we do it, and this Kommandant Wagner goes back to Entrepot without a single shot fired, the best he can hope for is that her court-martial goes before his."

Ronan nodded. "It doesn't matter what happens, now. Wagner has a chance of getting out of it—come back covered in glory. Think about Arcturus, what a walkover that was. The Jade Falcons were long gone. She finds another world like that, comes back? Publicly she'll be a hero, even if they shuffle her off out of the limelight afterward."

Sarris and Kojima nodded. Bel looked confused for a moment, then shrugged. "Doesn't change my mind. It'll go worse for him if Wagner gets away. And like you said, the Jade Falcons are gone. So it's not like they're headed into a trap."

"An hour is not a lot of time," Azarri said, speaking for the first time. "If we choose to make this attempt, could we? Could we be ready to go in an hour?" He looked at each of his comrades as he continued. "The 'Mechs are as ready as we can make them, yes. And we have sufficient vehicles and weapons for the soldiers we have. But even I know having the tools is not enough; we need to know how to use them."

"That depends on how right Jen is about Wagner's likely reaction." Ronan stood, crossed his arms, and tried to read the future. "The Two-Nine has a 'Mech company, but it's a scout company. According to the data she brought, they don't have anything heavier than a *Wolfhound*. The rest of the battalion is fast scouts and mechanized infantry. In a standup fight, we could do some real damage."

"Or they can go around us; the only thing we have that fast is Elia's hoverbike squads." Bel nodded her head at the infantry noncom.

"Only if they abandon their loggies," Ronan said. "Wagner is taking her logistical tail with her; that's what's holding their speed down. And she's a good enough officer to know she can't do anything without the parts and bullets to make her combat units work." He grinned and inclined his head at Buthra Azarri. "As we've all be educating ourselves these past weeks."

"So we *can*," Azarri said. "Now is only left to determine if we *should*."

"You all wanted this," Ronan said to the group. "We have the capital now; we can all just go home. Hell, I can probably sell all our stuff to Jen right now, and we can walk out of here filthy rich while they take what we've built. Knowing her, she'd probably take my *Gargoyle* out alone and try to stop Wagner. So we don't *need* to do this."

Bel frowned. "It'd be fighting Lyrans," she said. "People just like us."

"Like we were a couple months ago," Marianne Kojima put in. "Hell, if Fat Timmy keeps to form, soon they'll all be out on the street like we were."

"You all told me," Ronan said, glaring at each of them in turn, "when I said we had the cash, you told me you wanted to stay and build a unit. To go the mercenary route, to stay together, to keep soldiering. If we become mercenaries, then we don't always get to pick our opponents. We fight for money, not loyalty."

"Your ancestors only fought for the Lyrans," Sarris put in.

"Grayson Carlyle worked for the Mariks, don't forget," Bel put in. "And the Snakes killed his dad, so he was never going to go far from that border." Sarris bowed her head, acceding to the new information.

Bel looked Ronan in the eye. "Will Mom and Dad understand?"

Ronan swallowed. "They're not here," he replied. "Take ten minutes. Go poll your people. I won't run a military unit like a democracy, but they should all get a say in whether we become one."

Sarris and Azarri stood up to leave; Bel and Kojima stayed behind. Neither had "people" in the sense the others did. Ronan waited until the door shut, then shook his head. "I can't believe we're seriously considering firing on the LCAF."

Kojima shrugged. "Fat Timmy burned that bridge for us when he threw us out."

"We could make reinstatement part of the deal," Ronan said. "Try to, anyway." He crossed his arms and half-sat on a desktop.

"I wouldn't go back even if they asked," Kojima spat. She was an average, featureless woman in every way, but now strong emotion distorted her face. "I took the same oath you did, and they threw it back in my face. I walked away from friends and comrades I've known for years in the Guard, to come back here and be told I'm not trustworthy. I did it because I swore that oath, and it meant something. But loyalty goes both ways. I don't owe the LCAF a damn thing."

Bel looked at Kojima for a long moment, then looked at Ronan and nodded.

"Okay," he said, standing again and uncrossing his arms. "Let's get a head start on the paperwork, in case the vote comes back yes."

Thirty-four minutes later, Ronan stepped back into the hall where Jen Kipping crouched, waiting. She lurched to her feet when she saw him.

"I hope you brought enough *kroner*," Ronan said. "We have a contract for you to sign; you may not like all of it. Just so you know, there won't be any negotiations, either."

CHAPTER 7

"All units in position, Captain," Bel sent. Her *Hatchetman* was about 400 meters to Ronan's right, closing on him. Ronan adjusted his *Gargoyle*'s stance and eyed the horizon again. He felt like had to sneeze. Buthra Azarri and his astechs assured him there was nothing wrong with the *Gargoyle*'s air tanks, but Ronan still felt a tickle in his sinuses whenever he put the 'Mech's neurohelmet on.

"Roger," he replied.

Captain. It felt weird. His Lyran rank, hauptmann, was the same effective rank, company commander, but the English version felt unfamiliar. Still, mercenaries rarely used the rank structure of a regular military, so adjustments had to be made. He wondered if Bel was feeling the same thing; leutnant and lieutenant were the same rank, but maybe the extra syllable carried weight.

The dash out of the scrapyard had startled him. He hadn't expected his scratch unit to come together as well as it had, but once again Bel had surprised him. She'd been spending time with Sergeant Major Sarris, working out what a mercenary unit built out of the Arcturan expats might look like. And the two of them had been quietly spreading their ideas around.

As usual, the CO was the last to know.

"Still can't believe we're doing this," Bel added. Ronan looked at her 'Mech, painted in desert camouflage. He could just make out the insignia painted on her *Hatchetman*'s shin; a grinning skull set on a red field. He felt something—a sensation halfway between tingle and shudder.

"Too late to turn back," Kojima—*Sergeant* Kojima, she was now—put in. Her *Bushwhacker* was about a hundred meters to Ronan's left. The three of them were an effective barricade on the wide road that cut through the dusty, cracked-earth plain.

"Any word from the scouts?" Bel asked.

"Nothing yet."

"Over there, Sarge," said Private Tareen.

Sergeant Bill Ortiz shifted his weight on the hoverbike's saddle and lifted his rangefinder binoculars toward were the other hoverbike scout pointed. "Right where the satellite said they'd be."

"Got 'em," Ortiz said. The pair of scouts had stopped atop a dune that had grown on a rise; the sand was sharp-edged and biting, and they'd discovered quickly during test rides that if they didn't travel in echelon with the direction of the wind, the gritty sand would clog drive fans and even cut skin.

In his binoculars, about four kilometers away, he saw the leading edge of a battalion task force; a platoon of Packrat recon vehicles about a half-klick ahead of a dust cloud that had to be the rest of the Two-Nine.

Ortiz lowered the binos for a moment and looked around, considering. Standard operating procedure for a battalion in movement in friendly territory was forward outriders and a tail to sweep up anyone who fell behind, but didn't include provision for flanking scouts. Ortiz knew that doctrine as well as anyone in the Two-Nine; he'd been a Packrat driver himself in the Arcturan Guard. He'd crawled along at forty kph waiting for the whole battalion to catch up more times than he could count. He didn't envy those Packrat jocks.

"Tell the captain," Ortiz said, after a minute. "On schedule, no flankers. They're not expecting us." He shifted in his seat again, watching the other hoverbike scout put a hand to her helmet and send the information. When Tareen nodded, he turned back and raised the binos.

"Can't wait to see what happens."

Sergeant Glenda Manwaring snapped out of the haze induced by the warm sun and the Packrat's smooth operating vibration when Private Gomez yelped. "Contacts ahead, Sergeant!"

So far, the hours of the march from Entrepot to Bad Tölz had been dull, maybe the dullest hours of Manwaring's life. She'd been floating in and out, letting Gomez handle the driving and sensors, since the kommandant had made damn sure there wasn't any Lyran units in position to stop them before they reached the DropShips. Manwaring frowned and scrunched her face up, eyes squeezed tight, nose tight, trying to shake the cobwebs from her mind.

"Can't be," she said. "What's our position?" When Gomez read the coordinates off, Manwaring snorted. "There's no one to be out here," she said. "Intel was clear on that."

"Tell the sensors, Sergeant," Gomez said. "This says three BattleMechs."

"Don't be absurd," Manwaring said, but she toggled a channel to the platoon commander. "Sir—"

"I see them," Leutnant Klein said from his own Packrat. "Hold. I'm talking to the CO."

"One heavy or assault and two mediums, it looks like," Gomez added.

"IFF?"

Gomez squinted, reading the transponder code. "That *can't* be right..."

Ronan shuddered as a cold chill ran down his back when the first red carets for the Lyran recon battalion's outriders appeared on his HUD. The Packrats were already slowing down, letting the gap between the scout screen and the main body shorten. Right now, the main body was just a block of red on his strategic-scale map, reported by the hoverbike scouts and Lyran satellite reconnaissance.

"They've seen us," Bel reported unnecessarily.

"Question is how they'll react," Kojima put in.

Ronan licked suddenly-dry lips and sipped tepid water from the nipple inside his neurohelmet. He was suddenly conscious the rough weave of his cooling suit touching his skin.

Toggling the comm to a long-range, wide-band frequency, Ronan cleared his throat. "Attention, *Aufklärungsbataillon 29*. You are away from Entrepot Military Reservation without leave, in violation of the lawful orders of Hauptmann-General Timofey Bondayehr. You are ordered to halt in place and await new orders from higher. Comply immediately, or we will fire on you."

"Subtle," Bel snickered on the lance channel.

"*Aufklärungsbataillon 29*, respond." Ronan set the comm to loop his previous recording and ping him if there was a response.

"In a way, we're already winning," he told his two lancemates. "We've got their screen stopped; that will delay them. Even if they beat us, every minute we give Jen to get more forces in their way is another minute we win."

"If they beat us, we won't be around to care about that," Marianne Kojima said.

"Point," was all Ronan would say.

"It's a trick," Hauptmann Jaruwalski, the battalion operations officer, said. "It has to be."

"The 'Mechs are real," Kommandant Liesl Wagner said. She and her staff were in the working compartment of the battalion's mobile headquarters vehicle, nestled safely in the center of the road march order.

Now she stood, swaying with the motion of the wheeled vehicle as it slowed. Her firsts were planted on the edge of the holographic map table, currently set at strategic scale and showing the path from Entrepot to Bad Tölz. She glared at the pulsing red icon for enemy force right on their path for a moment longer, then switched her glare to Hauptmann Erskine, the intelligence officer. "You told me there wasn't anything that could get in our way if we moved fast."

Erskine, a heavyset woman with defensive eyes, shook her head. "There wasn't. Isn't. Even assuming instant alerts from the time we left Entrepot, there are no regular LCAF or Garrison militia units within ten hours of this position."

"And yet."

"I don't know who these people are or where they came from," Erskine said. "They shouldn't be there."

"But they *are* there," Kommandant Wagner said. "And the fact that they are, especially right here, means that Bondayehr or one of his lapdogs has figured out where we're going." She exhaled, slowly, then looked at Jaruwalski as she sat back down. "Options?"

"Steamroll them," Jaruwalski said immediately. "We don't have time for anything else. If Bondayehr put these people here, he has units on the way to the spaceport to get our ride. We have to get there first."

Wagner grunted, considering. She knew her battalion was behind her; she'd spent the last year carefully transferring out anyone likely to dissent. That hadn't been her plan, but when you're building the best damn recon battalion in the LCAF, you only want people in it who want to be in it. Every one of her soldiers was dedicated to the mission. They'd risk court-martial or worse for the chance to do their duty to the Commonwealth.

Just like she would. Like she had, more times than she could count, in her regular career.

"Can we bypass them?" Wagner asked. "A fight will slow us down, too."

"We can try," Jaruwalski said, hesitantly. "But with the log units, we're slow. They can hit us in the flank whenever they want."

Wagner knew he was right. The log units—the ammo haulers, the supply trucks, the medevac blowers, even the pair of Savior mobile repair vehicles—were critical if the battalion was going to face an enemy force at the other end. Unlike frontline units, which usually depended on their DropShips for depot-level repair, a militia battalion going off-world had to carry everything it might need along with it. The vehicles were thin-skinned and slow, most of them never intended to be in the line of fire.

"It's three 'Mechs," Erskine said incredulously. "Are three 'Mechs going to charge a battalion?"

"They're here," Jaruwalski shot back. "They wouldn't be out there broadcasting if they weren't prepared to back up their claim."

"It doesn't matter," Wagner abruptly decided. "The issue here is time, not what these people will do. We have an appointment we can't miss in Bad Tölz. Whether they fight or give ground, we can't slow down." She stood again, now that the mobile HQ had stopped. "Halt log section here; all combat elements are to form on the scouts. Put Charlie Company—" the BattleMech company, "—out front. Maybe four-to-one odds will convince them."

Jaruwalski nodded, spinning his chair around to face his own console, already talking quietly into his headset to pass the orders.

Wagner crossed her arms and looked at Erskine. "Do you think they're who they say they are?"

Her intelligence officer scoffed. "That unit died almost a century ago. They just stole the name is all."

"It's a powerful name."

Erskine only gave a Gallic shrug.

Wagner turned to a rating at the comm panel. "Connect me," she ordered.

Ronan heard an instant's static before a strong female voice answered him. "This is Kommandant Liesl Wagner, commanding *Aufklärungsbataillon 29*. Stand aside."

"Kommandant Wagner." Ronan wanted to swallow, but he didn't. "Ma'am, you are ordered to hold in place by direct order of Hauptmann-General Timofey Bondayehr. Failure to comply immediately will be grounds for insubordination. I am authorized to tell you anything less than instant compliance will escalate those charges to mutiny."

"That's a cute story," Wagner said. "I don't recognize your authority to issue me orders, son."

"Ronan," Bel cut in on the lance channel, "they're massing their combat elements with the scouts. I read a dozen 'Mechs at least."

Ronan frowned. "Kommandant, I don't want to fire on Lyran troops, but I will."

"We outnumber you four to one in 'Mechs alone," Wagner said. "Stand aside or be destroyed."

Ronan's hands squeezed the *Gargoyle*'s controls. "I can't do that, Kommandant." He made sure his radio was still broadcasting widebeam in the clear, so every receiver in the battalion could hear it. "You're operating against the lawful orders of your superior. The spaceport at Bad Tölz will be occupied before you can get there. The jump points have been interdicted." He paused. "Don't throw your soldiers' careers— their *lives*—away, Kommandant. There will be another day."

"The Two-Nine will do its duty to the people of the Commonwealth," Wagner said, and clicked the connection closed.

Ronan sighed. "All right then," he said to the empty air. He toggled his comm back to the main unit frequencies and tagged the all-unit channel.

"Okay, troops. The kommandant has declined to surrender. You all know your jobs. If we do this quick enough, maybe we won't have to kill too many of them to make them stop."

He paused. There was no other way to say it. In his mind's eye, Ronan saw his great-grandfather, nodding at him.

"Gray Death Legion, attack!"

CHAPTER 8

OUTSIDE BASTION
GARRISON
LYRAN COMMONWEALTH
26 OCTOBER 3151

None of the Legion 'Mechs moved when Ronan gave the order; that was per the plan. They wanted to let the Two-Nine come to them. But the rest of the Legion assets sprang into motion.

Ronan thanked the gods again that Bel and the sergeant major had spent so much time together without him knowing about it. They'd done enough staff work, and brought the NCOs into the planning early enough, that what would have been a suicidal standup fight might now actually turn into a win, if the orchestration worked out.

"Phase One," he sent.

Sergeant Ortiz had his hoverbike up on its fans before he heard "Phase One" in his helmet. At the captain's order, he and Private Tareen leaned forward on their pillion seats, face-shields down. The hoverbikes started skittering forward just from the change in weight, even before Ortiz twisted his throttle. Inside the plenum chambers, the blade incidence changed, driving the blowers forward.

"On the way," he signaled.

"Phase One," Staff Sergeant Skyler Padgit heard. She reached up and toggled the Karnov's power plant from standby to live; outside, on each end of the extended wings, the huge rotors began to spin up. The airframe began to groan, a sound that would quickly switch to a teeth-breaking, high-pitched vibration as the rotors got up to speed. Across the gully, she saw the other Karnov's blades begin to spin as well.

"Get ready," she said on the intercom.

"Already up," said her gunner, Private Patel.

A few moments later, they were airborne. Padgit added power, the nacelles on the ends of the wings tilted forward, and the helicopter quickly turned into an airplane.

Sergeant Major Elia Sarris looked down the line of infantrymen sharing the compartment inside the heavy armored personnel carrier with her as its drive fans spun up. The driver had already given her the agreed-upon hand-signal that meant Phase One. The soldiers in her squads looked back at her, waiting.

She held up a single finger.

Nods came back. It was too loud in the compartment to talk; the drive fans screamed. The floor moved in the disgusting way blowers always did when they first broke loose, like oil on a hot pan.

It wouldn't be long now.

As the recon battalion's 'Mechs got closer, the *Gargoyle*'s computer quickly ID'd and catalogued what was coming at them. The 'Mech company was at full strength, three lances of four 'Mechs apiece. That mean four targets for each of the Legion 'Mechs.

Or four 'Mechs shooting at each of them.

"Remember the plan," Ronan said. "We're not here to kill them. They're Lyrans, just like we are. We're just here to make them stop. I think the sergeant major will take care of that. We just have to hold the combat units here."

"Shouldn't be a problem," Bel said. There was something in her voice; Ronan looked at her *Hatchetman*. Bel was standing still, though the arm carrying the 'Mech-scale hatchet was swinging back and forth.

"Roger," was all Kojima sent.

Two of the oncoming lances were pretty standard Lyran scout lances: a trio of *Dart* light sprinters with a *Scarabus* lance commander. Those two lances had already separated on the flanks, clearly aiming at Bel and Kojima.

The third lance was most likely the company CO's lance; a pair of *Talon* fast snipers, a PPC-armed *Wolfhound* that was almost certainly the CO, and what sure looked like a 300-year-old *Javelin*.

That lance was headed right for him.

In Echo Company, he'd have had his fire lance already dropping LRMs around the lead 'Mechs, trying to slow them down, move them off-course, even do a little damage. Light 'Mechs were notoriously under-armored; it would only take a few hits from the Legion weapons to make them combat-ineffective. But he didn't have a fire lance. None of the machines Buthra Azarri's miracle workers had been able to get working were long-range machines.

Which meant those PPCs were going to hurt.

Sliding the *Gargoyle*'s throttle forward, Ronan leaned the 'Mech into a run to close the range. At 80 tons, a *Gargoyle* was an assault 'Mech, but it was as fast on the ground as a 55-ton *Shadow Hawk*. The speed might help protect him from long-range sniping from the Lyran lance.

A blue-white PPC bolt ate into the sandy soil a few meters from the *Gargoyle*'s left foot, exploding a huge puff of sand and smoke. Glass, melted out of the sand by the PPC's intense heat, shattered against the *Gargoyle*'s calf as Ronan passed. Two more PPCs sizzled past him close enough to raise the hairs on his arm from static electricity.

On his left, Bel's *Hatchetman* fired its own heavy PPC. The harsh bolt of infinitesimal lightning connected her 'Mech and the *Scarabus* charging toward her for a moment; when the instant ended, the *Scarabus* was stumbling, a massive cavity blasted into its right chest. The 'Mech immediately slowed and turned away; without its armor protection, the huge 300 extralight engine inside was exposed. Another shot there, and the fusion engine could be destroyed.

One down, eleven to go, Ronan thought.

His *Gargoyle* had two main weapons groups in this configuration, and this was the only configuration they'd been able to salvage, beg, borrow, or steal parts for. Azarri assured Ronan that once they had a sufficiency of parts, he'd be able to arm his OmniMech however he wanted. For today, though, he was stuck what he had.

In one arm, the *Gargoyle* carried the powerful Devastator 200mm Ultra autocannon, capable of blasting limbs off enemy 'Mechs in one salvo. In the other, he had a half-dozen extended-range medium lasers. Fired as a battery, the ER mediums could also be devastating.

He didn't have the heat sinks to fire them all at once, but luckily he didn't think any of the Lyran 'Mechs would be enough of a threat to require that much firepower all at once.

And besides, this whole part of the battle was a sideshow, anyway.

Bill Ortiz's drive fan screamed in the wind; the rooster-tail of sand and dust he was throwing up would be visible for a klick or more, but he was also sliding across the ground at just under 200 kph. Private Tareen was behind him by about twenty meters, offset ten to the left so she wasn't flying through his dust cloud. Ortiz grinned; this was *so* much better than Packrats.

Ducking his chin into his left armpit, Ortiz looked left. There, a cluster of trucks and larger, dedicated repair vehicles were halted on the cracked roadbed; if there was security, he didn't see it. He shifted his chin to his other armpit; on his right, the rear ranks of the Lyran battalion vanished into the dust cloud they kicked up just moving.

"Phase Two green," he sent.

"Phase Two yellow," he heard from the other hoverbike section, Vijaya and Ueda. The other pair of bikes was crisscrossing the stalled log element from the rear. "Looks like the convoy tail," Sergeant Vijaya reported. "Pair of Goblins." Ortiz's pair of hoverbikes never slowed.

Sergeant Major Sarris held on as the APC lurched into motion. The driver steered into a skidding turn that had the hovercraft flying sideways for a moment until the drive fans caught up and changed the vehicles' momentum. She gripped the shoulder straps of her five-point restraint tightly, with her knees locked around the rifle clamped muzzle-down between her legs.

A yellow light lit up in the infantry compartment. Sarris frowned. She looked to her squad and fireteam leaders and got nods back; they'd all seen it.

Sarris held her teeth a millimeter apart. The drive fans' vibrations traveled up her spine from the seat and shook every part of her against herself, but she ignored it. She tasted metal in the back of her throat. Her fingertips tingled. Adrenalin was an old and familiar companion, but she never got all the way used to it.

It wouldn't be long now.

A PPC shot from the *Wolfhound* nearly knocked the *Gargoyle*'s leg out from beneath it as Ronan heard the green report, then the yellow one. He couldn't spare any extra worry for the infantry just then: the Lyran lance was pressing him too closely, but the range had finally fallen to where he could reply.

Clan-built ER medium lasers were generally effective out to about 450 meters; the two *Talon*s had passed the slower *Wolfhound* and *Javelin*, and had just stepped past the boundary. Ronan settled his crosshairs on the leftmost BattleMech and squeezed the trigger for all six lasers.

Five of the beams hit. The *Talon* was moving well over a hundred kilometers per hour; two of the beams scattered damage across the 'Mech's chest, costing it not quite a ton of protection. The other three medium lasers, however, combined to blast the 'Mech's left leg off at the hip. The slender 'Mech, leaned into its run with its torso canted around so its weapons could bear, immediately fell into a skidding, rolling pile of broken and smoking 'Mech.

Before Ronan could celebrate, the other *Talon* slammed a PPC into his chest; the damage wireframe went from green to yellow. *Gargoyles* were powerful OmniMechs, but they gained their trademark speed at the expense of armor.

"Ow," Marianne Kojima grunted. Ronan looked; her *Bushwhacker* was staggering back from where the *Scarabus* had just backhanded her with its hatchet. The Legion MechWarrior steadied her bullet-shaped 'Mech, then pivoted. Her 'Mech was an old L1 configuration: instead of a mid-size autocannon and a bevy of missiles, it carried only an ER large laser and a class 20 LB-X autocannon. That massive weapon coughed now; the cluster munitions sparked all across the *Scarabus*, denting armor and getting lodged in actuators. The 'Mech moved away with a frozen knee actuator, but before Kojima could build on her attack, two of the *Darts* in the lance she faced put medium lasers into her armor.

There was just too many of them.

New carets appeared on his tactical screen as the Two-Nine's armored cavalry company roared forward out of the mass of the battalion, adding another dozen contacts.

Way too many of them.

In the mobile HQ, Kommandant Wagner watched the icons for the skirmish at the head of her column with a frown. She was down two 'Mechs already, and while the addition of her armored cav should be enough to seal the deal, she'd expected this group to break off long before now. Sure, they were getting a few early successes, but the end was inevitable; her more numerous machines would pull the trio of 'Mechs down like pygmies and elephants. Even if they tried to disengage, her units were fast enough to dog them into the ground no matter how hard they tried to run.

Not that she would chase them; she was on a schedule. She turned to Hauptmann Jaruwalski. "Assume they break in the next two minutes; can we afford the time to pick up our damaged units, or are we going to have to abandon them to make our rendezvous?"

Jaruwalski frowned. "I think if we bring the log section forward fast enough, we should be able to get at least two of the 'Mechs into the mobile field bases. We can do repairs on the way out to the jump point, I would think."

"Figure out exactly how many minutes we can spend on that—"

"Kommandant!" Hauptmann Erskine shouted. "Log section!"

Wagner spun to look at the strategic display. A cluster of red carets had suddenly appeared around the log section units clustered about two kilometers behind them.

CHAPTER 9

OUTSIDE BASTION
GARRISON
LYRAN COMMONWEALTH
26 OCTOBER 3151

The timing couldn't have been better if they'd planned it. They hadn't planned it. There hadn't been time. But Staff Sergeant Skyler Padgit led her flight of two Karnov gunships across the dune at 30 meters elevation just as the APCs bearing the Legion infantry slewed to a halt on next to the stopped Lyran logistical vehicles. The ramps dropped immediately; from one APC sprung unarmored trooper after trooper, about half of them lugging single-shot SRM tubes while the rest had infantry assault rifles.

From the other clomped the squat shape of Phalanx powered battle armor, a squad of four.

Padgit grinned and slid the Karnov up on its side, angling around the clump of vehicles. According to the scouts, the two tanks running shotgun were at the tail of the column, a pair of Goblin infantry fighting vehicles. Those were her targets.

"Target in sight," said Patel, her gunner.

"Then hit it!" She held the Karnov steady. "Shotgun first!"

A moment later, the airframe slammed to the side like the hand of God had grabbed on and pulled.

The Karnov UR tilt-rotor had been in service for literally centuries, mainly as a cargo-carrying VTOL. But a few enterprising engineers had taken a concept out of ancient history and mounted cannons in the cargo bay, turning the humble cargo aircraft into a gunship. It lacked the armor for sustained combat, and once it revealed itself it was quickly targeted, but the usefulness of timely and heavy air support was difficult to understate.

When the Legion salvage teams had found the two fusion-powered Karnovs, and determined they could be rebuilt, the sergeant major had stepped in. Staff Sergeant Antonio Castillo, the legion's senior mechanic, had horse-traded with Lyran quartermasters for a pair of Defiance Disintegrator 200mm autocannons. One had been mounted in each of the Karnov's cargo bays.

So from an effective height of about 120 meters, thanks to the slope down from the dunes, Padgit's aircraft coughed a salvo most assault 'Mechs would covet. The sleet of submunitions, a score of tungsten-alloy penetrators, sparked across and around the Goblin training its turret laser up to bear on them. This close the Karnov could turn faster than the tank's turret could traverse. The submunitions did little damage individually, but there were a lot of them, and they had an uncanny ability to find a chink in a target's armor.

And they didn't let the Legion down this time; the Goblin's turret abruptly halted as a shard of tungsten locked the turret traverse, and the tank drove off its left track into the sand. A moment later the crew hatches opened as the Goblin's crew bailed out of the crippled vehicle.

"Target disabled," Patel confirmed. A moment later the other Karnov reported the same.

Padgit, grinning like a wolf, changed frequencies. "Escorts disabled, Sergeant Major," she sent. "Orbiting."

"Roger," the sergeant major growled. She was panting, no doubt from running.

Sergeant Major Sarris had no more to spare for the chopper pilot. She heard the harsh chopping of the tilt-rotor's big propellers. But she was far too busy to look away from her task.

"Sergeant Morgenstern?" she barked.

"On it, Sergeant Major," Zuzana Morgenstern sent. She led the single squad of battle armor the techs had been able to get operational. The suits were old Phalanx charlies, support configured battlesuits with big mortars on their backs. For this mission, the mortars only had one purpose. "Firing."

Sarris looked to her left, where the other APC had unloaded. The four stumpy suits as one took a knee, planting one fist into the dirt to create a stable firing position, and ducked their head. On their backs, the stubby barrel of a heavy mortar poked up. In sequence a half-second apart, each mortar fired; the *crack* of 120mm mortars firing shook the sand around the suits.

Sarris looked right, toward the Lyran battalion main body. Four geysers of dust and dirt flew up as the rounds fell, each about thirty meters from the other. Moments later, great clouds of boiling white smoke began to billow.

It wasn't much of a screen, but it would do.

"That's all the cover we're going to get," she sent on her platoon channel. "Let's get this done." She turned back to the trucks.

The Lyran log section had huddled closer together; few of the vehicles mounted weapons, not even a machine gun in a pintle mount. The pair of big recovery vehicles, the saviors, had a small laser in a remote-controlled turret, but she'd leave those to Sergeant Morgenstern's squad, now that the smoke screen was laid. The Phalanxes were already back on their feet and sprinting toward the pair of bulbous Saviors.

"Engines and tires, boys and girls. Engines and tires. Don't hurt anyone you don't have to."

"The escorts are down," Hauptmann Jaruwalski said.

Kommandant Wagner pounded her fist on the edge of the holotable. Her eyes searched the table, looking for a solution, anything that would push down the grinding dread she felt gnawing at her gut. She didn't even look at the 'Mech battle taking place in front of her column. She recognized that now as a distraction, one that may have cost her the mission they'd left Entrepot to do.

On the table in front of her one of the retreating 'Mechs was almost behind the lines. She toggled her comm. "MechWarrior Gorman, come in."

"Gorman here, Kommandant."

"We've got infantry mixing up with our loggies. Get back there and deal with them."

"Yes, ma'am." On the holomap, the *Scarabus* accelerated toward the rear.

Wagner closed the channel, looked at the map again, then sat slowly down in her chair. "It's not going to be enough," she whispered.

Sergeant Major Sarris had built the Legion's first infantry squads very consciously. She only had four, not counting Sergeant Morgenstern's battlesuits. Two were rifle squads and two were SRM squads.

Each rifle squad was broken into two fireteams and a command element; each fireteam was three troopers. For this mission, each fireteam had one of the troopers carrying semiautomatic 12.7mm sniper rifles. Sarris knelt behind one of those troopers now, where he lay prone with the big rifle snugged into his shoulder.

"The engine block, son," Sarris said.

"Roger, Sar'nt Major."

A moment later, the big rifle barked out a single round; the recoil pushed the shooter back a centimeter or so on the soft sand, but the truck immediately in front of Sarris screeched and started belching black smoke as the engine ground to a stop against the big bullet. Many militaries classified the twelve-seven rifle an anti-materiel weapon, not just a sniper's weapon. That truck wasn't moving unless someone towed it.

"Good shot, son," Sarris told him. "Now do it again."

Around him, the other snipers fired at other trucks.

Staff Sergeant Padgit's Karnov was high enough that she could see over the smoke screen. Her sensors pinged the movement first, but her eye caught the flash off the 'Mech's cockpit canopy. She focused her sensors in that direction, digested the result, and swore as she jerked the aircraft around on a new heading.

"Simkins, on me," she ordered the other Karnov. "Sergeant Major, we've got a 'Mech on its way. Time's up."

"Roger," Sarris sent. Simkins just double-clicked her mic.

"Patel," Padgit said next, "load HEAP. We got a 'Mech on the way."

"Roger, loading HEAP."

The Disintegrator cannon fired two kinds of shells: the cluster round they'd hit the Goblin with, which was a packet of tungsten-alloy penetrators, or standard high explosive armor piercing shells that autocannons had fired for centuries. When you needed something put down in a hurry, 200mm HEAP was just what the doctor ordered.

Nose slightly down, rotors roaring, the Karnov sprinted over the smoke screen.

Across the road, Sergeant Major Sarris heard the hypersonic hiss-*crack* of the Phalanxes' MagShot Gauss rifles firing. Their mission was the Savior repair vehicles, specifically the heavy tracks the repair vehicles drove on. If they could break the tracks, the vehicles were helpless until they could crack new track.

"Time's up," Sarris shouted. "Everyone back on the APCs!"

Around him, the rifle squads stood up and sprinted back to the heavy hover APC. The *crump* of mortar shells sounded again, though this time the smoke shells fell in and among the crippled Lyran vehicles. Almost every truck had been disabled, or had wheels shot off, or tracks broken. Two of his troopers were wounded; not all the Lyran troops had hidden in their vehicles when they were getting shot at, but all they had were sidearms or a handful of submachine guns.

Sarris trotted back, stopping every couple steps to spin in place and take a look around. As she put her foot on the APC's ramp, she saw the four stumpy battlesuits sprinting back to their own APC, twice as fast as a man could move.

"Come on!" shouted the APC's driver, his voice loud enough to be heard over the snarling fans. "We got a 'Mech coming in!"

Grinning, Sarris stepped up the ramp and slapped the *close* button. The driver had the blower in motion as soon as the ramp was off the ground.

The sergeant major sat down in an open seat, racked her rifle, and secured her restraints quickly as the APC lurched into a turn. Her helmet clanged against the bulkhead behind her. She put one hand against her earpiece, toggled her transmitter, and shouted, "Phase Three green!"

Around her, the infantry platoon cheered.

Skyler Padgit held her course as the *Scarabus* raised its left arm. She'd had a course in 'Mech identification years ago, but while she recognized the model, she had no idea what weapons were in that arm. Lasers felt most likely.

She chewed the inside of her cheek for a moment. "Patel," she said, "you ready?"

"Roger."

"Simkins, follow me in." Two clicks came back.

Red and green light flashed past her; a few pulses hit the Karnov's nose, triggering alarms, but thankfully all of them missed the rotors. Padgit judged her angle, then used her rudder to kick the tail around. Normally she'd bank right to open the left broadside, but she needed to bank left to bring the autocannon's muzzle down to bear on target.

The *Scarabus* didn't slow down, and neither did she. The Disintegrator fired, this time hammering the Karnov's frame with the rhythmic *slam-slam-slam* of the HEAP cassette-round. Padgit craned her head around, trying to see the fall of the shot.

All the fire landed behind the hard-charging 'Mech. *Damn it*! "Hang on, Patel, we'll come around again!" She flattened her bank to extend the range enough to come around and hit the 'Mech again, from behind. *Except it's faster than I am...*

"Simkins is coming in!" Patel called.

Kommandant Wagner watched a relayed image live on a flatscreen. The first Karnov gunship missed wide, not slowing Gorman's *Scarabus* in the least. Jaruwalski and Erskine grunted with pleasure, the hungry sounds of predators who still see a chance to get at the prey. Wagner wanted to join them, but she waited...waited...

The second Karnov blew the *Scarabus'* right leg off at the hip. Gorman went down, skidding, crushing what was left of his extralight fusion engine shielding.

Wagner sat down heavily. "Signal the cease-fire," she told Jaruwalski. The operations officer stared at her uncomprehendingly. "It's over."

"But Charlie almost has the three 'Mechs on the ropes! Their infantry is retreating, and those gunships have to have shot their bolt. Our combat power is reduced, sure, but we can still do the mission! We have time."

Next to him, Erskine nodded earnestly in agreement.

"But we no longer have the means," Wagner said quietly. "Without the log section, we can't carry out the mission. Even if we make it off-world, we won't be able to repair our damage. We'll run out of ammunition. Hell, I'll bet you we can't even shove the techs and mechanics into the infantry APC and carry them to Bad Tölz."

She shook her head. "No, whoever the hell these people are, they did their job." She sighed. "It's over."

CHAPTER 10

Ronan looked up when Jen Kipping, sitting beside him, tapped his knee with hers. A lift opened at the end of the corridor. A woman in Lyran battledress but with no sidearm stepped out, flanked by two troopers in MP attire with sidearms. From the briefing Jen had given him, he recognized the woman as Liesl Wagner.

"That's her," Jen whispered.

"I know," Ronan whispered back. He stood as the trio approached. "Kommandant Wagner," he greeted her. The trio stopped, the MPs looking to Kipping and getting a nod. He held out his hand. "Ronan Carlyle."

"Carlyle," Wagner said, taking his hand. Her grip was firm and dry, strong even though his hand was quite a bit larger than hers. "The Gray Death Legion."

"Yes, ma'am."

"You're related, then?"

Ronan knew what she meant. "My great-grandfather, ma'am."

Wagner regarded him. "Didn't fall far from the tree, then, did you, Carlyle? That was damn sneaky, what you did to my battalion. I don't know a lot of MechWarriors who'd have held themselves out a distraction while the ground-pounders did the hard work." She glanced at Jen Kipping, who must've held a stoneface, because Wagner didn't react. "Grayson Death Carlyle had a great reputation, but it wasn't one for sneakiness."

"The mission comes first, ma'am."

"You can stop with the ma'am," Wagner said, grinning. "I don't think I'll be a kommandant much longer."

"Maybe not, ma'am," Ronan said, grinning back. "But so long as you are..." He shrugged.

Wagner nodded at him. Turning to Kipping, her demeanor cooled quite a bit. "Hauptmann-Kommandant Kipping," she said. "Still doing Fat Timmy's dirty work, I see?"

"I serve the Commonwealth," Kipping said. "I follow orders."

"You know the rumors are true," Wagner snapped. "At least a little. There are too many stories, too many similarities, for it all to be bullshit. Hell—" she inclined her head at Ronan, "—if his last CO can carve out a bandit kingdom on Arcturus, of all places, then the Jade Falcons *have* to be gone."

Ronan stiffened at the mention of General Regis, but Kipping didn't give him a chance to interject. "I think the rumors *are* true, Kommandant. But that doesn't change the lawful orders I'm given."

One of the MPs cleared his throat. Wagner glanced back at him, then at Ronan, then a lingering glare at Jen Kipping. "Take this lesson to heart, Carlyle," she said. "I took my battalion and tried to do the right thing by the Commonwealth and its people. You stopped me. I don't hold that against you—you were just doing your job. But this one—" she pointed at Jen, "—this one just follows orders, even when she knows they're bullshit. Learn to see the difference, boy. You're going to hold peoples' lives in your hand as CO of a mercenary group. Eventually, you're going to have to make decisions like this one." She glanced down the hall, at the waiting door behind which General Bondayehr waited to pass judgment. "For people like *that*," she spat.

A moment later she and the MPs were gone, inside the room. Kipping sat down, crossing one leg over the other, and sighed. "You may as well sit down," she said. "It'll be a minute."

Ronan turned so he could look down the hall and still see Kipping in his peripheral vision. "I see why her people followed her," he said. "That's a hell of an officer."

"She is," Kipping said. Her tone sounded sincere. Ronan twisted his head and looked down at her. "She *is*," Kipping repeated. "I never said she wasn't. She might have been the best battalion commander on this planet. Maybe one of the best I've ever seen. And her goal, for all that she went about it the wrong way, was the right one. We *should* be out there liberating our citizens if the Jade Falcons are gone. It's our duty."

Ronan frowned. "Then why..."

Kipping shrugged. "It's not *orders.*" She spread her hands. "You know that. Bondayehr should be turning loose every unit he can, instead of hunkering down on this rock like a hermit crab. But until someone either comes with new orders from theater or from Tharkad, he'll sit here. And so will we, because we're an army, not a rabble." She brought her hands back together in her lap and looked up at him.

"We follow orders," Kipping said. "We learned that in KSK 9, remember?"

"I remember a lot of things," Ronan said, sitting down. He wasn't thinking about KSK 9, though. His mind was wallowing in the emotions he'd been feeling the last time he'd been in this building.

And how it felt to get put out on the street with all his people.

Jen Kipping followed Ronan Carlyle into the general's office. She didn't even try to avoid sneering when she saw the JAG officer, Kommandant Lentz, standing at the general's shoulder. Ronan marched into the room and halted, standing, braced to attention, but didn't salute. Kipping braced beside him and did salute.

"Sit down, both of you," General Bondayehr said, waving at them without looking up from his noteputer. Ronan glanced at her, but remained standing. He relaxed to parade rest. She did as she was ordered, though in her heart she wanted to stand next to her friend. He deserved at least that.

He deserves a lot more than that, she made herself admit. She looked up at the tall, blond man with the wide shoulders and the set jaw and mentally rolled her eyes. Ronan Carlyle's pride had been evident the first day he arrived in KSK 9, temporarily detached from his cadre after graduating Coventry. He'd carried himself like the son of nobility he was, to be sure, but he also displayed a zeal for duty and talent for combat.

Looking now between Bondayehr, and Ronan, Kipping with struck with the sudden realization that the two were in the wrong uniforms; Carlyle should be wearing the Lyran fist, and Bondayehr the basic green battledress.

Finally, the general put down the noteputer and looked up. He frowned when he saw Ronan standing. "Something wrong with your chair, Captain Carlyle?"

"I'll stand, General," Carlyle replied evenly. The tension in his shoulders was evident, but his voice was calm.

Bondayehr regarded him, eyes flicking to Kipping, who made no response. He exhaled, crossed his arms, and looked up at the towering Carlyle. "I should congratulate you on the success of your mission, Hauptmann—"

"Captain, General," Ronan interrupted.

Bondayehr frowned. "Captain. Yes. As I was saying, I should congratulate you. You and your scratch unit did all that Hauptmann-Kommandant Kipping assured me it could." He smiled, a patently false smile that wouldn't have convinced a child. "But...I can't bring myself to applaud the assault and killing of Lyran soldiers." His voice hardened, in the last few syllables, into what Kipping imagined he thought of as his command voice.

Kipping bit back a snort. Her mind flashed back to an action no one would ever talk about, where then-Leutnant Carlyle and his *Gauntlet* had faced down two Jade Falcon OmniMechs on Dustball. She remembered the timbre of his voice as he refused the order to leave her behind.

Bondayehr's attempt at command didn't rank on the same scale.

"Neither I nor any of my people took any pleasure in it, General," Ronan said after a moment. "But orders are orders. Soldiers follow orders."

"Indeed," Bondayehr said. He sat there, fingertips tapping on elbows, staring up on the two-meter-plus height of Ronan Carlyle. "Well. Kommandant Lentz, here," he gestured at the JAG, "has a breakdown of your after-action report. And your payment." His mouth twisted into a moue at the last word.

Lentz stepped forward, took a noteputer from the stack on the general's desk, and handed it across the desk to Ronan, who tapped it live and looked down at the displayed numbers. Bondayehr never took his eyes off him.

That made Kipping nervous.

"This is less than we agreed upon," Ronan finally said.

Sir. Kipping realized what had been missing from the entire conversation. Ronan had not once addressed Bondayehr as "sir," giving him the honorific due his rank. He'd been careful to only say "general." And now he'd stopped that.

"The amount was adjusted," Kommandant Lentz ventured, "for damage assessed against LCAF equipment." He smiled with the same empty, reptilian eyes as Bondayehr.

From the side, Kipping saw the muscles in Ronan's jaw work. He lifted the noteputer again, tapped a few commands, swiped with his finger. The muscle in his jaw twitched again as his teeth clenched. "I don't see the delivery schedule for our salvage, either."

"*Salvage!*" Bondayehr blurted. "You destroyed Lyran combat equipment. We're hardly going to give it to you."

"Our contract specified that the Legion could keep anything we killed. The three downed 'Mechs, all the disabled logistical vehicles—that belongs to us."

"Your *contract*," Bondayehr spat, his smile gone now, "says what I say it says."

Ronan set the noteputer back on the general's desk. "That's not how contracts work, General."

"I think you'll find," Kommandant Lentz said, wading into the lull while Bondayehr bristled, "that the relevant documents will be filed with whatever terms we want, *Captain.*"

Kipping licked her lips, just the inside, just the tiniest amount. This was going to be delicious, and she wanted to *taste* it.

Reaching behind his back, Ronan opened the small document storage pocket at the small of his back and pulled out a small folio. He set it, open, with the letters facing the general.

"ComStar may be gone," he said, "but there're still plenty of guarantors of verigraphs. These are the terms Hauptmann-Kommandant Kipping negotiated with my company, gentlemen. This is one of four copies. Another has been placed in escrow with the local representative of the Mercenary Review and Bonding Commission."

Lentz goggled at the verigraph. The holograms worked into the document would display the genetic codes of the encoders and would vanish if the document's storage was modified in any way. For centuries, verigraphs had acted as the absolute record of truth.

Ronan leaned forward, putting his fists on the desk. "You will wire the payment, in full, to the accounts specified. You will deliver the salvage to the listed addresses in Bastion within seventy-two standard hours. Or my unit will sue the LCAF for breach of contract. And with this," he nodded at the folio, "I think the proceedings will be short."

"Who the *hell* do you think you are!" Bondayehr roared. He leaned forward, sputtering. He knocked the folio to the floor.

"The man you *kicked out of the LCAF!*" Ronan roared back. "The man who had to clean up your messes, who led the best soldiers on Garrison against people they used to call comrades because *you* couldn't keep control of them, *Timmy.*"

Kipping stood. She could see the tendons standing out where Ronan gripped the edge of Bondayehr's desk. "Let's all calm down—" she started.

"Get out," Bondayehr said.

"Payment," Ronan said. He straightened up, breathed in, exhaled, met the eyes of Kommandant Lentz and Kipping. "Delivery." He bent down, picked up the folio Bondayehr had knocked off the desk, and set it down. Then he nodded at Kipping, who looked down and up again, and strode to the door. He paused there, looking back. "Listen to the adults, *General.*"

And then he was gone.

Kipping turned back to the desk. Bondayehr trembled with rage. Lentz was flushed; sweat shined on his upper lip.

"Sir—" Kipping started, but Bondayehr slapped a hand on his desk.

"Get out," he whispered.

"Sir..." Lentz ventured, but Bondayehr shook his head once, violently.

"*Out,*" he repeated.

Kipping grabbed the verigraph folio on the way out.

In the hallway, Ronan Carlyle was gone. Lentz pulled the door closed, exhaled, and looked at her with a grin. "That was something," he said. From his tone it was clear he thought they were comrades now, having both survived the shared experience of that meeting.

Kipping jabbed him in the chest with the folio. "Deal with this," she said. "Per these terms. Before the deadline you heard in there."

"The general—"

"I'll handle the general."

Lentz frowned. "I don't know—"

Glad of the release, Kipping grabbed the collar of his battledress and slammed him back against the doorjamb. "Do you see any blue in my rank, Kommandant?" She lifted her chin, exposing the black triangle on her collar.

"N-no."

"Then take this a direct order. And before you try and argue I'm not in your chain of command, I'm a superior officer and a MechWarrior. Do you really think I can't give you orders?"

"N-no, ma'am."

"Then process the contract. Fully. Understand?"

"Yes, ma'am."

"Good." Kipping let Lentz go, smoothed his collar, and shooed him on his way. A moment later, she was alone in the corridor outside the general's office. She looked both ways, but the corridor was empty. Taking a deep breath, she worked her hands, waiting for the tingling in her fingertips to fade.

"I'd rather be fighting the Jade Falcons," she muttered before heading to the lift.

CHAPTER 11

**CASTEL
GARRISON
LYRAN COMMONWEALTH
29 OCTOBER 3151**

Bel was waiting in the hotel lobby when Ronan came down the next morning. He hadn't been able to muster up the willpower to hop the train to Bastion the night before, and anyway he—they—*the Legion*—had business in Castel.

In mufti, she sat in an overstuffed chair, a mug of light-colored coffee on the armrest. One side of her hair was tucked behind one ear. She looked for all the world like a young businesswoman waiting to meet someone for breakfast.

Which, Ronan told himself, *isn't that far from the truth.* "Have you been waiting long?" he asked as he walked up.

"Not long," Bel said. She brandished the coffee cup. "Besides, your hotel makes a fantastic latte." She set down the noteputer she'd been scrolling as he settled in across from her. "So. How'd it go?"

"You were right," he admitted. "They tried to cheat us."

Bel grinned. "Toldja."

"I left the one copy of the verigraph. The money was wired overnight, I checked this morning. And I got a message from Jen Kipping; the salvage trucks are on their way to Bastion." He rubbed his palms together. "I wasn't sure until I saw the money last night. I thought I messed it up."

"What do you mean?"

Ronan looked at the floor. "I called him Timmy. To his face."

When he looked up, Bel snort-laughed. "I'd have given real money to be there for that," she said, then giggled. "Wow."

Ronan stood. "So. If we leave now, we can catch the mid-morning train and maybe beat the salvage trucks."

Bel didn't stand. "Or..."

"Or what?"

"We had mail waiting when I got back to base," his sister said. "Two pieces stand out." She gestured with the noteputer. "Sit down." When he sat, she handed the noteputer over. "Just tap it live," she said. "The first one is from home."

"Home?" Ronan glanced down, then back at his sister. She nodded, smiling.

"A JumpShip just came in by way of Odessa."

Ronan swallowed. He'd sent word to his parents immediately after the debacle in Castel, of course, telling them what had happened, that he and Bel were safe, and that they were out of the LCAF. But with no hyperpulse generators to send the message faster-than-light, they'd had to rely on a JumpShip visiting Odessa, delivering the message via radio, and getting a response. It worked, but it was slow.

He tapped the message open. It was plain text. *Ronan*, it started, *you did everything right. People come first. See attached for what help we can send. All our love. Dad.*

Blinking, Ronan swallowed and looked up. "You looked at the attachment?"

Bel nodded. "It was encrypted, but it was one of the family ciphers. It's money. Local lines of credit if we need it, and a list of assets we can liquidate if we need to."

Ronan looked down at the noteputer so his sister wouldn't see his eyes. He'd never understood whether or not Gardner Carlyle had understood why he'd joined the LCAF instead of staying on Odessa and embracing life as The Honorable Ronan Carlyle, eldest son of the planetary baron.

Now he knew.

People come first.

It didn't matter if you were responsible for a planet or a group of abandoned former Arcturan Guards. People came first.

Sniffing, Ronan toggled the other message. "The second?"

"The second was me," a new voice said. Ronan looked up. At first his brain refused to process what he was seeing. Standing next to Bel's chair, also in mufti, with one hand on the chair back, was Kathleen McQuade.

"Colonel—"

McQuade interrupted him, raising a finger to her lips. "Just Kathleen for now," she said. "I'm a wanted woman on this planet, after all."

Ronan looked around without thinking. Bel rolled her eyes. "No one's watching, idiot."

Colonel McQuade sat down in the identical overstuffed chair between the facing pair Ronan and Bel filled. "I'm told you did good work the other day," she said, "by people I trust to know."

Ronan blinked. "Col—ma'am—*Kathleen*. How are you here? What are you doing here?" He was suddenly back on that parade field on Arcturus, feeling the weight of her judging glare as he walked toward the bus that eventually brought him here, to Garrison. "And how could you hear about the other day? You're a wanted traitor."

McQuade made a shushing gesture with her hands. "Not quite so loud with the traitor, okay?" She glanced at Bel, who made no reaction, then looked back to Ronan. "As for the rest, let's just say I know a lot of people who hate Timofey Bondayehr and officers like him, and they'll still talk to me, even when I'm *persona non grata*."

Ronan frowned. "How do you know we won't turn you in?"

McQuade sat back in her chair and crossed her leg. "I don't." She turned away to flag down a waiter and order a coffee. Pointed to Bel's cup. "Whatever she's having."

The pause gave Ronan time to marshal his thoughts. "We told them everything we knew," he said. "When we got here. When they interrogated us."

"Before they kicked you to the curb," McQuade said, nodding. "Of course you did. You couldn't do anything less and still be doing your duty." She shook her head at him. "We knew you would. It was the cost of letting you go."

"We talked about keeping quiet," Bel said. "A couple of us, on the ride here. But we couldn't see an upside."

"There wasn't one," McQuade said, nodding. "General Regis knew you'd tell all you could. But we also knew Garrison was the nearest planet, and that Fat Timmy Bondayehr was senior officer on-world. For all of Garrison's martial past, there wasn't anything you could tell the LCAF here that would threaten Arcturus. Or any of the other worlds of the Pact."

"Other worlds?" Bel asked.

McQuade winked at her. "So the risk was manageable."

"Did you argue to let us go?" Ronan asked quietly.

"No," McQuade said without hesitation. "I said we should machine-gun the lot of you and bury your bodies in the woods. But the general said we owed you more than that."

Bel sipped her coffee. "Wow."

McQuade was watching Ronan. "The thought occurred to me," he admitted. "I wondered if anyone else had thought of it."

"General Regis told us there was no point in reclaiming our ancient homelands if we did so with the blood of the people who got us there on our hands." McQuade shrugged. "She's probably right."

"Probably," Bel said. She looked at McQuade like one looks at an alligator.

"Time will tell," the Tamar colonel said. "Which brings me to the here and now. You're mercenaries now, yes?" When Ronan nodded, she nodded once, as if filing the information. "Looking for work?"

"You're joking," Ronan said. "A couple months ago you wanted to shoot us."

"It wasn't personal," McQuade said. "You were shooting at Lyran militiamen two days ago. Was that personal?" She sat up as the waiter brought her coffee. She took it with both hands, sat back, blew on the top, and sipped. From the face she made, she and Bel had very different tastes in coffees.

Ronan sat back in his chair. "The Legion is only about a week old."

McQuade nodded. "I knew that. Good choice, that. Taking up the old name."

"It was Bel's idea."

"I figured."

Ronan frowned. "You're not doing a lot of wooing here, *Kathleen*."

McQuade chuckled. "You served with me long enough, *Hauptmann*, to know I'm no wooer." She uncrossed her legs and sat forward. "Here's what I hope your plans are." She held up a hand before he could speak. "I was in operations. I make plans. Go with it."

"Okay," Ronan said.

"Today, the balance of *Aufklärungsbataillon 29* will be cashiered, just like you were," she said. At Ronan's raised eyebrow—*how could she know that?*—she held up her hand and rolled her eyes. "People talk to me, remember? Anyone in that battalion without interest is on the street." Ronan knew what *interest* meant. In the class-conscious LCAF, cronyism and social-generalism were rampant. "Anyone worth anything will do what you did, look after their people."

"Kommandant Wagner?"

"Arrested. Fat Timmy will ship her off-world for court-martial. She's out of the picture."

"They just wanted to do their duty," Ronan said, remembering the shock of being kicked out of the LCAF.

"Just so. Now you have some recruiting to do."

"Recruiting."

"If you don't think those recon troopers didn't notice how you went for mission-killing their loggies instead of, you know, actually killing them, you're not paying attention." McQuade reached into her pocket and pulled out a datacard. She handed it to Bel. "That's the personal comm of every officer and non-com above sergeant."

"Come on," Ronan said.

"I told you," McQuade said. "People like me."

"Must be your sparkling personality," Bel said, deadpan.

"Must be," McQuade said. She looked back at Ronan. "So. Recruit. Keeping digging equipment out of your rust pile. I can have transport here in four months. If you can have even the bones of a combined-arms battalion of at least a dozen 'Mechs by then, I can offer you a contract."

"A contract for what?"

"Retainer, most likely. In the Pact."

"I won't fight the LCAF," Ronan said.

"Plenty of other threats out there," the colonel said. She sipped her coffee again, made a gagging face, and set it down in front of Bel. "Call this a bonus."

She stood. "I'll be in touch in three months. If you're gone by then, I'll consider that a no. But if you're not, and you need a contract, well...we served together. I trust you." She glanced at Bel. "More, the general trusts you."

"I'll think about it," Ronan said.

"*We'll* think about it," Bel corrected.

"Do," Colonel McQuade said. "Be seeing you, Carlyles."

And she was gone.

Bel looked at Ronan, sipped her coffee, and set it on her knee. "Well, that was weird."

"Yeah..." Ronan's mind raced. He was thinking about all the people he'd left behind in the Arcturans, wondering how they were doing. What they'd think he if he reappeared at the head of a mercenary battalion. About what McQuade had meant by "worlds" of the Tamar Pact...

After a moment he shook his head, exhaled, and stood. "Come on."

"Where are we going?"

"To charter some busses," he said. "We know what happens when Bondayehr kicks you out of the LCAF. I want to make sure we're ready to meet those Two-Nines when they come out." He nodded once and rolled his shoulders. "Nobody should ever feel that abandoned."

Bel stood. "That's a fantastic idea, brother," she said. "And we can hire them on the drive back."

Ronan smiled, squeezed her shoulder, and pulled her toward the door. "That's for tomorrow. Today we just need to make sure they realize they're not alone."

He nodded once, to himself. "People come first."

BUSHWACKER
MEDIUM—55 TONS

GAUNTLET
MEDIUM—55 TONS

GARGOYLE (MAN O' WAR)
ASSAULT—80 TONS

HATCHETMAN
MEDIUM—45 TONS

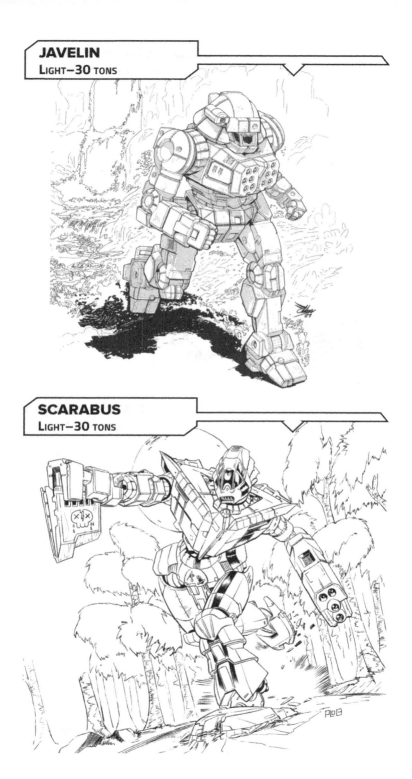

JAVELIN
Light—30 tons

SCARABUS
Light—30 tons

TALON
LIGHT—35 TONS

WOLFHOUND
LIGHT—35 TONS

MERCENARY'S HONOR

CHAPTER 1

CONDOR
CRIMOND
TAMAR PACT
21 JANUARY 3152

Curtain didn't wait for the skiff to bump the dock. He had his pack in hand and stood, arm ready, to let the momentum of the boat give him an extra-long step across the distance. He shouldered the pack as soon as his feet were settled on the rough ferrocrete, turned, and sketched a loose salute, really just a finger to his temple, to the boatman. "A favor is owed," he said in one of the tongues of the Emberá people.

"Pardon?" Curtain repeated it in English. "Not if your coin is good," the boatman replied. He turned the wheel, thrusters pushing the skiff back away from the dock and spinning the bow around at the same time.

Curtain nodded and turned away, toward the shore. *A favor is owed*, he thought, *no matter the coin*. He had paid the boatman's master, the captain of the oceanic fishing ship, for passage, sure. But he hadn't paid the boatman himself. And the passage from the ship to the shore had been skillful; the reefs on this side of Condor were difficult to see in the dark, not marked with buoys as they were on the Fort Beaufort side.

Curtain chuckled as he stepped off the dock onto the soft soil; it was unlikely he'd ever see the boatman again, so the favor likely had no cost. Which had no effect on the burden

Curtain put on himself. He wasn't so juvenile as to believe in fairness, but he understood reciprocity.

"What's so funny?" a woman's quiet voice asked.

And loyalty, he understood that too.

"I keep accepting burdens," he told her. "How is it, Andy?"

"I think you're supposed to tell me that," Andrea—Andy—Ishikawa said. Andy stood about a meter-eight, not tall but not remarkably short. She kept her black hair cut short, tight across her light brown skin in a skullcap. Her clothes were pure Condor jungle: thick-fabric fatigue pants with sealed boots and a jacket loose enough to not catch on the holster on her right thigh. The handle of a machete stuck over her left shoulder.

"Later," he said. "I don't want to tell it twice." He reset his pack on his shoulder and gestured for her to precede him down the path. She rolled her eyes and did so. It was a short walk to the jeep. The dirt roads through the Darien were impassable to the hovercraft they preferred on the big continents, and maintenance on tracks away from the Fort was hopeless, so they made do with wheels and tires.

"We'll have to lay over at Paulo's outpost," Andy told him. "We can't make it tonight."

"Fine," Curtain said. He hefted his pack into the rear seat and climbed aboard. He breathed deeply, drinking in the fragrant, wet scents of the jungle. He got a couple of the local insects, of course, but that was habit as well. He spit them out without crunching the chitin; in the high jungle, the bugs were thick, but none of the native Crimond insects found humans palatable. "I miss Paulo's wife's cooking." *You always miss home, when you choose it*, he knew. *Even the bugs*.

"Paulo's wife," Andy said, climbing aboard, "doesn't like you."

Curtain chuckled. "Everyone likes me."

"Not the woman who has to cook—you eat more than three other people combined."

"I have a high metabolism."

"You may as well be an Elemental."

"Founder forfend," Curtain said, affecting a shudder. He waved a few more bugs out of his face. "Are we going?"

"We are," Andy said. She pressed the button to start the jeep, and the fuel cell engine fired right up. The headlights were bright LEDs, brilliant in the darkening air even though there was plenty of light left. Clouds of insects swirled in the beams. Curtain chuckled again.

"Top's going up, I'm not having those things crawling in my hair," Andy said. Curtain said nothing, just spread his hands. The jeep's top came up out of the rear and settled over them quickly, then the vehicle jerked into motion. The top also cut off enough of the engine noise that they could speak without shouting.

"Give me the short version," Andy said.

"The rumors are true."

"Invaders?"

"Liberators, they call themselves," Curtain said. "From Arcturus. But not the Commonwealth."

"Not from the Commonwealth—like, mercenaries?"

"No, not like mercenaries."

Andy drove in silence for a moment, bumping over the rain-soaked track. "Curtain?"

"Yes?"

"Don't make me leave you out here."

"I don't want to tell it twice."

"Tell me," she commanded.

"There is, if the newcomers are to be believed, a new Tamar Pact," Curtain told her. The grin fell away as he recalled all he had learned, all he had heard. "The constabulary in Sol City folded right away, so by the old laws, I guess we're now citizens of the Tamar Pact."

"The old laws."

"Before the Clans came here, custom was if the invader defeated the defender, the planet was theirs." Curtain shifted in his seat; he was too big to really be comfortable in a jeep, and none of the accommodations on the ship had been to his size, either.

"That doesn't make any sense."

"History rarely does."

"Why would the people back then go for that?"

"To avoid fighting in the cities," Curtain said absently. His memory was reciting facts he'd learned in the *sibko* while his mind cycled again through his last few weeks. "To avoid total war, and reprisals, and the final dark age the Inner Sphere so narrowly avoided in the Succession Wars."

"Sounds like a bunch of cowards," Andy said.

"We weren't there."

"They expect us to hew to these old laws?"

"I didn't ask," Curtain said. "But you've been to the mainlands. What do you think?"

Andy snorted. "I bet the miners are already measuring their fuses."

Curtain chuckled. "I suspect you are right."

"Will they come here?" Andy asked a few moments later.

"Unless we are luckier than we've earned," Curtain said.

They drove the rest of the way in silence.

CHAPTER 2

SOL CITY
CRIMOND
TAMAR PACT
2 FEBRUARY 3152

"A car race."

"That's right."

Isobel Carlyle frowned. She couldn't be hearing what she thought she was hearing. "They surrendered the whole planet. After a *car race*."

"Yes." Her brother Ronan, tall, sandy-haired, earnest as any two second sons, rolled his eyes.

"That's the stupidest thing I ever heard."

"I know."

"What is wrong with these people?"

"Ask louder—I'm sure some of them will want to answer you."

Bel frowned and looked around. She and Ronan sat in an open-air cafe along the banks of the River James in Sol City, capital of the planet Crimond, newest member of the reborn Tamar Pact, a collection of worlds abandoned by the Lyran Commonwealth, abandoned by Clan Jade Falcon, pretty much abandoned by everyone. It was a young nation, less than a year old, but strong. And it was the employer of record for the Gray Death Legion, commanded by one Major Ronan Carlyle, also employing Captain Bel Carlyle, commander of scouts. A good number of the other patrons wore battledress, though the

Carlyles were the only ones in Legion gray. The rest wore the green shade known as "field gray" of the Lyran Commonwealth Armed Forces, though none of them served that organization any longer.

"So the whole thing is over?"

"Pretty much," Ronan said. He sipped his latte and looked across the river. "Be nice to have some downtime, I guess."

Bel looked around. "Then why did we even tag along?"

Ronan shrugged. "Orders."

The Legion had come to Crimond along with a battalion of the Third Tamar Jaegers—which, as far as Bel and Ronan were concerned, was really just Third Battalion, Twenty-Sixth Arcturan Guards, with some attachments. The Carlyles had been expelled from the Twenty-Six about six months earlier, when they refused to join the regiment in rebellion against the Archon. The Tamar Pact shipped them to Garrison as Lyran loyalists, where the local Lyran Commonwealth Armed Forces had promptly cashiered them as Tamar traitors.

And so the Gray Death Legion was reborn as a mercenary battalion. And, absurdly, hired by the group of people who'd kicked them out in the first place: the Tamar Pact.

The Jade Falcons had abandoned their occupation zone in a frenzy to race Clan Wolf to Terra. No one Bel trusted had yet come back with an answer of what had happened on Terra, or if the fighting was even over, but what was true was that the Falcons were gone. And worlds like Crimond needed protection. Or liberation. Or conquering. She wasn't one hundred percent clear on their exact role here.

Crimond, historically a Lyran Commonwealth world, had been conquered first by Clan Wolf, and then the Jade Falcons across recent decades. It was a sparse world, barely a billion people, spread across two continents, Metallerz and Chromastich. The majority of the planet's industry had been mining; both continents were dotted with abandoned "boom towns" where surface deposits were mined out before people moved on. It made for a population of fiercely independent people, all of them out for their own self-interest, who barely tolerated the so-called planetary government here in Sol City. Bel had no idea how the Jade Falcons had administered the world, but if whoever they left in charge wanted to surrender the whole planet a kilometer at a time...

"I don't understand—" Bel said, before the restaurant's kitchen exploded.

She didn't put together what had happened until she blinked herself back to awareness on the ground, crushed beneath Ronan against the stone railing, with the detritus of chairs, food, and drink splashed across her. Her leg was bent painfully beneath her and she felt the arm of a chair driving into her side, but Ronan shifted and the pressure eased. Her skin felt hot and prickly; her nose and sinuses were on fire, and her ears rang so loudly she couldn't hear anything else. There was grit in her eyes; they burned, and her arm hurt when she reached up a hand to rub at them.

Her whole body hurt.

She finally got her eyes clear and looked around. People were down all over. Some were moving, slowly like she was. Most were not. Ronan had gotten shakily to his feet, but was bracing himself with one hand on the railing. Bel watched him look around, then down at her. His mouth moved, as if he were talking, but all she heard was ringing.

"What?" she asked, or tried to. She couldn't hear herself.

He pointed at her with two fingers, then made a thumbs up and a questioning face. *He wants to know if I'm okay.* She shrugged and rolled to her hands and knees. They way her body felt, she didn't want to rush getting to her feet. She put her hand in something warm and wet; it was red when she lifted it.

That's blood.

Bel struggled to her feet, looking around. Muffled sounds were starting to penetrate the ringing, as if they were far away and deep underwater. Her head swam, but she found her balance. Ronan gripped her upper arm, stared into her eyes. She blinked and tried to focus.

"Okay?" he yelled. It sounded like he was across a football pitch. She blinked, then opened her mouth wide, trying to pop her ears. Maybe that would help. It didn't, but she nodded anyway, then looked past him, got a good look at the building.

The cafe had been on the raised porch of a restaurant housed in the cupola of a government building. The facade was wood painted to look like stone, between two native stone pillars. The facade was gone, the edges jagged and blackened.

It was a miracle they were alive.

Bel looked around, behind her, across the street and the square, toward the other buildings. She could see broken windows and people picking themselves up, and men and women in both military uniforms and the gray utilities of the local constabulary running toward them.

She looked back at where the kitchen had been.

"I got blown up," she whispered, or tried to.

SOL CITY
CRIMOND
TAMAR PACT
3 FEBRUARY 3152

The sentries outside the temporary Tamar command center at the Sol City spaceport were armored today, Bel saw, a pair of black-painted Infiltrator Mk II battlesuits with MagShots mounted and rounds in the feed tube. There was an unarmored infantry staff sergeant checking IDs against a noteputer, but the line was moving rapidly. He checked Bel and Ronan's IDs, frowned at their grays, and then motioned them inside with his chin.

The command center was a commandeered secure aircraft hangar on the spaceport's edge, where the civilian airport was attached. The hangar was probably where some noble kept his puddle-jumper, but the Tamar Jaegers had evicted him and installed what looked like the guts of two mobile headquarters vehicles. There was a section off to the side with chairs set up for the briefing they'd come to attend, but the crowd was still milling around. It was a little unsettling, seeing so many soldiers in Lyran battledress without the Steiner fist on their shoulders.

"Nice guy," Bel said. "The guy at the door."

"Just doing his job," Ronan said. He was standing a little stiffly, looking around. Bel looked around, resisting the urge to knuckle her still-humming ears.

"What are you looking at?"

Ronan flinched. "Nothing."

"You're looking for people you know," Bel said.

"We served in the Twenty-Sixth for a while," he said. "We were officers. We're going to know people."

"Far as I'm concerned, these people are all strangers," Bel said. "They kicked us out."

Ronan grunted. "Yet here we are."

Bel rolled her eyes. She still had moments where the sheer absurdity of the past six months shocked her. Seven months ago they'd all been aboard DropShips, headed for Arcturus from Kandersteg, all loyal soldiers of the Commonwealth doing their duty for Archon and nation. And then they'd been ejected from the family of their regiment, sent to Garrison, where the LCAF, the organization they had renounced their traitorous brethren to serve, rejected them.

And now here they were, working for their traitorous former comrades as mercenaries.

Home is the regiment, she'd always heard around her family growing up. An old saying, but one the Carlyles kept alive. The nascent Gray Death Legion had been formed out of that core of loyal LCAF soldiers who'd been cashiered on the order of Hauptmann-General Timofey Bondayehr. Fat Timmy, as his troops called him, soon repeated his mistake by ejecting the core of a Lyran recon battalion that had attempted to go rogue and, you know, free Commonwealth worlds from invaders. A lot of those recon troopers had joined the Legion after their forced discharges.

A handful of other former Lyran soldiers had applied and been accepted, too. Ronan was always careful to say that one successful battle was not a tradition of victory, but with the unrest along the former Jade Falcon border, Bel understood the need to feel like you were somewhere safe.

And even more after yesterday. *In fact...*

"Somebody gets a bomb in here," she said, leaning close to Ronan, "like yesterday? Whole liberation is over."

"One hopes not," Ronan said dryly.

The crowd began moving toward the briefing area, and Bel and Ronan drifted that way. Bel made for the last row of chairs, but Ronan touched her shoulder and shook his head.

She frowned, but then remembered. Scowling, she looked toward the front of the briefing area, but didn't recognize any of the officers.

The regiment's operations shop would be in charge of putting on the briefing. In the LCAF, it wasn't at all uncommon for the rank-conscious Lyran officer corps to play favorites by inviting more officers and senior enlisted than they set up chairs for, so those of junior stature could be shown their place in the pecking order. It was petty, but life was petty.

Bel looked around, seeing a couple of collar flashes for kommandants—battalion commanders—and more hauptmanns—company commanders—looking around and eyeing chair. There was already a mass of leutnants—lance and platoon leaders—standing along the sides and back.

Bel and Ronan, she knew, as attached mercenaries, were lucky to even be in the room. The Legion had only landed two days before, and they were still waiting on their liaison officer to appear. Even though Ronan held the rank of major, equivalent to the Tamar kommandants, she knew it wasn't at all the same thing.

"*ACHTUNG!*" You could take the soldier out of the Commonwealth, it seemed, but you couldn't take the German out of the soldier.

At the shout, every Tamar officer in the room who had sat jumped to their feet. All the standing officers clicked their heels, Ronan included. Bel did not. She'd be damned if she was going to kowtow to some Tamar dandy—

"Wow," Ronan whispered.

"What?" Bel asked. She was too short to see past the clutch of field gray backs. Ronan was tall, damn him. He should know better.

"The Tamar colonel—it's Gerald Torres."

"Torres—wait. The infantry colonel?"

"The same."

Bel blinked back surprise. "The general is progressive, I guess." In every military that had them, BattleMechs were the premier ground combat unit, commanding the most prestige and usually, the most authority. 'Mech officers rarely submitted to the control of officers from other branches like infantry or armor. In the past it had led to extreme cases like BattleMech captains giving "orders" to armor colonels.

As people started sitting down, Bel got a glimpse of the infantry colonel. He looked like most senior officers she had seen; older, with a middle-age paunch and a serious expression. He kept head shaved so close the light reflected off his near-obsidian skin. He took his seat in the front row, and those near him did the same.

The people who'd sat down earlier than the colonel now stood out to Bel. 'Mech officers, maybe?

"This is going to be interesting," Ronan muttered. Bel didn't know if he meant the briefing, or the contract as a whole.

CHAPTER 3

CONDOR
CRIMOND
TAMAR PACT
3 FEBRUARY 3152

"Hot as hell in here, *quiaff*?"

Bernard Blucher was glad he had his head half-inside the panel and didn't have to hide his expression at the Clan euphemism. "Sure is," he said, and kept focusing on trying to get the cable run free of the binding clips. The fault he was tracing had to be in this bundle somewhere.

Fort Beaufort had been built centuries earlier for the Star League Defense Force, and basically abandoned for half that time before the LCAF turned Condor into a harsh environment training facility in the 3010s. Since then, much of the original fort had been either scavenged, ignored, or shoddily rebuilt and rewired for whoever had occupied the sprawling complex. For much of that time, the entire island continent had been largely uninhabited, aside from short-term coastal settlements to support fishing operations or smugglers. It was only since the Clans came that people had moved to Condor en masse. First the Wolves, then the Jade Falcons, and neither had given a whit where the people went so long as they did what they were supposed to be doing.

The first clip broke under the pressure of his pliers, and he saw now why it had taken so much effort. He'd thought the whole clip was plastic, but the outer plastic was just a sheath for a narrow metal core. It had taken friction weakening, him twisting it back and forth, to make the metal warp and break. Blucher dropped the pieces and sighed, looking ahead at the four additional clips in the run.

"How long until you guys get the air conditioning restored?" Blucher closed his eyes. *The air conditioning. That's your priority.* "I'm just doing the wiring, friend." He reached for the next clip, but his forearm cramped. He gasped and dropped the pliers.

"You okay?"

"Arm cramped."

"Ouch."

"Yeah." Blucher flexed his hand a couple times, then picked up the pliers. The LED light on his headband cast weirdly-sharp shadows inside the panel casing. He went to work on the next clip in line.

Bernard Blucher had been on Crimond more than twenty years ago as part of the Lyran Commonwealth Armed Forces, a technical staff sergeant in a support team assigned to see about reconditioning Fort Beaufort for the LCAF. It was those desperate years around the Blackout, when everyone was suddenly afraid the Clans would appear out of the darkness and kill them all. The Wolf Clan appearing and taking the planet was almost anticlimactic. Blucher had spent the next ten years assigned to a technician caste work team focused on civilian infrastructure, until the Wolves abandoned Crimond and the Jade Falcons swept in. Not that he'd gone looking for it, but when the merchants had come through the camps for POWs who'd refused to become bondsmen, Blucher hadn't eaten in four meals, and he was getting scared. He'd managed to avoid the Jade Falcon castes after they took over; the Falcons were less inclusive, but Blucher had made a living subcontracting work from a Free Guilds contact, learning more about how Jade Falcon techs put things together.

When the Jade Falcon *touman* left, Blucher bought his way onto a fish trawler headed toward Condor, and then made his way to the fort. He didn't speak a word of Emberá, but neither did any of the others who were here from Clan heritage, and his experience with the Free Guilds gave him enough knowledge to fake being one of those. Soon enough, the idiots accepted him at face value and let him go wherever he wanted.

Nothing else appearing, Blucher had gone to what first brought him to Crimond in the first place: the old Star League fort. The Commonwealth would return for the Crimonds—and him—soon enough, he was sure. Not even the Blackout could keep away word that Crimond lay naked. The LCAF would come back, and they'd find Staff Sergeant Bernard Blucher still here, still working to learn what he could about the Commonwealth's enemies.

If he could ever get this *damn* cable run out and find the fault...

"What are you doing in there, anyway?"

Blucher closed his eyes. "Trying to get this place working," he said. Again.

"Why?"

"Because it's something to do."

"Sounds boring."

"You don't need to watch me."

"I got nothing else to do until Curtain gets back."

Blucher strained, and broke the last clip. He huffed and relaxed, letting his hand just lay with the pliers, then set them down. Grasping the cable bundle, he gave it a gentle tug. Nothing happened. He adjusted his grip and, now that the clips were all loose, worked the bundle back and forth across the space. If the wall mount was modular, like most of them here, then the bundle should come free after a minute—*there*. He grabbed the pliers and shimmied backward on his side until his head was free of the panel. Then he got to his hands and knees, and pulled the freed cable run out where he could see it.

"What's that?"

Blucher glanced over. The young man—*Blanton, his name is Blanton*—was about half Blucher's age, with short-cut brown hair and pale skin burning red in the Condor sun. His outfit was pure laborer caste, off-green utilities in a coarse, cheap, easy-to-extrude fabric.

Blucher put the pliers back in the case by his knees, then sat back into a sprawl. He held the end of the cable run up and looked at it. From the dust on the mounting, he might be the first person in 300 years to see it outside that panel. "It's a cable."

"For what?"

"That's what I'm trying to figure out," Blucher said. "I'm tracing a fault between two systems. The sending unit is working fine, but the receiver isn't getting it."

"Sounds boring," Blanton said.

"So does waiting for Curtain," Blucher muttered.

Curtain. Blucher had only met Curtain once, in passing, but he could tell even then that they weren't going to get along. Curtain was a bear of a man, a MechWarrior, though clearly freeborn. He lacked a Trueborn's haughtiness. He'd defaulted to being leader of the people of Condor less because of rank or caste structure, or even because he had a BattleMech, but because he was loud and willing to make decisions when almost no one else seemed to be.

"He went to the mainland to check the rumors," Blanton said. If he'd heard the sarcasm in Blucher's voice, he'd clearly ignored it. "About the invaders, you know?"

"Yes, I've seen the HV." Blucher began picking the strands of the cable run apart to check for physical defects. The old Star League techs had been wizards of technology by the standards of any age, but centuries of time was centuries of time, and entropy waited for no one. Metal fatigue, polymer corruption… it could be any of a hundred things breaking the connection.

Holovid on Condor was spotty at best, but because of that it ended up being one of the main social attractions for the Emberá and their guests. They'd all seen the imagery of the DropShips descending, the pronouncements of the neutered Jade Falcon constabulary that the invader would be ejected immediately. Blucher had snort-laughed at that: the Jade Falcons had barely kept track of what was going on across Crimond before they all pulled out. Now that the warriors were gone, they had no idea. Blucher, all the others here, had only made it because of that limited view.

He pulled the noteputer around from the pouch on the small of his back. The probes in his thigh pocket were already synched to it. The cables all looked good, so he was going to have to do a guide test on each strand to figure out where the break was.

As he was setting the probes against the first wire, Blanton's comm chirped. "Curtain's back!" the boy cried, jumping to his feet.

"Great," Blucher said.

"Aren't you coming?"

"Maybe when I'm done," Blucher said. He touched the second set of cables, watching the meter displayed on the noteputer's screen. Also good. Blanton was gone by the time he touched the third wire, thank all the gods.

There's no rush, he knew. Whatever the news, Condor was a small community. He'd hear about it eventually, even in passing. There was certainly nothing else to talk about. Blucher sighed and took the probes off the fourth wire. It was good. As was the fifth.

They were all good.

Blucher frowned and set the cable bundle down. He slid the probes back into their pocket and stared at the dusty floor for a minute, thinking. He'd traced both ends of the connection along this building. The fault should have been here. *If it isn't here*...he didn't know.

"Now I have to put all that back," he muttered. He had replacement clip-ties in his tool bag. While his fingers did their task, Blucher set his mind to tracing circuit diagrams.

He was trying to get the main control system here in the central Fort Beaufort Citadel fortress building to connect to the sensor outposts. Beaufort was a sprawling complex set at the base of the mountains, a couple kilometers from the wide river that more or less demarcated the mountains and jungle from the desert. It was a weird trick of ecology Blucher didn't even try to understand, that you could drive from sweltering, humid jungle to dry, moisture-stealing desert in less than an hour.

The sensor outposts extended up the side of the mountain and out toward the river, past the old, vine-shrouded defensive turrets. If he could get even a handful of them working again, and reporting back to the main control room here in the Citadel, he'd be able to give the Fort eyes. One man could sit at a console and see for kilometers.

That's what he wanted, more than anything. The Commonwealth would be coming back. They'd want to occupy

Fort Beaufort, and if Blucher had gotten even a few of the old fort's systems back online, that might go a long way toward convincing the LCAF not to look too closely at how he'd spent the past decades. If he could just get back in, he'd have an incredible amount of seniority, be overdue for promotion.

After he got the cable run secured together and then clipped back in place, he replaced the panel access cover and stood, brushing dust and dirt off his pants. There were great scuff marks where he'd knelt and worked in the dust coating the floor. *Gonna have to get someone to clean things up, too*, Blucher realized. There was certainly no chance he was going to pick up a broom.

Outside the building, the sun was starting to get low in the sky. Blucher stood and looked around, hoping fresh eyes would give him an insight. He'd already walked the track of the cable run, or as close as he could, between the building and the sensor outpost. It was underground, of course, but there hadn't been any obvious examples of disturbed soil. It was possible a burrowing animal or a tree root had dislodged something, but he didn't think so. He was just missing something.

Blucher sighed and turned toward the setting sun. There was always tomorrow.

CHAPTER 4

"I'm sorry, Major, but I don't have time for you today."

Bel Carlyle frowned and looked at her brother, but Ronan took the dismissal with aplomb. They stood in a makeshift cubbyhole office shoehorned into the space between two ten-meter shipping containers. The desk was a plank of polymer set across two fuel barrels, and from the smell, neither of the barrels had been cleaned before being requisitioned.

"I think you can make time, Hauptmann," Ronan said. "Seeing as you've got a countryside erupting in bombings and violence, and I've got a short battalion to help you catch the people responsible for it."

Bel eyed the Tamar officer. She knew him, or knew his name and face, anyway. He'd been a first lieutenant back in the Twenty-Sixth Arcturan Guards Regimental Combat Team, executive officer of one of the Third Battalion BattleMech companies, but she couldn't remember which one. His name was Eldon, it was stitched right there on the nametape on his battledress, but she had no idea what his first name was.

He was a hauptmann now. *I guess breaking an RCT into three light combat teams makes for some promotions*, Bel thought. Governor-General Sarah Regis of Arcturus, formerly Hauptmann-General Regis of the Twenty-Sixth Arcturan Guard, and her staff had broken up the old Twenty-Sixth to stand up the First through Third Tamar Jaegers. Based on the old Federated Suns LCT model, the short combined arms regiments offered a balanced force mix that was relatively easily transportable, but lacked the heavy hitting or staying power of a full regimental combat team.

"The Jaegers can handle some unruly miners," Hauptmann Eldon said shortly. "We certainly don't need trigger-happy mercenaries out there shooting up towns and turning the people against us."

"Where were you two days ago, Hauptmann?" Bel asked.

"What?"

"Two days ago." Bel reached up and brushed blond hair away from her forehead to expose the ugly, green-brown bruise on her skin. "When I got this at the Sol City bombing?" She let go of her hair and gestured around the makeshift office. "Were you here, sitting on your ass, waiting for someone to tell you what to do then, too?"

"Bel," Ronan said.

"How *dare* you—" Eldon started, but Ronan cut him off.

"Excuse Captain Carlyle, Hauptmann," he said. "She may be concussed. In all the emergency, there hasn't been time to get in to see a doctor." Before the Tamar officer could speak more, Ronan barreled on. "Now, my Legion's contract names you our liaison officer, and tells me I get my orders through you. I'm here for orders. If your orders are I keep a battalion of good soldiers sitting around, that's what I do. But we're a resource, Hauptmann. Use us. There has to be some task from the ops shop you can give us."

Eldon glared at Bel for a moment longer, before he shifted his eyes to Ronan. The other Carlyle was quite a bit taller, so he had to look up. Way up. Bel managed to control her smirk, but only just. She was seething, and it had nothing to do with any concussion. Eldon was a clear example of the worst kind of young Lyran officer she'd known at the Coventry Military Academy and after, in the Twenty-Sixth. The cocky, sycophantic generation convinced of the natural Lyran—or, she guessed, Tamar now—exceptionalism that it had done nothing to earn.

He looked down his nose at mercenaries, thinking of them as nothing more than money-hungry wannabes.

Which was fair. Bel knew of any number of mercenary bands that fit that description. But that wasn't the Legion. It hadn't been in their great-grandfather's day, and it wasn't true now, and this *dummkopf* ought to know that from Ronan Carlyle's record from the Twenty-Sixth and before, if nothing else. *Assuming the rat even took the time to look him up*, Bel realized.

"If I did that," Eldon said slowly, "it would only eat up my time because I'd have to get out there with you to give the requisite orders."

"Ah," Ronan said. "A small point of order, *Hauptmann*," he emphasized the rank beneath his. "My contract names you liaison, not commander. You give me objectives. I see that my Legion carries them out."

Eldon sneered. "As if I'm going to turn a battalion of *mercenaries* loose on a Tamar world."

Bel opened her mouth, but Ronan shook his head. She closed her mouth, but glared at him. Yes, okay, he was better at this sort of thing than she was, and someday she was going to have to learn not to let her temper get away from her, but it sure as shit wasn't *this* day.

"Due respect, Hauptmann," Ronan said, "but there seems to be a whole lot of angry, armed people out there who dispute whether the Pact is really in possession of Crimond."

Eldon simmered for a moment, but only a moment. "Fine." He dug around the piles on his desk until he found the noteputer he was looking for, then held it out. "Two taskings came in this morning," he said. "From the Three." The Three was the Third Tamar Jaeger regimental S3 shop, or operations shop, the staff function that oversaw planning and tasking. "Look these over and let me know which you think your mercenaries can handle without killing civilians."

Bel's face got hot, but she held her tongue as Ronan took the noteputer. "I'll be back within the hour," he told Eldon. The hauptmann just waved his hand as he went back to his desk work.

"I can't *believe* him," Bel said, as soon as they were outside the hangar. "Of all the close-minded, insulting—"

"Yeah, he's a prick," Ronan said, cutting her off. He led her over to the side, where a couple of locals had pushed some empty crates into a small nook that would give them a modicum of privacy. "Can we look at this?" He held up the noteputer. "Copy over to yours so we can both read? I want to get back in there before he changes his mind."

"Yeah," Bel said, pulling hers out. At a touch the file Ronan queued appeared on her screen and she sat down and started reading. The form of the tasking was familiar. The Tamars had just carried over the Lyran formats and practices they'd been trained on. She scanned the summary, the description, and the intent sections. Her brow furrowed as she read, trying to translate the mil-speak into simple concepts.

"This one is pretty simple," Ronan said. "A search and destroy they labeled as a capture mission, but if you read between the lines, they'll be happy with warm or cold." Bel looked over at him. His face worked, an innate sense of disgust warring with the righteous indignation of a fighting man for people who bombed indiscriminately. "What about yours?"

"Apparently there's a place called Condor," Bel said. "Island continent, way the hell out there. Deserted, they think. Or hope, rather, because there's an old fort there the LCAF used to use for hostile environment combat schools, mountain and jungle and desert, this says." She waved the noteputer. "Says they want the fort secured before anyone can get in there."

"They *think* it's deserted?"

"Apparently the locals never bother to go there," Bel said. "The place is supposed to be a shit hole. But there's rumors people have been moving there the last couple of years, and the Tamar Two—" the staff intelligence shop, the S2, "—is worried that if there's bombmakers here, and there's a fort there, and if the people there hate people like Eldon as much as we do..." She gave a Gallic shrug. "Makes sense."

"Yeah," Ronan said. He rubbed his short-cut hair, looking down, his go-to action for buying time while he thought. "Think we should take these back, let the others get a say?"

"I think you're the major and I'm the captain, and they'll do what they're told," Bel said. "And I think you're right, if we wait too long that prick Eldon will find a way to sideline us. And while we could all use a vacation, that doesn't help us. We got a reputation to build."

"Yeah," Ronan repeated. He looked like he'd tasted something sour.

Bel regarded him. In a lot of ways Ronan wasn't quite cut out to be a mercenary commander. The things that made him a good one far outnumbered the things that hindered him, but this was one of them. Bel understood the need for the Legion to build its reputation as one of the elite mercenary units of the Inner Sphere. There was a reason people remembered the Gray Death Legion name nearly a century after it had died. There was a reason Tamar had hired the Twenty-first Centauri Lancers last year, instead of the better-equipped Legion of Iron and Steel. That reason was reputation. Bel knew, even if Ronan didn't, that part of the reason Regis and McQuade and the others had hired the Gray Death Legion was to try and get another stamp of legitimacy. But the reborn Gray Death Legion needed exploits *now*, in this century, if it was going to endure.

Ronan was a good soldier, a talented MechWarrior, and a gifted leader. He was the right person to have in command of the Legion, unless the ghost of great-grandfather Grayson rose from the grave. There was no mission he could not complete, no force he could not lead.

But he needed someone like Bel around to ensure there was a *next* mission.

"Okay," Ronan said, "which of these do you think we should ask for?" He motioned with his noteputer. "I think this search-and-destroy thing should be pretty straightforward, unless something takes a bad turn. The locals, up around Kola, where this happened, they want these people caught. The local cops are getting tips. They just don't have the firepower to go in and get them out."

Bel smiled. "That's easy. Both."

"Both."

"Yeah. You go north and deal with the bombers. That's an important mission. I'll take my Commandos and go check out this Condor place."

"You want to split up?" Ronan frowned. "I don't know, Bel—"

"You don't trust me to do this?"

"Of course I do," Ronan said. And Bel knew he meant it. Being his little sister aside, she was a combat-tested veteran graduate of one of the premier MechWarrior academies in the Lyran Commonwealth. "It's just..."

"Just what?"

"It's too far for support if you need it," he said. "I haven't looked at the map, but 'way the hell out there' doesn't sound like close."

"It's not. But it's far enough that asshole Eldon can't interfere, either."

Ronan nodded. "Okay, let's go over these again real quick, make sure this is a good idea. We'll start with yours." He tapped the file open, skimming. "You weren't kidding. Way the hell out there. How are you even supposed to get there?"

"There's a note from the Three suggesting a DropShip," Bel said. "With a supplemental note saying there are oceangoing freighters here that could carry us, but that'd be slow. If the Jaegers will let us borrow one of those," she pointed out toward the spaceport, where the Tamar Jaeger DropShips sat nestled in blast pits, "then we can be there tomorrow."

"Okay, I see it."

"You think Eldon will go for it?" Bel had a moment's worry that her temper could cost them the mission. People like the hauptmann put a lot of stock in face, more than she did.

Ronan laughed. "A chance to get you off this continent? He should love it."

CHAPTER 5

CONDOR
CRIMOND
TAMAR PACT
4 FEBRUARY 3152

Bernard Blucher didn't have any friends in Condor, but he knew where to find people who thought like he did nonetheless. He was going to need help for this next part of his plan. It was more than one man could do alone, and he certainly didn't trust any of the Clan-bred locals or Emberá to help him.

It was just after dawn, so there were few people out and around. He walked down the street between rows of buildings converted to housing in South Six, a zone largely populated by the Emberá. Fort Beaufort was huge, covering easily a dozen square kilometers just in the primary defense zone. Support structures, buildings, machine shops, warehouses, all the stuff that grew around the fort organically like suburbs around a city, had slowly, over time, been claimed by the Condor settlers.

Outside each of the doorways leaned a notched post, like some kind of wooden ratchet or miniaturized ladder. Nearly all of them were turned so the notches faced the wall. That meant the Emberá resident was not receiving guests. One woman, tall and pale in the morning light, saw Blucher coming and twisted hers so the notches faced the wall before stepping inside and closing the door. Blucher rolled his eyes and kept walking. As if he cared.

He'd had an epiphany the night before, about his problem. If the disconnect between the outpost sensors wasn't physical, and it didn't seem like it was, then it had to be some kind of command interlock. A breaker, for lack of a better word, that had severed the connections from a central location. Blucher had been over the main control center in the Citadel a dozen times. It was not there, if it was anywhere. There was one place it might be, Blucher had realized.

But he couldn't get in there alone.

At the end of the street there was a warehouse whose vehicle-entry doors were missing. Smoke from cookfires roiled out of the openings, thick with the scent of Condor tinwood and cooking meat, but it couldn't completely mask the scent of unwashed human, vomit, and the sinus-clearing burn of still alcohol.

Blucher swallowed once and stepped inside, letting his eyes adapt. The group he needed would be here. They were always here—*there*. Blucher headed toward the dark corner where three men sat slumped against the wall on low, dirty benches.

"Sanchez," Blucher said, as he stepped close. "Want to make a few *kroner?*"

Istvan Sanchez looked up, bleary-eyed. Blucher saw him struggle to put a name to the face, but then the man grinned. "It's the Archon's boy," Sanchez said. "Hey boys, look, it's Kommandant Blucher. How's things, Archon's boy?" The other two, obviously still half-drunk as Sanchez was, grinned and chuckled listlessly.

"Things are good. How about it?"

"How about what?"

"I need help with something. I'm willing to pay. Should only take a couple hours."

Sanchez grinned wider. His teeth were brown. It turned Blucher's stomach. "We're pretty busy," he slurred, "but maybe you can speak to my assistants." He beckoned to his companions. One giggled, then burped and coughed at the same time and slid to the floor, unconscious.

"Never mind," Blucher said. He'd find some other way. He turned and picked his way across the dirty floor, through the low cloud of smoke and stepped outside onto the dock. He stood there for a minute, trying to clear his head. *The smell...*

"S-sir?" Blucher turned. A young man in low-caste greens, with olive skin and big shoulders, stood behind him,. "Sir, if you need help, I'm strong and good with my hands." The boy wiped his hands nervously. "If there's money in it, as I heard you say."

Blucher opened his mouth to snarl something, but then reconsidered. "You can work a prybar?"

"I was on the crew that took down the east wall last year, sir. I know my way around a prybar, yes sir."

"You got a name?"

"Rocker, sir."

"Stop calling me sir," Blucher said. "I'll give you ten *kroner.* Should take an hour or two. Over in Southwest Three. Bring a bar if you have one. That work?"

"I'm ready now, sir," Rocker said. "I know where we can get a bar along the way."

"Perfect. I'm Blucher."

An hour or so later, Blucher and Rocker stood outside a low, vine-encrusted nondescript bunker unremarkable when measured against any of the scores of other bunkers that littered the landscape. They'd passed a dozen or so that were visually indistinguishable from this one from the outside, but Blucher had seen the schematics in the Citadel. This bunker was a nodal command bunker. Beneath the ground ran lines of communication and control, invisible to the naked eye.

It was the perfect place to put an emergency cutout.

"We need to get in here," Blucher said, pointing. "The hatch is in the rear, but we may have to dig it out." He had an entrenching tool on his pack, if necessary, but luckily the recessed entryway was clear, just filled with brush. Blucher and Rocker cleared it quickly, ignoring the cloud of Crimond insects that flew out.

"Okay," Blucher said once they had it clear. "This usually works in two stages: I know how to release the lock, if it's even set. But almost all these hatches are rusted shut, or the track is jammed, or something. And there's a manual catch I have to hold down behind an access panel over there—" he pointed a meter or two to the left, "—while you get the door open."

"I understand," Rocker said. He eyed the thick hatch, tapping the tip of the 1.5 meter prybar a couple times, until he found a notch and leaned the tip into the bar. "Seems like a bunker this easy to get into would be easy to defeat."

"With the power on, there's a magnetic seal you'd need a DropShip engine to break," Blucher said, not really paying attention. He pried the hatch off with the special tool he'd found in the Citadel, then reached in and twisted a handle. It resisted at first, but released with a crunch of old dirt and grit. Inside the door, something moved with a heavy *thunk*. "Now, get it open," he ordered Rocker.

Rocker grunted and leaned on his bar. The tip slipped loose, and the boy nearly fell, but he caught himself, grinned, and stabbed the bar in harder. He swung against it with his full weight, using the full length of the bar for leverage. He jerked it rhythmically until something gave with a crunching *ting*, and the door slid open a centimeter.

Blucher grinned and let go of the release inside the wall. He replaced the panel, more out of a sense of habit than any need, and stepped next to Rocker. The hatch had slid open symmetrically, thank the gods, but there wasn't enough light to see inside yet. Blucher put his hand against the edge of the hatch and pushed, but it didn't move. He grinned at Rocker. "The hard way, then," he said. Rocker grinned back.

It took them most of an hour of sweating, swearing, and frequent breaks to get hatch open wide enough for them to slide through. Blucher slid on his headband LED light and took a look around. "Touch nothing," he told Rocker. "I don't think you can hurt anything, but I want to see where things were left when this bunker was sealed. That might give me a clue about what I'm looking for."

"*Aff*," Rocker said quietly.

The bunker layout was standard for a Fort Beaufort infantry redoubt. Blucher had been in a dozen just like it, which meant the officer's station would be right *there*... He stepped that way and gently lowered himself into the hard, steel seat. The seat cover had long since decayed to dust. The console was familiar, but covered in dirt. Blucher opened one of his kits and began to clean it, so he could see what he was working with.

"Is it safe to move?" Rocker asked. Blucher blinked; he had forgotten the boy was there. He twisted in the seat, shining his LEDs at the boy, who threw up a hand to block the sudden light.

"It is," Blucher said. He dug in his pocket and pulled out a ten-*kroner* coin. "Here." He tossed it to the boy, who snatched it out of the air even in the low light. "Thanks for your help. That's all I needed."

"M-may I stay?"

"Up to you," Blucher said, turning back to the console. He returned to his cleaning, watching for anything out of the usual. The old SLDF had usually built things to a pattern; it should be relatively simple to see if there was anything out of the ordinary on this console, but after another half-hour of cleaning, he hadn't found anything. He set back in the chair, sighing.

"No luck?" Rocker asked, from the door. He'd been using his feet to brush dirt and debris out the gap in the door, for lack of a broom.

"Not yet," Blucher said. He stretched, hands over his head, feet out beneath the console, trying to force his mind to give him a new insight. His mind was awash with ideas, but they were all ideas he'd already tried or discarded. Frustrated, he slammed his knees against the side of the console. His left knee just rebounded off the hard metal, as did his right. But above his right knee, a hidden, recessed panel popped open. Blucher felt it and jumped, thinking it was an insect. Some of the Crimond beetles grew as big as a human hand.

When he looked, though, he saw the hanging panel. And when he reached inside, he felt a heavy mechanical switch, like an old-style electrical breaker. He tugged at it until it slid into the other position, resisting the whole way. The console did not react in any way: there was no hum of power, no telltale ker-*chunk* of circuits resetting or anything.

Blucher licked his lips. *The damn thing has to do* something.

"Do you hear that?" Rocker asked.

"Hear what?" Blucher lurched forward, fingers probing gently for any more hidden panels. If there was one, there might be more.

"Sounded like thunder," Rocker said. "I will check." He eeled his way out the wrenched-open door and disappeared. Or at least that's what Blucher inferred from the way the shadows moved; he didn't look away from the console.

"Sir?"

"What?"

"I think you should come and see this."

Blucher frowned. "I've seen a storm cloud, Rocker."

"It is not a storm."

Blucher grunted and lurched up out of the seat. It took him a minute to get through the door because his belt got caught on one of the edges. He jerked himself free and stepped over, around the edge of the bunker, where Rocker stood, shading his eyes with one hand. "What?" There wasn't a cloud in the sky.

"There," Rocker said, pointing.

Blucher looked. He heard it first, the low-frequency rumble that sounded like distant thunder coming down off a mountain, but over and over again. He held his hand up to block the sun, as Rocker had, and looked where the boy pointed.

A distant speck was growing larger, trailing a huge contrail. It took Blucher a moment to realize what he was seeing. "It can't be..."

"Is it the invaders Curtain told us about?"

Blucher ducked back into the bunker, grabbed up his kit, stuffed it into his pack, and wriggled out of the bunker doorway again. By then the noise was louder. The DropShip was getting lower.

"Will there be fighting?" Rocker asked.

Blucher ignored him and ran toward the Citadel.

CHAPTER 6

CONDOR
CRIMOND
TAMAR PACT
4 FEBRUARY 3152

"Release those clamps before we are down and stable and I will see you're billed for the damage!"

Bel Carlyle rolled her eyes. From her vantage in her *Hatchetman*'s cockpit, ensconced in the 'Mech repair cradle in the *Union*-class DropShip's 'Mech bay, the deck officer was a child's toy, but Bel could well imagine the expression on the woman's face. She'd yelled the same way when her Commandos had boarded the ship. Clearly she, like the rest of the Tamars, didn't want the Legion anywhere near them.

Which was fine. Bel felt the same way.

She and Ronan had convinced Eldon to let them take both of the taskings from the Jaegers' operations shop, but he'd made it clear he expected both of them to fail. Bel had bristled, but Ronan had hustled them both out and into the sun.

"We got what we wanted," he'd told her. "Now don't screw it up."

While Ronan took the bulk of the Gray Death Legion and its support units toward Kola, Bel and her Commandos—technically B Company, Gray Death Legion—had boarded the Tamar DropShip for the suborbital hop across the ocean to Condor. *Union*s were designed to carry a full company of twelve BattleMechs, but she had only the three 'Mechs of her B1

Lance, and the four tanks and sixteen battlesuits of B2 and B3 Platoons, respectively. She'd also brought strands of both Combat Support and Service Support companies, to support her company. That left the *Union* pretty spacious, all things considered, but it also meant her tanks were lashed down like common cargo.

No one shot at us as we came down, Bel told herself. The tank crews and the DropShip's crew were getting the Myrmidons unlashed right now. There should be time to get them up and running before she had to debark. So for now, she ignored the haughty deck officer. She toggled her intercom open; so long as her 45-ton 'Mech stayed in the 'Mech cradle, she was hardwired into the ship's communication systems.

"Legion to CIC," she said, calling the DropShip's combat information center. "Anyone reacting to us yet? And where are we on a map?"

There had been stock aerial photography of Condor, and rudimentary maps that showed the basic geography and few notable locations such as Fort Beaufort available in Sol City, but nothing of any detail. Bel had requested the DropShip's tactical section run their automappers during the descent, to give the Legion at least basic tactical maps of the area. They knew—the Tamars knew, and their collaborators in Sol City knew—that there were people on Condor, but no one knew how many, if they were organized, armed, or otherwise.

Terra incognita, one of her support troops had called it. Whatever that meant.

Curtain stood at the foot of his 'Mech, the only BattleMech in the entire warehouse, and watched the armor troops scurry around. Andy Ishikawa stood next to him, hand on her holstered pistol, a half-smoked *culebra* strand cigar glowing in her mouth. She'd smoked the other two strands of the *culebra* Paulo had given her on the drive back. It made Curtain smile to realize she was finishing the gift now.

"Like a bunch of kids," was all she said.

"Indeed," Curtain said. He brushed some dirt off his cooling suit sleeve and glanced up at his 'Mech, thinking. "I only hope they listen to me out there."

"Be more sure of that if you'd bothered to train them," Andy said.

"To train them I would have to lead them."

"What else is making them listen to you, if not leading them?"

Curtain chuckled. "A thin line, to be sure. But when I came here, I gave up being a warrior. I have no desire to lead warriors." Andy frowned at him, then gestured at his cooling suit, and then his 'Mech.

Curtain chuckled again. "A thin line," he repeated.

"You think they're here to fight?" she asked, more quietly.

"We shall see?"

"Can you beat them, if they are?"

"I did not come here to bow."

"That's not what I asked."

Curtain smiled at her. "Yes, it was." He nodded at her and turned to climb up the 'Mech's access ladder. He heard her inhale, then exhale, and smelled the sickly-sweet aroma of her cigar, but then he was too high to hear, and had other things to concentrate on.

She was right, of course. He could have easily arranged these people into Stars, a Binary even. He could have given them ranks, and drilled them, and rewarded good behavior and punished poor performance. He'd been asked many times. He had always demurred.

He had a home now. One he'd chosen, and one that had embraced him. He would fight to protect it, yes. Any man or woman would do that. It did not make him a warrior, a leader of warriors. But as he reached the cockpit, and climbed inside, he desperately hoped he wouldn't have to.

"This is the best you could do?"

"Next time, *you* map a whole island in six minutes, lady," the DropShip officer replied. "CIC out."

Bel bit her tongue. She had no idea how one mapped an island through a camera in a descending DropShip, but the Tamars had done their best. She wasn't in a position to decide whether their best was any good. And besides—her internal voice changed to Kommandant Ogilvy, the Coventry tactics instructor—*no one enters battle with complete intelligence. An officer's job is to analyze, adapt, and react.*

"So get off the ship, Bel," she muttered, then touched a different intercom channel. "Legion here. Open her up."

Below her, on the deck, the deck officer waved to indicate she'd heard, then started talking on the DropShip channels. Bel looked at the other two Legion 'Mechs in the bay.

The largest, Lieutenant Nick Christensen's *Catapult*, was painted in the Legion's standard gray-black-green camouflage with the Legion grinning skull insignia on its shin. The 65-ton 'Mech was another salvage job out of the Garrison scrap heap, lovingly brought back to fighting trim thanks to Master Sergeant Buthra Azzari's amazing technical teams. Christensen was a taciturn MechWarrior, one of the former Lyran recon battalion MechWarriors who'd joined the Legion after their battalion had been cashiered by Fat Timmy Bondayehr on Garrison. Christensen might be the most skilled 'Mech pilot Bel had ever met. He was amazingly talented, able to hit targets with his PPCs while the *Catapult* ran flat-out. He was an otherwise average man, unremarkable in build or features, though he had smart eyes and an irreverent grin, as if he'd just heard a joke no one else had.

The other 'Mech, Sergeant Yurim Mbaruku's 35-ton *Talon*, was one of the machines captured from the Two-Nine Battalion. Yurim, another of the former Steiner MechWarriors, was a solid soldier and a talented scout. She was young, only twenty-two standard years old, but she'd aged fast in the fight against the Legion and the aftermath. She drove herself hard, more or less living in the 'Mech simulators. Bel liked her, and liked having her in her lance.

Her B1 Lance was short one 'Mech under establishment, but there were limits to even Buthra Azzari's wizardry. Both Ronan and Bel were confident the Legion would grow; she'd have a fourth 'Mech in her lance in due course.

Across the bay, the restraints holding Christensen's *Catapult* fell away. The birdlike 'Mech took a few tentative steps forward, out of the cradle, obedient to the directions the DropShip crewer acting as ground guide indicated. Bel watched another crewer headed toward the *Talon*. The deck officer herself pulled a paired set of light bars out of pockets and waved them overhead toward Bel's cradle. Bel brought the *Hatchetman*'s engine live and prepared to move out.

Her ground guide suddenly crossed the light bars in an X over her head as Bel took her first step. She twitched the *Hatchetman*'s throttle back to idle, waiting. Her helmet speakers burped static at her.

"Status change," she heard, in the CIC officer's voice. "Unknown 'Mech and tanks detected."

"What is it?" she asked. "Just one? Any ID?"

"Retransmitting," CIC said.

On her heads-up display an inset flat image appeared, showing a heavily-magnified image of a hunched-over BattleMech stalking out of a warehouse. Hovercraft and fast wheeled vehicles scurried around its feet, and Bel thought she saw soldiers carrying rifles hanging off the sides of some of the vehicles.

"No solid ID yet," CIC reported. "But that's either a *Hauptmann* or a *Regent*. We've carried them often enough."

"Agreed," Bel said. "Any comms?"

"Nothing from them."

"And from us?"

"I think that's your job, merc." There was a pause. "Get out there and keep that thing away from my ship, yeah?"

Bel bit back a snort. "Will do."

Curtain had to slow his *Regent* to keep from stepping on Hector Alessandro's Joust at one point, but he chose to laugh rather than curse. Hector's son Felipe must be in the driver's compartment; Curtain knew Felipe never remembered to check what was behind him when he braked. The Joust suddenly lurched forward, treads tearing the gravel. Curtain could well imagine old Hector, in the gunner's seat, seeing the *Regent* looming off-balance, surmising what had happened, and smacking the back of young Felipe's head.

"Like herding cats," he muttered.

A half-dozen tanks and APC swung back and forth around him, all of them anxious to get out and meet the invaders, but none willing to move out from beneath the protective shadow of his 'Mech. The Alessandro tank was the heaviest and in the best shape, but all of them showed signs of disrepair. He knew his own 'Mech, in the old days, would have earned a technician team ten lashes with a neural whip. But there were no technicians in Condor to help him, so the *Regent* showed every scar, every weakness.

"We going to ride right up to the DropShip?" Andy asked. Her jeep was lagging behind, with a half-dozen heavily armed infantry hanging off it, but she had a headset radio.

"Perhaps," was all Curtain said.

The invader DropShip—he recognized it as a *Union*-class 'Mech hauler—sat on the far corner of the ancient spaceport pad adjacent to the fort. Most of the pad was ruined, the ferrocrete undermined by years of neglect, invasive roots, and weathering, but the invader ship had managed to find a relatively secure patch. The dead space between them was going down with every step.

"Ship like that will have guns of its own," Andy added.

"It doesn't need them," he said. "Look closer."

There was a pause. "Shit."

Curtain chuckled, but didn't respond. BattleMechs, at least two, were striding down the 'Mech ramp and onto the tarmac. A ship like that could carry six times that many. And he had only his *Regent*.

"Shit" is probably the right response, he thought.

Bernard Blucher burst out of the stairwell access atop the Citadel, chest heaving, out of breath. Rocker was right behind him, although the punk was not nearly breathing hard enough. Blucher stared toward the DropShip, wishing he'd brought a set of binoculars. It was too far for him to see if the ship carried any insignia.

"There's Curtain and the others," Rocker called. Blucher, hands on his knees while he gasped for breath, twisted that way. The ex-Clanner's big 'Mech stomped toward the invaders' DropShip. From the dirty black exhaust smoke and the dust being blown up around its feet, the rest of the yokels were with him. Blucher frowned and looked back at the DropShip. Large shapes moved in its open 'Mech bays.

"I wish there was something I could do to help," Rocker said.

Blucher took one last look, looking back and forth while he wheezed, then nodded and waved at the door. "Good idea. Let's get down to the control room and see if our work paid off."

CHAPTER 7

CONDOR
CRIMOND
TAMAR PACT
4 FEBRUARY 3152

Bel Carlyle glared at the magnified image of the *Regent* OmniMech on her HUD and ground her teeth. "I'm gonna need my tanks."

"They're coming," the Tamar deck officer replied. "We're freeing the last one now."

"Great," Bel said. She touched a control to change frequencies. "Alexei?"

"Sixty seconds or less, Captain," replied Lieutenant Alexei Komljenovic. He commanded the tanks of B2 Platoon. "I'm watching them undog Sergeant Durston's track right now."

"Very good," Bel said. "Form behind the 'Mechs when you get down."

"Roger."

"Sergeant Xi, hold the DropShip, got it?"

"They won't get past us, Captain," the commander of her battlesuit platoon said. The old Purifier battlesuits weren't going to add much to a standup fight, if it came to that, but they might be enough to keep the Tamars from abandoning Bel's company here if they decided to run. Nothing *inside* the DropShip could fight them.

"Nobody shoots unless I say so," Bel said, starting her *Hatchetman* moving forward a few paces. "Could be they just want to say hi."

"In an assault 'Mech," Lieutenant Christensen put in.

"That's how we'd do it back home," Sergeant Mbaruku said with a chuckle. The Lyran Commonwealth had, for centuries, favored BattleMechs at the heavier end of the spectrum, which led to a lot of bad jokes.

"I mean it," Bel said.

"Do not fire," Curtain radioed.

"What if they shoot at us?"

"Then you shoot back. But we will not fire first. There is no reason to make an enemy before we even know their name." He squeezed and relaxed his hands on the *Regent*'s gunnery controls. "Besides, my weapons shoot farther than any of yours. If there is any shooting to do, I will do it."

A chorus of "*okays*," and "*rogers*" and one sullen "whatever" answered him. Curtain grinned and focused his attention on the DropShip and the 'Mechs. Three had appeared, and now paused a couple hundred meters from the DropShip. The *Regent*'s powerful computer drank in information and threw up inset panels in his HUD for each enemy machine. All were Inner Sphere-built machines, and none were OmniMechs. The leading 'Mech, a 45-ton *Hatchetman*, intrigued him. He had never seen one of the barrel-chested 'Mechs with his own eyes. He zoomed in on the 'Mech's namesake hatchet and chuckled. *As if enemies are trees to be cut down.*

Curtain was not sure what to expect. All he had learned on the mainland last month told him they must be from this new Tamar Pact, or its proxies. They had assumed control of the world from the Jade Falcons, but they'd arrived on Condor far faster than he'd expected. Truth be told, he'd hoped they'd never come to Condor, but he'd known they would.

What they wanted, he didn't know. Most of his contacts agreed they were little more than Lyrans with a different flag. Rumor was they were founded by Lyran defectors. With the whole of their former nation as an enemy, perhaps they might not want to get in another fight.

But they were here.

The *Regent*'s sensors chimed; new red carets appeared on his HUD as a platoon of medium tracked armor trundled down the ramp and onto the field behind the trio of 'Mechs.

Curtain sucked air through his teeth.

The four Myrmidons of B2 Platoon arrayed themselves in echelon behind the B1 Lance trio of 'Mechs. As they came to within a hundred meters, Bel started her *Hatchetman* walking forward. After a few steps, she spread the 'Mech's arms wide and ensure her targeting systems were on standby. The *Hatchetman*'s passive sensors absorbed every bit of information they could, but she ran no active targeting systems.

"Attention," she sent on an unencrypted frequency. "This is Captain Isobel Carlyle of the Gray Death Legion." She stopped, not sure how to go on. "Uh, take us to your leaders?"

The range between the two forces was down to two kilometers or so. Neither force was moving fast, but neither had stopped.

"What is a Gray Death Legion?" a man's voice replied. Her computer painted the *Regent* as the sender. His accent was Clan.

"We are mercenaries, under contract to the Tamar Pact," Bel said. Her palms had begun to sweat a little at the speaker's accent. Together with the presence of the Sea Fox-inspired *Regent*, that suggested some uncomfortable things. *I hope they know the planet's already been surrendered*, she thought. *I do not want to have to tell that stupid car race story.*

"I was not aware there was a Tamar Pact."

"It's new."

"Must be," the man said. The *Regent* and its support stopped advancing, the 'Mech standing still and the tanks shifting to either a halt or driving back and forth in circles. Bel halted her force as well. "What are your intentions on Condor, Gray Death Legion?"

Bel's mouth felt dry. "To secure it in the name of the Tamar Pact, which has accepted responsibility for this planet from the Jade Falcons."

"Accepted responsibility," the man repeated. Bel heard the wry grin in his voice, clear as day. "Offered freely, I imagine?"

"The Jade Falcons surrendered." She really didn't want to have to explain *how*.

"And the rest of the people, on the mainlands? They have offered this Tamar Pact their obedience?"

Bel's bruised head and body throbbed while the restaurant kitchen exploded behind her eyes inside every blink. She thought of the rest of the Legion off on its counterinsurgency mission. "They have."

The *Regent* spread its own arms. "Tell me," the pilot said. "You mentioned 'securing Condor.' Do we look insecure?"

Bel bit her lip.

"You do not," this Captain Carlyle replied.

Curtain grinned. She sounded young, very young, but she was doing an admirable job holding her own.

She continued, "The fact remains that the Tamar Pact is now the legitimate government of Crimond."

"We were not consulted," Curtain said.

"You prefer the Jade Falcons?"

"We prefer to govern ourselves." There was no response, so Curtain pressed on. "The Jade Falcons left us alone."

"And the Lyran Commonwealth treated this island as a protected military reservation," Carlyle said. "The past is less important than the present."

"There are children here," Curtain said, "and some nearly grown, who have never seen a Lyran Commonwealth flag. They have surely never seen a Tamar Pact flag. We want nothing to do with the mainlanders. Go back and tell them that." He lowered the *Regent*'s arms, sensing the end of the conversation approaching.

"I have orders," Captain Carlyle said. "Perhaps we could meet and talk, outside of these machines?"

"That depends on your intentions," Curtain said.

"My intentions are to talk."

Curtain opened his mouth and then closed it. Finally, he said, "I need to confer."

"As do I. Shall we say five minutes?"

"*Aff.*"

"He's a Clanner," Sergeant Mbaruku said immediately. "You heard the *aff.*"

"He's not talking like a Jade Falcon," Bel said. "Nick?"

"While you were talking," Christensen said, "I was taking a close look at their kit. Look at this." A series of flat, still images flickered across her HUD.

Bel squinted, swiping through them. "What am I looking for?"

"The infantry, first."

Bel swiped until she found a magnified image of a woman in infantry kit hanging off the running board of a wheeled vehicle. She was in simple green battledress with a helmet, a rifle of indeterminate make slung across her back, and several large satchels. A shiny metal rod stuck up over her shoulder. "What I am I looking at?"

Christensen snorted. "And you're the one always lecturing us about the old Legion. *Look.*"

Bel frowned and looked again. The woman held onto the truck with one hand; in the other, she gripped what looked for all the world like some kind of ice ax, except instead of a hook it had a flat, disk-shaped metal head. The ax had a lanyard slipped over her wrist. Bel had no idea. She couldn't see the rifle well enough to ID it, and as for all the kit bags...*oh.*

The bags were satchel charges, blocks of explosive in bags with friction fuses. Bel looked again at the ax, imagining it as electromagnetic. "Anti-'Mech infantry," she whispered.

"Bingo," Christensen said. "Just like in the old Legion."

"Damn," Bel said. *"Damn."*

"Whoever these people are, they're serious," Christensen said. "We get in a scuffle, I'm shooting at the groundpounders first, while they're far away. Worse than battle armor. You can *feel* a battlesuit hit you."

"Yeah."

"The rest of its pretty standard, beat-up armor. Close-ups on the *Regent* show old damage, even some rust. I'm not sure what their tail is set up for, but they look like they're away from supports."

"With a whole military base right there?"

"Doesn't mean they're using it," Mbaruku said.

"Fair."

Bel swiped through the rest of the photos, but nothing jumped out at her. "I think we need to try and get a sit-down with these people," she said. "I don't want to fight them. That will cost, and even if we win, they'll just hate Tamar. We need to find out if they're hostile, or just ambivalent."

"You kinda asked that already," Sergeant Mbaruku said.

"Then let's hope for the right answer."

"We should *take* them," Felipe Alessandro said.

"Felipe!" Hector barked.

Curtain just grinned.

"We shoot at them, hell, we kill them all, more will just come," Andy Ishikawa put in. "No harm in hearing them out."

"What if we don't like what they say?"

"It will be easier to deal with them outside their 'Mechs," Curtain said. "Andy is right. Besides, we don't know how the mainlanders are treating these Tamars. It could be they'll be happy to leave us alone, if we we're no threat."

"So, what, we invite them for drinks?" Felipe asked tartly.

"Yes," Curtain said. He toggled his radio open. "Captain Carlyle?"

"I'm here."

"We invite you to enjoy the hospitality of Condor," he said. "For one night, at least. So that we may speak more, and come to an understanding." He paused, mind working. "You may come, and six more. I will send a vehicle. The rest of you are welcome to stay in your 'Mechs, near your DropShip. So long as no armed unit approaches the Fort, we will hold the peace."

"Personal weapons?" Carlyle asked. "We have no intention of becoming hostages."

Curtain grinned again. "Within reason."

"Whose reason? Yours or mine?"

"I guess we will find out. In thirty minutes?"

"Agreed, if you tell me your name."

"Curtain. I look forward to it." He closed the channel. "You all heard?"

"I suppose I'm going to get them?" Andy asked.

"If you would."

"No one better. That way Felipe and Hector can stay here on watch."

"Now, wait—" Felipe began, but there was the sound of an impact. Then Hector's deeper, slower voice.

"We will watch them."

"Nick, you're in charge until I get back," Bel said. "Alexei, I want you to send me Sergeant Carillo, okay?"

"He's on his way, ma'am," the armor platoon commander replied. "Standard ground mount?"

"Body armor and sidearms only," Bel said. "No shoulder weapons."

"Roger."

"Sergeant Xi?"

"Captain."

"I want two of your troopers out of armor," Bel said. "Pick big ones. Same deal, battledress and sidearms only. People who know how to keep their mouths shut and eyes open."

"Know just the two, ma'am."

"And get with Staff Sergeant Gleason. I want someone from the Two-shop and Four-shop along."

"Roger."

"Rally at my 'Mech in ten," Bel said.

"Roger."

Bel set the *Hatchetman* into standby and unbuckled her neurohelmet. She racked it above her head and climbed out of the command couch to get to the locker beneath it, where her own body armor was stored. Her cooling suit was already painted in the Legion trademark gray digicam. It would take her half the ten just to get dressed and down.

She leaned over to peer through the narrow viewport, across the field, toward the fort and the bustling ruins around it.

I wish Ronan were here, she thought, and then hated herself for thinking it.

CHAPTER 8

"Hold the *verdammt* light!"

Rocker didn't say anything, but the light shifted to where Blucher was under one of the consoles, fingers grasping for a specific circuit. He finally saw the gap in the seated cable runs and jabbed his hands forward, seating the one he held. He slithered out from beneath the console, wiped dust off his elbows, and lurched upright with a grunt. The light followed him.

Blucher stepped across the aisle to another console, held his breath, and pushed a button. He waited, not moving, tongue poking out from between his lips, eyes on the ceiling. Rocker, seeing where he was looking, directed the handlight that way.

Blucher snorted. "Just wait."

"For what?"

"You'll see."

It started as a hum, and Blucher smiled. His hands clenched into fists as the first glows of light flickered in the overhead LED lights. The covers were all dirty, giving everything a rotten, lime-brown tinge, but Blucher didn't care. He looked around, seeing activation lights coming online on several of the consoles.

"You did this?" Rocker asked.

"*I* did this," Blucher whispered. "Me, and not anyone else." He leaned over and touched a control; behind them, an armored door clanged shut, driven by magnetic rams. If the sound was a little crunchy from dirt in the mechanisms, Blucher didn't care. He pressed the button again and the door ground open.

A flatscreen flickered to life on the wall in front of him. The image was grainy, and the screen was missing several rows of dead pixels. But he could make out the shapes of BattleMechs.

Grinning, Blucher sat down and worked the console. So far as he knew, no one had activated this secondary control post in a century or more. The LCAF had operated out of the main control room, which barely functioned. They'd written Fort Beaufort's other functions off as ruined by time. But Bernard Blucher had found it.

The image on the screen was gun-camera footage from one of the vine-covered PPC turrets. If it functioned, then the subterranean fusion reactors had come back online, too. Blucher chuckled; if any of the locals had found their way down there, they'd sure be surprised at the *thrum* of the reactors spinning up. Deeply buried, the newcomer DropShip might not even detect them.

"This is amazing," Rocker said. "We have to tell Curtain!"

"Hell with Curtain," Blucher said. "This fort is *mine*." But before he could say more, what he was seeing through his gun camera registered. There was no fighting. Both Curtain and the newcomers had stopped, more than a kilometer apart, it looked like. "What's going on?"

"How should I know," Rocker said, petulantly, "when I've been here with you in the dark?"

Blucher sat back, frowning. He didn't understand what was happening. It had taken him too long to get this room up and running; he'd expected to see the two forces fighting. If they weren't fighting, they were talking. And if they were talking... *they might come here.*

Blucher stood and moved to another console. He sat down and called up a schematic, then took out his noteputer and started taking stills. The noteputer was too new to link directly with the old Star League computer system, but its camera worked fine.

"What are you photographing?" Rocker asked.

"Schematics," Blucher said. "Things I still need to fix."

"Why?"

"So I can get more of the fort working."

"More than this?"

"More than this," Blucher told him. "Get ready with the light again, will you? As soon as I'm done here, we're turning all this off again. I need to get back to South Six." *In case I need help*, he didn't say. With what he didn't yet know. Several potential outcomes were running around his head at the same time, one chasing the next. He needed more information.

He took the last photo, then slid the noteputer into its pouch. He returned to the first console, put his finger on the button. "Ready?"

Rocker didn't move. "Why do you not wish to tell Curtain?"

Blucher fought the urge to roll his eyes. "I don't answer to Curtain."

"He is our leader."

"Not mine."

"But—" Rocker frowned. "Then why are you here?"

"For this," Blucher said, indicating the walls and ceiling with his free hand. "For the Fort. Because I knew I could do this, bring it back to life. No one else could, but I did."

"Are you..." Rocker cleared his throat. "Are you our enemy?"

"My enemies were the Jade Falcons," Blucher said sincerely.

"Mine, too," Rocker said. He brandished the handlight. "Ready."

Blucher pressed the button, shutting down the systems he'd activated. All the consoles and lights went off. If everything was still working, deep down below the reactors had shut down again.

He was relieved Rocker hadn't realized that Blucher hadn't actually answered his question.

By the time Bel got down from her 'Mech, wearing her ground mount and with a big Python pistol snugged into her thigh holster, one of the Myrmidons was returning from picking up the crew she'd called from the DropShip. The squat tank trundled up with four figures hanging off the body, clutching handholds on the turret. All wore gray Legion digicam and carried sidearms, though two clutched heavy combat noteputers as well. The tank lurched to a halt and all four jumped down, while a fifth climbed out of the turret.

"Staff Sergeant Gleason with a party of four, ma'am," a short, thickset woman with one of the noteputers said, nodding. The Legion did not salute. That didn't do anything but point out officers for enemy snipers, especially while they were all just standing in the open.

"You could have sent someone, Gleason," Bel said.

"My job, ma'am," Gleason said. Mira Gleason was assigned to the Legion's S2, the battalion intelligence squad. She was the senior NCO of the small detachment of headquarters troops Bel had brought to Condor with her. "I assigned myself."

"Glad to have you with me," Bel said, grinning. She nodded to Sergeant Perathoner, from the S4, the logistics squad, who clutched the other big noteputer, then looked to the man climbing down from the tank. "Sergeant Carillo, good to see you."

"Good to be seen, Captain." The dapper young man, sergeant-commander of the Myrmidon even now reversing away from them, nodded and clapped his hands together. "I assume you'll want my opinion of their armor, ma'am?"

"Right in one," Bel said. She looked at the two big infantry troopers. "Private Peat, Private Atwater. Sergeant Xi give you instructions?" The battlesuit troopers both grinned, but it was Peat, big, bald-headed and brown-skinned, who answered.

"Bring the captain back alive, ma'am," he said.

"And remember we're not in armor, and not invisible," Atwater added. He was wiry where Peat was bulky, but he looked sure of himself.

"What about the rest of us?" Sergeant Carillo asked.

"Sergeant Xi didn't say nothing that about that, Sergeant," Peat said, still grinning.

"Guess you're big enough to hide behind, it comes down to it," Staff Sergeant Gleason said.

Bel smiled while the others laughed, then cleared her throat. "Here's the deal. The head guy over there, Curtain. He said we can come into town." She gestured across the field, where the big *Regent* still stood unmoving. "We have no idea who these people are. So think of yourselves as guests at your grandmother's house, okay? Our job is to learn all we can." Bel met each Legionnaire's stare until she got a nod from each of them.

"We walking, ma'am?" Sergeant Carillo asked.

"They're supposed to be sending a ride."

Carillo nodded. "I think I see it coming." He pointed, and Bel turned and looked where he pointed. A wheeled jeep was tearing across the broken ground, top down. Bel saw the outline of a driver and no one else.

"That's probably it." She turned back to her group. "You're all armed. Protect yourselves. Guests, not prisoners. Atwater and Peat, try and keep an eye out. All of you, keep an eye on the people around you. But I'll tell you now, any of you put your foot wrong, especially if any of you shoot someone, I will personally squeeze your balls off." Staff Sergeant Gleason coughed. It may have been a laugh. "Ovaries too," Bel added.

"How long are we going for?"

Bel shrugged. "Until we get back." She turned and looked up at Christensen's *Catapult*, looming overhead. "Nick? You heard all that?"

"Roger," the 'Mech's speakers boomed. "Call for us, and we're coming, Captain."

"Hopefully we won't need to," Bel said, as the local jeep pulled up in a wash of wind and small, particulate sand. She shaded her hands with her eyes and regarded the driver.

"One of you Carlyle?" the woman asked, climbing out.

"I am," Bel said.

"Andy Ishikawa," the woman replied. She sketched an informal salute. "Well met, and all that."

"Likewise."

Ishikawa regarded the group. If her eyes lingered on their sidearms, Bel didn't see it. She did stare for a moment at Gleason and Perathoner's noteputers. "I'm taking it on faith those aren't bombs?"

"I can turn one on, if you wish?" Staff Sergeant Gleason said, brandishing the shock-resistant case.

Ishikawa shook her head. "No, you want to haul that shit around with you everywhere, more power to you." She gestured to the jeep. "Pile on, and we'll get out of here. Curtain told me to take you to the warehouse in South Six. That's more or less our common area." She eyed the two big infantrymen. "I think we'll all fit. Maybe."

Bel shrugged. "We're along for the ride. Let's go, people."

The Legion people found seats or, in Gleason's case, sat on her noteputer case, which in turn rested on Private Peat's lap. The private looked resolutely straight ahead, but Gleason smirked when Bel met her eyes. Ishikawa nodded and jerked the jeep around in a tight turn that threw everyone off-balance.

"I appreciate the ride," Bel said, or rather shouted. The wind made it difficult to hear.

"No problem," Ishikawa said. She glanced at Bel, then smiled. "I seem to spend a lot of time playing taxi lately."

"What can you tell me about this place?" Bel asked.

"Nothing Curtain can't tell you himself."

"I wouldn't mind a head start."

Ishikawa made a waving-off gesture with one hand before putting it back on the steering wheel. "Not my place," was all she said.

"It's beautiful country," Bel offered a moment later. When Ishikawa glanced at her, she pointed off toward the looming, green-covered mountains. Their driver barked a short laugh.

"You haven't met the bugs yet," was the last thing she said.

Curtain stood on the *Regent*'s shoulder long enough to see the Legion party board Andy's jeep, then swiftly climbed down to the waiting skimmer. As soon as he settled into the small passenger seat, the driver, another of Hector Alessandro's many children, spun the fans out of idle and adjusted the blade incidence to push them forward. They would beat Andy to South Six easily.

"You won't bother me if you lean a little toward the center," the driver said. She was young woman, maybe twenty standard years, with long, jet-black hair and what was once called a Mediterranean complexion. "You're a big guy—makes it hard to trim the fans with all the weight on one side."

Curtain laughed and leaned closer to her, close enough he could smell the slight scent of either perfume or shampoo, he couldn't tell which. "Better?"

"Be better when we get there," the girl muttered. "Like a damned giant, you are. Stay out of my lap, though. You're not my type."

Curtain's laughter echoed from the surrounding buildings as they sped down the center of the debris-strewn street toward the South district.

CHAPTER 9

CONDOR
CRIMOND
TAMAR PACT
4 FEBRUARY 3152

Bel's first experience with the common people of Condor was a matronly older woman handing her some kind of lizard that had been barbecued on a stick. One of its four eyes rolled in the socket when she took the skewer. Bel swallowed and smiled at the woman. "Thank you."

The woman grinned yellow teeth, ducked her chin, and backed away. Bel smiled again at her, then stared at the lizard. The skin had started a sandy brown, it looked like, but had been blackened by the fire. The legs were stumps. If the lizard had had toes, they'd been burned off in the cooking.

"It looks disgusting," Curtain said, where he sprawled in a chair too small for him, across the table from her. "But it tastes like bacon."

Bel frowned at him, brandishing the skewer. "You're joking." The big man spread his hands and shrugged. Bel waited, sure she was being twigged. She had a lifetime's experience with men bigger than she was making jokes at her expense. Ronan had done it as long as she could remember. But Curtain's face didn't have that sort of anticipation Ronan's always had, waiting for her to walk into the joke facefirst.

"D-do you just bite in, or do you peel it?" She looked around. "Do I get a fork or anything?"

Curtain crossed his arms and said nothing. Bel grimaced and looked to the other person sitting at the table, Staff Sergeant Gleason. She made a no-way face and crossed her own arms. Bel sighed and glanced around the ersatz cantina. It was filled with people of all shapes and ages, sitting at tables or in corners, most of them drinking or eating, or both.

Andy Ishikawa had deposited them here, in some place she called "South Six," which turned out to be a sprawling warehouse-like structure that had been subdivided internally into spaces, some large and some small, similar to indoor markets Bel had been to on other worlds. People lived or worked, lounged or sold, as they wished inside it. Andy had led them to this small cantina, near the center, where she'd met the *Regent* MechWarrior, Curtain.

He was clearly Clan-born. It was obvious in the way he spoke and his—to her—weird social cues. But he was also congenial, with a boisterous laugh and a curious lack of pretension. He'd invited her to sit and, so far, resisted her every attempt to turn the topic of conversation to more serious matters. The woman with the lizard was only the latest straw and, Bel hoped, the last one.

She looked at the other person sitting around the small table, Andy Ishikawa, brandishing the lizard. "No hints?"

Andy sighed, then rolled her eyes. "It's cooked to crackling," she said. She made a twisting motion with her hands. "You break the skin, then peel it and eat it. The skin does taste a little like bacon, at least if nona over there used enough salt while she cooked it. But the inside is like an oily birdfowl—duck, if you've ever had that."

Bel frowned and turn the lizard over. The eyes rolled again, which made her want to gag. She reached her free up hesitantly, grasped the blacked torso part between the legs, and squeezed gently. The skin felt dry and broke easily under her pressure. It cracked into easily-grasped edges. She reached for one, then glanced back at Andy. "Peel it."

She nodded. "At least, that's what I've seen other people do."

"Other people—you've never done this?"

"Oh hell no. I order bacon. I didn't grow up in the forest. I'm from Sol City."

Bel set the lizard down on the table and glared at Curtain, who laughed his booming laugh again. People around them glanced their way, then shared looks and went chuckling back to their conversations. Curtain, for his part, twisted in his chair so that he could face the old woman who'd brought the lizard. He steepled his fingers and sketched a seated bow over them, saying a few words in a language Bel didn't recognize. The old woman nodded back, then looked at Bel with crinkled eyes and shrugged.

"What was that you said?" Bel asked, when Curtain faced her again.

"A favor is owed," he replied.

"I don't recognize the language."

"It is the words of the Emberá people," he said. "They were the first to come here, when the Wolf Clan landed, seeking the freedom to continue their way of life. They settled here, around the Fort and up into the mountains. Their culture, as far back as anyone can locate, had been jungle based, so they took to this place well. As the rest of us arrived, over the last fifteen years or so, they have been very welcoming."

"How many of you are there?" Staff Sergeant Gleason asked.

"No idea," Curtain said. "We have never attempted a census, but certainly thousands. Perhaps many thousands. I travel more than most across Condor, and I meet new people every time I visit a place again."

"And you owe no loyalty to the planetary government in Sol City?" Gleason pressed. That was her job, both because she was an intelligence analyst by training and because it was also her job to protect Bel in the conversation.

"The mainlander government," Andy corrected her. "It's a big planet. And no, none."

"We all left the mainlands behind," Curtain added. "We have no wish to return. There is a limited trade, of course, most of it illicit and unofficial. Mainly the fishing vessels, or transoceanic WiGEs. To my knowledge, no one has come here the way you did, in a DropShip, since the Emberá came here."

Bel nodded. She had grown up admiring the big wings-in-ground-effect seaplanes that carried cargo across Odessa's oceans. And while no one in Sol City had anticipated so many people being here, Curtain's story about the isolationist policies of the denizens matched the lack of information available on the mainland.

"So," Andy said. "Let's get down to it, shall we? What's a Tamar Pact when it's at home?"

Bernard Blucher stood leaning against a wall support across the aisle from the cantina where Curtain sat with the newcomers, hands in his pockets, trying to look unobtrusive while he eyed the group. The newcomers didn't look Lyran, but they didn't look exactly not-Lyran, either.

He'd sent Rocker on his way with one last task and an extra payment, and hoped the boy would keep his head down. For a former Jade Falcon, he was harmless enough, but Blucher had lived long enough among two Clans to recognize that Clan civilians could be just as timorous, if not more, as any Inner Sphere wage earner.

The two women, or one woman and one kid, both in gray digicam, talked and laughed with Curtain and his favorite sidekick, that pain in the ass Ishikawa. The kid had one of those burnt lizards the locals liked so much. Blucher had tried one once, when he'd been really drunk. He didn't remember what it tasted like. But he remembered what it'd looked like when he'd thrown it up the next day.

A pair of big men in the same gray digicam the women wore were coming down the aisle toward him. Blucher lurched upright and walked toward them. He smiled as he got closer. "Don't think I've ever seen uniforms like those before, lads."

"We're from off-world," the leftmost said. He was tall and bald, with brown skin and piercing almost-black eyes. "First time visiting Condor."

"Didn't need to be told that," Blucher said, holding out his hand. "I'm Blucher. Where you boys from?" He shook first the bald man's hand, then the hand of the younger man.

"Kandersteg. Sweeney Peat." the younger man said. His accent was pure Lyran. It gave Blucher a flash of hope.

"Arcturus. Aaron Atwater." the other man said.

"Arcturus?" Blucher feigned surprise. "Last I heard, the Jade Falcons held Arcturus. The Commonwealth finally get its act together and kick them off-world?"

"Not exactly," Atwater said, exchanging glances with his companion. "The Twenty-Sixth Arcturan Guards RCT landed and liberated the world."

Blucher grinned. "That sounds like the Commonwealth coming home to me!"

"Not exactly," Peat, the bald man, said. "They turned their coat. Declared it the capital of a new Tamar Pact. Took a bunch of other worlds the Jade Falcons abandoned."

"Yeah, funny how things work out," Atwater added.

Blucher was confused. "Funny?"

"I was in the Twenty-Sixth," Atwater said. "On Arcturus. A bunch of us didn't want to go rogue, and they let us go. Back to Garrison, a couple hundred of us and Hauptmann Carlyle, as he was then."

"Then," Blucher repeated.

"Yeah, then. I didn't even get time to go and see my family. I got to comm them, see they were still alive and tell them I was. That was it. Then the boot. Then we get to Garrison, and the sonsabitches arrested us like we were the traitors. Put us in cells, questioned us. As if we were the ones who went turncoat, right? Then they cashiered the lot of us." Atwater spat the last part. "Put us on the curb with nothing but the clothes on our back."

"No way," Blucher said.

"Believe it," Peat said. "I was in a different unit, *Aufklärungsbataillon 29*. On Garrison. Our kommandant told us we were on a recon mission in the OZ, right? We were on the march, headed to the ships, when this bastard and his lot—" he play-punched Atwater in the arm, "—got in our way and blew out our tail. Arrested the kommandant and the senior officers, they were all in on it. Turns out we were away without orders. But just like him, they arrested all of us. Called us rot. Shoved us out of the LCAF like we were trash. But Mr. Carlyle was there when we got out. Waiting, with busses. Got us fed, got us put up, let any of us join up as wanted. Gave the others money to get home if that's what they wanted."

"Carlyle," Blucher repeated.

"Yeah, himself," Peat said. "Major Carlyle, now."

"Major of what, if you're out of the LCAF?"

"The Gray Death Legion," Atwater said, with strong sound of pride. "He's one of *those* Carlyles."

"I don't understand."

"We're mercenaries now," Peat said. "The Gray Death Legion is back. And under contract to the new government on Tamar."

"Now I'm *really* confused," Blucher said. He glanced at Atwater. "You refused to go rogue, you said. Got yourself shipped off-world. And now you're fighting for the same people you refused to join?"

Both Peat and Atwater grinned. "It gets confusing," Atwater said, slapping Blucher on the arm. "But it's like this. I tried to do right by the Commonwealth, but the Commonwealth did very wrong by me."

"Both of us," Peat added.

"Yeah, both of us. Loyalty goes both ways, right? So yeah. I don't want to fight anyone from LCAF. I know Major Carlyle doesn't either. But Tamar's coin is good, and I know the major's got my back. I know I can trust the people around me, yeah?" He shrugged. "Hell, I can get back to Arcturus and see my family a lot easier now than before."

Blucher stared. He'd imagined a lot of ways this conversation could have gone, and this hadn't been one of them. He knew Curtain had come back with news about the "the invaders" but he'd never bothered to learn the details. He'd been too busy and, if he was being honest with himself, sure it'd be the LCAF coming to rescue the world.

He hadn't expected kingmakers and mercenaries.

"What about you, friend?" Peat asked. "I can hear a bit of Commonwealth in your voice, can't I?"

Blucher blinked at him, mind whirring, then smiled. "Not in a lot of years," he said truthfully. "You guys seem happy, though—any chance I can meet your CO?"

CHAPTER 10

CONDOR
CRIMOND
TAMAR PACT
4 FEBRUARY 3152

"So let me get this straight," Bel said, ignoring the cooling lizard-on-a-stick on the table. "There are Emberá here. Plus odds and sod from both mainlands." The Condors seemed to disregard both Metallerz and Chromastich equally, from what she could tell. She would, too, in their place, just from the names. Ridiculous. "And on top of all that, expats from both the Wolves and the Jade Falcons?"

"Yes," Curtain said simply.

"And you all get along?"

"As much as anyone does."

"I don't understand."

Andy Ishikawa chuckled. "The mainlanders, they like to put each other in boxes. You're in charge, and I'm not. I do this, and you do not. We're not like that. Condor is big enough that we can all just do what we want."

Bel frowned. "The mainlanders, or the Clans?"

"Perhaps both," Curtain said, with a grunt. "Certainly my mother's people are strict; no society with castes can be described otherwise. In the old days, back before the Clans returned to the Inner Sphere, there was always the so-called Dark Caste. Bandits, the Clans called them. They would have fit in well here on Condor. They were merely people who rebelled against labels and laws and rules."

"So you're anarchists," Bel said.

"Tell me," Curtain said. "The mainlanders. When your Tamars landed and deposed the Jade Falcons' left-behinds. How did the mainlanders react? Parades, warm embraces, shared drinks?"

"Bombs," Bel said. She reached up and brushed her hair back off her forehead. "Personal experience."

"I suspected," Curtain said. "The mainlanders are miners, in the main. Blasters. They know explosives well, know how to use explosives to literally move mountains. When they see obstacles, they blast them. So when your Tamars arrived, and removed an obstacle—the Jade Falcons—you expected them to welcome you with open arms. Or at least change out the flag and the address where they send their tax revenue, by the old laws. But instead, your Tamars became a new obstacle, because what the miners want after this long under the Jade Falcons is self-determination. So they turned to the tool they know best for removing obstacles."

"Bombs," Gleason said, frowning. "That was well-articulated, Curtain."

"Thank you," Curtain said, grinning. "I had a long ride in a foul-smelling boat to work it out."

"And you Condors?" Bel asked. "What tool do you lean toward for removing obstacles?" She prodded the end of the skewered lizard in front of her. "Exotic foods?"

"We just want to be left alone," Andy said.

"So do we all," Staff Sergeant Gleason said, with a knowing look at Bel. "But help me understand. You all looked pretty organized when we landed. How do you manage that with no leadership?"

Andy laughed. "Easy—he's in charge." She pointed at Curtain.

Bel squinted. "You're in charge."

"Yes," Curtain said.

"But you just said people don't want to be told what to do?"

"They don't. So I don't tell them."

Bel opened and closed her mouth, which made Curtain erupt in one of his great belly laughs. Andy just grinned. "I came out to face you when you landed," Curtain said. "The others just came along, and thankfully most of them listen to me when I talk."

"Because you're the leader."

"Because I will step on them with my *Regent* if they don't."

"Right..." Bel said.

"Why don't you tell us why you're here," Andy put in, "and we can talk about that for a while."

"Yes," Curtain said. "Tell us about 'securing Condor for the Tamar Pact.'"

Now Bel grinned. "To be honest, we didn't expect to find you here. Our information said this whole island was deserted." She shared a glance with Staff Sergeant Gleason, then decided to go for it. "My orders were to secure the Fort for Tamar."

"Fort Beaufort," Andy said. "That wreck? You're welcome to it."

"Perhaps," was all Curtain said.

"May we tour it?" Gleason asked. "Make our own examination? That way we can tell our superiors if it's really a pile of rocks not worth any attention."

"I will take you over there myself," Curtain said. "Whether or not we allow you to 'secure' it may depend on how exactly you define the verb 'to secure.'" He glanced at Andy, who made a Gallic shrug. Then he returned his gaze to Bel, who frowned slightly.

"I just can't believe no one told us you all were here."

"Few people rush to correct an invader's records, I expect," Curtain said. Gleason nodded firmly in agreement. "But I will reiterate: do we look insecure?"

"You do not," Bel said, "and I will need to seek new orders in light of that." She pushed back a little from the table. "In fact, I think it wise that I do that now. Is there a place I may have privacy?"

Curtain nodded. "I will show you."

As they walked out into the aisle, Bel nodded to Privates Peat and Atwater, where they stood talking to a local. Carillo and Perathoner had remained outside the building, talking to a couple locals huddled around a ramshackle Giggins APC.

"Your mother's people," Bel said to Curtain as they walked.

"Mmm?"

"In there, you said your mother's people could be very strict. You were talking about the Clans."

"So I was."

Bel felt absurd walking beside him; he was nearly twice her height. "They are not your people?"

Curtain grinned. "These are my people," he said, nodding to the passersby, who all returned his nod with smile or a wave. "When I was young, my mother told me I could be anything so long as I earned it. So I became a warrior—yes, a freeborn one, but that doesn't matter as much as it used to—and found it was not enough."

"Not enough," Bel repeated. "To be in the one percent of a Clan."

"But still at the very bottom of that one percent," Curtain corrected her. "From the inside, the warrior caste was no different from my mother's caste. Full of internecine fighting and backstabbing, men and women who say one thing and act another. The glory my mother had taught me about, the purity of purpose and sense of service, was absent."

"So you left."

"So I left."

"And took your 'Mech with you?"

Curtain grinned. "I did, but not that one. That one I traded a gullible Sea Fox trader for."

Bel grinned back at him. "What did you trade him?"

"My old 'Mech, of course," Curtain said. "But also certain 'treasures' from the Fort here that I may have claimed were relics of the ancient Star League." He spread his hands. "Items that have no value in and of themselves. They cost only what people are willing to pay."

"That's a very capitalist thing for a freeborn Clan warrior to say," Bel told him.

"You are not the first Lyran I have met," he said, laughing.

"That's the head honcho she's with, Captain Carlyle," Private Atwater told Blucher, as she walked past with Curtain and the others. He and Peat both nodded to the diminutive officer as she walked past, but Blucher just glanced at her and went back to his discussion. Movement behind the two infantrymen caught his eye: Istvan Sanchez, hands in his pockets, nodding at him.

"Will you guys excuse me?" Blucher asked. "I need to see a guy about a thing, if you catch my drift."

"We should check in with the captain anyway," Private Peat said. "Nice to meet you, Blucher."

Blucher shook their hands again and walked slowly down the aisle, threading a needle between people until he stood next to Sanchez, who pretended not to know him.

"What the hell's this about, Archon's boy?" Sanchez snarled under his breath. "You send that tinspawn kid to us—"

"You heard about the invaders?" Blucher asked, cutting him off.

"Everyone has."

"Well, I was just talking to two of them. You and your boys got a choice, Sanchez."

"What kind of choice?"

Blucher licked his lips. "The Jade Falcons are gone. The invaders on the mainlands, they're called Tamars, and they're Lyran renegades."

"Renegades," Sanchez snorted. "That must chap your ass, Archon's boy."

"At some point the Archon will come fix the books," Blucher said. "Think about those rumors we heard years ago, about that guy Widmer way the hell out on Buena?"

"So what if she does," Sanchez said. "No skin off mine."

"You know everyone on this island," Blucher said. "I need you to get anyone like me—Archon's boys and girls, whatever you call us, people who still believe in the Commonwealth—to the Fort. You and your boys. Right now, like in the next hour."

Sanchez abandoned the charade and faced him. "What are you talking about?"

"These Tamars, they want the fort. I can keep them away from it. But I need people to watch my back. That's sure as shit not you, I get it. But you know the right people."

"Why would I do that?"

"Because I can pay you," Blucher said. "Six thousand *kroner*, right now. And you can loot the bodies when I'm done."

Sanchez laughed in his face. "You don't have six thousand *kroner*."

Blucher reached into his thigh pocket and pulled out a palm-size tool carrier. It flipped open on a hinge, revealing ranks of delicate electronics instruments. He dug a thumb into the seam and lifted the whole tool assembly free. Beneath it, hidden between the tools and the outer shell, was a single thousand-*kroner* note. "Don't I?"

Sanchez stared, but Blucher could already see the wheels of avarice turning behind his watery brown eyes. "And I'll sweeten the deal."

"How's that?"

"I'll make sure you get pardons when the Lyrans come back. Blanket."

Sanchez snorted again, disbelieving, but with the thousand-*kroner* note staring him in the face… "How?"

Blucher laughed. "I'll have given an entire fortress on a remote island to the LCAF when they come to kick renegades back off their planet. They'll give me anything I want. Me—and the people who helped me."

"You're crazy," Sanchez said, but he couldn't tear his gaze away from the thousand *kroner*. Blucher gave it to him, set it in the open palm of his hand.

"Five more just like that," he promised, "when the people I want show up at the fort."

"What am I supposed to tell them?"

Blucher closed his fingers over Sanchez's, covering the *kroner*. "Tell them the Archon is asking for their help."

Curtain held the door open for the tiny mercenary officer to enter. The room was one of the few built into the structure of the building, with solid walls and a roof and a door that closed. There was little inside but a desk, some rotten chairs, and the detritus of years of passersby tossing in their trash, but it was private.

"No one will bother you while you speak," Curtain said. "And no one will listen. You can speak freely."

"You won't be offended if we take our own precautions," the other mercenary woman, Gleason, said.

Curtain grinned at her. She was clearly older and more experienced than the young captain, but deferential nonetheless. That spoke to a commendable amount of professionalism inside this Gray Death Legion. "I would be offended if you did not."

"Thank you," Captain Carlyle said. She grinned suddenly. "I won't try and butcher the Emberá version, but... a favor is owed." Curtain smiled broadly, and said the phrase again in the Emberá tongue. Carlyle mouthed it silently, then shook her head. She looked past him. "Go get the others, Private?"

Curtain turned; two large men in the gray Legion battledress were behind him. One of them, nearly his own size, with a bald head and a serious expression, was staring hard at Curtain. *Because I am putting his captain in a locked room*, he realized, and stepped back with a flourish.

"We'll be quick," Carlyle told him. "Then we want to see the fort?"

"I will show you," he promised her.

CHAPTER 11

"So," Bel said to the group as soon as the door was closed. "What have we learned so far?"

The enlisted Legionnaires glanced at each other until Sergeant Carillo cleared his throat. "I haven't seen all their equipment, ma'am, but the APC outside is *way* behind on PMCS." He glanced at Sergeant Perathoner, but continued. "It's a miracle it's still running, ma'am."

Bel nodded. PMCS—preventative maintenance checks and services—was the nearly every day work it took to keep military vehicles up and running. Testing systems, switching spares in for defective components, making sure the oil was changed. No matter whether the Legion was in combat or not, Master Sergeant Buthra Azarri's technical teams were always in motion, making sure the Legion's 'Mechs, tanks, and battlesuits were ready to go at a moment's notice. A single MechWarrior may command a BattleMech in combat, but it took a half-dozen or more other people's work to keep that 'Mech in fighting trim.

She trusted Carillo to know, too. Lieutenant Komljenovic, the Legion's senior armor officer, expected his tank crews to pitch in and help with PMCS wherever possible, for two reasons he'd explained to the Carlyles: first, because a tank crew lived and fought as a unit, and sometimes the margin between life and death was knowing how to fix something that broke or was damaged in combat. It wasn't enough to just be able to crack track. And second, because it made his crews partner with Azarri's mechanic teams, forced them to work together, to get to know each other as people. That sort of friendship was invaluable in a mercenary company. Ronan and Bel had wholeheartedly agreed.

"I noticed the rust," she said to him. "Even on the 'Mech. You think the rest of their force is like this?"

"Ma'am, if I may?" Sergeant Perathoner interrupted. At Bel's nod, she nodded at Sergeant Carillo. "While the sergeant was inspecting the outside, I was talking to the crew. They have no logistical function, or really any organization at all. The vehicles are largely personal vehicles or family affairs. There's no pool of equipment to draw from: if they expend rounds, if something breaks, they're on their own to fix it."

"How the hell do they keep anything running?" Staff Sergeant Gleason asked.

Perathoner shrugged her slight shoulders. "They're resourceful people."

"Or this Fort is a lot less a wreck than we've been led to expect," Bel offered. She raised her eyebrows, making it clear it she meant it as a question, but all she got back was shrugs. "Could they be making up their tail—" in military parlance, a "tail" was shorthand for the logistical effort it took to keep a military force in action, "—out of old storehouses, either Star League or LCAF?"

"Ma'am, I couldn't tell you that yet," Sergeant Perathoner said.

Bel nodded and looked to Staff Sergeant Gleason. "And the Two shop says?"

"Ask me again after our tour," Gleason said, grinning.

"Fair enough." Bel turned her attention to the two infantrymen. "Okay, boys, what about you?"

Private Peat spoke first. "Ma'am, they seem like nice people, but out of touch, you know?" Atwater nodded.

"Out of touch like they're outcasts from planetary society, on a planet formerly held by an insular Clan, in a galaxy without working hyperpulse generators?" Bel grinned at him. "Out of touch like that?"

"Exactly like that, ma'am."

"I saw you talking to one of the locals. What did he want to know?"

"State of the universe, ma'am," Atwater put in. "He sounded ex-LCAF, from a long time ago, if that makes sense. Like maybe he was here when the Wolves first took over? He never came out and said it, but he seemed real broken up we weren't the LCAF finally come back. And when we explained about Arcturus and the old Twenty-Sixth..." He glanced at Peat, who nodded. "Well, ma'am, it seemed like he couldn't quite wrap his mind around it."

"I know the feeling," Bel said. "We all do."

"Yes, ma'am."

Bel nodded, mulling over all the things her team had said. "What you've all said matches my impressions. I'll add, so you all know what's going on. The guy in charge, Curtain, he's a pistol."

"Big guy," Private Atwater said.

"And that," Bel agreed. "But he's being completely hospitable. Short version is, the people here left the mainlands—what they call the other two continents—by their own choice. They don't want anything to do with what goes on back there. They just want to be left alone."

"With a Star League-era fort nearby," Staff Sergeant Gleason said.

"With that," Bel said. "Which brings all of this back around to why we're here, and what's next. Curtain has agreed to give us a tour of the Fort. You all put your heads together and decide which parts we want to ask to see. We can't spend a week crawling through every nook and cranny. But I want us to get a solid read on the state of it."

"Roger," Staff Sergeant Gleason said, for the group. "And while we're doing that?"

Bel pulled out her pocket comm. "While you're doing that, I'm going to see if I can get that Tamar DropShip to retrans back to the major and our esteemed liaison officer, and see what they say about the new circumstances."

Outside the small room they'd stuffed the Legion party into, Curtain stood with Andy Ishikawa, watching people walk by. He leaned against the wall, arms crossed, just waiting and enjoying the peace that came from being among his people.

"What do think of them?" Andy asked.

"They seem like good people," Curtain said. "Young, certainly this Captain Carlyle is young, but among my mother's people, that is the norm. They could have just blasted their way in, but they are taking the time to try and understand us."

"Doesn't mean they won't change their mind later," Andy said.

"No, it doesn't. And they are people under authority, so even if they might wish not to, they may be forced into it."

"What will do then?"

"Defend ourselves."

Andy grunted. "You're really going to show them around the Fort?"

Curtain nodded. "Their commander and the mainlanders, they envision a shining lost fortress sitting in the jungle, just waiting to be occupied and used as a base against them. We know better. Fort Beaufort is a wreck for any military purpose. No one has even been able to get most of it to power up."

"I guess." Andy watched an old man hobble past, carrying a bundle of tinwood logs in his arms, then bit her fingernail. "Can we win, if it comes to a fight?"

Curtain waited until she met his eyes. "I do not know."

"He's coming," Ronan Carlyle said. His voice, coming from the small flatscreeen on her noteputer, was haggard. He wiped a big hand across his forehead, smearing the dirt there. "Should be just a minute."

"How is it there?" Bel asked.

"Ask me again later," Ronan said. "We found the bombmakers—or at least, the police did. We just gave them backup. There are people who will fight it out with a cop, but will just sit down when you send battlesuits in on them."

"That's good." Bel was confused—that was unequivocally good news, but her brother didn't sound happy.

"Yeah," Ronan said. "It's just while we were taking down the ringleaders, their people were blowing up three more bombs across Kola. We've got hundreds dead here, Bel. Including a platoon of Tamar Jaegers infantry who parked their APC in the wrong spot. Eldon, all the Tamars, they're red-hot right now." He blew air out his cheeks. "Here he comes. I hope you've got good news. We're doing our job here, no one can say we aren't, but it isn't a happy place to be."

A moment later, the image shifted as Ronan stood up and Hauptmann Eldon sat down. He looked like he hadn't slept in a week. And it hadn't been a week since Bel had seen him last. "Captain Carlyle. What's your status?"

"Sir, we arrived safely, and—"

"Not what I asked, Captain."

Bel blinked but bit back the retort her temper shot forward. "Sir, our status is good."

"Very well. Status of the Fort?"

"We're touring it shortly, sir—"

"Call me back when you've done that." Eldon made as if to stand up.

"Sir—*Hautpmann!*"

"What?"

"Sir, our information was out of date. Condor is not deserted. There are people here. Locals. Long-established and in control of the local area around the fort."

Eldon frowned. "Explain."

Bel shook her head. "The details would take too long, sir. Suffice it to say they are organized and they live here. I mean here as in the Fort grounds, sir. At first glance the place is a wreck. Everything's overgrown, buildings are falling down—"

"Tell me about these locals. Are they hostile? Jade Falcon remnants?"

Bel breathed in and held in. *Interrupt me one more time*, her temper muttered, but she kept it inside. "No sir. Not so far.

But they are armed. At least one 'Mech that we've seen, and a handful of fighting vehicles."

"Do they object to our occupying the Fort?"

"You haven't seen it, Hauptmann. It'd be like occupying a ruin."

"Again, Captain, not my question."

"I'll tell you when I call you back, Hauptmann. Their leader is the one taking me on the tour."

Eldon sighed. He blinked once, hard, a long blink that squeezed his eyes together. Bel knew that blink. She had done it a hundred times cramming for exams on Coventry. The blink that told the pain in your head from stress or allergy or lack of sleep or even hangover that you didn't have time for it. She felt her first instance of empathy for Hauptmann Eldon. She knew she'd never like the man. But at least now she knew he was human.

"Your orders stand," Eldon said, "and I see nothing changed yet to suggest to the Three that we change your tasking. Get a look inside. Get me an order of battle on these people for the Two shop. Do they report through Metallerz of Chromastich?"

"Neither, sir," Bel said. "They want nothing to do with the planetary governments on the mainland. That's what drove them out here in the first place, a desire to be apart from the people on those two continents."

"They separatists?"

"No more than you, sir. You formed the Pact because the Commonwealth wasn't doing its duty to the people out here. As far as the Condors are concerned, the people on the mainland, the people you're trying to get to stop blowing each other up, are the Commonwealth."

Eldon stared at her. Then he blinked again. "Call me back after your tour," he said before standing up. Ronan sat back down and put in the earbuds so he could talk to her.

"You hear any of that?" Bel asked.

"All of it."

"What do you think?"

"I'm not sure equating the new star nation he's a part of to a bunch of anarchists in the jungle was the wisest course of action, but other than that..."

"They make a good first impression, Ronan."

"I trust you. But remember you're under orders."

"I don't forget," she told him.

"Go have your tour." Ronan grinned. "Remember Grandad telling us the stories his parents told him about Nagayan Mountain? Maybe it'll be like that."

"Sure," Bel said. "*After* the flood." She licked her lips. "Ronan, be careful, okay?"

"I think I'm supposed to say that to you."

"I have good people here. I'll be okay."

"So do I," Ronan promised. "We're doing the job. You do yours, and it'll all work out."

Bel nodded, smiled, and killed the transmission. She sat there for a minute, thinking, then slapped her own thighs and stood. *Let's get this done.*

CHAPTER 12

CONDOR
CRIMOND
TAMAR PACT
5 FEBRUARY 3152

The Fort Beaufort Citadel was a solid mass of ferrocrete, rust-stained thick steel and surreptitious armor bulkheads. It towered over the scenery, dwarfing everything except the sprawl of mountains to one side. The main entrance, designed to welcome dignitaries, was a sprawling, transpex-lined affair that drew natural morning light, and was meant to impress. Today, of course, the transpex was covered with dust, dirt, and the creeping encroachment of vines as the jungle fought its own war against the fort, but some small amount of light still got through.

It was there Bernard Blucher met his "recruits." True to his coin, Sanchez and his crew had rounded up about twenty men and women. They were a motley bunch, uniformly older, like Blucher himself, old enough to remember a time before the Clans came to Crimond, and probably—also like Blucher—bitter enough to want to do something about it. There was nothing so formal as an "LCAF Association" on Condor, but Blucher recognized several of them from chance conversations over the years.

"What're we doing here, Blucher?" asked a portly man in the front of the group. He was dressed as the others were, in jungle wear, with an old shotgun slung across his chest and a bandolier of shells around his waist. Blucher recognized him. "I got up early for this."

"Simmons," Blucher greeted him. "All of you. I'm glad you're here." He wouldn't say anything so petulant as "thanks for coming," that would give them the chance to say no thanks. "You all know about the invaders?"

"Can't help but know," said a tall, wiry woman with spiky brown hair a few steps behind Simmons. Blucher didn't recognize her. "We all saw the DropShip come down, didn't we? They probably saw it through the canopy, a day deep in the Darien."

"You hear the details?" No one spoke. "They're traitors to the Commonwealth. Twenty-sixth Arcturan Guards turned its coat when it landed on Arcturus, turned its back on the Commonwealth, declared something called the Tamar Pact. Now they're here because the Jade Falcons are gone."

"Good for them," Simmons said. "What are we doing here?"

"What were you in the LCAF, Simmons?"

"Gunner," Simmons said. "In a Rommel tank."

Blucher looked to the next person he recognized. "Petersen. You?"

"I was a scout," said the average height, skeletally thin man with a wicked scar across his cheek and a shock of white hair. "Unarmored."

"I was an electronics NCO," Blucher said. "And a damned good one."

"If I wanted to recollect the old days, Blucher..." Simmons growled.

"The Commonwealth with be here soon," Blucher said quickly. "I know it and you know it. It's only a matter of time. And when they get here, I'd much prefer Fort Beaufort was in our hands. Not in Curtain's. Certainly not in these damned Tamar bastards'. *Ours.*" He paused, looked across the group, then smiled. "And operational."

"Yeah, I'm done here," Simmons said. There were murmurs of agreement.

"I can get the turrets working," Blucher said quickly. "I've already done it. I have a secondary command post we can occupy, and barricade ourselves inside. We can get the invaders and Curtain's fools fighting each other, we can secure this building and only let people we trust inside. With no Curtain, and with us holding an activated fort beneath them, the invaders won't come back."

"You're dreaming," Petersen said.

"You all swore the same oath I did!" Blucher snarled. "We can do this, for long enough. And when the Commonwealth comes back, they'll know we did our duty despite the years and the Clans."

"How?" a voice in the back called. Blucher wanted to grin, but didn't dare. "How did you do it?"

"Because I'm very good at my job," he said. "Come on, and I'll show you. We'll do this right now."

He turned and started walking for the stairwell. Blucher was afraid to look over his shoulder to see how many were following him, but from the sound, it was not zero.

The Legion party bunked overnight in the South Six complex, using materials provided by the locals. They kept a watch all night, but true to his word, Curtain's people did not bother them until the man himself came to take them to their ride to the fort.

Andy Ishikawa's jeep was insufficient to hold all the Legion party members plus Curtain, so instead they decided to pile into the heavy wheeled APC Sergeant Carillo had been inspecting. Andy and Curtain climbed in without hesitation, but Bel looked at Carillo. The dapper tanker caught her look and shrugged.

"Worst that happens is we break down," he said with a grin. "Be a good way to get our cardio."

"I hate cardio," Staff Sergeant Gleason said firmly. She stepped past them and up the ramp into the infantry bay. The driver fired up the APC's engine as Bel climbed aboard; she got a whiff of pungent, sickly-sweet diesel exhaust. The APC's entire 20-ton frame rattled from the engine vibrations.

Bel sat down next to Curtain, close enough that they should be able to talk. Andy Ishikawa, who'd been sitting on Curtain's other side, got up and crossed the bay to sit across from them, giving them a modicum of privacy. The ramp cycled up and the

APC lurched into motion. Bel, with the awareness that small people all had around large people, braced herself for Curtain to lurch with the acceleration into her, but he held himself in place.

"What did your commanders say?" Curtain asked. He spoke loudly, to be heard, but the words would not carry far in the raucous noise of the infantry bay.

"To call back after the tour," Bel told him with a grin.

"How did they take the news?"

Bel shrugged. "As well as anyone. They're curious about you. Afraid, I think, because they don't know whether or not you could be a threat."

"We are a threat to no one."

"To believe that requires trust," Bel said. "You're smart enough to know that."

"Or distance," Curtain replied, nodding. "We came out here because we chose distance."

"You're still on the planet," Bel said carefully, "and the planetary government—"

Curtain's snort cut her off. "The planetary government was the Jade Falcons. They ignored us. The mainlanders have their own concern. There is no reason we should submit to their oversight." He made a small gesture with his hand, half brushing off, half knife-hand. "It is a long sail by boat to get here. I know. I have done it many times."

"It's a short trip by DropShip," Bel said. Curtain stared at her. She gave a Gallic shrug. "I have done it."

He frowned, but didn't look away.

"Look," she told him. "These Tamars, they've built their whole star nation on the ideology of protecting those who can't protect themselves. That was their justification for breaking away from the Commonwealth, that Tharkad was too far and too distracted to know how to keep the people of Arcturus and the worlds around it safe."

"'For your protection' has been the invocation of almost every conqueror in history," Curtain argued.

"My point," she said, raising her eyebrows, "is that I think they'll leave you alone. They'll want to be sure of the legitimate military concerns, like making sure Fort Beaufort is the ruin you say it is. But they're not tyrants. Not that I've seen."

"Tyranny is often done in the dark," Curtain said. Bel nodded. She didn't disagree. Neither of them spoke further.

The APC soon slowed, before coming to a stop. The rear ramp banged down, shining in bright light. Bel and the others climbed out, into an entryway before a huge, rust-stained ferrocrete building. Vines and other creepers climbed every wall, finding notches and pores in the ferrocrete to anchor their roots.

"The Citadel," Curtain said, gesturing grandly. "Headquarters of Fort Beaufort." He grinned at the Legion party. "Beware the smell inside." Andy Ishikawa laughed and shook her head as Curtain led them inside.

The atrium inside must have been incredible when it was new and clean, Bel decided. Now it was dirty and—as Curtain had warned—smelled of the thick cloying scent of organic decay. Animals had defecated in this room in the past, she was sure. Each of the Legionnaires, as the came in, gasped and held the backs of their hands over their noses.

"What the..." Andy said, before stalking off to the right. Bel looked where she was headed, and saw a crew of three men crouched against a wall, passing a bottle back and forth. "Sanchez!" One of the men flinched, spilling liquor down the front of his shirt.

"Friends of hers?" Bel asked Curtain.

"Layabouts," Curtain said, shaking his head. "But they do not usually do their drinking here."

"Don't know how they *can* drink in here," Private Atwater said. He was pinching his nostrils shut and breathing through his mouth. Bel sympathized.

After a minute talking to them, Andy kicked one of the men in the leg. All three scrabbled to their feet and scurried out a side door, down what Bel took to be a hallway, while Andy walked back over to them.

"Assholes," she muttered. To Curtain, she said, "Sanchez said Blucher hired him to get a bunch of the old Lyran loyalists here a little while ago. Paid him well, though he wouldn't say how much."

"Why?" Curtain asked.

"Didn't say."

"Did you say Blucher?" Private Peat asked. Andy looked at him, clearly surprised, and nodded. "We met a Blucher a little while ago." He described the man Bel had seen the two infantrymen talking to.

"That's him," Andy said. "What did you talk about?"

"The news, mostly. The last couple years."

"He say anything about coming here?"

"Nothing."

Bel looked from Andy to Curtain. "Is this something I need to worry about?"

"No," Curtain said. "Bernard Blucher and those others Andy described, the so-called Lyran loyalists, are old men and women who pine for an earlier age, before the Clans came. We are several versions of reality past them."

He clapped his hands together once. The sound echoed from the distant walls. "I propose we start at the top and work our way down, from the roof. That will give you the best view of the grounds. And this way, we do the climbing while we are fresh."

"Climbing?" Staff Sergeant Gleason asked warily.

"Elevators haven't worked the whole time I've lived here," Andy Ishikawa said, leading them toward a doorway marked STAIRS. "I hope you like steps."

"Cardio…" Gleason muttered mournfully.

"This is a lot of damn stairs, Blucher," Simmons growled from behind him.

"We're almost there," Blucher said. From the noise, it sounded like almost all the people Sanchez had gathered had followed him down. "This landing." He stepped out, into the corridor, shining his handlight so the others could see the floor. "If you give me a minute, I'll get the lights on down here."

"These lights never worked the whole time I been here," Petersen said.

"That's because I wasn't here," Blucher said. He slid through the door he and Rocker had gotten working, remembering the way it had ground on dirt and dust as it dogged tight. He sat down at the CO's console, just as he had before, and flipped a few switches, before touching the recessed panel open. He tripped the breaker. "There."

"There, what?" Simmons growled.

"Wait for it."

"If you dragged us all down here into the dark to play games," Simmons started, but stopped when Blucher extinguished his handlight. One of the overhead LEDs flickered as the power warmed up, just as it had yesterday.

"You're kidding..." Petersen whispered.

The lights in the room came up full, and the consoles sparkled to life. On the big main screen, the image Blucher had left up yesterday, of the field where the invaders, this Gray Death Legion, stood facing the frozen *Regent* and the rest of Curtain's "militia."

"All this time..." Peterson whispered.

"Tell us your plan again," Simmons commanded.

Blucher smiled. He didn't hear bluster in the gruff man's voice anymore. Instead, he heard something quite different. Something he doubted Simmons himself had felt for fifteen years or more.

Hope.

CHAPTER 13

**CONDOR
CRIMOND
TAMAR PACT
5 FEBRUARY 3152**

The view from the roof of the Citadel was *almost* worth the climb up.

Bel stood with Curtain and the others, hands on hips, breathing heavily and trying to hide it. To distract herself from the burning in her lungs and the stabbing pain in her side, she looked around. Behind her were the green-topped mountains, rising like a wall. It was hard for her to imagine that there trails, even vehicle paths, up that wall. But she'd met several Darien traders and hunters who spent much of their time up that mountain, in the jungle.

In front of her were the sprawl of Fort Beaufort and, farther out, the squat shape of the Tamar *Union*-class DropShip and the Legion 'Mechs, still standing their guard against the Condor armored vehicles. She'd told Lieutenant Christensen it was okay to retire aboard the DropShips, but he'd demurred, citing the need to be able to respond quickly if their situation there in the fort changed.

Curtain's *Regent* still stood out there, too, like a statue. She pointed it out. "Does it feel like you left your toys out?"

"I could ask the same of you," he said, jutting his chin toward where her own *Hatchetman* stood silent vigil as well. "But we came to see things closer than that. What do you think of the Fort from up here?"

Bel shook her head. "It's as you said: a ruin."

"How much of it is populated?" Staff Sergeant Gleason asked, or rather, gasped. She had struggled with the stairs.

Curtain looked at her, grinned, and then shrugged. "By now, a person has probably been inside everything one can access without power," he replied. "But permanently? Most of us live outside the Fort, though South Six is more or less always populated. It serves as our bazaar, as you saw."

"So if I were to have an infrared sight hauled up here..." Gleason pressed.

"You would see animals, to be sure," Curtain said. "The odd person out prospecting for an artifact that might change their fortune. But I would be amazed if you found any large groups of people outside of South Six."

"Kids," Andy Ishikawa put in. "Out hiding from their parents, doing what comes natural."

"It's a natural defensive zone for infantry and tanks," Sergeant Carillo put in. "But only because of the rubble. Gives endless opportunities for ambushes from cover and concealment."

"If you had the manpower," Curtain said.

"Yes, if that," Carillo agreed. Bel and Gleason shared a look, and Gleason shook her head slightly. Bel agreed; she hadn't seen any sign the Condors could bring that much manpower to bear.

"You would do better to send archaeologists," Andy said. "This was a Star League fort, once."

Bel grunted. She was starting to think Andy was right.

"Simmons, you sit there," Blucher said, pointing. "Anyone else ever fired a vehicle-scale weapon before?" A few hands went up. "Good. Spread yourselves over there. Concentrate on the PPC turrets, then lasers. There's no chance any of the cannon or missile feed tubes aren't solid masses of rotted ammunition. But the energy weapons may still work."

"What are we shooting at?" Simmons asked.

"Anything that moves," Blucher said. "The DropShip, if you can reach it."

Simmons chuckled. Blucher looked that way; the old man was sitting leaning forward at the console, hand wrapped around the gunnery controls, a childlike smile on his face. "We want them to think they're shooting at each other," he said. "So let's synchronize our shots."

"My turret's frozen," one of the woman who'd stepped to the other consoles said.

"Not frozen," Blucher said. "I haven't turned on the power to the turrets yet." He turned to the dozen or so people left. "Any of you got security experience?" A hand went up. "Good. Get the rest of these people organized. We need to hold this room, no matter what."

"Hold it against what?" the hand-raiser asked.

"What's your name?"

"Giorgio."

"Against anything that comes near it, Giorgio." Blucher raised his voice. "All of you, listen up. The moment we step off, we're Lyrans again. It's us against Curtain, us against this Gray Death Legion. We have to hit them hard and fast, and scare them into leaving us alone until the Commonwealth gets here."

This is insane, he waited for someone to shout. He knew it was, but he didn't care. He was talking like the LCAF was days or weeks away, and he had no idea. It could be months. Years, even. There was no way they could hold off a determined assault down a stairwell for *years*. Hell, they didn't even have food with them. Any one of these people could say the words and break the spell. Blucher knew it like he knew the sun would rise.

But no one spoke.

He set his fingers on the power controls. "Who has the mercenaries?" Three hands raised. Blucher's fingers moved. "Do not fire. You have power." He turned his head to look at Simmons. "You have Curtain's damned 'Mech?"

Simmons growled. Blucher touched a key. "You have power."

This is insane.

"Fire."

Bel was opening her mouth to suggest they start down, when blue-white light flashed momentary shadows across everything. She flinched, leaping to the side, moments before the report of PPCs cutting loose clapped across the sky like heavy thunder.

"Odin's *balls*, what was *that*!?" she shouted.

Across the distance, Curtain's *Regent* was smoking and falling over from multiple PPC hits. It collapsed with a crash, into a pall of smoke and dust. Bel, confused, looked toward Christensen's *Catapult*. Nick had the skill to hit the *Regent* and take it down with one barrage, but she had no idea why he would do it.

The Legion *Catapult* was down as well, smoke rippling from heavy hits to its shoulder and side. Mbaruku's *Talon* was also down. She didn't know if either of the MechWarriors were in the cockpits; her orders had been to stand by the machines, in case the situation changed, but with the *Regent* standing empty there was no need to sit in the command couch for days on end, weapons at the ready.

"Who—" she started, but stopped at the sound of pistol slides being racked.

Private Atwater stood with his sidearm leveled at Curtain; Private Peat covered Andy Ishikawa, while Staff Sergeant Gleason stood with hers drawn, but not aimed. "Step away please, Captain," she said. "Carillo, get her sidearm." She jerked her chin at Andy.

"Do it and you lose an arm, Sergeant," Andy growled. Her arms were up, but she glared the armor sergeant into stillness.

"What are you doing, Staff Sergeant?"

"Ma'am, those were turrets. Fort Beaufort turrets."

"Impossible," Curtain said.

Bel turned and looked at the smoking Legion 'Mechs. While she watched, another barrage of PPC blasts pounded the *Regent* and the *Catapult*. She pointed. "Then why are they shooting at the *Regent*?"

"Plausible deniability, ma'am," Gleason said.

"Staff Sergeant," Curtain said calmly, "you have my word I know nothing of this. Until this moment I would have told you on the honor of everything you hold dear that those turrets were solid blocks of rust. I have never, since I set foot on this island, seen one move, much less fire."

"We can't even turn on the lights on," Andy insisted.

"Someone did," Gleason said.

Bel ground her teeth. "Staff Sergeant. Lower your weapons. That is an order."

"Sir, all due respect—"

"Andy," Curtain said. "Your pistol. Set it on the roof."

"Eat shit."

"Do it," Curtain said with steel in his voice. He looked at Gleason. "She will do it, Staff Sergeant. Then you will not be pointing guns at us, and we will not be pointing guns at you. And we can talk."

"Staff Sergeant." Bel put her best command voice into it. "I gave you an order."

"Lower 'em," Gleason said. The two infantrymen did as they were ordered.

"Now—" Curtain said, but Bel shushed him. She pulled her comm out of her pocket and snapped it live.

"Christensen?"

"Here, Captain," Nick Christensen replied. Bel heard the pain in his voice.

"Status?"

"Taking fire," he replied. "Yurim and I are both in the cockpit, but they hit us before we could get out of standby. Yurim isn't answering, ma'am." There was a grunt. "I'll be on my feet in twenty seconds."

"It's not the Condors. Understood?"

"Understood. I see their 'Mech is down. Do they know it's not us?"

Bel looked at Curtain. "I'm doing that next."

"Orders?"

"See to your safety," Bel ordered. "Any means necessary, Lieutenant."

"Roger, ma'am."

"Good hunting."

Bel ended the call. "Do you need to contact your people?"

Curtain shook his head. "I left Hector Alessandro in charge. He won't shoot at the wrong thing, and he'll keep everyone else in line."

The PPCs cut loose again, but by now Christensen had his *Catapult* on its feet and moving. The blue-white beams missed behind it, blasting the soil into fragments. He twisted at the waist and replied, not at the turret blasting at him, but at the vine-covered blockhouse targeting Yurim Mbaruku's *Talon*. Both the *Catapult*'s PPCs struck the glacis, but the ancient armor held.

Bel pointed out there. "Now. What do we do about that?"

Blucher had put the gun camera footage up on the main screen. Every time the quad PPC turrets fired, the room erupted in cheers. Blucher didn't even try to keep himself from joining in. He zoomed in on Curtain's *Regent*, on the ground, being hit again and again like a lightning rod in a storm.

"Hey, who's that?" someone asked.

Blucher looked toward the voice. The scout, Petersen, had sat down at unoccupied station and poked some buttons. He'd gotten the console live. Blucher got up, walked over, curious to see what the station controlled.

It was a security station. The camera display was a 4x4 grid of sixteen flatscreens. About half of them, irregularly, were blank because the cameras were dead. The rest were flickering in and out, but one was clear: the roof monitor. There were people on the roof. One of them was tall, larger than the others. Blucher frowned, leaned closer.

Curtain was on the roof.

People were holding guns on him.

Blucher jerked back and ran for the doors. "Giorgio!" he screamed.

"What?" a distracted voice said from behind him, from inside the room. Blucher spun, eyes searching, until he found the man who'd claimed security knowledge.

"They're on the roof," Blucher told him.

"Who's on the roof?"

"Curtain. The mercenaries. Right now."

Giorgio looked up at the ceiling. Blucher slapped his arm. "Get up there. Kill them all. Without them to lead the rabble against us, we can control this whole island. Go. Now." Blucher pushed him toward the door. "*Now!*"

Giorgio nodded, and rushed out the door.

Behind them, the PPCs fired again, to cheers.

"Blucher," Andy Ishikawa spat. Bel and Curtain looked up from their argument about whether and how to storm the main control room. "It has to be Blucher."

"From downstairs," Bel said, as the memory caught up with her.

"That snake Sanchez," Andy went on. "He told me Blucher called together his Lyrans. And Blucher's some kind of tech. It has to be him."

"One man got this old Fort working?" Curtain asked.

"Stranger things have happened." Bel looked at Private Peat and nodded. "Let's get moving. We'll sweep down. We don't know how many there are, who they are, or where they are. We're not armed for it. And they know the ground."

"Sounds like fun, ma'am," Peat said. He nodded at Atwater. "You ready?"

"Armor just slows me down anyway," Atwater said with a grin.

"Andy," Curtain said. "Go get your gun."

Andy looked at Gleason, who nodded.

Bel looked at the group and grinned. "Well then, friends," she said, "let's see if we can go get ourselves kill't."

CHAPTER 14

Legion Lieutenant Nick Christensen desperately needed a nap. He'd been unstrapped in his cockpit when the targeting alarm blared, but by the time he'd gotten the neurohelmet down off its cradle the PPCs had already hit and his 'Mech was falling. He'd barely had time to jerk his head and fling the helmet off before he struck; having that much weight on his head, unsecured, when the *Catapult* hit the ground could have killed him.

Instead, it had still hurt like all hell, and he'd banged his head against the side of the cockpit. He was going to have a knot there, he knew; he could already feel the pressure against the inside of the neurohelmet. But he'd deal with that later. Right now he was too busy staying alive.

"Nick," Alexei Komljenovic said, "where do you need us?"

Christensen blinked, trying to think. According to his computer, there were four heavy turrets, what looked like armored quad PPC emplacements, firing. Three of them were tracking the Legion side of the pad, while one was pasting fire toward the local tanks that had burst into motion when the local 'Mech had gone down. Targeting indications were that two more might be active, but they looked like laser emplacements, too far out of range to hit him so long as he kept moving.

"If you can, get in there and fry those turrets," Christensen said. "If you can find any kind of defilade to get there, get some support over to the locals, too."

"The locals?"

"They're getting shot at too, Alexei."

"Roger," the tank officer said, and closed the channel.

"Roger," Christensen repeated. He swung the *Catapult* around again. As the bullet-shaped 'Mech's nose passed one of the turrets, he hit again with both his PPCs. One missed wide, but the other blasted at the armor and foliage covering the squat turret. If it had any effect, he didn't see it.

"Must've hit my head harder than I thought," Christensen muttered. A deflection shot like that against a still target should have been a clap shot.

Descending the stairwell was maybe the most terrifying time of Bel's life, and that was saying something given she'd just been blown up less than a week earlier. But as she trailed the group, pacing Staff Sergeant Gleason, with Andy Ishikawa behind them, holding her Python in a two-handed grip pointed down the center of the stairwell, it was all she could do to keep her hands from shaking too bad.

She'd been in combat before, but that was different. She'd been in a BattleMech. Sure, MechWarriors died all the time, but they had armor to protect them. It took a lot to get through a 'Mech's armor, and she had time to shoot back.

But here, now, someone could just appear out of the dark and put a bullet through her head, and she'd be dead and explaining herself to Odin or Saint Peter or whoever before she even knew it. She licked her lips and concentrated, telling herself it was just adrenalin.

"At least it's not that dark," Gleason whispered.

"What?"

"The lights are on," Gleason said, rolling her eyebrows at the wall, where small, inset LEDs cast light down on every landing. "We had to use handlights coming up, remember?"

"Yeah," Bel said. She did remember, but it still seemed plenty dark.

"I can't imagine how the lights even still work," Andy said, from behind them. She was half-backing down the stairs, one step at a time, watching their six. "It's been centuries."

"And the guns," Gleason put in. "All the times we hear the techs talk about PMCS, and those guns are still shooting all these years later? With fricking vines growing on them?"

"Star League knew how to build," Carillo put in, from two steps beneath them. "And most of the circuitry is solid-state, so it lasts."

"We can discuss maintenance later," Curtain said, from farther down, in the middle of the group. "For now, we must learn how to quiet them."

"Agreed," Bel said.

"Sure we shouldn't be sweeping these floors, ma'am?" Private Peat asked. They were at a landing, about halfway down to the atrium. The door onto the floor proper was ajar, but half-covered in brush and debris. Maybe a fifth of the lights were on, and two of those were flickering.

"I'm sure," Bel said. She pointed to the floor with her Python. "Look at the dirt. Fifteen or twenty people came through here this morning, there'd be a bigger mess."

"Told you," Atwater hissed.

"Besides," Bel said. "Curtain says they're not using the control room on the main floor. That means they went down, and that make sense. You bury secondary control posts and fallback positions, so if you lose the main post in a strike you don't lose the others. My bet is they went down, and we're going to have to smoke them out." She motioned the party into movement again.

"Good eyes on the dirt," Andy Ishikawa told her, a minute later.

"Back on Coventry I hung out a lot with the infantry," Bel said. "Not that I want to fight this way, mind. But they're good people, and they taught me a lot."

"I wonder how Nick and the others are holding up," Gleason said, into the silence.

"I'm sure he's doing his best," Bel said. "Best thing we can do is get down in here and silence these guns."

"Gung ho, ma'am."

"What?"

Gleason chuckled. "Something my old man used to say, when I was a kid. Means "right on," or something like that. He never told me where he learned it."

"Sounds Capellan," Andy said.

"Could be, for all I know," Gleason told her.

"Two more flights," Private Atwater called back.

Bel shivered. *Cortisol, in my muscles*, she told herself, but silently prayed it'd feel different in the open air of the atrium.

Blucher tapped the controls around the screen Petersen had activated, but none of the other camera feeds would come up, and none of them were stairwell cams or showed the main atrium. The party on the roof had drawn weapons and disappeared back into the stairs, but Blucher had no idea how fast Giorgio and his people could get up there.

It was a lot of steps.

"Son of a bitch!" Simmons snarled. Blucher looked that way. "That bastard Alessandro just took out one of my barrels with his damned laser!"

"Shoot back," Blucher said. He made sure he was looking away before he rolled his eyes, but Petersen saw him. The scout grinned at him.

"The hell you think I been doing?"

"Missing," Blucher muttered.

Petersen snorted.

Bel sighed in relief when they made it to the atrium floor without incident. The eight of them gathered on the landing as Peat and Atwater took opposite sides of the door. Curtain himself gripped the door handle, nodded at the two infantrymen, and then jerked it open. Peat, opposite the door hinges, led the way out, but Atwater was right behind them, following by Carillo and Perathoner.

"It looks clear," Atwater called.

A shotgun blew divots out of the wall above the doorway. The report was concussively loud. Bel's ears rang, even as she half-heard, half-felt the patter of dust and debris fall from above her. Gleason grabbed her arm and flung her down behind a counter. Another shotgun fired, and now Peat and Atwater were firing.

The standard Legion sidearm was a Mauser & Gray automatic pistol, same as the old Twenty-Sixth Arcturan Guards. Peat and Atwater both advanced, alternating steady, aimed shots, until both had emptied one eight-round magazine. Then they ducked behind separate concrete pillars to reload. Meanwhile Gleason and Perathoner, with the same weapons, banged out their own shots. Bel could tell from the sound the two staff NCOs were just trying to keep the other side's heads down.

Bel looked down at her Python. She'd declined an MG; she liked the Python, it fit her hand better, and it carried half-again as many bullets as well. But she couldn't even see what they were shooting at. "What do you see?" she shouted to Atwater.

"Two men at the door across the way," Atwater said. "Was three."

"Dressed like locals," Peat added.

Curtain grunted. "Blucher's Lyran loyalists, no doubt."

Bel glared at him. "Can we get down these stairs behind us, flank them?"

"They do not connect."

Andy Ishikawa stood up, leaned around her won concrete pillar, and *brapped* off five bursts from her TK Enforcer pistol. Peat and Atwater took advantage of the fire and sprinted to the sides, making for closer concrete pillars.

"There are going to be more than two," Curtain said.

Bel stared at him. "Why don't you have a gun?"

"I have never needed one."

"You know how to use it?" Curtain nodded. Bel put her Python on safe and handed it over. "Be my guest."

There was a flurry of shots, and then Peat shouting. Bel looked around her cover, saw him waving, and charged across the floor. While she was running Atwater leaned around the doorway and fired a few shots down the stairwell. What sounded like a machine gun answered him.

Bel slipped on a vine and slid the last few meters to the wall. She came to rest next to a still-warm body leaking red, and older man with a straggly, reddish-gray beard who was missing the top of his head. Peat leaned down and pulled the Gunther MP-20 off him, then started slapping the dead man's jacket, looking for magazines. She looked away and concentrated very hard on *not smelling anything*.

"Here you go, ma'am," he said. She looked and found Peat holding out a Python. Bel looked, but Curtain still held hers. "He liked the same gun you did, ma'am."

"Great," Bel muttered, and took the dead man's gun.

"Any grenades?" Atwater shouted.

"No," Peat replied. He glanced at Curtain, who had been searching one of the bodies, but the big man shook his head.

"Be better if it were yes," Atwater said, and danced back. Buckshot rang off the doorframe. Atwater hissed and slapped his shoulder.

"You okay?" Bel called.

"Ricochet, ma'am," Atwater said. "I'm okay."

"Due respect, ma'am," Peat said, "we got two choices. Me and Atwater can probably hold this door, if you or Mr. Curtain can go for help."

Bel looked at Curtain, but he shook his head. "No one I trust is nearby."

"And that doesn't stop the PPCs," Bel added. "Second choice?"

"We assault down, ma'am," Peat said. His voice was steady, but she could tell he didn't want to do it. "We're not armed for it, and we're not in armor."

"I understand, but we can't—" Bel said, but was interrupted.

"*Grenade!*" Atwater shouted. Before anyone could stop him, the young private danced forward, sweeping his foot along the floor. Bel heard the *thunk* of something metal hitting the wall and then the floor, and then Atwater was back. The fire from below abruptly cut off.

The grenade exploded. Smoke and debris blasted out the doorway. Bel covered her ears and her eyes, but tried to look around.

She saw Peat and Atwater disappear into the stairwell, Curtain immediately behind them. Bel opened her mouth to shout, but then her trained officer's mind caught up with what had happened. The loyalists from below had, at best, stunned themselves with the grenade that Atwater had kicked back. At worst—for them—they were all dead from shrapnel and blast effects. Whichever it was, this was the best opportunity the Legion was going to get to clear the stairwell, and the infantrymen—and the Clanner—had taken it.

Bel lurched to her feet. "Come on!" she yelled at the others. Then she stepped into the darkened, smoke-choked stairwell to follow.

CHAPTER 15

CONDOR
CRIMOND
TAMAR PACT
5 FEBRUARY 3152

By the time Bel got into the stairwell, Peat and Atwater had already reached the first landing; it was dark, still smoky, and two of the LEDs were flickering. Both Atwater and Peat fired, Atwater two aimed shots from his sidearm, and Peat a three-round burst from the confiscated Gunther MP-20. The reports were shockingly loud in the confined space. Bel yelped and tried to pop her ears, opening and closing her mouth, trying to swallow. The ringing was different from the restaurant bomb blast: higher pitched, and almost echoing.

"Do not stop!" Curtain shouted. The big man crouched by one of the bodies and came up with a shotgun and a bandolier of shells. "They may rally if we delay."

"You heard the man, Private," Peat said to Atwater. He glanced at Bel. "Ma'am, get these peoples' weapons and follow, okay? We may need the ammunition."

"Go," Bel said. She crouched by one of the bodies, a woman who'd been shredded by shrapnel from the grenade. She'd carried a rifle Bel didn't recognize, but the barrel was bent. Bel tapped around her jacket, looking for a sidearm or a magazine.

Sergeant Perathoner knelt across the body from her, searching that side. After a moment she muttered "Oh, goddess," twisted aside, and threw up on the floor. She recovered in a few seconds, wiping her mouth and going right back to her search. "Sorry, ma'am."

"I'm not far behind you," Bel said. She found two small, five-round or so magazines filled with long, thin rifle cartridges. She slid them into her jacket pocket, then stood. "Ready?"

Across the landing, Sergeant Carillo straightened, holding another shotgun. "No extra rounds, ma'am, but ready."

Staff Sergeant Gleason and Andy Ishikawa both just nodded. "Better go before my brain catches up with what we're doing," Andy said. Bel grinned at her and turned to follow the three skirmishers down.

Two landings down, there was another burst of fire.

And a yelp of pain.

The sound of guns in the stairwell was loud enough to shake the wall panels. Blucher swore and got back to his original console, looking for the control for the door. Petersen, the scout, stood and followed him over. He put his hand on Blucher's shoulder.

"Not yet," Petersen said.

"They get in here—"

"We still got people out there," Petersen said. "We lock the door, they can't get in. We lock the door, we can't get out. If you think Giorgio and his people can't hold them, we're better locking the room and getting out of here. Better to be moving than trapped in a steel box underground."

Blucher frowned, thinking.

An explosion shook the floor.

"Grenade," Petersen said. He stepped closer to the door. He had a long, slender rifle slung over his back, but he'd drawn his coat back to clear the holstered sidearm on his hip. He leaned out the door just far enough for his eye to see, then leaned back in and smiled at Blucher.

"Still a couple floors away," he said. The scar on his face glistened in the lights when he spoke.

Blucher turned back to his console. He called up a schematic of this part of the Citadel's sub-levels and swiped through image after image, until he found this room and the surrounding floor.

"There's not another stair access on this floor," he said, "at least not that goes up." He touched another set of images. "But if we go down, it's a bulk storage floor. There it should let us cross to the other side and use those stairs."

"Those stairs are blocked," Petersen said.

"Then we go up, cross somewhere else. We'll be behind them."

Petersen nodded. Another burst of fire echoed out of the stairwell.

"Look, you just keep them off us!" Simmons yelled. "We almost got these bastards!"

Blucher looked at the screen; the humanoid Legion 'Mech was still down and burning, but the other one, the bullet-nosed one, was still limping around and firing. The Legion tanks had sprinted across the field and were helping Curtain's left-behinds advance toward the laser turrets.

"No, you don't," he muttered.

He looked back at Petersen and nodded. The white-haired man nodded back.

"I'll check the route," the scout said.

Sergeant Carillo leaned over the railing, butt of the shotgun in the air, and fired two quick blasts down the stairwell. Despite the reports Bel heard the shot ricochet like sand against stone. Carillo ducked back and dropped the empty shotgun. He leaned back against the wall, drew his sidearm, and grinned at her.

Bel grinned back. At her feet, Staff Sergeant Gleason ripped a self-sealing bandage out of its packing and wrapped it around the bleeding wound in Private Atwater's upper right arm. The boy sat braced against the wall, pale and breathing hard, and winced when Gleason drew the bandage tight. The staff NCO patted his shoulder and stood.

"He should be okay for a minute, but he lost a lot of blood," she told Bel.

Bel snorted at the absurdity of the statement. "I know, it's on that wall over there." She pointed to the spot where Atwater had been hit; there was a large spatter of blood on the wall.

"Captain?" Private Peat said.

"Private?"

"They're pulling back out of the stairs, ma'am. It could be this is their floor. Or it could be a feint."

"This is it," Curtain said. He had claimed a shotgun of his own, and was feeding shells from a bandolier into the receiver. "Even if they were soldiers once, they have been hunters for decades. They are not thinking about tactics right now."

"The door is a strong point," Peat said, nodding. "And we can't count on them using their own grenades against us."

"Then we will just have to be better shots," Curtain said. He looked past Bel. "Sergeant?"

"I'm ready," Sergeant Carillo said.

Bel opened her mouth, but Curtain held up a finger. "I am not protecting you, Captain. It is merely a question of mass and you are, if you will excuse the observation, not a tall woman."

Private Atwater laughed.

Bel glared at him. "Fine."

Peat nodded. "I'll empty this to drive them back," he said, brandishing the Gunther, "and then it's shotgun and pistol work, yeah?"

"As you say, Private," Curtain said. Carillo, stepping past Bel, nodded.

"Fine," Bel repeated. She drew the Python and clicked the safety off. "I hope all you big tall men don't get in my way, though. I'm not a great shot."

Curtain's grin was a white Cheshire smile in the darkness.

Peat stepped off, charging around the corner with the submachine gun's stock extended and snugged into his shoulder. He had it set for single-shot, rather than burst, but he was banging out two rounds for every step, and he wasn't walking slow. He made it halfway down the final set of stairs to the loyalists' landing before the Gunther ran dry. He tossed it to the side, out of the way, and immediately transitioned to his pistol, staying close to the wall.

As soon as the Gunther stopped shooting, Curtain, striding down the stairs close to the railing, began booming out shots from the shotgun. He got them the rest of the way down the stairs to the doorway. Bel expected him to stop, flatten himself against one side, and let Peat or Carillo stack behind him, but instead he stepped right through.

Bel charged down the steps.

Giorgio, bleeding from two or three small wounds on his face, shoved his way into the control room. "They're coming down and we're not stopping them," he gasped to Blucher. "I need more men."

Blucher looked around. Simmons was on his feet, shotgun in hand. One of the Legion tanks had found enough cover to get close to slag his turret with paired plasma cannons. The others were still plinking at the Legion 'Mech, but both had been degraded.

"Time to go," he called to the room.

"Can't believe you can't stop a half-dozen mercenaries with pistols," Simmons said, shoving past Giorgio. "Some security expert you are."

"You can do better, Simmons, be my guest," Giorgio snarled.

"Out the door and down the hall, two lefts and fifty meters is another stair," Blucher said. "We go down one level, then across, then back up four levels, then cross back to this side to get above them. We'll be back on the surface before the figure out where we've gone. Hell, we can come up behind them."

"They're good," Giorgio said. "I never thought—" A fresh burst of firing, an automatic weapon from the sound, erupted. Blucher pushed himself up from the console and ran for the door. That sounded close.

As he shoved past Giorgio, a shotgun started blasting. Blucher stepped into the hallway, expecting to see Simmons there firing, but the shotgun was firing from inside the stairwell. Shot ricocheted everywhere down the hallway. Two of Giorgio's men, huddled against the wall about six meters back, snatched at their arms and legs as pellets hit them.

"Shoot back—" Simmons shouted, but Blucher didn't hear the rest.

Curtain stepped through the door. *Curtain.* Of all the people—

Simmons roared a challenge and fired. His shot blasted a hole in the wall a meter to Curtain's right. Curtain blew him off his feet in a welter of red gore, then dropped his shotgun. Blucher stared, saw Curtain standing staring back.

"It's him!" Blucher yelled. He reached into the control room, grabbing for Giorgio, and dragged him out. "Shoot him!"

Giorgio stumbled out, off-balance, but he had his rifle, a semi-automatic civilian rifle in military styling. He jerked it up, squeezing the trigger too soon. Bullets blew divots out of the floor. A tall, gray-clad man burst through the door behind Curtain. Blucher recognized him from the prior day—*Peat, his name is Peat*—even as the new man raised a pistol and put two rounds into Giorgio's chest. The rifle kept firing, Giorgio's fingers still clenched on the trigger. Curtain dove to the side.

"Run!" Blucher shouted at the others still in the. He spun around, his own directions echoing in his head—*two lefts, then fifty meters to a stair*—and lurched into a stumbling run.

"Blucher!" someone shouted from behind him. "Stop!"

Blucher ran. There was a *bang* behind him, and then suddenly he was on the floor, and his left leg was on fire. He tried to push himself upright, but his leg felt like it was buried in lava. He rolled onto his back, screaming, but he knew he had to get to the corner, get around it, crawl if he had to...

He looked back, seeing the corridor upside-down.

Petersen was there, aiming his rifle, white-haired and grinning like an executioner.

Bel came through the door right behind Sergeant Carillo. She saw Curtain on the floor and turned to help him. He was already half-upright, looking down the hall.

"Blucher!" he shouted. "Stop!"

Bel looked. A man was running in the opposite direction. Sergeant Carillo, in front of her, glanced back at Curtain, then at her. His pistol was leveled. She nodded. Carillo sighted and fired. Blucher—if that was Blucher, she'd never met him—collapsed, his leg bloody.

"Nice shot," she said.

Carillo turned and smiled sheepishly. "I was aiming for his back." Bel opened her mouth to say something, but her eye caught motion behind Carillo. A man was leaning around the corner of the hallway, a rifle leveled.

"Down!" she shouted. Carillo obeyed, dropping like a stone and rolling onto his stomach, pistol leveled. Curtain, however, just stared at her. He hadn't seen the newcomer. He was facing the wrong way anyway, toward her.

Bel, with a lifetime's experience wrestling with larger, stronger men and a military academy's training, put her foot behind his, swept her arm across his chest and pivoted her hips. Leverage did what raw strength could never, and dropped the massive man to the floor. She fell atop him just as high-powered rifle shots rang out. The wall above them cratered, showering them with debris and dust.

Curtain, on his back, wrapped his arms around her and rolled so his back was to the shooter. Bel slapped at him, trying to get her arm free to shoot back.

On the other side the hall, Private Peat fired four quick shots.

Down the hall there was a clatter of metal on the floor.

"Clear," Peat shouted. "Staff Sergeant, Andy, I need your help!"

Curtain stared at Bel, face inches from hers. His infuriating, wry grin broke open again. "A debt is owed," he told her.

CHAPTER 16

KOLA
CRIMOND
TAMAR PACT
7 FEBRUARY 3152

When Bel climbed out of the APC, Ronan was there waiting for her. He looked like he hadn't showered in three days. His hair was mussed and oily, his skin sallow, with dark circles under his eyes, and his grays were wrinkled and dirt-stained. His left hand was wrapped in a bandage.

"You look like shit," she told him.

"Sir."

"You look like shit, *sir*."

"Better," he said with a grin. He looked past her to the rest of the party climbing out of the PPC, and raised an eyebrow. "This looks like more people than you left with."

"I did a little recruiting," she said. "Is Eldon here?"

"Inside." Ronan frowned. Bel knew what he was looking at, but refused to turn around. She couldn't face that damned grin right now.

"Then let's go inside," she said. "Staff Sergeant, see that our people get looked after, would you?"

"Roger, ma'am," Gleason said from behind her.

"I'll take the big guy with me," Bel said.

The Legion headquarters in Kola was a high school, it looked like. The playing fields, football and baseball from the way the stands were arranged, had been turned into vehicle and

'Mech marshaling areas. The Legion's two Savior repair vehicles had their mobile field bases fully deployed and were working, repairing damage. A pair of infantry with the silver gorgets of Sergeant Major Sarris' headquarters security platoon stood with TK assault rifles in tactical carries by the door, but nodded Ronan and Bel through.

"What's been going on here?" Bel asked.

"Wrapping up," Ronan told her. "The Jaegers' Two shop thinks we've gotten all the cells, but they did a lot of damage. Turns out they had a couple converted IndustrialMechs no one knew about. No one killed, but the docs are plenty busy with a couple wounded. And the civilian wounded, of course."

"Of course," Bel said. She let Ronan lead her down a hallway into an interior gymnasium. The Legion support staff had set up tables and appropriated portable dividers to break it into rough room. Bel nodded to staff NCOs she recognized, and saw Hauptmann Eldon standing in a corner, swiping through a noteputer.

"Hauptmann," Bel said, bracing to attention.

Eldon glanced up, then swiped his noteputer off and held it behind him. "Captain Carlyle. You never called me back."

"I'm here now, sir," Bel said.

"Your mission?"

"Complete, sir," Bel said. "Fort Beaufort is secure. And, it seems, semi-operational."

Eldon blinked. "You said it was a ruin."

"That's what I'd been told, yes, sir."

"What you'd been told."

"Yes, sir."

Eldon frowned, glanced at Ronan, then over Bel's other shoulder. "And who is this?"

"This is Sergeant Curtain of the Legion," Bel said. "A MechWarrior, lately commander of the Condor Defense Force."

"The Condor...what are you talking about?"

"Lyran loyalists were able to reactivate a portion of the Fort's defenses, sir, and turn them against both us and the locals, the Condor Defense Force. With Sergeant Curtain's help, we were able to recapture the fort's control center and detain the ringleader."

Eldon just stared.

"He's wounded, but I left him with the Jaeger MPs back in Sol City. Seemed like a matter for the judge advocate general, not us mercenaries."

Eldon opened and closed his mouth. Bel watched him attempt to process what he'd said before he visibly took control of his thoughts. "The Fort."

"If I may, Captain," Curtain asked.

"By all means."

"Hauptmann Eldon, the people of Condor have no quarrel with the Tamar Pact, so long as you respect their sovereignty. They have no wish to be associated with the governments on Metallerz or Chromastich, but they don't object to a Tamar garrison occupying and restoring Fort Beaufort, either. My— er, *their* conventional forces now hold the Fort. As soon as a designated Tamar commander is named, they will withdraw." Curtain grinned. Bel wasn't looking, but she just knew it. "But you should hurry—none of them really know how to use the weaponry they are guarding."

The Legion's liaison officer just stared, again.

"Captain Carlyle's people treated us with the respect due peers, Hauptmann," Curtain added. "And when pressed, fought and shed their blood alongside ours. If all your Tamars are as honorable as they are, you will find no quarrel with the Condors."

"I...see," Eldon said, though he clearly did not.

"If there's nothing else, Hauptmann," Bel said sweetly, "I'd like to go file my report and see to my wounded?"

"Of course," Eldon said, bringing his noteputer back out. "Good work, in the end, Captain Carlyle."

Bel smiled at the dismissal and turned away, drawing Curtain and Ronan with her, acting in every aspect the well-behaved mercenary officer. But inside, she still seethed at being around Eldon.

Prick.

Back in the hallway, Ronan touched Bel's shoulder to stop them, and turned to face Curtain. "Sergeant?"

Curtain grinned. "Your sister kindly enrolled me in your Gray Death Legion, Major Carlyle. I look forward to serving with you. She has told me a great deal about you."

Ronan nodded. "Uh-huh." He looked at Bel. "Sergeant?" he repeated.

Bel shrugged. "He wanted to join, he's a good MechWarrior, and he comes with a *Regent*."

"You just met him."

"Oh, don't give me that," Bel said. "We hired all those Two-Nine boys and girls sight unseen."

"That was different—"

"How was that different?"

"Those were trained Lyran soldiers—"

"He's a *Clanner*, Ronan. He could probably blow you out of your *Gargoyle*."

"In a simulator, of course," Curtain added. Both Carlyles turned to stare at him, but only Bel was grinning.

Ronan, frowning, stared at Curtain for a moment, the looked back at his sister. "Any other surprises?"

"Couple of infantry, couple of tankers," Bel said. "Oh, and a real angry woman named Andy Ishikawa. She comes with Curtain. They're not together or anything, she just likes to give him a hard time."

"I don't understand," Ronan said.

"We have a saying on Condor, Major," Curtain said. "We say 'a favor is owed.'" He repeated it in the language of the Emberá. Bel was starting to recognize the sounds. "It means what it says. To your sister, and her companions, however, many of us owe a *debt*."

"So you joined out of obligation?"

"We joined for the opportunity," Curtain said. "To repay the debt."

Ronan glared at Bel. "You can't just follow her around," he said. "If you're going to be in the Legion, you're going to be under discipline. You're going to serve where we say, do what we say. This is a military unit, not a social club."

"That is understood. Your sister raised the same points."

"She did?"

"I tried to talk them out of it," Bel said with a shrug.

"She did," Curtain confirmed.

"But they're good people," Bel went on. "Good in a fight. Good to each other. They'll be good for us, Ronan."

"And when we go off-world?" Ronan asked. "We're mercenaries. Our next contract could be on the far side of the Inner Sphere."

"I find," Curtain said, "that as I get older, the urge to travel gets stronger."

Bel snorted.

"Fine," Ronan said. "Fine." He glared at his sister, but offered his hand to Curtain.

"Welcome to the Gray Death Legion."

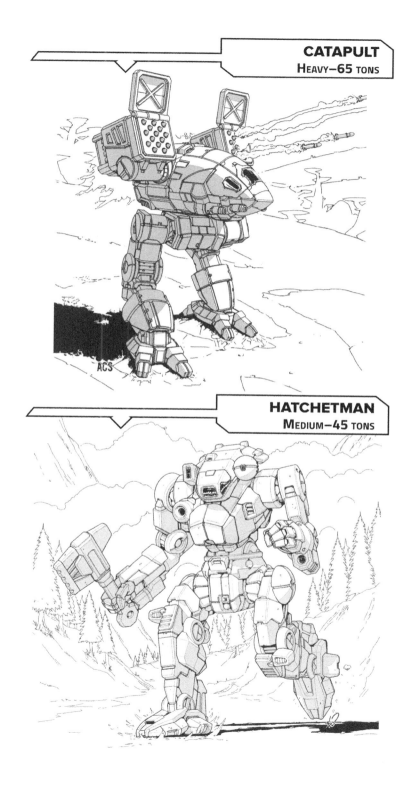

CATAPULT
HEAVY—65 TONS

HATCHETMAN
MEDIUM—45 TONS

REGENT
ASSAULT—90 TONS

DECISION AT PANDORA

CHAPTER 1

PALACE OF THE GODS
DELIVERANCE
PANDORA
TAMAR PACT
28 APRIL 3152

The tremble of Kommandant Hakima's lower lip gave her away. Elam Nobu, baron of Pandora by the grace of the gods and Governor General Sarah Regis of Arcturus, controlled his own emerging grin. His face was a politician's face, long accustomed to showing nothing but what he wanted it to show, but he still felt the little thrill every time. There was no sensation quite like the knowledge you *owned* another human being.

"There is no reason this recording need ever see the light of day," said Nessa Deschanes. She stood next to Nobu in a suit as expensive as a down payment on a house. "So long as you continue to do your duty to the people of Pandora."

Katherine Hakima looked up at that. She glared at Deschanes, glanced at Nobu, but then looked back at Deschanes. "My duty," she said. Nobu noticed the wet eyes, the reddening skin, but also the stone in her gaze and the hint of steel in her voice. "This—" she stopped and visibly swallowed. "This has nothing to do with my *duty.*"

"Nonetheless—" Deschanes started, but Nobu held up his hand. *Exactly as we planned*, he thought.

"Of course it does not, Kommandant," Nobu said, speaking for the first time. "What you do in your off-hours is no concern of the governor general." He paused, not out of necessity, but because his instincts told him to. "We are all free citizens of the Tamar Pact, after all." Now he showed a frown. "But..."

Hakima couldn't ignore the silence for more than a few seconds. "'But' what, my lord?"

Nobu shook his head regretfully. "If people *were* to find out..."

"But she just said—"

"I said there is no need," Deschanes put in. "I never said it could not happen." A pause. "If this had come to the Deliverance scandal media, for example, instead of the lord baron..."

Hakima's mouth closed audibly.

"The resurgence of the, shall we say, sensational media coverage a free society encourages has been quite swift after the Jade Falcons' defeat," Deschanes added.

Nobu was careful not to smile like a shark. Sensational media—scandal media, to give it an accurate name—had returned with a vengeance as soon as the Tamar Jaegers liberated the planet Pandora, and since his arrival Nobu had been careful to ensure he controlled as much of it as possible. Nothing direct or obvious, of course. He owned the companies that owned the companies that owned the media companies and the like.

Life on Pandora under the Jade Falcons had been strict. Certainly here in Deliverance, the planet's capital city. The Falcons had controlled what messages reached the people as securely as they could, and they had little appetite for the sort of headline-generating, fact-tangential news the lower masses consumed like air and water.

Nobu, given authority over the planet by Governor General Regis' new Tamar government on Arcturus, had made getting control of its media his first priority.

He saw the calculation in Hakima's eyes. She'd come into his office expecting to be exposed, probably cashiered, potentially disgraced. The Tamar Armed Forces had largely carried over the old Lyran Commonwealth Armed Forces code of military justice when they'd seceded from the Commonwealth. The rules might have been more honored in the breach than the observance, but there remained those ancient codes about "conduct unbecoming an officer of the Commonwealth." *Or the Pact, as it were, for* the TAF. *I don't care what two—or three—consenting adults do together, but there are people who* would.

"Then...I am grateful that the lord baron was able to intervene," Hakima said. She had composed herself. Nobu had to hide another grin—he'd done this so many times he knew what would come next: her blush-reddened face would quickly take on the pallor of stale oatmeal. "It seems that I am in your debt."

"I seek only the safety and security of the people of Pandora," Nobu said, allowing himself a humble smile. He leaned back in his plush chair and spread his hands expansively. "It is the officers and troops of the TAF who keep us safe, Kommandant. If I can do the same for you, while you do the same for all of us, it is only *my* duty."

"Thank you, my lord." Her face was already starting to cool. *She will likely throw up before she gets out of the palace,* Nobu knew. He wasted a few more moments on reassurances, then nodded to Deschanes to escort the woman out.

"I will check on the kommandant in a week or so," Deschanes said, when she returned. "To make sure she fully understands."

"She understands fine," Nobu said. It was always the same, so simple. People did things, things they regretted later, things that would cause them terrible trouble if exposed, and then did whatever was necessary to keep the news from getting out. He licked his lips, thinking. "With her, we have three of the five battalion commanders, correct?"

"Correct," Deschanes said. "I may have a line on Leutnant-Colonel Bredell's executive officer, and one or two of his operations staff, but the rest are all off-worlders and haven't had time to get in trouble yet."

"Nothing from our Malthus contacts on any of them?"

"No, my lord."

Nobu grunted. Much depended on securing the loyalty of the leaders of the Tamar garrison battalions on Pandora. Kommandant Hakima would be key, if she didn't do something ridiculous like run and confess to her CO or shoot herself. She commanded the Thirty-Seventh Panzer Battalion; the panzers were the lynchpin of Bredell's garrison. *If she could be controlled...*

Nobu tapped his fingers together. "Go talk to Keeling," he told Deschanes. "In person. Remind him we will pay top *kroner* for anything about the people we don't have any leverage over."

"Yes, my lord."

"And tell him we may need the equipment for the Guards' battalion sooner than we thought."

"Of course."

Nobu nodded her away and then spun his chair toward the big Transpex window facing out across Deliverance. Irwin Keeling had secured control of Red Devil Industries, a defense company responsible for producing several chassis of BattleMechs and armored vehicles, even before Nobu had arrived. Keeling was also the head of the Malthus criminal syndicate here on Pandora. He was an ally of sorts, but the worst kind: he and Nobu were only joined in their own self-interests. Keeling wanted access to the larger—and more easily corruptible—military contract market of the Lyran Commonwealth. Being a satrapy of the Tamar Pact, a rebellious breakaway nation not even two years old and surrounded by enemies, was not a profitable long-term solution. Whoever took Pandora away from the Tamars would undoubtedly install their own corrupt flunkies.

And Nobu—he tapped his fingers again—*Nobu wants everything he lost when he came to this godsforsaken place.*

CHAPTER 2

**HOME GUARD HEADQUARTERS
DELIVERANCE
PANDORA
TAMAR PACT
2 MAY 3152**

"Zee?"

Staff Sergeant Zahara Khaled looked up from her report. "Yeah?"

"Can you take a look at this?"

Zee put down the noteputer and its endlessly detailed—and boring—logistics analysis of the forming Pandora Planetary Guard and stood. She stretched, listening to her neck and shoulders pop, and walked over to Sergeant Henderson's table. "Whatcha got?"

William Henderson was too big a man to be working in a space as small as had been assigned to the Tamar Home Guard garrison's intelligence staff. He was an infantryman, a squad leader in the Forty-Second Motor-Rifle Battalion, but he'd been reassigned here while recuperating from surgery. He was tall, over two meters, and had to keep his leg braced straight out in front of him, which made hunching over the small tables difficult. But he was a soldier, and a good man. He didn't complain.

"The news," he said.

"Oh," Zee said, laughing. "Kevinsson, or Parendoupolos?"

"Kevinsson," Henderson said, grinning.

"Let's take a look."

The Deliverance HV media had split pretty quickly once the Tamars had taken control. The more staid, just-read-the-news kind of people the Jade Falcons had preferred, who had more sinecure positions and were used to being government mouthpieces, had more or less just asked for the new scripts and kept on keeping on. Their senior representative was Hester Parendoupolos. She was calm, collected, and only reported news she considered factual. To Zee's trained eye, that didn't mean it was completely factual—everyone editorialized—but she was closest.

On the opposite end of the spectrum was Yao Kevinsson. Where Parendoupolos was calm, Kevinsson screamed. Where Parendoupolos at least claimed journalistic standards, Kevinsson openly scorned them. "I'm just having a conversation," he liked to scoff when pressed. *Right*, Zee had thought the first time she'd seen a clip of him. *And Malvina Hazen was just promoting a political ideology.*

"I was watching last night's segment," Henderson said. He held up earbuds and pointed to where the HV was set for double normal playback speed. "He doesn't say anything new, but he ran some fresh stock footage of the Palace of the Gods, and I caught something." He slid his finger along the playback indicator until he got to the scene. "Right here."

Zee leaned over to get closer to the small HV projection. "*— and of course the Tamars say they're here to protect us. We're helpless, right? We need some army from some other planet to come here and keep us safe? What a load of—*"

Henderson stopped the HV. "Did you see it?"

Zee frowned. It had been people coming and going from the Palace, a long shot showing the lines of them, and then a close-up of random passersby zoning out through the security line. She'd been more distracted by Kevinsson's usual xenophobic rhetoric. "Play it again. This time on mute."

Henderson complied, and the scene burst into motion, this time silently. Zee's mind absently filled in the words she'd already heard, listening to what parts of the conversation Kevinsson's producers synced up with the talk track. It was part of learning how people thought—

"Wait," Zee said. *That woman...*

"You saw her too?"

"It can't be."

"Facial recognition says it is," Henderson said. He slid his finger back, scrolling until the HV stopped on a holo of a middle-aged woman with tight hair and a stern face. "Kommandant Katherine Hakima."

"The Three-Seven Panzer CO," Zee filled in as her mind raced. "When was this?"

Henderson shrugged. "Could be any time, but the weather looks right for the last week or so." He tapped the edge of the desk. "From the traffic, I'd put it in the afternoon. Foot traffic in and out of the palace is only that heavy in the mid- to late-afternoon."

"Meetings, late lunches, early dinners," Zee agreed. Few things in the universe were as predictable as the habits of bureaucrats. She frowned. "She's in mufti."

"I noticed that."

"So, not official business?" Zee stood up straight to think. "If she was there on orders, she'd be in uniform. And probably not in the mob lines going through security."

"That's what I thought, too," Henderson said.

"No chance she was on orders?" She looked across the room. "Gina? Can you pull the daily calendar of the Three-Seven Panzer headquarters unit for the last week or so?"

Sergeant Gina Fritsch grinned. "Billy already asked, Staff Sergeant."

Zee turned so her back was to Gina and cocked an eyebrow. "*Billy?*" she whispered.

"Gina's nice," Henderson said. He was pale enough that the flush crawling up his neck was visible. "But the calendar said there's no official reason for her to be at the Palace."

"Talking to the baron," Zee surmised.

"Or anyone else, innocent or not," Henderson extended. "Most of the civic business for the city is run out of the Palace of the Gods. Maybe she needed a library card."

Zee chuckled. "Right." She glanced down at the frozen image. "This is good work." Henderson grinned. "See if you can lock down a date and a time. And start looking back at a couple months of this kind of footage. See if there's anyone else we know." She paused, considering, but decided as soon as she thought of it. "Not with your eyes. Use the computer and facial recognition. Feed it any Tamar officer hauptmann or above."

"On it, Staff Sergeant," Henderson said, mirth forgotten. "And if the staff sergeant will permit, she is a very suspicious person." His grin returned.

"Part of the job, *Billy*," she said, grinning back before walking back to her own station. She sat down, picked up her noteputer and swiped the logistics report off the screen. Then she tapped an access code and opened a private document. Her list.

Kommandant Katherine Hakima, she wrote. Then she sighed.

Hakima wasn't the only name on the list, but it was the only one with a Tamar battalion commander's slot. She skimmed the list again, not that it wasn't already burned into her brain, and then closed the file.

"The coincidences are congealing," old Staff Sergeant Heinz would have said at this point. Zee's favorite intelligence instructor had been firm that a good spook was not allowed to believe in coincidence, but they were allowed to count them. Not for the first time, Zee wondered what the crusty staff sergeant would have thought about where she was now.

The general's announcement back on Arcturus had been a shock, to Zee especially. She was a staff spook; she was supposed to know what was going on before it happened, but she hadn't had any inkling of Hauptmann-General Regis' plan when they landed. It had seemed like an eyeblink before the commanders announced the secession.

Those had been tense days. So tense that its happening, less than a year ago, defied belief. Zee had been a junior logistics analyst, a sergeant, when Hauptmann Ganz had passed out the message sheets and told everyone they had 24 hours to consider whether they wanted to be a part of the new Tamar. Zee recalled the crinkle of the yellow paper, how thin and flimsy it felt to carry such weight. Staff Sergeant Gleason, her section chief, had let them each decide, but Zee hadn't been able to follow Gleason to the evacuation DropShip the general offered to anyone who wanted to return to the Commonwealth.

It felt wrong, no question. Zee knew she was betraying the oath she'd sworn to the Archon. They all had, to form the Tamar

Pact and take the people of its worlds under their protection. But like the general, Zee felt she had a higher duty as a soldier to those people she was now sworn to protect. She knew her oath to the Archon and the Commonwealth was valid, but she saw the people on Arcturus and the other worlds around them. Oaths to a woman and a nation light-years away in space and time crumbled beneath the weight of duty Zee felt to the small children she saw playing in the streets of Malcheema, all of them looking slightly undernourished from lack of critical nutrients.

Arcturus and the worlds around it were literally starving for protection and support. Against that, some words said when she was younger to a woman she'd never even met meant nothing. Like all the rest, like Governor General Regis herself, Zee had felt driven to *act*.

Zee blinked. She glanced around the small room, wondering if anyone had noticed her sudden reverie, but everyone else was heads-down at their tasks. She swallowed, blinked again to clear her thoughts, and leaned forward.

Now she was the staff sergeant, senior enlisted member of the intelligence shop assigned to Task Force Bredell, the Tamar garrison on Pandora. Hauptmann Candiz—who'd been Leutnant Candiz when they all turned their coats—was officially the CO of the Two Shop, but he spent more time with the colonel dutifully regurgitating Zee's reports as if they were his own. Zee had never expected to become the Old Lady of her own shop this fast, but she was far from alone in that.

The transition of the Twenty-Sixth Arcturan Guards RCT into the Tamar Armed Forces had meant explosive growth for everyone. The professional core of the RCT had been broken up as companies became battalions and battalions became task forces to garrison the new worlds of the Tamar Pact as the Home Guard. Leutnant-Colonel Bredell had been a kommandant in his first battalion command in one of the armor regiments. Now he was the senior Tamar officer on Pandora.

And at least one of his officers is visiting the Palace of the Gods in mufti, Zee mused, turning back to the task at hand. Her mind replayed the list she'd just added Kommandant Hakima to. Something was rotten on Pandora. She could smell it. But she couldn't put her finger on it.

Pandora had seemed happy enough to join the Pact once the Jade Falcon remnants were defeated. It was a prosperous world, made so by the BattleMech factories of Red Devil Industries and the Quickscell Corporation's armored vehicle foundries. Recruitment into the burgeoning Pandora Planetary Guard was high, outpacing even mainline TAF recruiting. Soldiers in the battledress of the TAF rarely had to buy their own drinks in the Deliverance bars. It should have been an easy posting, but...something didn't sit right.

First, elements in the media *hated* the Tamars. Yao Kevinsson and his cronies, who made a living saying the opposite of whatever the more respectable journalists said, had declared a *de facto* media war against the Pact and its *occupying army*. Zee would have ignored him—every world had blowhards who would say the sky was falling for ratings and advertising income—except his opinion was appearing in other places, other media, where it shouldn't. That took money. More money than could be justified by Kevinsson's backers. So much money, it made Zee nervous.

And then there was Hauptmann Cadmus Petrov.

Petrov was a company commander in the Four-Two Motor-Rifle Battalion, Henderson's battalion. He was a cad, a nobleman's son from back in the Commonwealth who drank too much, bet too much, and borrowed too much. Zee was looking forward to the day the governor general's inspectorate caught up with him. She knew, because her shop had intercepted the police reports, he'd gotten drunk one night in a Deliverance speakeasy and beaten two locals near to death before the cops got him.

But there had been no charges.

The locals had disappeared out of the hospital, all their fees paid, and as far as Zee could ascertain, out of Deliverance and possibly off the Kaos continent altogether. There was no way Petrov had the pull for that. Not here on Pandora. Not without local help.

Cadmus Petrov was the first name on Zee's list.

That list had been far too long even before she added Katherine Hakima's name to it.

Zee frowned and pushed her chair back. "I'm going to get some air," she said to the room.

"Good idea, Staff Sergeant," Henderson said. "You get out there soon enough, you might see that new battalion coming down. I think they're due today."

"New battalion...?"

"The mercenaries."

Zee rolled her eyes. "I know I'm in charge of intelligence, Sergeant, but I can't be expected to know everything." There had probably been an update on incoming troop movements, but she was looking for more well-hidden prey than people who blasted down into the spaceport.

Henderson grinned at her. "The Gray Death Legion, Staff Sergeant."

Zee gaped. "You're joking."

"You should read the dailies, Staff Sergeant," Gina Fritsch said wryly. "You always tell us, 'Don't neglect the newspapers.'"

"I—"

"Wonder if we'll know any of them," Henderson said. "From the old days." He raised his hands over his head, stretching. "Two guys from my platoon took off with them, back when."

Zee glared at him, then half-walked, half-ran out the door.

CHAPTER 3

Ronan Carlyle really wanted to reach up and pinch the bridge of his nose. The incipient headache brewing there was becoming an old and familiar companion. Trapped as he was in a small cubbyhole compartment on an *Overlord*-class DropShip, sitting on the tarmac of a spaceport, waiting for the ground to cool enough to disembark his mercenary battalion, he didn't welcome the additional pain.

"Tell me again," he said to the man sitting across from him. "Without the rancor this time."

The man, whose gray Legion battledress had CAI spelled on its nametape, worked his mouth. Ta-heng Cai—he went by Tang—was the newest Legion officer. He'd been the senior survivor of a shattered mercenary company in Tamar employ on Crimond, Fitzroy's Fusiliers. He'd only been a Legionnaire a couple of months, and had spent a lot of that time aboard ship in the simulators, working to integrate his former Fusiliers into the Legion.

The Fusiliers had been decimated by the partisan bombing campaign the Legion had helped put down on Chromastich, going from a company of BattleMechs and tanks to half that. Their contract voided by combat losses, the Fusiliers had been penniless and deeply in debt to their Tamar employers. They'd been forced to surrender equipment, a pair of pilotless 'Mechs and a handful of tanks, to settle the debt.

Cai had found Ronan Carlyle on Crimond and begged him to take the survivors into the Legion. Ronan and the other Legion leadership had complied, and used the Fusiliers to flesh out the bones of a third company. Ronan had named Cai its captain.

The Legion has developed a habit of taking in orphans, Ronan realized. It had grown from the orphan corps of loyalists who'd refused to join the mutinous Twenty-Sixth Arcturan Guards at the founding of the Tamar Pact and grown with recruits and carryovers on its last contract on Crimond, people like Captain Cai.

"Staff Sergeant Ojima refused a direct order," Cai said, evenly. "During the last exercise sequence. I ordered him to ground his hovertanks and hold a line; instead, he sent his platoon on a flanking run to the right."

"And the result?" Ronan asked.

Cai frowned. He reached up and scrubbed his hand through his short-cut black hair. "He pushed the enemy into our engagement zone," Cai said through gritted teeth. "My 'Mechs took them apart."

"I see." Ronan leaned back in his chair. "Staff Sergeant Ojima has been a blower commander and a platoon leader since before there was a Legion, Captain Cai. Since the days of *Aufklärungsbataillon 29."*

"Sir," Cai said. His face worked. He clearly didn't like that statement.

"Speak freely, Captain," Ronan said.

"Sir—" Cai started, then stopped. He visibly got control of his emotions. "Sir, there has to be discipline. If I give an order, it has to be obeyed. It doesn't matter what the result was. I can't have platoon leaders freewheeling in the middle of a battle." He stopped, blinked, looked down, then back up to meet Ronan's eye. "I know I asked to be here, sir, but if this is how you run your Legion—"

Ronan grinned as Cai's sentence stopped abruptly. He let the silence hang a few beats, then set his palms on the tiny desk in front of him. "There are two parts to this, Captain. Three, really, but let's take the first two." He waited until Cai nodded.

"First, you are completely correct. There has to be discipline. Orders must be obeyed. When we're done here, you will bring the staff sergeant to me, and I will make that clear. Non-judicially, but meaningfully nonetheless. We train like we will fight, and orders are orders."

"Yes, sir," Cai said. His posture had changed, a touch of haughtiness in the way his back straightened and his shoulders went back. Ronan saw it and knew he had done it in the right order. *Now, can he take the medicine along with the candy?*

"The second thing is, the staff sergeant acted correctly."

Cai frowned. "Sir?"

"You're a Nagelring grad, correct?"

Cai nodded.

"Served in the Lyran Guards before you went mercenary?" Another nod.

"Then you learned the long wall in school." Ronan spread his hands. "Same as I did, at Coventry."

"Yes, sir..."

"The wall teaches us to trust our armor and our weapons, to trust the MechWarriors to our right and left, and know we will just blow the enemy off the field," Ronan said. The Lyran military had always been heavier, 'Mech for 'Mech, than most of its opponents. The Lyran Commonwealth Armed Forces had long ago evolved a tactical doctrine that basically amounted to stand-and-deliver. "That works when you have an *Atlas* at each shoulder. It doesn't work when part of your 'wall' is hovertanks."

"Major—" Cai started, but Ronan raised a finger.

"I'm not done." He clasped his hands together. "The Legion is a young battalion. We're still figuring out some of this stuff. We've got mostly former Lyran service here, with a smattering of other states and former mercenaries like yourself. Even one Jade Falcon, if my sister can be believed. We haven't had time to establish *Legion* doctrine for any of this. But we will."

A knock on the door interrupted him. "Come," he said. His sister, Captain Isobel Carlyle, stepped inside. He waved her to silence and looked back at Captain Cai. She frowned, but said nothing.

"Here's one thing I *know* we will be adopting: we're going to use our assets to their fullest potential and avoid as much as possible using them for roles they're not intended. That means we're not going to use blowers for roles intended for assault armor. Clear?"

"Yes, Major," Cai said.

"Understand me, Tang," Ronan said, using his nickname to show the formal part of the conversation was over, "when I say 'Legion doctrine,' I don't mean mine. You will contribute— you and your people, the former Fusiliers—because you have experience my longer-service people lack. You have to push back when you see stuff like this. Just like I have to push back when I see it, and why Bel has to do the same."

"You yell at me when I push," Bel teased.

"I mean it," Ronan said, ignoring his sister and staring at Cai. "We're on Pandora for six months at least. This is a quiet little garrison post where we can get our kit polished and our doctrine solidified. I'll have us out in the field every day I can manage it. We have to work this out, and fast, so we can start training on it." He pointed at Cai. "You have a part in that. But we must listen to our experts, like Ojima, too."

"Yes, sir," Cai said. "I understand, I think. You're not saying what Captain Fitzroy would have said, and you'd have my tactics instructors at the Nagelring apoplectic, but I get it."

"He had the Coventry instructors that way, too," Bel put in.

Ronan sighed. "Why are you here again?"

"Skipper says we can disembark in ten minutes or so."

"Great." Ronan stood, half-filling the tiny compartment that was already crammed with three people. He held out his hand. "Go get Staff Sergeant Ojima. I will put the fear of the dark gods in him, and then you can be the good cop and compliment him on that flanking run."

Cai stood and shook his head. "Understood, sir. Thank you."

"There will be discipline, Captain. There must be. You are entirely correct. But we all have to keep learning, too."

"He angry Ojima ignored him?" Bel asked as soon as Cai was out of the compartment.

"Not your business," Ronan said, sitting back down behind the desk.

"You could hear him shouting two decks down."

"Ten minutes, you said?"

"Eight or nine now, yes," Bel said.

"Thank the gods for that," Ronan muttered.

"Did you mean that, about being out in the field?" Bel stepped around and plopped into Cai's chair.

"You know I did," Ronan told her. "We have to get this battalion organized. We've spent the last year going from world to world, battle to battle, adopting people as we go. Good people, in the main, don't get me wrong. But they all still fight the way they were trained. We need to get everyone on the same page."

Bel held her hands up in mock surrender. "No argument from me. Besides, this is good ground for that."

"You've never been to Pandora," Ronan said.

"I haven't, but the Legion has."

"The Legion—oh, crap," Ronan said, shutting his eyes.

"A century ago. We fought the Jade Falcons to a standstill. Needgate. Vandmaal Crossing. Names from our history, brother mine."

Bel had always been fascinated by the history of their family's mercenary regiment. She'd annoyed anyone who would listen telling stories of the old Legion. She'd named her cadet company Carlyle's Commandos, in honor of old great-grandpa Grayson's dad's mercenary unit. It was a miracle she hadn't named the *Shadow Hawk* she'd driven in Lyran service *Boss Lady*, just like great-grandma Lori Kalmar.

Ronan opened his eyes and stood. *Maybe if I get out of here...*

"I've been thinking about a sim," Bel said. "Recreating the Vandmaal Crossing fight, but making the opponents Hell's Horses..."

Ronan couldn't get the door open fast enough.

"Hope no one arrests us this time," Bel said as the massive bay doors cracked and started whining and groaning down. The breeze washing in was hot and stale, tainted with the lingering scent of burnt air. Ronan's sinuses prickled. Ozone.

The light was soft, and there was an undercurrent in the air of something smelling vaguely of cinnamon.

Ronan grunted at his sister's statement. He still woke up in the night sometimes, sweaty, thinking about that first landing on Garrison when Jen Kipping had arrested him and all the other loyalists from the Twenty-Sixth Arcturan Guards RCT.

"Eight months," he said.

"What?"

"It's been eight months," Ronan said. "Since we landed that day on Garrison. Feels like a lifetime ago."

"Huh...you're right."

The *Overlord*'s ramp slammed down with a *thud* that made the deck vibrate. The wash of warm air, with the pressure of a whole planetary atmosphere, had already washed out the cooler, drier recycled air they'd been breathing this whole transit. Ronan felt sweat on his forehead and upper lip, but ignored it as they stepped closer to the edge of the ramp. He raised a hand to block the sunlight.

Deliverance spaceport looked like so many others he'd seen: gray, dirty, with fire-blackened pits of ferrocrete and long, distant runways where the aerodynes landed. A squat, fortress-like terminal building huddled in the near distance. In the middle distance, spaceport vehicles scuttled back and forth: road trains of reactions mass, luggage carriers, cargo haulers. Black-smoke-belching WorkMechs lifted cargo from low trailers and carried it up the ramps of cargo DropShips, while white-painted spaceport security blowers lifted curtains of dust and soot wherever they went.

A small, three-wheeled jitney sped toward them, weaving between the various cargo carriers. Ronan indicated it with his chin. "Sure hope that's not the cops."

"Not funny," Bel replied. "I hope it's the portmaster. I'd like to get off this boat, get out into the fresh air." She sneezed suddenly. "Great. I'm allergic to Pandora."

"It's the ozone," Ronan said, still watching the jitney.

"Not my first time," Bel said, sniffling. She glanced behind her. "You tell everyone else to wait?"

"No." He glanced back too. The bay was empty. Normally at seal-break, the bay would be full of people desperate for fresh air, to see a sky again, to know there was reality outside the DropShip's thick hull. But this time, aside from two crew in their coveralls, there was no one.

"We're totally getting arrested," Bel said.

"We're not."

The jitney rolled to a stop at the foot of the ramp. A short woman climbed out, stepping quickly across the still hot ferrocrete and onto the lowered ramp. She carried a noteputer in her left hand; her uniform, if that's what it was, was navy blue with gold piping.

She met Ronan's stare every step of the way. "Crew or passenger?" she asked, as she got close enough.

"Passenger," Ronan said. He half-turned, gesturing. "There are some crewers—"

"You Carlyle, then?" the woman asked, cutting him off.

"What?" Beside him, Bel made a sound, half-grunt, half-laugh.

"Your name. Is it Carlyle?"

"It is. How—"

"Good. This is for you." She held out the noteputer. When he didn't reach to take it, she shook it. "Here. It won't bite."

"What is it?"

"A bill," the woman said.

"I didn't get your name," Bel said.

Ronan stared at the noteputer, nonplussed. His hand half-rose.

"Oh, for—" The woman reached out, grabbed his wrist, and jerked his hand into contact with the noteputer. "There. Was that so hard?"

Ronan frowned and took the noteputer.

"My name's Guyon," the woman said to Bel. "Port Lieutenant Guyon."

"Bel. A pleasure."

"Bel..."

"Short for Isobel."

"You got a last name?"

Bel chuckled. "Depends. You got another noteputer somewhere?"

Ronan had tapped the screen live and scrolled the document already called up. The words were plain enough, but what they said didn't make any sense. "This is a bill."

"He always this sharp?" Guyon asked.

"Most days," Bel said. "While he's processing whatever that is, what are the customs processes for people like us? Incoming military units, I mean." She rolled her eyes as if to indicate the military DropShip they stood on. "We got just under 400 people waiting for some fresh air and real gravity, if you know what I mean."

"You're cleared," Guyon said. "Incoming Taffy mercs, right? I've got the paperwork on file already. Unless you hired a bunch of people between here and the jump point when you sent the manifests?"

"We did not."

"How can I have a bill?" Ronan blurted, brandishing the noteputer. "I literally haven't set foot on this planet yet." He pointed. "See? It's down there."

"That's right, it *is* down there," Guyon said as if to a very bright child. Bel snorted.

Ronan, frowning, brandished the noteputer. "You break that, it gets added to the bill," she added. "That's spaceport property."

"A bill for what?" Bel asked.

"Storage," Guyon said. "On your behalf, a bonded warehouse has been engaged for two months. Fees due on arrival, per the contract. Says you'll take possession right away."

"Two months ago, we were on the way from Crimond," Ronan said.

"Slow transit," Guyon observed.

"How much is it?" Bel asked. Ronan held the noteputer out so she could see the screen. She leaned in, shaded the screen, read the number, then slapped his arm. "You cad, that's nothing. Pay the woman."

Ronan rolled his eyes. "We haven't even set up banking on Pandora yet!"

Bel rolled her eyes back. "Of course we did. Radios work just fine—I did that two days ago, during transit." She took the noteputer, swiped, did a search, and a few moments later handed it back to the port lieutenant.

"So," Bel asked, as Guyon confirmed the transaction. "What did we just pay for? What's in the warehouse?"

Guyon shook her head. "I haven't been inside—it's a bonded warehouse, remember—but the rumor mill says it's a BattleMech."

CHAPTER 4

DELIVERANCE MILITARY SPACEPORT
DELIVERANCE
PANDORA
TAMAR PACT
2 MAY 3152

Zee's Tamar Armed Forces ID was enough to get her onto the tarmac at the spaceport, but it took almost half an hour to cadge a ride on a cargo hauler to get her close to the newly arrived DropShip. By the time she got there, the new mercenaries, this Gray Death Legion, were already debarking. A pair of BattleMechs stood obvious sentry duty over the sprawl of people, but Zee's experienced eye made out the organization in the chaos. Platoons and companies moved together, getting ready for their movement.

She couldn't have explained why she'd come. She just wanted to see, she supposed.

Zee's father had enjoyed genealogy in his later years. Her twice-great grandfather had escaped the Draconis Combine during the Fourth Succession War, carried away as a war refugee on a Lyran military ship, and settled on Porrima. His diaries contained mention of a shunned second-cousin, Hassan Ali Khaled, who had been banished from Shaul Khala and become a mercenary in the Gray Death Legion. It had been a curiosity for a young Zee, a nugget of history in her own family's twisted genealogical tree, a note her father used to share his fascination with genealogy with his bright, favorite daughter.

And now she was here, and so was the Gray Death Legion. It felt weird.

She shook the reverie off and concentrated on seeing what was in front of her. "You can learn a lot about a force by the way it behaves in garrison," Staff Sergeant Gleason had taught her. "Especially in transit." Zee beat the last of her childhood nostalgia down and tried to see with professional eyes.

The Legion looked professional enough. She'd already noted the clear subunit delineations, which usually meant one of two things among mercenary units. In the more common case, the unit CO was a screaming martinet who forced his unit to be parade-ground-colored birds, always looking professional for potential employers, always making sure the onlookers understood what they were paying for.

Eying the blocks of people, she didn't think that was it. The people inside them were too relaxed. Sure, they moved with purpose, but she could see clear signs of joviality and frivolity among the sub-units, lots of laughing in the ranks, a sense of comfortable confidence. *No*, she reasoned, *these people are the second kind*.

The less-common case was unit pride. What was sometimes called *esprit de corps*. The Legion soldiers were soldiers, people under discipline, but with the confidence discipline gave them. Their attitude said they had nothing to prove to anyone, not each other, not their employer, and certainly not any random onlooker.

It wasn't the way Zee's task force had unassed the DropShips, she recalled. Task Force Bredell had been a mix of quiet disquiet, pomposity, and derision for their new posting.

Even as she made these realizations, her trained mind was assessing more details. The subunits moved together, lances and platoons, but there were subtle differences. That group over there moved like a Lyran infantry company. Zee could almost feel her knees itching to straighten into a goose step. The mass of support personnel behind them moved completely differently, wrong to Zee's Lyran-trained senses, but still comprehensible and similar.

It made her brain ache a little trying to parse it out.

She'd walked closer as she watched, not really paying attention. She was still 50 meters away when a Purifier battlesuit shimmered out of its adaptive camouflage and held up a gauntlet.

"Please stop there, miss," the battlesuit trooper said, their voice heavily digitized by the helmet speakers. *"This area is restricted."*

Zee frowned. "Restricted?"

"While the Legion debarks, it's not safe," the trooper clarified. *"Lots of heavy equipment moving around, too many people. Can't let you in. But you're welcome to stay there and watch, if you want."* The chuckle was digitized into a terrorizing caw. *"Lords know I'd like watching the 'Mechs moving around, if that's what I came for."*

"What if I'm a spy?" Zee challenged playfully. She added a smile.

The Purifier waved its arm, as if to indicate the whole spaceport. *"We're out here in plain view of the gods and radar, miss. Take all the pictures you want."*

Zee laughed, looking past the battlesuit. She opened her mouth to add a new jest, but her eyes washed across a figure and then snapped back. *It can't be—* "Staff Sergeant!" she shouted. Without thinking, she took another step forward.

"Ma'am, *stop!*" the Purifier pilot barked. All trace of levity was gone from their voice. The arm, raised as a bar across her path, pivoted around like a turret to point at her, palm raised.

Zee stopped, but frowned. "It can't be her—Staff Sergeant! Staff Sergeant Gleason—*Mira!*"

A head turned among the group of pogues across the tarmac. Zee smiled and waved like a kid. The woman raised a hand to shade her eyes from the sun then started walking over. The Purifier didn't move, but another shimmering hulk *clunked* closer.

"Long time, Staff Sergeant Gleason," Zee said as the Legion NCO got close enough to hear her. She shifted her weight, but there was a warning growl from the new Purifier.

"It's okay, Private," the staff sergeant said. She sidled close, set her hands on her hips, and smiled wryly. "I know her. How you doing, Zee?" Her eyes flicked to Zee's rank tabs, and her smile widened. "Staff Sergeant Zee, no less."

"Thank *God* you're here, Staff Sergeant," Zee said, her eyes burning.

The three-wheeled jitney had never been intended to carry someone as tall as Ronan, but he made do. The ride was rough. Three wheels didn't make for a sturdy center of gravity on turns, and Port Lieutenant Guyon threaded her way through the spaceport ground vehicles with an almost manic glee. Ronan braced his knee against the front corner of the dashboard where it met the small side door and prayed the end would be quick when it came.

When the jitney pulled up in front of the warehouse with a final lurch, he unfolded and staggered out, desperate to get fresh blood flowing to his lower legs.

The bonded storage facilities were along the opposite edge of the spaceport, a row of towering warehouses large enough to roll a DropShip inside them. Guyon took them to one of the smaller buildings off to the side; these were only fifteen or twenty meters tall.

Ronan wished Bel were here. He hated admitting that, but he did. As the Legion's XO, it was her duty to ensure the battalion debarked and got started on its way to the cantonment. She couldn't be away from the ship right now, and besides, the bill was addressed to him.

As Guyon led him toward the building's personnel entrance, she gestured toward the blocky lock panel on the door. "It's keyed to you," she said. "Thumbprint biometric, looks like."

"Where in the hell did you get my thumbprint?" Ronan demanded. When Guyon just shrugged, he frowned and stepped forward. The thumbprint scanner was beneath a clear plastic weather cover. He lifted it and shoved his left thumb against the scanner, held it there. The scanner was warm. He thought he felt a tingle of vibration.

The lock *thunk*ed open.

"I guess it really is you," Guyon observed. Ronan just glared at her before he jerked the door open.

The air inside the warehouse was warm and stale. The persistent scent of cinnamon was still there, but dulled, as if it hadn't been refreshed for a long time. Ronan had felt it burning his sinuses ever since he climbed into the jitney. It was dark, with only a pool of light from the small LED over the personnel door.

Guyon stepped through behind him. "What?" She spread her hands. "I want to see what's in here, too."

"It's dark," Ronan told her. "That's what's in here."

"Hang on..." Guyon stepped to the side, out of the circle of light. Ronan waited where he stood. His eyes began to adjust to the darkness; he thought he saw the dim shape of something huge in the back corner of the warehouse. "Here we go." He heard a heavy breaker being closed, then the warehouse lit with a flicker of old sodium lights and brighter LEDs. He blinked, clearing his vision, then looked.

"Stone's *balls*..." Ronan whispered. A BattleMech stood there, as promised. But it was one he'd seen often in his childhood back on Odessa. Tall, hunched-over, mean-looking, painted in mottled black and gray camouflage. A grinning white skull set against a red background on one shin.

"Okay..." Guyon said, her voice trailing off.

"It can't be," Ronan whispered. "That's his *Marauder.*"

"Whose *Marauder?*"

"It can't be..." Ronan repeated, ignoring her. He started walking closer. The *Marauder*, 75 tons of fighting BattleMech, stood quiet and dark. Now that he was over the initial shock, he saw it was secured to a tracked crawler, the kind of vehicle techs used to move disabled 'Mechs into repair cradles after battle. It had clearly been driven off a DropShip and stored here. *But how did it get here?*

"Whose *Marauder?*" Guyon repeated.

"*His,*" Ronan said.

At the base of the 'Mech, near the crawler cabin, he stopped and looked up. As a child, he'd stood at the foot of this 'Mech he didn't know how many times, feeling as small as he did now, looking up at all twelve meters of machine and history and feeling just as incapable, deep inside his darkest thoughts.

He knew he was capable, knew it intellectually, could look at his own performance dispassionately. That was a skill that had been pounded into him on Coventry in the academy.

But that wasn't the same as *knowing it* in his gut.

In his gut, Ronan Carlyle was still that small boy standing in his family's museum, looking up at the weight of history and expectation and feeling doubt.

"His *who*?" Guyon persisted.

Ronan spun, the whorl of emotion in him bursting into irritation he couldn't wholly control. He opened his mouth, closed it. He squeezed his eyes shut for a second, getting control of his emotions.

"Grayson Death Carlyle," he told her. "My great-grandfather."

"Ah," Guyon said. It was obvious she was aware of how close he'd come to snapping at her. She pointed past him. "There's a note."

Ronan turned, looked. A noteputer hung from a strap on the handle of the crawler's door. It was in a hardened case, meant for outdoor military use, and emblazoned with the insignia of the Odessa planetary militia. He unhooked it and turned it over. It had another, smaller thumbprint.

"Do I need to explain how those work again?" Guyon prodded.

"You really are an unpleasant person," Ronan told her.

"I get that a lot." She flared her eyes and jerked her chin at the noteputer. "We doing this today?"

Ronan half-closed his eyes and exhaled, controlling his temper again. He pressed his thumb against the scanner until the noteputer *clicked* open. He pried the hardened case apart and touched the screen. A simple text message appeared.

Ronan,

News is hard to get, but from what we hear, you need this more than the museum does. We had a little work done. Colonel Torres tells me everything you need is in the cockpit. Bring it back in one piece.

I understand why you're doing what you're doing, even if I don't completely understand what you're doing. I think your grandfather would have, though. And I trust you to know what's right.

Your mother and I have never been more proud of you and Bel. Keep each other safe.

Dad

Ronan snapped the case shut and looked up at the *Marauder* again. He ignored the burning in his eyes. Now that he'd been warned, and the initial shock was past, he saw the differences his father's note mentioned. The PPC barrels were a little more angular, and the overhead GM Whirlwind cannon was now something else, something with a thicker, squared-off barrel.

"The port storage fees are complete?" he asked Guyon.

"They are. Do I get to see the note?"

"No." Ronan held the noteputer against his side. "I'll have a team in here no later than tomorrow to remove it. Thank you for keeping it safe."

"My duty," Guyon said softly. He looked down at her, but she only shrugged. "What? You don't have a monopoly on duty, MechWarrior. I know my job."

Ronan nodded and looked back up at the *Marauder*. As a boy and a young man, he'd always felt the oppressive weight of his family's legacy. Always. It was on his shoulders to carry that legacy forward. He'd always felt that way, no matter that no one, not even his father, had ever even hinted that. He'd stand beneath this BattleMech in the family museum, thinking of his great-grandfather, wondering how Grayson Death Carlyle had stood so long under the weight of his accomplishments.

His face was warm. His eyes burned. His hand squeezed the noteputer so tightly the hardened case creaked. His mind, however, was steady. Resolute, even.

The world—hell, the universe—could roll onto his shoulders, but he'd be damned—*dead*—before he let his family down.

CHAPTER 5

PALACE OF THE GODS
DELIVERANCE
PANDORA
TAMAR PACT
3 MAY 3152

The smell of onions from the omelet he'd ignored since he sat down grew stronger the longer it sat on the corner of his desk cooling, but still Elam Nobu ignored it. He was sprawled back in his comfortable chair, holding the HV remote and pressing the back-30-seconds button again. His thumb came up from its most recent press.

"*—and now we have* new *mercenaries here to* protect *us*," Yao Kevinsson whined from the holotank. "*More Taffy bootlickers, here to keep us* safe. *Safe from who, I want to know? The Jade Falcons are gone, and it doesn't seem like they're coming back—*"

Nobu paused the holo again. His teeth ground together as he—again—controlled his temper. He should have known this was coming—that *they* were coming, these mercenaries. Things were too close for him to have missed this.

But you can't watch everything.

The office door slid open and Nessa Deschanes stepped through, cradling a noteputer and wearing her usual stern expression. Nobu set the remote down and sniffed. He pushed the plate of cold eggs to the edge of his desk as she crossed the room.

"It is the Gray Death Legion," Deschanes said. She stopped in front of his desk and stood. "That is confirmed."

"Fantastic," Nobu said flatly. "I recall the stories from my childhood. I thought it was dead."

"A new one," she said. "A combined arms battalion under contract to the TAF. My sources didn't know if they fell under the task force's direct command." She frowned, looked down at the noteputer, but didn't tap it live. "It goes without saying: we don't know anyone in this new battalion."

"Yet you say it anyway." He stopped his teeth grinding by force of will. "Do we know anything?"

"Less than we will by the end of the day," Deschanes said. "My people are scraping the port authority records now. I have already sent the request for whatever the Taffies have on them to go to our people in the task force."

Nobu nodded. He huffed. "We should have seen them coming."

"I checked the logs. There was a transit order for a Taffy auxiliary unit tagged with nothing more than an ID. We did see them coming. But that was ten weeks ago. We've been busy."

By and large, the distance between a planet and its customary jump points averaged a week to ten days, but not Pandora. Thanks to a relatively rare feat of system mechanics, the customary points were set *sixty-eight* days out. It made for a thriving interplanetary economy; for one thing, few DropShips carried two months of reaction mass, so huge refueling stations and "water buffalo" in-system craft carried mass to them at in-system rendezvous and waypoint stations.

"We can't change it now," Nobu said. "Let's not get hung up on it. I want to know everything you learn about them as you learn it. They're a wild card in a deck, and we don't have time for wild cards."

"We will know more soon," Deschanes repeated.

"Good," Nobu said, closing the conversation. "Now—"

The door to his office slid open before he could say another word. Two men walked in, one small, one large. Nobu controlled the reflexive moue of distaste the smaller man engendered and ignored the larger. Irwin Keeling, the shorter one, was a toad of no breeding and less courtesy who used the underworld power he'd amassed to show anyone he considered beneath him that he didn't care about their opinions.

"You don't have an appointment," Deschanes said coldly as she moved to stand in front of Nobu's desk.

"I don't need one," Keeling said. "The little man out there, the secretary, he tried to tell me the same thing." He wore a dark suit of conservative cut, but the slight sheen of the fabric told Nobu it was made from *daigumo* silk, imported at great expense from the Draconis Combine. Nobu had six similar suits himself. Cleaning them was impossible, so he only wore them for special situations.

"The baron is a busy man," Deschanes persisted.

"Nessa," Nobu said, bowing to the inevitable. "Irwin. Good to see you. We weren't expecting you."

"Yes, *Nessa*," Keeling said, frowning at her. "Elam." He stepped around one of the two chairs in front of the desk and sat down. His giant bodyguard stood behind him on the left. "I've come because we need to get things moving."

"Thing *are* moving."

"In the wrong direction."

"Nonsense."

Keeling smiled, a condescending little twist of the mouth that made Nobu want to have Deschanes smack him across the face. "What about this new Taffy battalion that just landed?" He glanced up at Deschanes, who still stood next to him, smoldering. "My people tell me you don't know anything about them."

"Your *people* don't know anything more," Deschanes said acidly.

"They know there was a BattleMech waiting for them at the port," Keeling said, looking back at Nobu.

Nobu kept his expression still, but felt cold between his shoulder blades. "We knew about that," he said. Or they would shortly, but Keeling didn't need to know that. "Is that all you came to talk to me about?"

Keeling grunted. A beat of silence hung in the air, just enough to make it awkward. "As it happens, no it isn't. I actually came to talk business. We need to make a change to our arrangement."

"What kind of change?"

"Personnel," Keeling said. He made his little smile again.

Nobu felt sweat on his lower back. He was suddenly aware of the way his chair reflected his own body heat back at him. His skin felt clammy. He shifted, crossing his legs and folding his hands in his lap. Arguing with people like Keeling made his skin crawl.

Their arrangement, as Keeling called it, was nothing that could ever be put down on paper. There could be no records of the planetary government colluding with a criminal syndicate like Keeling's Malthuses. The Malthuses were meticulous in the record keeping of their own legitimate businesses, but something like this...no. Which meant there was no contract for Nobu to fall back on. No legalese to protect him against partners who wanted to renegotiate the deal at the last minute...

"Personnel," Nobu made himself repeat.

"Yes." Keeling motioned to the huge man behind him. "You've met my friend Hector Jurasco, yes?"

"We're acquainted," Nobu said. He hadn't known the thug's name was Jurasco, but he was Keeling's shadow. Nobu had taken him for a bodyguard. More than two meters tall, easily 120 kilos, with balding hair shaved short and a permanent frown. He had the look of a gym bodybuilder, the kind of cretin who liked to stare at himself in the mirrors while he lifted heavy things over and over again.

He's probably dying to tell me about his nutrition plan, Nobu thought.

"He's a veteran."

"Of?"

"The military."

"Whose military?" Deschanes asked, from the side. She'd quietly slid across the room until she was behind the other chair, next to the one where Keeling sat.

"The Lyran military," Keeling said, not looking at her.

"Thank you for your service," Nobu said, glancing up at the big man. "Now, Irwin—"

"I want him to command the PPG."

It took half a second for the words to process inside Nobu's mind. When they did, it was all he could do not to burst out laughing. Instead, he said, "I think Colonel Benchley would object to that."

The Pandora Planetary Guard—PPG—was Nobu's ace in the hole. His position made him titular head of any planetary protection entity, and he'd rammed through the PPG as soon as he was secure. Raised from Pandorans, the PPG was a militia force "dedicated to the protection of Pandora from all threats." Along with several regiments of unarmored infantry, a combined-arms battalion of 'Mechs and armored vehicles was currently assembling, using equipment from the Quickscell Corporation and Keeling's own Red Devil Industries. The PPG was the one thing both sides of the scandal media supported. It was the patriotic thing to do.

It was wholly Nobu's creature. He controlled every officer company commander and above, and a significant percentage of the NCOs. It would be the instrument, along with the suborned elements of the Taffy garrison battalions, that kept him alive and in power long enough to return Pandora to the Commonwealth. The return of Pandora and its industry—as well as the regiments of trained troops—would ensure he received a hero's welcome instead of a hangman's noose.

The Tamars had stolen this world from the Commonwealth. It was only fair play to steal it away from them.

"Colonel Benchley objects to what you tell him to," Keeling said. "Jurasco is the right man for the job."

"Jurasco," Nobu repeated, looking at the man.

"Hi," Jurasco said. His voice was deep, gravelly.

"You're Pandoran?" Nobu asked.

"Got papers say I am," Jurasco said.

"Your LCAF rank upon exit?" Deschanes asked.

"Hauptmann," Jurasco said.

"Of?" Deschanes persisted.

"I had a company of the Donegal Guards," Jurasco said.

"You're a MechWarrior," Nobu said.

"I was. I remember how."

Nobu wanted to sigh, needed to sigh. But he didn't. "What if I decline?" he asked Keeling.

"You can kiss your 'Mechs goodbye," Keeling said.

"We had a deal."

"Look—I make the most desirable product in the Inner Sphere. I got Taffy quartermasters sniffing around every week, asking when they can get more of my production for themselves. I don't *need* to sell you those BattleMechs. I can move them all, this afternoon, with a snap of my fingers."

Now Nobu did sigh. "All right." He made himself smile at Jurasco. "Welcome to the Pandora Planetary Guard, Colonel Jurasco." *There will be some way to control him*, Nobu told himself. There would have to be.

"My lord," Jurasco replied.

"I'm glad that worked out," Keeling said, standing. Jurasco stepped back to make room. "I understand the first tranche is being delivered this afternoon. I think I'll go oversee the delivery with the colonel here."

"Come by after," Nobu said, this time to Jurasco. "We'll administer the oath then, get you fitted. I'll speak to Colonel Benchley in the meantime. I trust you'll keep this under your hat until we make the announcement, Irwin. The media, you know."

Keeling made a brushing-off gesture. "Of course, Elam. I leave all that to you."

"How dare he," Deschanes said as soon as the door closed behind them. "How *dare* he." She was half-turned, staring at the door. Her fists were bunched tightly enough Nobu could see her white knuckles from his chair.

Now Nobu let out the tension he'd been controlling. "He dares because he can," he told her. "Get Benchley in here ASAP. I need to give him something more useful to do."

Deschanes turned away from the door. "What might that be?"

"I have no idea," Nobu said. "I'll think of something. Once you've done that, get out and meet these new mercenaries. I need to know if they can be bought. Adding another battalion would mean we don't need to count on Keeling anymore. That would be nice."

"My lord..." Deschanes hesitated, but then went on. "My lord, you can't possibly believe you can trust a mercenary battalion we know nothing about, even if they were willing to turn their coat."

Nobu snorted, thankful he could now that Keeling was gone. "You think we can trust Jurasco?"

"Jurasco can be dealt with."

"So can these mercenaries," Nobu told her. "Go."

"What if they can't be turned?"

"Then we'll deal with them," Nobu said. "Better now, before they're organized."

CHAPTER 6

CAMP DELMAR CLAY
DELIVERANCE
PANDORA
TAMAR PACT
3 MAY 3152

A lone Gray Death Legion infantry trooper stood half-hidden behind a tree, trying to stand straight and get their whole body behind the trunk. Rounds impacted against the tree trunk, kinetic and laser both, blasting chunks of the purple sapwood away. It was soundless, but everyone in the hangar saw the Legion trooper open their mouth and scream. Finally, they found a last bit of courage, leaned around the trunk and fired back until their laser rifle's capacitors were empty.

A shot took the Legion trooper's head off at the neck.

The holo ended.

The lights came up in the hangar. Ronan stood from where he'd been sitting with Bel and Tang Cai. "That was recorded a few hundred klicks from right here, almost exactly a century ago, by a squadmate's helmet cam. The original was sideways, because that squadmate was already dead." He paused, looking around the space, watching the faces of the assembled Legion.

"You are all soldiers. You understand that what we do means we may die. Our friends may die, our comrades may die. Our ultimate job, if it comes right down to it, is to make the enemy die for their side before they can kill us." Ronan paused and looked across the assembled faces, trying to read the room.

He'd assembled the entire Legion in the hangar for this, combat personnel and support staff alike. In the Lyran military, Ronan had been exposed to the divide between combat arms and rear echelon troops, how the MechWarriors had lorded their lofty status over everyone else. He'd always despised that attitude.

It took a team of seven, at minimum, to keep his 'Mech running. A technician sergeant and two groups of three assistant technicians—astechs—who worked under the sergeant's direction. In addition to those people who put their hands directly on his BattleMech, there were the logisticians who ensured there was a ready supply of ammunition and replacement parts across interstellar distances without working HPGs. And that didn't even take into account the administrators who ensured the Legion had the funds to purchase that materiel and the recruiters to replace retirees and combat losses.

It all came down, in Ronan's opinion, to the belief that everyone in a unit should understand that the unit as an organism only survived if every part did its job. That meant the combat personnel should respect the support staff, yes.

But it also meant the support staff should respect the people who went out and put themselves inside a bad guy's ten-ring.

"Tomorrow, the combat companies will head out for a week of field exercises. We have a lot of dust to shake off. Then we're going to come back here, refit and fix whatever breaks, and go out and do it again. And again. And again, until we have firmed up what Legion doctrine is for all of this." Ronan glanced back at Cai and Bel, then faced the group again.

"We have a lot to do to get ready for that, so we're going to dismiss to companies. I want you all to think about where we are, how we got here, and where you want to go. Your Gray Death Legion is already building a reputation to rival the old Legion. But it takes each of you, individually, doing your part to build it." Ronan took one last look across the room, then nodded. "Dismissed to companies."

As the room broke up, Bel and Tang Cai stood up and stepped closer. Ronan looked at Cai first. "Tang, hold down the fort. I have to talk to someone, but as soon as you've turned your lances and platoons over to their COs, come find me in my office."

Cai nodded and stepped past. Ronan looked at Bel and frowned. "Where is she?"

Zee Khaled stood in a small room off a BattleMech hangar, alone. She wore mufti, but still felt like the walls had eyes. It was the spook in her; she knew how easy it was to bug an office in a disused 'Mech hangar. She'd ordered it done any number of times.

No one knew she was here.

That didn't make her feel any better.

The room's only door opened, and three people stepped inside. She knew one of them, Staff Sergeant Gleason. The others were younger and shared enough features that they had to be the brother-and-sister mercenary commanders, the Carlyles.

"You're Khaled," the big blond man—Ronan—said.

"I am."

"You can trust her, Major," Staff Sergeant Gleason said. "I know her from back in the day. We trained together. She's good people."

"Not good enough to come to Garrison with us," said the other Carlyle, Isobel.

Zee bristled, but contained her reaction. It was a natural way for Isobel to feel. Lord knew there had been nights and hours where Zee had second-guessed her decision to stick with the governor general. *Still...*

"From where I stand, Captain," Zee replied, "you weren't good enough to stick with us. But here you are now, taking the governor general's money."

The small blond woman smiled, nodding at the point scored. "She sounds like you," Isobel said to Gleason, who inclined her head. "What can we do for you, Staff Sergeant Zahara Khaled?" Isobel's brow twitched. "Khaled..." she repeated.

"A distant relative, actually," Zee said.

"Seriously?" Isobel's expression changed completely and instantly. "You're related to the Assassin?"

"Not why we're here," Staff Sergeant Gleason put in.

"No, it's not," Ronan said. "Why are we here, Staff Sergeant?"

Zee took a deep breath. "I pulled your contract."

"And?"

"I've come to ask if you have sealed orders," Zee said. She held up a hand. "I know you probably wouldn't tell me if you did. But there's some shit going down here—" she stopped. "Sorry. I need to know if you're here about the thing I can't tell you about."

Ronan Carlyle didn't speak. He blinked. Then he looked at Gleason. "What?"

Gleason chuckled. "You're going to have to give him a little more, Zee."

"I can't. You know that."

"Sealed orders," Ronan repeated.

"She means secret orders," Bel put in. "As in, your eyes only, burn after reading, maybe even torch the building just in case." Her expression was pure amusement. "I think you can assume we don't, Staff Sergeant. Which is what we'd say if we *did* have them, of course, but my brother's poker face is terrible."

"Secret orders," Ronan repeated.

"I didn't think you would," Zee allowed. "There really hasn't been time for my reports to get back to Arcturus and for them to have turned a mission around."

"What's going on, Zee?" Staff Sergeant Gleason asked. "You can trust us."

Zee chewed on the inside of her cheek. She trusted Gleason implicitly. She trusted Gleason's experience more than she trusted her own if she was being honest, but it still felt unnatural. She did need the help; she couldn't explain why, but her gut was telling her things were coming to a head. And Gleason was just sitting there.

"There's something rotten on Pandora," she said in a rush. No one spoke. Zee closed her mouth, trying to regain her control.

"Like...spoiled?" Isobel asked.

"Like treason," Zee said. "Against the Pact."

Ronan blinked a couple times. Isobel crossed her arms and chewed on her lip, brow furrowed. Zee ignored them, concentrating instead on Mira Gleason. "You remember we all went to Garrison the last time this came up," Gleason said.

"You know what I mean," Zee persisted.

"I do," Gleason said.

"I don't," Ronan said. "Explain."

Zee gave them the short version of her private file, ending with Kommandant Hakima at the Palace of the Gods just before the Legion arrived. The Carlyles listened, clearly out of their depth, but doing their best to keep up. Zee included them in the conversation because they were the decision-makers, but she was really telling the story to Staff Sergeant Gleason.

"Pretty thin," Gleason said when she'd finished. Zee shrugged.

"Thin," Ronan said.

Bel sighed. "You really need to find a way to say words other people didn't beat you to, brother."

Ronan scowled at her, then looked back at Zee. "You're telling me someone is intriguing against the Pact. But what I'm hearing is a how-to guide for being a Lyran officer. Spend more than you have. Find a patron. Get influence, and use that to advance your career."

"It's more than that," Zee said. "It goes into the Palace, maybe all the way up to the baron's office. It's a *lot* of money these people are spending, if I'm right, Major."

"Show me," Ronan said.

"I...can't."

Ronan turned his hands palm-up. "I don't know what you want from me, then. Our contract is with the Tamar Armed Forces; we're in garrison, but we're really here for training. We didn't get any secret orders about spy work."

"I want your help, if it comes to it," Zee said.

"Help you," Ronan said. "With what? What does your CO say about this?"

"He doesn't know," Zee admitted.

"Leutnant-Colonel Bredell?"

Zee shook her head.

"So, you're telling me you want my help for a counter-coup against a coup that hasn't happened yet, that your own chain of command doesn't know about."

"I don't know for sure how deep the rot goes," Zee insisted. She felt her face getting warm. She'd walked into this room expecting these kinds of rebuttals; they were only logical. Her theory had a lot of holes in it, but Gleason had taught her every tapestry was just a collection of loose strings until someone found the order in them, and second, to trust her gut.

"The rot doesn't go this far," Staff Sergeant Gleason put in. "You're safe here, Zee." She pushed off from where she'd been leaning against a wall. "Major, captain, I think we can agree to keep this between us?"

"Of course," Isobel said, and Ronan made an agreeing sound. He opened his mouth, but a knock interrupted him. The door opened to reveal a Legion corporal with Signals collar flashes.

"Sorry, Major, Captain, but there's a woman at the gate. Says she's here to see you, Major."

"A woman," Ronan repeated.

"Gods," Isobel said, rolling her eyes. "Come on. You're doing it on purpose now." She looked at the corporal. "Is she on the schedule?"

"No, ma'am."

"Then send her home," Isobel said.

"Yes ma'am, we tried. She says she's from the local baron, though."

Cold sweat broke out between Zee's shoulder blades. She watched Isobel and Ronan share a look, and then turn to look at her. They both made the same face, raising an inquiring eyebrow. It was all Zee could do not to laugh at the absurdity of it.

"It's not about her," Gleason said. "She knows better."

"Then I guess I better go see what it's about," Ronan said.

"I am Nessa Deschanes," the woman said. They were standing in the foyer of the cantonment main building. The cantonment dated back to the Succession Wars era, thick ferrocrete with chipping paint. The general tenor of the interior was *depressing,*

never-ending attritional war. "Personal assistant to the baron of Pandora, my lord Elam Nobu."

"Charmed," Ronan said. "Ronan Carlyle, major, commanding the Gray Death Legion." He heard Bel, who stood one step to his right and one step back, stifle a snort. "How can I help the baron, ma'am?"

"Is there somewhere we can talk?"

"Here is good," Ronan said.

"Indeed." Deschanes wore a severe expression and demeanor and something else, something that set Ronan's hackles on edge, beneath it all. He couldn't put his finger on it, but he didn't want to let this woman any deeper into the Legion's cantonment than he had to.

"Indeed," Deschanes repeated. "Major, the baron merely wishes to welcome you to Pandora, and to learn more about your Gray Death Legion. He prefers to keep close relationships with the senior military officers of all Tamar units on-planet." She paused. A plastic grin, clearly intended to be conspiratorial, appeared, but Ronan had seen a thousand just like it. "He is titular commander of the Pandora Planetary Guard, you see. I think he likes to learn what he can from other military leaders."

"I'll have a copy of our contract and our table of organization and equipment sent over," Ronan said. "According to the letter of our contract, we're attached to Task Force Bredell, under the leutnant-colonel's authority, but not direct command. I'm sure the leutnant-colonel or his staff can inform the baron of anything he wishes to know about the Legion's disposition."

"I'm sure," Deschanes agreed. "Still, the baron prefers face-to-face meetings. Might it be convenient to visit him tomorrow, at the Palace of the Gods? We know well the toll the long transit to Pandora takes on travelers; perhaps the baron can help you alleviate any lingering supply problems?"

"I regret that that will not be possible," Ronan said, not regretting it at all. Even if he hadn't just come from Zee Khaled and her nebulous warnings, everything about Deschanes and, by extension, her baron, rubbed him the wrong way. He'd heard all these words before, when he'd been courted for patronage while in the LCAF. A company commander wasn't much of a prize for scheming nobleman, but Hauptmann The Honorable

Ronan Carlyle, heir to the barony of Odessa, was something else indeed. "Let's talk," and "maybe I can help," dressed up however flowery, were always the gateway ploys. A call could be made. Supplies found. Thus, the unending back-and-forth of favoritism began. Ronan tasted metal just thinking about it.

"I will be in the field with my battalion for the foreseeable future," he continued. "Perhaps it will be convenient when I return."

"Your diligence to your duty does you credit," Deschanes said, without a hint of compliment in her tone. "When will that be?"

Ronan spread his hands apologetically. "Regretfully, I can't yet say. We're staying out until I'm satisfied with the Legion's performance."

"Ah," Deschanes said. She glanced at Bel, but must have gotten nothing back. "In that case, I will take up no more of your time, nor stand in the way of your duties to the Pact."

Ronan inclined his head. "Thank you for your visit, and please thank the baron for his interest. It is humbling to know our efforts have been noticed."

As soon as she was gone, Bel blew out a big breath. "Wow."

"Right?"

"If something is rotten here, it may be starting there," Bel said. "Maybe we should take Khaled seriously?"

Ronan shook his head. "Not our mission. And I meant it—we're in the field until I'm happy."

"You're never happy."

"Better pack a lot of food, then."

CHAPTER 7

RED DEVIL INDUSTRIES
DELIVERANCE
PANDORA
TAMAR PACT
5 MAY 3152

"He sent the woman," Jurasco said.

Irwin Keeling looked up from his noteputer. "And?"

"They're not interested," Jurasco replied. He stood in Keeling's office at Red Devil in his new PPG uniform, all black and red and gold. "From what I heard, the mercenary CO told her to pound sand. Then they pulled out the next day, damn near all of them, and headed for Vandmaal."

Keeling had seen the name on maps, but it meant nothing to him beyond that. "What's down there?"

"Nothing. Trees. I expect that's why they went. Word is they're on a training mission."

Keeling sat back in his plush desk chair. "Training..." He knew what that meant: low-powered lasers, paint-filled kinetic and explosive ammunition, throttlers and limiters. All the stuff they had to put the fresh new 'Mechs through as part of acceptance trials.

"No word how long they'll be out there, but at least they can't get in anyone's way." Jurasco stopped talking.

Keeling tapped his lower lip with a stylus and considered. "You're read-in on Nobu's plans, yes?"

"Such as they are, sure," Jurasco said. "I'm the CO."

"And his people will follow you?"

Jurasco grunted. "I'm the CO."

"How soon could we go?"

"Plans say six hours from when Nobu gives the word," Jurasco said, after a moment, "but he won't say that word. He's too scared. Back at the Nagelring, we called it analysis paralysis. He's running down every angle, building his PPG to some imaginary goal, suborning all the Taffy people he can get his grubby fingers on. He's too scared to actually move."

Keeling continued tapping. "What if I gave the word?"

"You?"

"I say it to you. You say it to whoever needs to hear it. The whole thing swings into motion, and even Nobu can't stop it. Will it work?"

"Depends when you say it," Jurasco hedged.

"What if I say it now?"

"Now?"

"Right now."

"Nobu will never go for it."

Keeling chuckled. "By the time he finds out, he won't have any choice. It'll be rolling by then. You can't stop a rockslide with a shovel." He set the stylus down. "Will it work, though?"

"It might..." Jurasco said, clearly thinking. "If we waited until tomorrow, let's say..." he went silent. Keeling let him think. He'd known Jurasco a long time. He knew when the other man's mind was working, how long it usually took to think through a problem.

"It could work," Jurasco finally said. "I'd need the ready 'Mechs from the security force here, potentially, and you'd need to sit on Cartwright out at Quickscell."

"I can do that," Keeling said. He paused. Now that he was leaning toward acting, he considered not acting. It was an exercise he'd taught himself when he was young and coming up, a stress-test on any big plan. Would it be better to wait? They'd get stronger, to be sure, but any day, another Taffy task force could appear at the jump point. More time swung both ways.

Cartwright at Quickscell was no problem. He was the worst of all things, an honest man. Cared about his employees, wanted to turn a profit, worked by the book. He'd gotten the job under the Jade Falcons and kept it after because he kept the production quotas up every quarter. Keeling wouldn't even have to sit hard on him; he'd be so scared of events he'd lock his own plant down tight and sit it through.

And Keeling knew things Jurasco didn't. There was a Lyran-flagged freighter inbound, due in a couple weeks. If it arrived and found the system inclined to rejoin the Commonwealth, it could jump out and summon a Lyran task force to secure the planet before the Taffy yokels could react. It was two months' travel to the jump point, sure, but lightspeed was faster, and that transit distance would give the Lyrans time to react.

"Do it," Keeling said. "Nobu's too scared to act. Let's act for him."

"What if he reacts poorly?"

Keeling chuckled. "Who do you think the Commonwealth will be more likely to choose, Jurasco? A disgraced nobleman they've run out of their space once already, or the man who returned a modern BattleMech factory to the fold?"

PALACE OF THE GODS
DELIVERANCE
PANDORA
TAMAR PACT
5 MAY 3152

Deschanes burst in without warning. Nobu looked up from where he'd been conversing with his social secretary. "Nessa?"

"Get out," Deschanes said to the secretary. Her voice was like ice. *"Now."*

Nobu nodded the young man away and waited while he gathered his case and strode quickly out of the room. As soon as the door panel slid closed, Deschanes stepped closer. "Keeling made a move."

"What?"

"I just got a confirmation code," she said. "A go-code."

"A go-code..." Nobu stood up suddenly. "He couldn't! I'm the only one—" He stopped. "Oh, no."

Deschanes nodded. "Jurasco."

"That son of a bitch," Nobu said. He sat back down slowly, eyes unfocused, mind racing. "We have to stop it."

"We can't," Deschanes said. "It's too late."

"But—"

Light flashed from behind Nobu, from outside the window. It silhouetted Deschanes in stark profile against the wall for a half-instant. He spun his chair around; as he did, the building rattled almost imperceptibly as the ground shock reached them, a moment before a low rumble shook the thick transpex window.

Smoke roared into the sky from the direction of the Tamar Armed Forces military headquarters. The top floors of the building were aflame. Nobu recalled hearing the size of the bomb they'd planted there, but the numbers hadn't meant anything to him.

Seeing the damage, now they did.

"*Damn* him," Nobu whispered.

HOME GUARD HQ
DELIVERANCE
PANDORA
TAMAR PACT
5 MAY 3152

The first thing Zee felt was pain. A wracking cough tore at her chest. Her lungs burned and her throat felt like it was full of hot sand. She felt grit in her eyes even while they were closed. Her ears rang. She didn't move, despite a terrifying fear, waiting until her body started reporting again. Everything hurt everywhere, but nothing was screaming for immediate attention. That was good. She hunched her shoulders and felt debris move on her back, but it wasn't heavy.

Acoustic tile, her mind filled in. *The ceiling collapsed.*

She worked her way to her knees and elbows and risked wiping her eyes. She blinked rapidly, feeling the grit lessen as her tear ducts did their job, and wiped at the corner of her eyes with the backs of her hands. When she risked a cracked eyelid, the light was low and flickering.

"Khaled," she called out, or croaked. She worked her mouth and tongue, spat, swallowed, and tried again. This time it felt recognizable, but she barely heard it through the ringing in her ears. "Call out," she ordered.

It had been just Henderson, Fritsch, and her in the intel shop. "Bill? Gina?"

There may have been a noise in response. Zee rocked back into a kneel on her heels, ceiling tile and other debris cascading off her back. She looked around, squinting and working the last of the grit out of her eyes. The ceiling had collapsed completely. She was looking at broken ductwork and the skewed thin-metal frames the tiles had hung on. An emergency light on the wall was dangling from its wiring, blinking haphazardly.

"Gina! Bill!"

"Here." She twisted around to see a desk lift and slide to the side; Bill Henderson emerged from beneath it, one hand pressed against the side of his head. He was covered head-to-toe in dust and dirt, as if he'd just come off the infantry mud course. Zee imagined she must look the same. She worked her mouth and spat again. It felt like she had crap in her sinuses.

Taking a deep breath, she pushed herself back onto her heels, careful to feel for pain in her back or legs. Nothing beyond the general tenor of "ow" appearing, she stood. Her balance was sketchy but coming back; she put a hand on a ferrocrete column next to her. It trembled. She snatched her hand back.

Zee blinked and willed her mind to reset. "Gina?"

"He—here," Fritsch said, emerging from beneath a chair and an overturned shelf case. "What happened?"

Zee spat again. "Bomb," she said. "We'd have gotten an alert from anything else. Time to go."

"We under attack, Zee?" Henderson asked. The big infantryman was on his feet, dabbing his head and looking at his bloody fingertips.

"No, I don't think so," she said. "Feels like just one bomb. Just the one blast. If it were an attack, the hits would keep coming. Doesn't mean it's not cover for something else, but..."

"A bomb," Fritsch repeated.

"I think so. But it doesn't matter. We evac. Hit the burn boxes, wipe the drives, smash everything you can find. Two minutes. Then we bug out and find out what's happening."

"You sure, Staff Sergeant?" Henderson gestured around. "If it's just one bomb, this is a lot of work to destroy..."

Zee pulled a stack of noteputers from beneath the wreckage of her desk, ejected the datacards, and crushed them beneath her heel. "Look around, Bill. We won't be back in this office, and it'll be unsecure the whole time. Destruction protocol. Carry what you think is most important, but the rest goes. We're not leaking secrets to a salvager on my watch."

All three of them bent to the task. Zee put several noteputers and a collection of datacards into a messenger bag and slung it over her shoulder. At the end of two minutes, the room looked even more destroyed. Fritch had hoisted a bulging ruck onto her shoulder, and Henderson...

Henderson was securing the chin strap of an infantry helmet. He already wore a combat ruck and had an old but serviceable AX-22 assault rifle hung on a sling across his chest.

"That's what's most important?" Zee asked.

Henderson grinned. "If we need it, it will be." He reached down, ejected the AX's magazine, banged it against his helmet to clear dust, then reseated it and shot the charger. "Time to go?"

"Time to go," Zee confirmed.

"Go where?" Fritsch asked.

"Rally point for building evac is two blocks west, out of the direct line for emergency response," Zee said. "As you would know if you paid attention in the safety briefings." Fritsch had the good grace to gulp. "We will head in that direction, gathering what intelligence we can, and rally with the rest of the team."

"So, follow SOP is what you're saying," Henderson said.

"Follow SOP," Zee confirmed. The ringing in her ears was already fading, or else she was getting used to it, but now that she was up and moving, she felt sweat cloying the crud that had slipped down the back of her battledress where it rubbed against her skin. That was going to purely suck down all those flights of stairs.

"And when we find out what's going on?" Fritsch asked.

Zee thought about the list, her private list, still on one of the noteputers in her messenger bag. "We act accordingly."

PALACE OF THE GODS
DELIVERANCE
PANDORA
TAMAR PACT
5 MAY 3152

The water in the glass on Nobu's desk trembled in concentric rings as the heavy tread of BattleMechs approached the Palace of the Gods. He stood with his back to the desk, looking out the floor-to-ceiling transpex windows, fuming. Deschanes sat at a small desk off to the side of the large office, trying to get a handle on what was happening.

A single 'Mech stopped in the courtyard of the Palace. It was big, hulking, with a bulbous head and canopy, the latter of which cracked open to reveal a man in a red and black combat suit. The man began to climb down.

"That's him," Deschanes said from behind him. "Jurasco." Nobu grunted. "He says his lance is here to guarantee your personal security until you can be moved to a secure location," she added.

"*My* personal security," Nobu spat.

"Per the plan," Deschanes said without emotion.

Nobu spun away from the window. "The plan. *My* plan. The plan he and that asshole Keeling co-opted and launched *without me*? *That* plan?"

Deschanes said nothing.

Nobu swallowed and breathed out, desperately trying to regain his balance. He didn't want that toad Jurasco to see him flustered, not under any circumstances. He moved to the desk and sat down.

A short while later, the door to his office slid open. From outside, in the foyer where the planetary staff worked, came the sound of chaos as people dashed around, cried, shouted, or did whatever they chose as a reaction to stress. For now, Deschanes and he were following the script they had worked out across the last several months. If Jurasco forced them off-script, Nobu would deal with it. *Somehow.*

Jurasco strode in, his face impassive but his body language haughty. *More haughty than usual*, Nobu corrected himself. The cretin stopped before the desk and braced as if to attention. "My lord."

"How *dare* you," Nobu said.

"Would you prefer to argue about the past, or focus on the opportunity I've presented to you?"

"*You've* presented to me." Nobu glared at him. "Not you and Keeling?"

"Water under the bridge," Jurasco said. "I look to the future."

"We are not ready," Nobu said.

"We will never be your definition of ready," Jurasco said. "But here we are. I have come to escort you to your bunker, my lord. The releases to the news media are queued and ready; per the schedule, they go public in about seven minutes."

"Six," Deschanes said, from the side.

"If I choose to release them." Nobu steepled his fingers and looked over them.

"If you do not, you squander this opportunity," Jurasco said. "It will not come again. Leutnant-Colonel Bredell is dead. So is much of his staff. Arcturus will send new leadership, and you will have to start again. What will the state of the world be then? What will the state of the Commonwealth be? What if the Jade Falcons return?"

"That is not for you to decide," Deschanes said. Nobu, who'd known her long enough, heard the slight tremble of emotion in her voice.

"It is decided," Jurasco said. "Get up, my lord. It's time to go. The next stage of the plan is critical. It will go so much easier if you make the announcement live."

Nobu wanted to work his mouth, to spit, but his politician's calculating mind was taking over. Putting aside the betrayal and the loss of control, Jurasco was right. However they had gotten here, they were in the situation Nobu had planned for for so long.

The plan could still work. Except... "What about the mercenaries?" he asked as he stood.

Jurasco wasn't talented enough to hide the smirk of condescension as Nobu did, but the baron ignored it. "They're out of town," he replied. "If we get this sewed up tonight, it'll be over before they know about it."

Nobu shook his head. "Not good enough. I want them eliminated."

Jurasco shrugged. "I anticipated as much. B Company of the Guard battalion is already headed toward their cantonment. It's only a matter of hours."

Nobu took a last look across his desk, then sighed. It still rankled. But much of life rankled. You could rage against it—or you could seize opportunity when it came to you.

"Nessa," he said, stepping around the desk, "I want to be on the phone with Yao Kevinsson in the car."

CHAPTER 8

HOME GUARD HQ
DELIVERANCE
PANDORA
TAMAR PACT
5 MAY 3152

The sun was setting by the time Zee and the others reached the ground floor. The stairwells were clogged with dusty, coughing people, some in uniform, some not. Everyone was too dirty to make out details, but the shapes of battledress were discernable beneath the grime. Almost no one carried a shoulder weapon, which made Bill Henderson stand out. Henderson had never been a small man; he stood out already.

Zee's whole body flickered with new pain every step down the stairwell. She couldn't imagine what Henderson's knee must feel like, but she put that out of her mind. Getting outside was more important than pain.

Outside, people milled about. Some moved through the crowd toward designated rally points, either singly or in clumps. Everyone was uniformly covered in gray dust. Zee recognized a handful of people in the moving groups from the old Two-Six Arcturan she knew had seen the elephant. Veterans were hard to faze; they'd deal with the shakes later, after the mission.

"Let's go," she told her people, and led them through the throng. Others of her group may have been in another part of the building; if so, she wanted to make sure they were safe. The rally point was also where her CO would expect to find her.

If I still have a CO...

Zee twisted as the bodies clumped together, trying to look up. The entire top of the skyscraper was afire. It was way too many floors to try and count, but her task force HQ was on a high floor, and no other target in the building made sense. Hell, you needed a TAF ID to get above the sixtieth floor anyway.

Which means a TAF trooper carried that bomb up there.

Zee's intelligence-trained brain clicked into place. Yes, someone who was not in the Tamar Armed Forces could have spoofed the uniforms and IDs and gotten access past the security systems and patrols and placed an explosive. But Mira Gleason and Zee's other mentors had pounded the simple maxim of Occam's Razor into her over and over again: the simplest solution was often correct.

"Looks steady," Henderson said. Zee glanced at him; he was half-turned so he could look where she looked, but he kept his head on a swivel, checking to see if the pressure in front of them had lessened. He caught her glance and shrugged. "The building, I mean. Fire, sure, but the ferrocrete's rated for, it and if the wracking stress didn't do it in the bombing..."

"I'll take your word for it," Zee said. Then she spat. Again. Everyone around them was coughing or sneezing or spitting, or all three. The dust made it impossible not to. She glowered at the mass of people, then looked at Henderson. "Can you make a hole?"

Henderson grinned. The rifle was slung across his chest, muzzle-down, and he let go of it to make a megaphone of his hands. The rifle slid back against his body armor, drawn by its sling. He called, "No, dammit, don't throw up *here!*"

Space opened in front of them as people shoved into their neighbors to clear the supposed vomit area. Zee twisted sideways and pushed into the mass. She felt Fritsch grab the strap of her shoulder bag, and knew Henderson would bring up the rear.

A minute later, they were past the crush. Zee stepped to the side and put her hand against cool brick. She leaned into a nearby building, relishing the sensation of free air and the lack of crowding. Claustrophobia wasn't a fear she suffered from, but that many people...

"Staff Sergeant," Henderson said in a low voice.

Zee looked up at him. He had grabbed his rifle. While she watched, he pushed it out and back, testing the play on the sling. She opened her mouth to ask what he wanted even as she looked where he was looking.

Three people knelt on the ferrocrete at their designated rally point a half-block away. All of them held their hands behind their heads. A short squad of TAF infantry stood around them, weapons not leveled, but at the ready.

"No one move," Zee said. She glanced around, up at the buildings and back at the crowd, as if she were a gawker, while her mind raced. There was no reason, none, that her people, or anyone in the intelligence shop, should be on their knees in the street. *None.*

The weight of her pack, and the heavier weight of the list of names, pressed down on her shoulders. She looked up again at the burning top of the building. A fresh wash of metal flushed the back of her throat.

As she turned back to the street, the wall she leaned against flashed to life. It was a sidewalk newspanel flatscreen. She squinted against the bright lights and stepped back, staring like everyone else nearby.

Yao Kevinsson's soft, mopey face appeared. There was no sound, but subtitles ran across the bottom of the screen.

—ATTACK AT THE TAFFY HQ TONIGHT THE WORK OF TRAITORS AND OFFWORLD MERCENARIES, SAYS SOURCES LINKED TO HIS LORDSHIP BARON NOBU—

"How can they know that already?" Fritsch asked.

"They can't," Zee and Henderson said at the same time. They looked at each other and Henderson nodded at Zee.

"They can't," she said. "If for no other reason, the people who would tell them are either on their knees over there or standing here with me."

"I don't understand," Fritsch said.

"It's a coup," Zee said. "Or a rebellion or something. All the nuggets we've been seeing, they're connected somehow. And it's not someone at the baron's office. It's the baron. It had to be. There's no other way even a toad like Kevinsson would be saying this drivel."

"So what do we do?" Henderson asked.

Zee looked at him. "Do?"

"I already went back on one oath, Staff Sergeant," Henderson said. "I'm not doing that twice."

"Do you think the mercenaries are really in on it?" Fritsch asked. She was watching the chyron scroll past, repeating what Zee had already read, but clearly not fully processed.

"They just got here," Henderson said halfheartedly.

"No, they're not in on it," Zee said. "I met them."

"They just got here," Fritsch repeated in a completely different tone, one that said *you can't possibly know that*. The professional soldier in Zee's mind approved. She'd just said something incredibly naïve, and Fritsch was correct to call her on it.

But Zee nonetheless believed it.

"We go to the mercenaries," Zee decided. "Bill, we need a car."

"Let's go a couple streets over, then," he suggested. He stepped away from the wall. Zee made ready to follow.

Fritsch didn't move. "How do we know we can trust them?"

Zee pointed toward the kneeling people. "Do you think you can trust that?"

Fritsch looked that way, then back. The flickering light of newspanel painted the dust plastered to her face by sweat a weird morass of pastels. "Maybe it's just a precaution."

Zee stepped closer to her. "I won't make you come with me, Gina. You can go surrender to them, or you can go and hide until it's all over. But I'm going to the mercenaries, because they're the only people I can be reasonably sure aren't involved. And I think Bill is going with me."

"I am," Henderson said. "Come with us, Gina."

"I—" Fritsch stopped, looked back at the kneeling group. While she did, one of the guards slung his weapon and pulled a set of plastic restraints from his belt, then stepped close to one of the kneeling prisoners.

"Hell with that," she said. "Let's go."

CAMP DELMAR CLAY
DELIVERANCE
PANDORA
TAMAR PACT
5 MAY 3152

Camp Delmar Clay, named for an old Legion hero who'd died in the Clan Invasion, was far enough outside the city that only the light and smoke was visible. The duty watch in the security shack had hit the alert button as soon as the first news reports arrived, and it was sheer luck that Master Sergeant Buthra Azarri, senior Legion technician, was nearby.

The Sikh was the senior Legion leader still present at the camp. Major Carlyle had taken all the officers and combat elements to Vandmaal for in-the-field training, and wasn't due back for four more days. The Legion ran *very* light on officers, preferring to let enlisted experts carry the team leadership load.

"Anything new?" Azarri asked, ducking back into the guardhouse.

"No," said Private Tiffany Surla. "Just repeating the nonsense about us bombing the Taffy HQ." The private was one of the two squads of rifle infantry left behind as base security.

Another woman, Staff Sergeant Susan Osmonoglu, stepped into the small shack. "Anything new?"

"No," Azarri said, as Private Surla frowned at the new arrival.

"No word from the major?"

"They are under emissions control," Azarri reminded her. "The next scheduled comm check is tomorrow morning." He stepped out of the shack and looked through the gate toward the city. The city glow was dirty and diffuse, broken by the pillar of smoke rising until the high-altitude winds caught it and spread it like a blanket across the sky. He stepped back inside.

"Private Surla," he said. "Rouse your sergeant and the rest of the security force. Camp Clay is now on lockdown, under my authority."

As the private nodded and bent to her task, Azarri turned to Osmonoglu. "Susan, I want everything necessary to bring the battalion to full combat readiness loaded on anything that will move. Call it an exercise, if you must. But I want us ready to bug out and join the rest of the Legion ASAP."

"That will take hours," she said. "Are you sure?"

Azarri inclined his head toward the small flatscreen in the shack, still playing a loop of footage from downtown. "Are you not?"

"We don't have orders for that," she protested.

"I just issued them," Azarri said with quiet dignity. "Now, please attend to it."

"If you say so," she said, then turned and ran for the hangars, already shouting into her comm.

Azarri stepped back outside.

Something is happening, he thought. *I do not know yet what it is.* But Azarri knew his duty. The Legion had nothing to do with the bombing, but people in stress, certainly people without firm leadership, sometimes reacted to chaos with violence. He stepped back inside.

"Issue the pre-evacuation order, as well," he told Private Surla. "No one is to depart. Instead, form up on the supply convoy. We will all go and join the battalion."

"Yes, Master Sergeant," Surla said, her eyes wide.

Azarri stepped back outside. *Now the only question is whether or not we will have time.* As soon as he asked the question, he knew the answer. They would not. It would not matter how many minutes or hours they did get. There would not be enough. He stepped back to the doorway.

"Change of plans: every vehicle is to depart as soon as it loaded and proceed independently to join the major and the battalion."

Private Surla nodded again.

DELIVERANCE
PANDORA
TAMAR PACT
5 MAY 3152

The vehicle Henderson chose was a seven-passenger family van, fuel-cell powered, with faded, semi-rusted edges and a suspension that had been built sometime around the Second Succession War. Zee sat in the passenger seat, one leg up on the dash, chewing the cuticles of her fingers. Henderson drove, his rifle on the floor between their bucket seats. Gina Fritsch sat on the first bench in the back.

Traffic was a snarl, both because the whole city was panicking and because armored vehicles painted in the black and red of the Pandora Planetary Guard blocked certain intersections. Zee frowned as they passed another roadblock, crewed by a bored-looking infantry squad who just made "turn-left" hand motions until Henderson obeyed.

"Why isn't anyone else asking questions?" Henderson asked.

"What?" Zee blinked and looked at him.

Henderson indicated the rearview mirror with his chin. "Like those troopers. HQ explodes, and they already have orders? There's a contingency plan for this that has them blocking streets?" He shook his head. "I haven't been a soldier forever, but this isn't my first day. There's no way whoever is left at the top of the chain of command put all this together while the debris was still settling."

"Some of them *are* asking questions," Zee said. "But they have orders. In the absence of authority, you follow the last order given. Right now they're scared, reacting, but someone up there is giving orders."

"Who is it?" Fritsch asked, from the backseat.

"If we assume they called the whole task force staff in before they blew it..." Zee thought for a moment. "Next in line is probably the CO of the Three-Seven Panzer." She blinked and put her feet down to sit up straight. "Kommandant Hakima."

"Who we think might be dirty," Henderson said, nodding.

Zee opened her mouth, but new flashing lights in front of them stopped her. Another squad of PPG infantry was deployed in front of their tracked APC, armed but making traffic-control motions with their hands. Behind them the twin minigun barrels in the APC's turret pointed straight at the line of traffic, a less than subtle sign of menace.

"What now?" Henderson muttered.

"Listen," Zee said. She touched the window control and slid the glass down. She tried to ignore the sound of engines idling in the synthetic canyon of the city street... "There."

"I don't hear anything," Fritsch said.

"There," Zee said again. "It's—"

"'Mechs," Henderson said, pointing.

The infantry squad blocking the street turned with everyone else to watch as the twelve-meter-tall war machines strode past, moving slowly at maybe twenty KPH in deference to the crowded streets. Zee counted at least seven, and saw more shadows past them, as another force moved parallel down another street.

"More PPG," Henderson said. "I heard they were getting 'Mechs."

"From Red Devil," Fritsch put in. "It was on the news."

"*We* don't even have 'Mechs," Zee said.

"The mercenaries do," Henderson told her.

Zee made a face. "What direction are those 'Mechs going, Bill?"

"South, maybe southeast."

"What's out there?"

"Nothing, until you get to...oh." Henderson grinned wryly. "The mercenaries."

"We have to get out of this traffic," Zee said. "*Now.* We have to get in front of this column and warn them."

"You mean get in front of 'Mechs," Fritsch said, disbelief clear in her voice.

"Standard route march speed for LCAF 'Mechs in movement is 45 KPH," Zee recited. "This thing is faster than that. We can warn the mercs, make sure they're ready."

Henderson eyed an alley, muttered a curse, and cranked the wheel over. "Not much faster," he said as he pressed the accelerator.

CHAPTER 9

Ronan felt like a trespasser in the cockpit of Grayson's *Marauder*. The 75-ton BattleMech had been lovingly restored by the Odessa militia technicians, including completely replacing the cockpit. It even had that new-'Mech smell.

But it didn't feel like *his*.

In the heads-up display in front of him, he saw the 'Mechs and tanks of C Company attacking a fixed position held by Bel's B Company command lance and her battle armor platoon. It was a completely one-sided attack; the C Company machines outmassed and outclassed Bel's medium lance, but that was the point. No reasonable commander ever looked for a fair fight. Bel's unit was going to lose, and everyone knew it. What Ronan was watching for, and what the exercise was supposed to be measuring, was how costly she could make C Company's victory.

Motion at the edge of his HUD made him look away. A big, scarred *Regent* stalked up next to him. It was Curtain, the ex-Clan, ex-a-lot-of-things who had come back from Condor with Bel. He commanded Ronan's A2 Lance in A Company. Ronan had found him to be a font of quiet wisdom and an absolute demon in combat. After their first sim, Bel had pulled Ronan aside and whispered, "Now I'm *really* glad I didn't have to fight him." Curtain's lance would have this position tomorrow, but the rumor mill said he expected his lance to actually win.

If anyone can do it, Ronan thought.

"Major," Curtain sent. "How goes the engagement?"

"It turns out that when you know the playbook," Ronan said, "you can find ways to beat the playbook. Tang sent his tanks around the flanks, a move right out of the Lyran doctrine manual for combined-arms operations. The problem is, Bel learned that same doctrine on Coventry, and she makes a hobby of putting herself in the other guy's shoes."

"So Captain Cai is taking greater losses than he expects," Curtain said.

"He is," Ronan said. "And he's not going to like this, either." He toggled a separate channel open. "Padgit. Go."

"Roger, Major," came the reply.

"Reinforcements?" Curtain asked. When Ronan grunted, Curtain chuckled. "But for which side, I wonder?"

Ronan grinned like a shark. "Neither," he said. "What can I do for you, Lieutenant?"

"I have been unable to raise Camp Clay," Curtain reported. "I wished to deliver the morning logistics report, as the senior technician requested, but there was no reply."

Ronan frowned. "Radio or landline?"

"I tried both," Curtain said.

"Buthra is kind of obsessive about that kind of thing," Ronan said offhandedly while his mind worked. "You trust the landline?"

Curtain chuckled again. The *Regent* waved one of its arms, indicating the landscape. "This is not so different from home," he said. "There are no mountains, and the forest has nothing on the jungle, but I know what to look for. I used a forest ranger station. It was empty, but the carrier signal was there."

"Strange," Ronan said. Movement across the field caught his eye. An old hover APC converted to carry cargo instead of infantry was scuttling across the field. He recognized it as one of the logistical vehicles Azarri and his technicians had salvaged out of the scrapyard on Garrison what felt like forever ago.

Ronan frowned. *We didn't bring any log vehicles with us.*

A red light blinked on his comm board, the emergency channel. He toggled it live.

"—situation in the city went to shit, Major. Come in."

"This is Carlyle. Say again."

"Major, thank the gods," a woman's voice said. "Private Gale Crumlin, Charlie Technical Company, sir. Are we the first to reach you?"

"The first what?"

There was a pause. "We are, then. Shit. Sorry, sir..."

"Private, what's going on?"

"You haven't seen any news since last night, have you sir?"

"Wait one," Ronan said. He touched his comm board, set it to all frequencies. "Exercise cancelled. Rally on me." Then he focused his attention on the APC now slowing in front of his *Marauder*. "Now, what's on the news that I should have seen?"

"There was a bomb, sir," the astech said. "Taffy HQ got blown up, and the locals think we had something to do with it."

CAMP DELMAR CLAY
DELIVERANCE
PANDORA
TAMAR PACT
6 MAY 3152

"You should not be here, my lord," Deschanes said as the limo's drive fans spun down and the vehicle's weight settled on its skirts. Light flashed through the rear window slits as the news vans around them slid to a stop and the spotlights flashed to bright, LED-powered life.

"*They* are here, so this is where I need to be." Nobu indicated the light with his chin. He didn't want to be here, either, but he understood the necessity, just as he understood the necessity of the discreet body armor sewn into his overcoat. "What is the security situation?"

"Jurasco says it is secure," Deschanes said, derision dripping from her words. "I have confirmed through my own sources the compound was essentially empty when the Planetary Guard company finally arrived to secure it."

"Great," Nobu muttered. He levered himself across the seat and touched the button to open the gull-wing door. A moment later he was out, in the brisk midmorning sun and the cool, dry air. He sniffed and stifled a sneeze. There was a harsh taint in the air, the telltale smoke of burning plastics mixed with something chemical that singed his sinuses. "Great," he repeated under his breath.

Reporters crowded near, followed closely by holocam operators with heavy, multi-lenses cams on body harnesses that minimized motion to capture a clean, stabilized holo. Jerky HV tended to make people change the channel. That was bad for ratings. All of them shouted—as respectfully as one could attempt to shout over one's peers, but shouting nonetheless— for his attention, yet there was little doubt about who his first call would be.

"Yao," he said, pointing.

"My lord baron," Yao Kevinsson said, "what can you tell us about the state of the manhunt?"

The manhunt. Nobu smiled inside. *So many people just regurgitate the script they're given. It makes everything so much easier.* "I can tell you it's going well," he said with all due mock severity. He wanted to grin, but this wasn't the time. The top of the Taffy HQ building was still smoking. "The fact that we're standing where we're standing should prove that."

The night and the morning had been profitable, even if the mercenaries' support staff had escaped. Nobu had been forced to admit the plan might have been as ready as Keeling and Jurasco had evidently believed it was. The scripted news snippets and his delicately choreographed play of rumormongering had put public opinion exactly where he wanted it.

The original plan had been to pin the attack on the loyalist TAF officers he hadn't been able to suborn. *That would have worked,* he thought, *because there were so few who would have escaped the bomb and my carefully curated cast of turncoats.* But the presence of the mercenaries had given everything a very convenient off-world frame, and Nobu had seized it.

Now he had the world believing the loyalists were in league with the offworld mercenaries. The mercenaries, who no one really knew anything about, had disappeared without a trace. And who had conveniently left this cantonment they could stage in any way they wanted for the HV people.

"What particulars can you give us, my lord?" Kevinsson persisted. "Within operational security, of course."

"Well, I can assure you all Deliverance itself is secure. There have been no more attacks, and both the new commander of the loyal Tamar garrison forces, Kommandant Hakima and Colonel Jurasco of the Pandora Planetary Guard have both assured me that no one can approach the city. The sixth columnists inside the Tamar garrison have been apprehended and secured. And as you can see, the mercenaries..." Nobu just spread his hands and looked around. *Go ahead and fill in the blank however you like*, he thought.

"The mercenaries are not in the city," a woman's voice said clearly. Nobu looked to the side and successfully hid his moue of distaste. "They were not here last night, isn't that right, my lord?" asked Helen Parendoupolos.

"Enough were here that we have captives," Nobu said. "Now if you'll excuse me, I must go and check in on progress with those captives." He smiled a tight, polite smile that said courtesy but not pleasure. Appropriate for the morning after a failed coup attempt.

"See that she's kept away from anything important," Nobu said *sotto voce* to Deschanes as they walked. Across the sea of pavement strode a pair of Planetary Guard BattleMechs. Nobu knew they'd be headline holo images on every news network. He approved. Especially the black-and-red paint scheme.

Nowhere did they show the Tamar coat of arms.

But if anyone noticed that absence, it would be Parendoupolos.

"Of course, my lord," Deschanes said.

A few minutes later, they entered a building guarded by two infantry privates in PPG red and black; both had the good grace to snap to attention as the baron passed through the door. In the anteroom stood Jurasco, looking at a noteputer.

"Have you salvaged anything out of this mess?" Nobu said, without preamble.

"Quite a bit," the big man said. "We took seventeen prisoners."

"Seventeen."

"Yes, sir. Including, as it turns out, the mercenaries' senior technician."

Nobu sighed. "A mechanic."

"Senior, yes."

"You want me to parade a *mechanic* out in front of the newspeople?" Nobu gestured at the door he'd just come through. "You've got PPG BattleMechs out there, a couple burning cars so the smells and sights are right, and a mechanic."

"And sixteen others."

"Are any of those sixteen named Carlyle?"

Jurasco frowned. "You know they're not."

"Any MechWarriors?"

"No."

"Officers?"

"No."

Nobu took off his soft leather gloves and slapped them against his thigh. "Then you have nothing." He glanced at Deschanes, but she said nothing. "What's next?"

"Next, we take down the mercenaries in the field," Jurasco said. "I have the strength, with the Guards battalion and what I can pull from Red Devil. Keeling has had the ready 'Mechs repainted as PPG machines. The layman will never know any different."

"And you can do that?"

"My lord?"

"Defeat the mercenaries?" Nobu glanced around. "Your 'Mechs were late last night. And we still don't know how many mercenaries got away."

Jurasco laughed. "The mercenaries are on a training exercise, my lord. They have paint rounds and their lasers are dialed down. It'll be easy."

Nobu sighed. "This needs to go right, Jurasco."

Jurasco grinned like a wolf. "Trust me."

VANDMAAL CROSSING
VANDMAAL
PANDORA
TAMAR PACT
6 MAY 3152

The vehicles appeared all throughout the morning and early afternoon, having driven all night. Singly or in pairs, or in one case a trio of ammo carriers. Amazingly, the bulbous, road-clearing bulk of a Savior repair vehicle even made it, overloaded with techs and astechs on every surface. It had immediately deployed its mobile field base and begun converting the Legion 'Mechs and tanks away from training configurations and into combat readiness.

There was no one on Pandora Ronan wanted to get into a gunfight with. But if the gunfight was coming, he and his people were going to be ready.

"You know this is nuts, right?" Bel was saying. She, Curtain, Ronan, and Tang Cai stood in the shade of the MFB in a close circle, listening to the speaker's story.

"Yes," Zee Khaled said. "But it's happening."

Ronan looked past her to the bulk of Grayson's *Marauder*, where it stood nearby in standby. It had been the first machine through the MFB, piloted by a technician while Ronan met with what passed for the Legion's staff. After a moment of searching its familiar shape for insight and finding none, Ronan looked back down at Khaled.

One of the last vehicles had been a civilian van with Khaled and two of her people, along with Staff Sergeant Gleason from the Legion S-2 and two of her people they'd grabbed from Camp Clay before escaping. The drive had apparently been a working session, while the big Tamar infantry sergeant drove.

"Nuts," Bel repeated. She looked around at the group. "How can anyone believe this?"

"Right now, people believe whatever they see on HV," Gleason said. "It's proven psychology. They've taken a body blow to their sense of the world. To their sense of reality. Until they find some equilibrium, people are going to trust things they already trust."

"So, the crazies get crazier," Cai said. Gleason nodded. "Great."

"We weren't even *there!*" Bel said.

"Of course not," Gleason said. "We were out of the city. To make sure we had an alibi while our allies did the dirty work. We're probably out here planning our final assault on the city, where we'll force everyone into Clan-style castes. It'll be a hundred times worse than when the Clans were really here."

"At least," Zee said, nodding.

"Or that's what they'll say on the news," her woman, Fritsch, put in. "Especially Kevinsson."

"And the people will believe it." Gleason didn't sound pleased, but she did speak with finality. "Believe it, Captains, Major. Eventually it'll calm down, and then people will care about the truth. But now?" She shook her head.

"What's our play, then?" Ronan asked. "Do we get on the news, too? Present our story?"

"We have a story?" Cai asked.

"'We had nothing to do with any of this' is our story," Ronan blurted.

"Won't work," Gleason said. "For every reason I just said."

"Then what do we do?"

"Nothing would be best," Gleason said. "We hide out here long enough, people will calm down. Some reason will return."

"Can't do that," Khaled and Bel said at the same time. Khaled gestured for Bel to go first.

"Buthra and the others," Bel said. Ronan grimaced.

At least a dozen, maybe more if no more vehicles appeared, Legion support staff had never made it out of Camp Clay. The stragglers said Azarri was still there, trying to get transport for the last few people together. Gleason and the other spooks had been in one of the last vehicles, and they'd actually *seen* Pandora Planetary Guard 'Mechs on the horizon as they'd left. If their comrades had been taken into custody, or worse...

"I have the whole battalion to think about," Ronan said. He looked at Khaled. "Why do you say I can't do nothing?"

Khaled shrugged. "The other guys, whoever they are, can't let you. They sent 'Mechs after your cantonment. You weren't there. Now they'll come after you here."

Ronan looked around the circle, meeting each person's gaze, and got grim nods in return. Even Tang Cai, who looked like he was treading water with a ten-kilogram weight tied to his feet, nodded firmly.

Ronan looked back at the *Marauder*. His fingertips tingled. Cold sweat trickled down his back. In his bones, in his soul, he knew they were right. Whoever was behind this, they'd already declared war on the Legion in the court of public opinion. The real thing couldn't be far behind. Not if their plot, whatever it ultimately was, was going to succeed.

They couldn't.

They'd need scapegoats, if nothing else.

"Okay," he said, his gaze hardening as he looked back at the group. "Then let's get ready for them."

CHAPTER 10

It had taken a bit of searching, but Legion Sergeant Jack de Klerk had found a tree stout enough to hold the weight of his Gray Death Infiltrator battlesuit. He'd dug the armored fingers of his left hand into the tough bark and sapwood, locked the actuators into a clamp, and settled in to watch the remote feed from the sensors his squad had deployed across their gridline about an hour earlier, just as the sun was breaking the horizon. Yesterday had been another rough day in a series of rough days, and he relished the stillness.

Much of Scout Platoon had come from the old *Aufklärungsbataillon 29*, the Lyran recon battalion that had been cashiered on Garrison. Jack had been a squad leader there; he'd brought two of his troopers along into the Legion, but his third, Private Amina Kizito, had been a trooper in the Twenty-Sixth Arcturan Guards, and had come to the Legion with the major and the others. They all shared a lot of history and, more importantly, shared being handled roughly by the LCAF. They were all Legion lifers now.

Jack chuckled, alone in his helmet. The other Quokka squad—that's what the grunts called the Gray Death Infiltrator—under Sergeant Kamoku Hach were all former

Fusiliers, and while a lot of that dead mercenary unit's officers had been Lyran, its infantry was pure Armed Forces of the Federated Suns. All three privates had been trained in a different school than Hach and the others, and it showed. Every leader in the Legion understood why they were out here trying to get on the same page, but the effort was painful. It was like learning to walk a different way.

And then yesterday happened.

There hadn't been any idea that Deliverance could go up behind them. The moment they arrived on-planet, the major had put them straight into the field, trying to shake off the dust of the two-month transit. Hell, they'd expected to return there in another four days' time. Three suits were downchecked with real, not notional, damage from training mishaps. One of the C Company 'Mechs was limping on a frozen ankle actuator.

But for the bad guys to attack the noncombatants at Camp Clay...

Jack wasn't naïve. He knew there was no such thing as a noncombatant in a combat zone. He knew the easiest way to hurt someone was to threaten something they had to protect, someone who couldn't fight back. And he knew fair fights were for suckers.

But still, it rankled him that the Pandorans were too cowardly to come out and face them 'Mech to 'Mech. War was a profession like any other, and like any profession it had certain things *you did not do*. Knowing they were almost certainly coming, that there'd be a chance for payback, was the only thing that made this interminable waiting worthwhile.

The indicator in Jack's helmet heads-up display chirped at him; the magnetic anomaly detector in one of the remote sensors had gotten a scent of heavy metal. He opened the inset window and looked at the take. His eyes widened. *'Mechs*. He released the hold on the microservos holding his left hand to the tree, ready to move.

"They're coming," he told his squad. All four of the battlesuits would have gotten the alert, and he'd trained all three privates well enough they should recognize the signature of 60 to 80 tons of concentrated metal. Then he toggled the Scout Platoon frequency.

"Contact," he sent, and read off the coordinates before slugging the sensor report. He released his death grip on the tree trunk, flexed his hand, and then dropped the four meters or so to the forest floor. He already knew what the next orders would be. Hadn't they just been out here practicing this very scenario in this terrain?

"Move to confirm the contact," Sergeant Hach replied. "I'm sending this up the chain."

"Roger," Jack replied. He sent his squad the rally signal and charged the capacitors of the Gauss rifle in the battlesuit's right arm. He felt the balance of his suit shift as ammunition moved out of the ready magazine and into the feed tubes. *Thank the gods above and below for those techs*, he thought. Doing the next part with training rounds would have purely sucked.

As it was, he readied himself for a run. Normally his squad would reposition via stealth Cavalry helicopters, but the birds had another task this morning.

Time to get some back, Jack thought. For themselves and for the techs and others who'd made it out of the city.

And especially for the ones still there.

"The scouts have a signal," Bel sent.

Ronan's map display in the *Marauder*'s cockpit pinged with an update, showing unknown contacts along the direct route between Deliverance and the Vandmaal Forest.

Ronan eyed the position and grunted. "Right where we expected."

"Everyone can't be as smart as us."

"Well, me at least."

"Funny."

Ronan sighed. "Nothing new from the city? Nothing about Azarri or the others?"

"I'd have told you if there were."

Ronan squeezed and relaxed his grip on the *Marauder*'s controls. He imagined his great-grandfather sitting here, doing the exact same thing. Grayson's surviving journals and after-action interviews confirmed he felt many of the same things

Ronan felt now. Knowing he wasn't alone in this fear, this dread, had always given Ronan comfort, but not today. Today he worried he wasn't living up to Grayson's legacy.

The Legion didn't *have* to fight. There were courts of inquiry in every nation that would indict him for engaging in hostile acts on behalf of a handful of people he didn't actually have proof were being detained illegally. He was risking the lives of every other member of the Legion, as well as the new Legion's reputation, by offering combat to the approaching Pandoran forces.

Hell, there was no proof the version of events Zee Khaled presented was accurate. It could be the story permeating the local newsnets from the media was true: insurgents inside the Taffy garrison could have tried and failed to stage a coup. It was possible, certainly.

But it *felt* wrong and, more to the point, it was unlikely. That was ultimately what had swayed Ronan and the rest of the Legion leadership. It required too many things happening in too close proximity to chaotic events to hold credulity. He walked through the logic one more time.

Could insurgents have gotten a bomb into Taffy HQ? Certainly.

Could the decapitated Tamar Armed Forces organization have reacted with such immediacy to interdict the intelligence staff outside the HQ building? Zero chance.

Could the state of readiness of the Pandora Planetary Guard be so high that they could react and lock down the city within minutes of the explosion? Also zero chance. Even assuming the contingency plans were made and trained on, it would take longer than that just to get the units assembled and moving.

And, most damning, was there any evidence at all the Legion was involved?

None.

Ronan shook his head. Khaled was right. Something was rotten, and even if he didn't know exactly what it was, nothing in the laws of war required him to roll over and let someone who was acting shady take the Legion into custody, or worse.

"Send word to Khaled's team," he told Bel, "and let's do this."

"Roger," Bel confirmed.

Ronan squeezed the controls one last time. The decision was made, and he wasn't going to second-guess it. He'd given his word—and the word of the Legion—to Arcturus when he'd signed the contract with Leutnant-Colonel McQuade. He wasn't going to go back on that.

And he was going to get his people back.

NEAR DELIVERANCE
VANDMAAL
PANDORA
TAMAR PACT
7 MAY 3152

Zee Khaled held herself around the waist, clutching the straps of her restraint harness, staring at Bill Henderson as his helmeted head lolled against his own restraints, hard asleep. She'd learned the same tenets in basic training as he had—don't sleep when you want to, sleep when you can—but she'd never been able to sleep in helicopters.

A tap on her shoulder brought her head around. Staff Sergeant Gleason sat next to her, offering a wired headset that was plugged into the helicopter intercom. Zee took it and put it on over her boonie cap. The roaring vibration of the helicopter's almost-empty infantry bay lessened to an annoying hum.

"The Legion is about to make contact," Gleason said. Her voice was tinny but clear, and Zee could see her mouth form the words, so it was enough.

"PPG or TAF?" Zee asked.

"No word yet," Gleason replied. "My money is on PPG. Taffy armor wouldn't be enough to roll us up, even if we were stuck with paint rounds."

Zee nodded. That was her expectation as well. She looked around the compartment, trying to get what was actually happening to sit neatly in her head. The plot she'd been tracking, fearing she was imagining, had exploded into something far more dangerous and quick-moving than she could have expected.

And now she was in a stealth helicopter, with a team of mercenary infantry, going back to the lion's den to try and convince one of the lions they had chosen the wrong allies.

"You think it'll go to shooting," she said to Gleason. It wasn't a question.

The older woman looked away into the middle distance, thinking. After a moment she met Zee's stare and shrugged. "Always a chance it won't," she replied, "but I think it will. These people seem committed. They can't leave a loose end like the Legion rolling around. And they've sent 'Mechs."

"What about your Major Carlyle?"

Gleason chuckled. "He's got some rough edges, but he's hell itself in a fight, and once you get his sense of responsibility engaged, it takes an act of God to move him from what he thinks is right." She shook her head. "He doesn't want to fight, I can tell you that. But he's not going to back down either. We don't know about our people left behind. He'll fight for them."

Zee nodded. That matched her own quick read, but Gleason had known Major Carlyle longer. She breathed in and out consciously. The tingling in her fingertips told her adrenaline was flowing. She needed to manage that response.

Gleason poked her in the arm. "What about you?" She made a circle with her finger, indicating the helicopter. "This going to work?"

It was Zee's turn to shrug. "Hell if I know. But I have to try."

Gleason nodded and sat back. "Then you know how Major Carlyle's going to decide."

VANDMAAL FOREST
VANDMAAL
PANDORA
TAMAR PACT
7 MAY 3152

Hector Jurasco's mouth twitched every time his *BattleMaster*'s left foot slammed down. He sat eleven meters above the ground in the bulbous head of the 85-ton BattleMech, feeling invincible.

"No contacts, Colonel," said his Alpha Company commander, Hauptmann Edson.

"Roger," Jurasco said. He repeated the title in his head: *colonel*. He'd always wanted to earn that rank, back in the LCAF. It had driven him through the academy. It had driven him through his first field commands, and it had finally driven him to take the risk that had cost him his commission. It was too hard to climb the Lyran rank ladder without *interest*, without a powerful patron who could grease the wheels of Lyran martial society. He'd always resented that.

And now he was a colonel.

Because of interest.

Jurasco grinned and shook the thoughts off. He wasn't the man he'd been at twenty-seven. He saw the world through different eyes now.

"Sir," Edson started, then stopped.

"Something on your mind, Hauptmann?" Jurasco asked. He guided the *BattleMaster* around an obstacle, a three-meter boulder sticking out of the ground.

"I wanted you to know you can count on Alpha, Colonel," the boy blurted. And he was a boy, maybe twenty-four, a year or so younger than Jurasco had been when he'd gotten his first company command. "We haven't had a chance to exercise, to show you what we can do, but—"

"You wouldn't be here if I didn't know that, Hauptmann," Jurasco said.

"I know that, sir, and I appreciate it. It's just..."

"Just what?"

"Sir, barracks rumor was this would be a cakewalk, chasing down mercenaries with their machines in training mode, in the ass-end of everywhere." Edson's voice firmed up as he spoke. "Some of the boys and girls, well—Bravo and Charlie Company troopers, you understand—suggested you brought us because you knew it would be easy, like it was all we were good for."

It is all you're good for, Jurasco didn't say. But that was true of Bravo and Charlie, as well. Jurasco might have been long years out of the LCAF, but he remembered just fine what a well-oiled machine a BattleMech company could be. None of the Pandora Planetary Guard companies were anything close to that. They were all either green as grass or so old and out of practice they were still driving their new 'Mechs as if they were their old ones. Plemmons in Bravo Company insisted on using his *BattleMaster*'s hands like the clubs his old *Marauder* had.

The PPG didn't have access to the training academies of the Lyran Commonwealth. It had to do with what it had, and what it had was TAF rejects, militia, and the pilots out of the Red Devil security forces and test pilot pool.

Including young Hauptmann Edson, who owed his rank to his father's contributions to Red Devil's Malthus-backed "charities."

"You're here in case it's not that easy, Hauptmann," Jurasco said. "And I'll tell those other companies that when we return with a whole mercenary battalion of prisoners. The baron will probably give you all medals."

"Do you think there's much chance of that, sir?"

"I don't think there's any chance of that," Jurasco said honestly. "They came down here with regulated lasers and paint rounds. You see any 'Mech hangars around here? You think they can rearm out of trees?"

"No, sir..."

"But?"

The hesitation in Edson's voice was clear. "It's just...I read a report, sir. Said maybe some of the mercenaries' support staff got away."

Jurasco looked at Edson's 'Mech, another *BattleMaster*. He hadn't ordered any staff appreciations. That Edson had gone looking for the data was a good sign. He might make a good officer yet.

"Even if they did, what can they do? Bravo Company was on their base almost before they knew we were coming. You might be a crack MechWarrior, Edson, but can you stop a 'Mech lance without your 'Mech?"

"No, sir."

"Neither can a bunch of techs repair 'Mechs with tree branches and rocks," Jurasco told him. "If they don't surrender, we'll blow them all out of their 'Mechs and take them as scrap."

"Absolutely, Colonel," Edson said. "We're ready."

A red caret appeared on Jurasco's heads-up display. An enemy BattleMech.

"You better be," he whispered.

CHAPTER 11

VANDMAAL FOREST
VANDMAAL
PANDORA
TAMAR PACT
7 MAY 3152

The position where Ronan and the others had chosen to meet the enemy was along the edge of the Vandmaal Forest, where it abutted a lengthy series of low, rolling hills covered in brown-green low grasses and other plants. The armored scouts had done their jobs, planting remote sensors out on the moors and retreating into the tree line to monitor them. Now it was the rest of the Legion's turn.

Now it's my turn, Ronan thought.

He looked to his right, where Curtain's A2 Lance stood waiting with the rest of the company. Sergeant Ibiza had taken over his old *Gargoyle* with every grace, but Ronan still looked at the familiar machine and felt out of place in this *Marauder*. Ibiza stood with their lance, ready to fight if he gave the word.

Ronan squeezed the *Marauder*'s controls and looked forward. He had a job to do.

Scout Platoon's sensor data had already been relayed to every 'Mech, tank, and battlesuit in the Legion. The Pandorans had sent a company only; Staff Sergeant Khaled's information was they had most of a battalion available, which told Ronan and the other officers the Pandorans believed the Legion was still stuck down here on its training mission with paint in its shells and lasers dialed back to sunburn power. The Legion's leaders had convened a hasty plan to lean into that belief, but Ronan had doubts.

"You *always* have doubts," Bel had said when he'd voiced them to her and Ta-heng Cai.

"The other two companies could be out on our flanks," Ronan had persisted. "Or coming up behind. We could be doing exactly what they want us to do."

It was Cai who had cleared the fog.

"So what if they are?" he had said. "We can't do anything else but what we're doing. We're innocent of this attack. Our people are at risk. And we're not going to go quietly into internment and give up our 'Mechs and tanks while they sort it out, right?"

"Right," Bel had said.

"Right," Ronan had echoed, knowing Cai was right.

"Right," he whispered now. Cai was still right.

The first Pandoran 'Mech appeared from beneath a small rise, an old *Lineholder* someone must have pulled out of a militia armory somewhere. It was painted in Pandoran red and black, but it had clearly seen better days. Its left hip actuator was out of tune; the machine wasn't slowed, but there was a noticeable hitch in its step.

Its lancemates, and then the rest of the company, followed.

"Amateurs," Curtain huffed on the officer's channel.

"See how they're bunched up?" Cai added.

"Right out of the manual," Bel confirmed. "That's a column of twos, but they should be in movement to contact. If we had any artillery, we'd be ripping their ass off right now."

"Shame," Cai said.

Ronan ignored the chatter. He watched the rest of the 'Mechs. They all looked of a piece, cast-offs and left-behinds he'd expect to be available to a corporate security force on a planet producing BattleMechs, except for the quartet of what were obviously new-build *BattleMasters* from Red Devil Industries and one menacing *Onager*. Khaled had been right about that collusion, too. The *Onager* was painted red and black, but switching to an IR detail scan showed other paint symbols beneath the fresh Pandoran paint.

"Curtain," he said. "If this goes up, the *Onager* is our primary target. For evidence, so try not to blow it up."

"As the major wishes," the former Clansman, former Crimond island-dweller replied. "A debt is owed."

Ronan rolled his eyes. He changed frequencies.

"That's far enough," he sent on an open frequency. None of the Pandoran 'Mechs, the closest about three kilometers away, stopped.

Ronan changed the tone of his voice. "Maybe you didn't hear me. This is a military exclusion zone, under the authority of the Tamar Armed Forces. Halt, or you will be fired upon."

The column of Pandoran 'Mechs spread out into a rough skirmish line, but it was very rough: there were three clear clumps where the Pandoran lances were not maintaining proper separation. Ronan knew the front 'Mech in each diamond would be the lance commander, because he'd stood in that exact position on the parade field countless times.

Amateurs.

"Gray Death Legion, you are ordered to stand down," a man's voice said. The voice came in a sneering tone, one Ronan had heard any number of times in the LCAF. "By order of Baron Elam Nobu." The *Marauder*'s computer painted a *BattleMaster* on the left wing of the center lance as the sender. He was broadcasting on an unencrypted channel, so anyone with a receiver could hear.

"For what reason?" Ronan replied, keeping his voice even. He very much wanted this man to think he was a brainless mercenary commander, intent on getting his way by taking advantage of every loophole he could find in his contract.

"You don't know what orders are?"

"I wasn't aware my chain of command included the lord baron," Ronan said. "My orders come through Task Force Bredell from the TAF." He injected a little haughtiness into his own voice. "I really must insist you vacate this area. Our exercises aren't open to planetary militia." Ronan put just a hint of sneer into the final words, knowing it would rankle.

"All of Pandora is under the baron's authority," the sender said. Ronan's act must have hit home, because he could now hear just the barest hint of impatience in the man's voice.

"Including you. As the baron's personal representative and the ranking military officer in the Pandoran Planetary Guard, I order you again to stand down. You will place your BattleMechs into powered standby and dismount; your tanks will park, and the crews will exit their vehicles. Your infantry will exit their battlesuits and lay down their weapons. Sidearms are to be placed on the ground next to you."

"That sounds suspiciously like arrest, whoever you are," Ronan objected. "I will have to clear this with task force headquarters. I'm not sure how Leutnant-Colonel Bredell will feel about this." Inside his neurohelmet, Ronan's mouth twitched into the first hints of a wolf's grin. Now that it was here, now that it was *happening*, his doubts were falling away. He could see the next few moves as clearly as if he were sitting across a chess table. *And now you say...*

"That will not be possible," the voice said. "I am Colonel Jurasco, commander, PPG. Bredell and the rest of the Taffy staff are dead, as you well know. The baron has already uncovered proof of your collusion. Surrender now, or we will blow you out of your machines and execute the survivors as pirates." He paused, as if for dramatic effect.

He's recording this for the news, Ronan realized. His mouth settled into a firm line. Just as he had expected it to go.

"We don't allow terrorism here."

"As I well know?" he forced out, maintaining his façade, but his attention was already half on last-second checks of the *Marauder's* weapons and the Legion's deployment.

"The whole planet knows you were involved with the bombing."

"What bombing?"

A text crawl appeared on his HUD, a message from Bel: *JUST SHOOT HIM ALREADY.*

Ronan ignored it.

"The bombing you and your conspirators orchestrated to decapitate the Taffy command structure. If it hadn't been for the baron's dedication and diligence, you might have gotten away with it. But your cohorts have already been captured and confessed. It's over. No one else needs to die. Surrender."

Ronan grimaced. It was a terrible script. Anyone with two brain cells to rub together would see through it, but Gleason had also been right. Right now, no one was rubbing any brain cells together. Right now, people were reacting emotionally. And by the time they started thinking critically, it would be too late for the Legion.

"We're on a training mission," Ronan said, putting a pout into his voice. "We couldn't have done any bombing. We just got here!"

"The confessions say otherwise. Surrender. This is your final warning."

"You'd fire on defenseless 'Mechs?"

"Says the man who orchestrated a nighttime bombing in the middle of a city."

"We had nothing to do with that!"

"That's just what a guilty man would say."

Ronan decided he'd played enough of his part. "You're not getting our 'Mechs," he said, letting a bit of steel into his voice. "Back away now. This is your final warning."

The other man, Jurasco, couldn't hide the undertone of satisfaction as Ronan finally agreed to what he'd wanted all along: the chance for a fight. "I knew you'd say that." The channel clicked closed.

FINALLY, Bel sent.

Ronan keyed the Legion frequency. "Just like we planned," he sent. His company commanders, and Curtain who was standing in for A Company while Ronan ran the battalion, double-clicked acknowledgments.

The *Marauder*'s gunnery controls felt natural when he squeezed them, the first time that had ever happened. Ronan breathed deeply through his nose. Grayson Carlyle had fought his way into history in this very 'Mech, and he'd done it by always standing by his word, or by standing by what was *right*.

Ronan had never expected how easy it felt to know he was right, and to be content to do whatever was necessary to accomplish it.

In front of him, the edges of the PPG company burst into motion.

DELIVERANCE
VANDMAAL
PANDORA
TAMAR PACT
7 MAY 3152

The helicopter pad atop the news building could take the converted Cavalry helicopter's weight, but if the rooftop crew had ever seen a stealth-armored military helicopter before, they were hiding it very well. All four of them stood gawking as Gleason wrenched the side door open and stepped down. Bill Henderson, awake now, preceded Zee out of the compartment. She climbed down and swallowed. The small team of Legion infantry stayed where they were, though all of them surreptitiously checked the readiness of their weapons.

"Relax," Gleason half-said, half-shouted as the Cavalry's rotors wound down, and the noise became merely annoying, instead of deafening. "It might work."

"Might," Zee said, without much conviction.

"Y-You can't land that thing here," one of the rooftop crew said. She was a short woman in early middle age, with close-cropped hair beneath a ball cap emblazoned with the company logo, a trident upthrust through a valknut.

"Bill us," Henderson said. Zee almost chuckled as she watched the woman's eyes track from Gleason and Zee, the two women who were clearly in charge, to Henderson. Then all the way up, to the tall man's face and his set expression, and then back down to his chest, where his fingertip tapped just outside the assault rifle's trigger guard on the selector-switch for single-shot or burst-fire mode.

"Bill you..." she said, but Henderson had already stepped past her. Gleason followed without expression, but Zee grinned wryly at the woman and took up the rear.

The door into the rooftop foyer was unlocked and slid open as they approached; the elevator was directly across from it. Henderson strode right over, head tracking right and left like a tank turret, and pushed the call button.

"Floor?" he asked, as the doors slid open.

"Parendoupolos is on eighty-two," Staff Sergeant Gleason said. The trio stepped into the elevator, and the doors irised shut. The drop was short but soft, and the doors opened. A corporate security guard stood there, in civilian-grade body armor done out in black with a stun stick holstered along his thigh. He turned and glanced into the car when the doors slid open, then did a double take. His hand dropped to his stun stick, but Henderson *tsk*ed and indicated his rifle. The guard stepped back, arms away from his body.

"Come on," Zee said. "Let's get this over with before they have a chance to react." She led the trio across the hallway and into a newsroom bullpen. Clear transpex-walled conference rooms dominated one side of the large room, beneath a larger-than-life holotank built into the walls of the room itself. Zee searched for the familiar skullcap of tightly coiled iron-colored hair...*there*.

"Are we under arrest?" Hester Parendoupolos asked calmly. The collection of people around her, all young and eager-looking staffers, all somewhat disheveled, just watched expectantly. One of them raised a palm-sized 2D recorder, but lowered it at Parendoupolos' gesture.

"We're not here for that," Zee said. "We're bringing you a story."

"In one of the mercenaries' helicopters," Parendoupolos said. Zee had never met her in person. Up close, she exuded even more of the aura of authority that came through the HV so clearly. Zee had the distinct feeling that if Hester Parendoupolos told Zee her name was actually Omi Kurita, she'd have to pull out her ID and double-check.

"We got a deposit," Staff Sergeant Gleason said.

"With one of the mercenaries," Parendoupolos added. She looked at Gleason. "That explains the battledress."

Zee looked down. She and Henderson both wore the field-green undress of the TAF, but Gleason's Legion battledress was a tiger-striped digital pattern in grays and dark greens. In low light or at night, it would be featureless and indistinguishable, but here, under the bright newsroom lights...

"The Gray Death Legion had nothing to do with the bombing," Zee said, anxious to get control of the conversation.

"Obviously," Parendoupolos said, as if Zee had said water was wet. "And?"

"And—" Zee stopped. "Obviously?"

"Young lady, give us some credit," the newscaster said. "We make our living assembling facts out of collections of indications, rumors, and inference. It doesn't take a genius to understand that no mercenary battalion, no matter how famously named, could coordinate decapitating the federal military leadership they're under contract with within a day of landing on a new planet."

"Thank you," Gleason said.

"These are just facts," Parendoupolos replied. "Leaving aside the timing, no member of your battalion, nor anyone we can track you interfacing with, has entered the building where the Tamar headquarters was located, with the exception of Staff Sergeant Khaled here."

"You know who I am?"

"Richard?" Parendoupolos said. A man near the end of the table tapped a few times on his noteputer screen then held the device up so Zee could see it. She'd never even imagined seeing her face beneath a *WANTED* sign, but there it was.

"Apparently you're one of the ringleaders in the criminal conspiracy," Richard added.

"I'm a what?"

"Does that make me an accomplice, Staff Sergeant?" Henderson put in.

"N-No—no," said Zee. "That doesn't matter. Those are all lies."

Parendoupolos smiled kindly. "I have heard that before."

Zee opened her mouth, but before she could babble more, Staff Sergeant Gleason cleared her throat. "While Zee finds her words, Ms. Parendoupolos, first let me compliment you on the completeness of your research. I suspect you already know the story we came here to give you?"

"Obviously. You came to tell me the baron is endeavoring to secede Pandora from the Tamar Pact." She said the words so matter-of-factly, with that same quiet absolute conviction, that Zee at first didn't believe what she'd heard.

"You know," was all Zee could get out. Parendoupolos just gestured around the room. Richard, at the end, waggled the noteputer. "Then why haven't you *said anything*?"

"Because there is no proof," the newscaster who'd survived broadcasting the Clan occupation replied. "It is all hearsay."

Zee pointed to the wall, and through it, toward the destroyed Tamar HQ. "There are a lot of dead people who would argue against it being hearsay." She brought her hand back, thumping it hard into her chest. "People *I* know."

"Indeed there are," Parendoupolos said. "It remains, however unpalatable the truth may be, that there are, as yet, no facts to report. And in journalism, one must have proof before one reports the news. Otherwise, we're no better than that beast Kevinsson."

"But it's *happening*."

"Zee," Gleason said, but Zee ignored her. She opened her mouth, but Gleason's comm chirped with a message. Everyone in the room turned to Gleason as she read the message. Zee already knew what it would say.

"Shots fired," Gleason said, putting the device back in a pocket.

"Is that enough of a fact to get you to *say something*?" Zee asked Parendoupolos.

CHAPTER 12

VANDMAAL FOREST
VANDMAAL
PANDORA
TAMAR PACT
7 MAY 3152

The Pandoran center didn't wait for the wings to move in. While Ronan watched, the whole line burst into motion, each lance moving at its best speed to close the three-kilometer distance with the Legion. They'd be close enough for long-range sniping in a minute or so, depending on how spread out they let themselves get.

"How's this, Major?" Sergeant Takira Kim asked. Ronan looked and found the sergeant's *Stealth* in his HUD. The 'Mech was positively pacing and pointing back toward the forest, away from the approaching Pandorans. Past it, Sergeant Owczarz's *Scarabus* brandished its hatchet as if to make a point.

"Perfect," Ronan told him. A glance around at the rest of the battalion showed similar disarray, as if the common MechWarriors and tankers were arguing with their officers about retreating. Judging by the amusement in Sergeant Kim's voice, the whole Legion was getting into the swing of it. "Just perfect." At the rear of C Company, Sergeant Prohacka's entire platoon of hovertanks broke ranks and scuttled toward the tree line, as if to find a path through the forest that wouldn't rip their fans out on tree stumps and fallen logs.

The Pandorans had come to Vandmaal expecting the Legion to be helpless, armed with training munitions and powered-down weapons. Unlike HV trash like *Immortal Warrior*, 'Mech-scale lasers couldn't be just dialed up and down in power with a vernier in the cockpit. It took technical hours to get the inhibitors removed and the capacitors rewired. It took getting beneath the armor and into the mechanical innards of a machine.

Ronan wanted the Pandorans to believe that was what they were facing for as long as possible. That was what the apparent disarray in the Legion ranks was all about. He wanted the Pandoran commander—Jurasco—and the common MechWarriors to think the Legion's discipline was breaking down. He wanted them to believe the Legion rank-and-file were about to rout because they were being asked to stand against an enemy with a sword when all they had was plastic picnic utensils.

"Tang?"

"Ready," Captain Cai said immediately.

Ronan nodded. C Company, on the Legion left, was in as much apparent chaos as the other companies, but the four 'Mechs of C1 Lance were still clustered together, and Prasad's *Trebuchet* and Duglosz's *Arbalest* had moved about 100 meters closer to the Pandoran line of advance.

*Trebuchet*s and *Arbalest*s were long-range missile BattleMechs. The Legion technicians and armorers who'd fled Camp Clay had left powered-down paint rounds as first flight of missiles in each 'Mech's magazine. LRMs were commonly among the first weapons fired at an approaching enemy, so the Pandorans should expect some fire.

So much the better if the first rounds showed them exactly what they wanted to see.

"The Pandorans fire first," Ronan reminded them.

"I want those 'Mechs taken with as little damage as possible," Jurasco told Captain Edson. "If we can get them repaired, that adds most of two companies to the Planetary Guard 'Mech force."

"Understood, sir," the young officer said.

Jurasco kept his *BattleMaster* at the rear of the command lance formation, having let one of the PPG MechWarriors take his place on the flank. He didn't need to be the one shooting fish in a barrel if Carlyle and his lackeys didn't have the good sense to surrender. He'd done plenty of shooting during his LCAF days.

Still, he kept his eye on the mercenaries, and couldn't help snorting in contempt. They were running around like scared rabbits, as if they had any chance of escape. Even if they got away today, where would they go? Keeling and Nobu controlled the media, the security forces both aboveboard and below, and the means of transportation off-planet.

"*This* is what Nobu was so afraid of?" Jurasco muttered. Keeling had been correct to advance the timetable. This collection of mercenary cowards didn't deserve to be called a battalion.

The leading Pandoran 'Mechs reached the extreme ranges of long-range missile fire and triggered a barrage. It was a paltry five missiles from an ancient *Lineholder*, but it scared the mercenaries into action. One of the mercenary 'Mechs, surely panicking, turned and rippled off about thirty LRMs in return.

The *Lineholder*'s fire missed wide, high-explosive warheads destroying a dozen square meters of grassy moor. The mercenary 'Mechs turned and ran for the forest, not even waiting to see what their fellow *Trebuchet*'s barrage did.

Jurasco laughed as the missiles burst across the *Lineholder*. The mercenary's gunnery was better than the Pandoran's, but instead of high explosive crushing armor, the *Lineholder* emerged from a fog of blue paint.

"Run them down," he told Edson.

"They took the bait," Ronan muttered as the Pandoran company advance became much less tremulous. He toggled the all-Legion channel. "It's time, Gray Death Legion. Suck 'em in."

The chorus of acknowledgements had a definite edge of hungry anticipation Ronan approved of. His *Marauder*, currently "chasing" the other three 'Mechs of A1 Lance, was at the rear of their "formation," but in just a few seconds, as the range to the main body of the Pandoran company fell to half a kilometer...

"Hit 'em," he growled, and wrenched the *Marauder* around. Every other Legion 'Mech and tank, as if tied to his by strings, did the same. He dropped the targeting crosshairs across the blocky shape of a leading *BattleMaster*, waited for the golden tone of a target lock, and squeezed the triggers of Grayson's *Marauder* for the first time in a full-power combat shot.

The old Magna PPCs had been retrofitted on Odessa with modern, Clan-spec extended-range particle projector cannons. They actually took up less space in the *Marauder*'s gauntlet forearms, but did half-again as much damage. Both PPCs spat scintillating gouts of ions at near-lightspeed that connected the *Marauder* and the *BattleMaster* for an infinitesimal second. The lightning-sharp instant ended, filling Ronan's cockpit with a wash of blistering heat and the chirping of recharging capacitors.

The Pandoran *BattleMaster*, contemptuous of what it expected to be training-grade weapons, crashed to the ground in a tangle of smoking, crushed armor plates, making a temporary, very short 85-ton landslide.

Ronan shivered. He never knew whether it was because his cooling suit shot fresh coolant through its mesh of tubes, or because no shot had ever felt so *right* in his entire career.

Around him, the rest of the Legion attacked.

When the *Marauder* had first turned, Jurasco had grinned. One of the mercenaries was showing a spine, at least, which would make it easy to dispose of them. Maybe the merc thought Jurasco would be naïve enough to let his company get close enough for physical combat. The PPCs had flared to life, and Jurasco had kept grinning. Even training PPCs were visually stunning. It would be a good show on battleROM footage. Nobu and his news people would love it.

Then Captain Edson yelped across the comm, and his *BattleMaster* hit the ground, smoking.

"What?" Jurasco asked. He blinked.

More Legion 'Mechs fired PPCs, lasers, and long-range missiles at his company. Pandoran 'Mechs, too confident to even evade, just walked into the fire—which was devastatingly accurate. PPG machines shook and fell beneath their caresses.

Edson's lancemate, the *Onager* whose pilot Jurasco could never remember, twisted beneath the fire of a Legion *Regent*. A slender *Talon* that had almost reached the tree line before turning and sprinting back toward the fight donated another PPC. The Red Devil-built assault 'Mech collapsed, half-crushing its right arm in the process.

Alarms blared in the *BattleMaster*'s cockpits as Legion targeting systems swept across Jurasco's own 'Mech. LRMs flickered into the air, and a laser wiped armor off his left shin.

All of this happened in a span of seconds.

Hector Jurasco needed more time than that to process what was happening.

He didn't get it.

The LRMs descended.

The BattleMaster*'s armor is thick*— was all he had time to think.

"Almost feel sorry for them," Bel said.

Ronan opened his mouth to reply, but Tang Cai beat him to it. "Don't. We don't know about Master Sergeant Azarri and the others."

Ronan felt a wash of kinship with Cai just then. He and the other orphans had joined the Legion freely, but they hadn't come from that first forming crucible on Garrison. They were neither old Two-Six Arcturan nor Twenty-Ninth Recon.

But they were Legion through and through.

The *Marauder*'s PPCs chimed recharged, drawing Ronan back to the situation at hand. He settled the crosshairs on the *BattleMaster* barely struggling to its feet and fired again. This time he added the overhung silver bullet Gauss rifle above his canopy. The *Marauder* shook with recoil.

The PPCs both cut into what would have been the gut of a human, slashing and crushing the armor there. The flickering exchange of fire was near-instantaneous. The *BattleMaster* was rocked back, trying to twist to avoid the fire, when the Gauss hit. Traditional Gauss rifles fired a single, heavy slug of metal at hypersonic speeds. The impact devastated anything it struck. But the silver bullet Gauss rifle broke that heavy round into fifteen flechettes, so instead of firing one large hammer, it fired fifteen needles.

Metal striking metal at those velocities *sparked*. The *BattleMaster* glittered for an instant as the projectiles struck. Several ricocheted away like miniature orange lasers.

One sliced through the *BattleMaster*'s bulbous canopy like a beam of light.

The *BattleMaster* toppled.

The entire tempo of the battle had changed in that first exchange of fire. The Pandorans had thought they were chasing an unarmed rabble, mercenary troopers who wouldn't obey their own officers, armed with training lasers and paint rounds. They had advanced with the righteous certainty that the Legion, running away from them, couldn't hurt them.

The first real exchange of fire had frozen them.

Worse, it had halted the physical momentum of their attack. The Legion, turning back as one and advancing back toward them, had reversed the direction of the fight. The Pandorans, shocked to be struck with full-power weapons, shocked to see the disarray in front of them resolve itself into choreography, had more or less *stopped*. They had certainly stopped mentally.

Now, the Legion was chasing them.

Now, they were outnumbered.

And Ronan had just killed a senior officer, if not the company commander.

Curtain's *Regent* stalked forward and hit the *Onager* again; the Pandoran assault 'Mech had been trying to get back to its feet, but the PPCs cut its legs out from under it. Curtain kept advancing, closing to the extreme range of his autocannon, and then unleashed the 200mm Ultra at its full rate of fire, chewing up the *Onager*'s side and legs. If the 'Mech could have, it would have curled into a fetal ball, trying to protect its head. When Marianne Kojima stalked her *Bushwhacker* close enough to cough a cloud of LB-X projectiles, the *Onager* shut down, its hip and shoulder actuators shredded. A3's heavy hover APC scuttled forward, Void battlesuits holding grab-bars on the sides.

Bel and her B Company advanced toward the flank, hitting the Pandoran lance there over and over again. Her Myrmidon platoon combined its plasma cannon fire and cooked a Pandoran *Archer* until its ammunition gang-fired and blew out the explosive panels in its back.

Tang Cai and C Company had gone the other way; Sergeant Ojima's Pursuit Platoon was scuttling around a Pandoran *Griffin* that had let itself get separated, while Tang and the 'Mechs of C1 Platoon kept the others distracted. Ronan watched Sergeant Prohacka's Drillsons and SM1s lining up for an attack run that would gut the distracted Pandoran 'Mech lance.

It still felt *right*.

But Ronan knew what he had to do.

Hector Jurasco had his *BattleMaster* walking backward, firing at the Legion 'Mechs, but he wasn't hitting anything.

"Sir—Colonel—the captain's down, sir, what do we do?" one of the Alpha Company MechWarriors shouted.

"Fight back!" Jurasco growled.

"They're killing us, sir!"

"Kill them faster!"

Jurasco squeezed his triggers, but his weapons hadn't cycled yet. The Gray Death Legion company in front of him, really two lances, kept advancing faster than he was backing up. If he was going to get out of this ambush, he would have to turn around soon and make a run for it. Not that *BattleMaster*s were particularly swift.

"All A Company units," Jurasco snapped. "Charge them."

"Sir?!"

"You heard me. They're a rabble. This is a feint. We're professionals, and they're mercenaries. We can take them, but we have to stop running." Jurasco tried with all his wit to put iron into his tone. It was important that Edson's lackeys understand their orders. They had to distract the mercenaries long enough for him to break contact and head back to Deliverance, get with

Keeling, and figure out their next move. If he could gather the other two PPG companies and everything Keeling could give him from Red Devil, he could come back here and crush the Legion.

"Pandoran commander," said the Legion commander, on an unencrypted channel, "you are outnumbered and outmatched. Surrender now, and we won't kill any more of you."

As if to punctuate the mercenary commander's words, a Pandoran 'Mech on the far left of the field collapsed in a cascading ammunition explosion, punctuated with a sharp *boom* as its Gauss rifle capacitors detonated sympathetically. The shockwave rocked every one of the *BattleMaster*'s 85 tons.

"Charge, I said!" Jurasco growled. "That's an order."

Instead, the last command lance 'Mech raised its hands and powered down in surrender.

"Shit," Jurasco muttered. He turned the *BattleMaster* around and slammed the throttle to its stops. A pair of PPG 'Mechs kept firing, but the rest were already surrendering.

"Halt or we will fire on you," the mercenary, Carlyle, said. His voice had none of the hesitation of earlier. He sounded as certain as a rockslide.

Jurasco had heard that tone before, at his court martial. He urged the *BattleMaster* forward. The comm channel clicked closed.

"Curtain," Ronan said. "On two?"

"A debt is owed," Curtain said. "On two."

"One," Ronan said, settling the *Marauder*'s crosshairs across the lumbering *BattleMaster*'s back. He waited until the battle computer painted it gold in target lock. "Two."

The *Marauder* and the *Regent* fired at the same time, two ER PPCs each. All four struck the *BattleMaster* in the back, obliterating the thinner armor there and eating at the vital machinery inside the chest cavity. One or more of the blasts destroyed the gyro housing, making it impossible to balance the 85-ton machine. It crashed to the ground.

Ronan touched a toggle to change the frequency. "Katine, make sure we get whoever is in there."

"Roger, Major," Sergeant Katine Kondracki replied. Across the field, the squat heavy hover APC carrying her squad of Void battlesuits scuttled past the surrendering PPG 'Mechs. Bel and B Company were finishing off the last two Pandoran holdouts.

"Tang, secure the surrenders," Ronan ordered. "Keep them isolated. When Gleason gets back, I'm going to want interrogations. And make sure none of them even see this Jurasco after Sergeant Kondracki's people pry him out of that wreck."

"On it, Major."

Ronan looked around. He had been confident of victory, but he hadn't expected it to be *this* easy.

CHAPTER 13

DELIVERANCE
PANDORA
TAMAR PACT
7 MAY 3152

"You'll cover the battle," Zee said incredulously, "but you won't report on Nobu?"

Hester Parendoupolos shook her head, the same as she had for the last hour. Zee sighed, resisting the urge to rub at the headache beneath her temples.

"By now the battle is probably over," Staff Sergeant Gleason put in. She was leaning against the wall, mindlessly watching the news chyron on the holo playing in the other room with no sound.

"How did you survive this when the Jade Falcons were here?" Zee raised her hands as if the answers would fall from the ceiling. "There's no way you could have *waited for the facts* for the things they told you to say."

Parendoupolos smiled and gestured at the room. The other newspeople spoke as one. *"According to the Jade Falcon Clan..."* they intoned, then chuckled.

"So, say 'according to unnamed sources,'" Zee tried. She waved. "Hi. I'm an unnamed source." She pointed to Gleason. "There's another one."

Parendoupolos opened her mouth to reply, but Gleason's comm chirped again. She pulled it out, read the message, and seemed to relax her whole body. She looked up, winked at Zee, and then addressed the newsroom. "We won," she said, and read off a series of coordinates. "Get your people there fast enough, and maybe the major will give you an interview."

Two of the newsroom staffers stood and dashed out of the room. Zee watched them go, gaping, until Gleason stepped close and pulled her up by the arm. "Time to go to phase two," Gleason told her.

"Phase two?" Parendoupolos asked.

"Sorry," Gleason said. "Maybe you'll see it on the news." She nodded Bill Henderson out of the room and stepped after him. As they waited for the elevator to the roof, she touched her comm. "We're on our way." The elevator opened, and the trio bundled inside.

Outside, the security guards just watched, a confused expression on their faces.

"I can't believe her," Zee said.

"Never mind her," Gleason said. "Get your head right about the next part."

"The next part..." Zee blinked. "You really think it's necessary?"

"You've been here longer. How is Nobu going to react to his people losing? To having his narrative upset?"

"Badly," Zee said.

"Right. So, we need to trim a little more of his support system out from beneath him." The elevator door slid opened to the roof. Across the distance, the Legion helicopter's blades were already spinning.

"We could just go directly there," Zee said.

"They'll arrest us," Gleason told her.

"They might not."

Gleason just laughed and pushed her toward the helicopter.

"—and so, Yao, I really think it's only a matter of time before we get these pernicious mercenaries under control, and then we can get to the bottom of what's been going on," Elam Nobu said. "I think we owe that to the people of Deliverance, indeed, the people of all Pandora." He smiled. "And to the governor-general, of course."

"Of course," Yao Kevinsson agreed. "I think I speak for a lot of Pandorans, my lord, when I ask: when will it be enough?" He looked away from the baron and into the HV lens, going off into one of the bloviating diatribes he'd made his career on.

A lot of Pandorans, Nobu thought, sneering in his mind. *How many Pandorans? Which ones? What are their names?* Nobu understood how the game was played: tell people their ignorant, inane thoughts were correct. Reassure them there were "many people" just like them. Make them feel like their decision is now supported. And then feed the paranoia and fear that created the nonsense in the first place. *This would all be so much more difficult if the "average person" applied even a gram of critical thought to what they saw or heard.*

Nobu looked back to Kevinsson, as it felt like he was coming to the end of his sequence of "just asking questions." Nessa Deschanes appeared behind him, out of the HV's pickup. She raised both her eyebrows, a rare show of emotion for her, and looked to the right.

Nobu made a gesture with his hand, and to his credit Kevinsson didn't hesitate. "We'll return after this short message," he said. And then the HV camera indicator went dark. Nobu stood, ignoring the curious newscaster, and stepped close to Deschanes. Kevinsson was a toad, but he was smart enough to know when his betters didn't need him around.

"Jurasco is out of contact," she told him.

"I don't know what that means," Nobu said.

"He reported encountering the mercenaries. He was confident he'd be able to sweep them up with no trouble. Now he's not responding to hails."

Nobu frowned. "Why would he do that?"

Deschanes regarded him for a moment. In anyone else, he would have read it as disappointment. "Because he is unable to reply."

"Unable?"

"Perhaps the mercenaries defeated him," Deschanes said.

"You said they were training. Paint rounds and the like." Nobu's mind went into overdrive, trying to sort through half-understood words from the prior day that were getting jumbled with the remainder of the speech he'd meant to make on Kevinsson's show.

"Perhaps they weren't," Deschanes said. "And I did not say that. Jurasco did."

"Whatever," Nobu said. "They're in Vandmaal, not terra incognita. Call down there. Get a park ranger or something. If there was a battle, people will have heard it."

"I should have thought of that," Deschanes said dryly.

Nobu stared at her. "You already did." She nodded. "And?"

"There was a battle, that much I know. I don't yet know who won."

"Jurasco—"

"Could have been defeated. Could have been killed, but our forces may have triumphed. Could have broken his radio. We can't know until we know."

Nobu bit back a snarl. "Fine. Get with Keeling. Assume Jurasco's been defeated and the mercenaries are coming. Tell Benchley he's back in charge of the PPG until and unless we hear from Jurasco. But get with Keeling first. He started this. If it's going to come apart, he can do his part to try and hold it together."

Deschanes nodded, then looked meaningfully past Nobu to where Kevinsson sat in his HV studio, trying to look like he wasn't trying to listen. Nobu looked back at him and ignored the childish smile that appeared, like an attentive student trying to get the instructor's affection.

"Turd," Nobu breathed, barely loud enough to be heard.

"Yes, but useful," Deschanes said.

"I'll get out of this as quickly as I can," Nobu told her. "While I'm doing that, figure out what the hell is going on."

"Good day, Lieutenant Guyon," Staff Sergeant Gleason said. She and Zee stood in Guyon's cramped office in the Deliverance spaceport terminal. "Major Carlyle has spoken highly of your professionalism."

"If he's looking for another secret BattleMech, he's going to have to keep looking," the port authority lieutenant said. Zee frowned, but Gleason only chuckled.

"*Captain* Carlyle, his sister, told me you didn't miss much either," she said. "We need your help."

Guyon made a show of trying to look around them at the closed door. "I'm not sure what I can do for you, Staff Sergeant," she said. "Doesn't seem like you have much business at the port. Unless you're looking for the offworld passenger terminal? I can direct you, if you're lost."

Gleason gestured at the pair of extruded-polymer seats in front of the desk. "May we sit?"

"Free planet," Guyon said.

"Is it?" Gleason asked, as she sat. Zee sat down beside her, keeping her tongue. They'd discussed the plan, of course, but Gleason had a great deal more confidence than Zee did that this was going to work.

But then, you thought Parendoupolos would work, Zee told herself.

"Supposed to be," Guyon said. "Speaking of which, I've got a bulletin somewhere here saying I should be detaining anyone wearing that little skull emblem." She pointed to the shoulder of Gleason's battledress, then she looked at Zee. "Your face sure seems familiar, too."

Zee opened her mouth, but Gleason spoke first. "Will you be detaining us, then?"

Guyon stared at her for a moment. She breathed in, and then back out. "Like I said, the bulletin is here somewhere. I'm sure I can find it if I need it." She waved a hand at her immaculately organized desk. "I am, after all, a very disorganized person."

"A curse," Gleason agreed.

Zee just looked back and forth. There was a conversation going on here at a level she wasn't quite getting. She got the subtext just fine, knew Guyon had just agreed to hear them out even if she had reminded them she could change her mind at any time. But it seemed like Gleason and Guyon were also talking about something *else*.

"While I look for that," Guyon went on, making no effort to look for anything, "maybe you can tell me why you're here."

"You recall Major Carlyle, our CO?"

"I do. He seemed really excited about a BattleMech."

"He strike you as a conspiratorial mastermind?"

Guyon actually snorted. "He seems like he probably needs his sister to explain jokes to him."

Zee stiffened, but Gleason only held her soft grin. "She has, on occasion," the staff sergeant allowed. "His talents lie in other areas. Leadership, strangely enough. Organization and training. And combat."

"Military man, model one-A," Guyon agreed. "I've met a hundred of him."

"And you watch the news?"

"When it's on," Guyon said. Zee heard a touch more guardedness enter her voice.

Gleason sat back in her thin, extruded plastic chair, making the feet chatter as they spread to accommodate her weight, and folded her hands in her lap. "Then I'll just ask you to do some basic arithmetic, Lieutenant. You met Major Carlyle a week ago when we landed." Gleason held up two fingers in her left hand in a V. "The baron would have us all believe in the space of days, he masterminded the assassination of the Tamar Armed Forces command." She held up her right hand, also with two fingers, then crossed them together. "Does that equal four, Port Lieutenant?"

Guyon licked her lips. "None of that means I'm willing to betray my oaths. I know my duties."

"Exactly as Major Carlyle told me you'd say." Gleason lowered her hands, then inclined her head toward Zee. "May I introduce Staff Sergeant Zahara Khaled of the Tamar Armed Forces?"

"Staff Sergeant," Guyon said.

"We need your help, Lieutenant Guyon," Zee said.

Guyon held up a hand. "You just heard about my oaths."

"We did," Gleason said.

"I did," Zee agreed. "I'm going to ask you to work in faith with those oaths, Lieutenant. Both to Pandora and to Arcturus."

Guyon spread her hands on the table. She looked back and forth between the two intelligence NCOs. Zee watched the wheels turn behind the other woman's eyes as she weighed her options. So far, no one had said anything incriminating, and

Guyon could ensure her position in the new regime by reporting or attempting to detain both of them.

Gleason had said she wouldn't. Carlyle—both Carlyles—had agreed on that before Zee and Gleason left Vandmaal. Zee had taken them all at their word.

"Ask me to do what?" Guyon finally asked.

Zee smiled as she thought angels might. "Very little," she said. "Just a ride."

VANDMAAL FOREST
VANDMAAL
PANDORA
TAMAR PACT

Ronan Carlyle stood at the foot of his *Marauder*, wearing his cooling suit sans neurohelmet. Bel stood nearby, leaning against the other foot. She was looking up at the *Marauder*'s underside.

"How many times did we stand right here as kids, back on Odessa?" she asked. "Grayson's *Marauder*. Damn. Mom and Dad must really love you."

Ronan shook his head. "What are they saying about Sergeant Winsor?"

"Should recover," Bel said. "The rest of his crew the same, though Private Sirki should be in a hospital. She's got third-degree burns on both hands."

"We'll get her there as soon as we can," Ronan said. Winsor's Drillson hovertank had taken a PPC hit during the battle, destroying the tank's internal heat buffers; the temperature inside the tank had blasted as hot as a BattleMech cockpit before the crew could bail out. All were burned from evacuating across the heat-blasted armor. Thankfully, the rest of the Legion's damage in the recent battle was just equipment, which the escaped technicians were already putting right with the aid of a Savior mobile field base.

"Here he comes," Bel said, jerking her chin. Ronan looked.

Curtain's hulking form was immediately recognizable. He was half-directing, half-dragging another man in old Lyranstyle MechWarrior garb by the neck. Behind them, an infantry trooper with an assault rifle held at port arms followed.

"Go get an update from the techs," Ronan told Bel. "I want to be on the road back toward Deliverance as soon as we're rearmed. Anything they can't fix in an hour will have to wait."

Bel nodded, but didn't move.

"Bel?" She held up a hand until Curtain got close enough that Ronan could see his controlled grin. A few meters away, Curtain shoved the prisoner hard enough the man stumbled a few steps before falling to his hands and knees. Ronan frowned.

Bel stepped forward and spat on the ground in front of the man. She turned and gave Ronan a dazzling smile. "On the road in an hour," she repeated back, and then walked away.

Ronan watched her go, then turned back to the man on the ground. He'd settled back into a kneel on his heels, breathing deeply and rubbing at the scrapes on his palms from when he'd fallen.

"You're Jurasco?"

"*Colonel* Jurasco," the man confirmed.

"Are my people in Deliverance unharmed?" Ronan asked.

Jurasco grinned. "Define 'unharmed.'"

Curtain stepped closer, but Ronan stopped him. "Are they alive?" he asked, more quietly than he had spoken before.

"They were when I left," Jurasco said, with a glance at Curtain. The flush in the Pandoran officer's face was bright and sweat-sheened; Ronan imagined the infantry hadn't been especially careful prying him out of the wreckage of his BattleMech, and certainly Curtain was not a man given to showing enemies—especially defeated enemies—much grace. "What happened to them after I left, I can't say. They were to be interrogated."

Ronan held his tongue, letting the incipient flash of rage rush through him and dissipate before he spoke. "If my people have been harmed," he said with quiet, stone-hard sincerity, "I will see you and all your cohorts prosecuted to the full extent of the law."

Jurasco snorted. "The law. Who do you think the law is on this planet, merc?" He grinned, showing teeth so white they must have been done cosmetically. "Who do you think you're going to get to arrest us? The baron is against you. Malthus is against you. The people are against you. According to the news, you assassinated the Taffy CO and are on a rampage of conquest, intending to keep Pandora for yourself."

"That's lunacy," Ronan blurted.

"It's what people believe," Jurasco said. "The truth is whatever we say over and over again until people believe it." He chuckled. "And anyway, it won't matter when the rest of my regiment gets down here and kills you."

"Your regiment. You have a few companies at most." Ronan jutted his chin past Jurasco, at the field where the Legion had gutted his company. "One less, now."

"It'll be enough," Jurasco said. "The baron will bring the Taffies in on you if he has to."

Ronan opened and closed his mouth. Keeping that from happening was Khaled and Gleason's job back in Deliverance, and he hadn't heard anything from them. He glanced at Curtain, who glared back with the most amazing combination of placidity and menace. As if the big man was happy to burn the whole world down, and laugh while he did it, but was in no particular hurry to get started.

"Keep him isolated from the others," Ronan told Curtain. "When we get back to Deliverance, we'll need him for a witness." He ignored the way Jurasco snorted in disbelief. "Put the others in APCs. Have the troopers be friendly. Get them talking. I want to know what the common MechWarrior is thinking about all this."

"*Aff,*" Curtain replied. He reached down and jerked Jurasco up by his collar.

Ronan let the big man drag the prisoner away, then leaned back against the *Marauder*'s cool armor. He wanted to think Grayson Carlyle must have had it so much easier. He'd been in declared wars among combatants who'd been fighting quite literally for centuries. He hadn't had to worry about whether or not his employer was going to turn on him.

Except, even as he tried to think that, Ronan knew it wasn't true. Not at all. One of the old Legion's formative crucibles had been the betrayal at Sirius and Helm. The recovery of the first Star League memory core often overshadowed that betrayal, but not in the internal Carlyle family histories. There, Carlyle and others in the Legion had recorded how it felt to be stabbed in the back by Duke Garth of Irian.

And again, near the end of the old Legion, in the Federated Commonwealth Civil War. Betrayals all around.

Is this what it means to be a mercenary? Ronan wondered. *To be a cat's paw for anyone who can use you to their advantage?* Then he snorted. If Bel had heard him say that, she'd have climbed up on a stool to smack him in the back of the head.

That's just life, she'd have told him. And she'd have been right.

Ronan shook his head and turned toward the *Marauder*'s mounting ladder. The time for reflection was past. He still had people in harm's way in Deliverance.

And a baron needed to learn the price of betraying the Gray Death Legion.

CHAPTER 14

PANZERABTEILUNG 37 CASERNE
DELIVERANCE
PANDORA
TAMAR PACT
7 MAY 3152

"No, I'm sorry, Private, but it needs to be Kommandant Hakima's signature," Port Lieutenant Guyon said sweetly. "I know it's a hassle, but it's your own regulations, and when the IG team came through last year, they fired one of my friends over this very thing. I'm not risking my kids' food because an officer can't walk five minutes to sign for an intelligence pouch."

In the second row of seats in the Port Authority van, Zee Khaled suppressed her snort.

"Wait right here," the gate guard, a private, said, and retreated inside the gatepost.

"I don't like it either," Guyon added. Then she rolled her window back up against the chilly evening wind. She glanced over her shoulder at Zee, rolled her eyes, and then shared a knowing grin with Staff Sergeant Gleason, who sat in the other front seat.

"Do COs actually come down here to sign?" Gleason asked.

"I'm told Leutnant-Colonel Bredell delegated it, with orders in writing, to his chief of staff," Guyon said, "but that's just a rumor. Your girl back there can tell you better from the Taffy side."

Gleason twisted in her seat to look over her shoulder at Zee, an eyebrow raised in question.

"No idea," Zee said. "Hauptmann Candiz never told me where he got the pouches from."

"Hang on," Guyon said. "He's coming back." She slid the window down again. "What's the word?"

"She's coming down," the young man said. "You're to wait here."

"Right here?" Guyon made a gesture. "We're kind of blocking your gate. Maybe we pull through right over there, next to your guardhouse, so you can watch us real close while we sit inside this warm van and wait for your kommandant to come out in the cold?"

The private looked back, past the end of the spaceport van, where a line of vehicles was waiting, then back toward the guardhouse and gate sergeant Zee knew was there. He jerked a thumb. "No farther inside," he said, and activated the gate barrier.

"Thank you, Private," Lieutenant Guyon said brightly. She slid the window back up and pulled the van through before parking in the indicated space. Then she set the vehicle to idle, adjusted the interior heater, and looked over at Staff Sergeant Gleason. "When they arrest you," she said, "I'm going to tell them you held a gun on me."

Gleason just chuckled.

Zee said nothing, but inside she was going a thousand kilometers a minute. She was a wanted person by the Tamar Armed Forces, sitting on a Tamar Armed Forces military installation, surrounded by solders with guns and rifles and powered armor.

In a thin-walled panel van with a noisy fuel cell engine.

Unarmed.

Here to tell a traitor it was time to turn her coat a second time.

"Still nothing from the south?" she asked.

Gleason shook her head. "No, but that's good news. If the Legion had lost, it'd be on the news by now. We know there was a fight. So the major kicked ass and didn't bother with names, per usual. We're on plan."

"That's a lot of faith," Guyon observed.

"Not really," Gleason said. "Just psychology." She glanced back at Zee, grinned, and then directed her attention at Guyon. "It comes down to how people act in their own best interests. Or their perception of their best interests. If the Legion had been defeated, it'd be all over the news. Nobu, and the toadies he has running everything for him, would not be able to resist. We'd be seeing battleROM excerpts on every HV broadcast. Every news channel would be full of interviews with victorious Pandoran military officers, cut away with shots of defeated Legion troopers being led away in chains. Pictures of our destroyed BattleMechs. Nobu is a creature of public opinion. He manipulates it as well as anyone I've ever seen, but he can't not act in a way that serves that purpose."

Guyon thought for a moment, then shrugged. "I can see that. I don't know that I buy it yet, but it makes sense on the surface." She raised an eyebrow. "And your side?"

"Silence serves us," Gleason said. "Major Carlyle is not interested in the spotlight. Sometimes that hurts us, but not today. Today we turned Vandmaal Forest into a black hole of information. It won't last much longer. It can't, not with this many people on the planet. People will find the battlefield, or spot our 'Mechs in movement, or just see the smoke and come investigate. But for as long as it lasts, Nobu and his people went south confident of victory and then fell off the edge of the map." Now it was Gleason's turn to shrug. "That will play hell with Nobu's narrative. He has newspeople primed to tell the story he wants. They've made the graphics. They've written the headlines. All they're waiting on is filling in the dates and the details. But the Legion has thrown that off."

"But how does that help us here, now, with Kommandant Hakima?" Zee put in. She couldn't help it. Her doubts were getting away from her. She already knew the answer, had known it since the contingency plans were made days ago. But she wanted to hear it.

"Like all of us," Gleason said, ostensibly for Guyon's benefit, but because she knew Zee needed the reassurance, "Hakima will work to her own self-interest. That's why she succumbed to the baron. But when that is no longer her own self-interest, she will come around."

"You're putting a lot of faith in people protecting their self-interest," Guyon observed.

"We are," Gleason said. "And sometimes it backfires. Because people are driven often by emotion rather than logic. And because they want irrational things."

"Here she comes," Zee said, pointing with her chin at the woman in the bulky parka who had just appeared out of the nearby building.

"But no one wants to be on the losing side," Gleason said softly.

"Keeling is withdrawing the BattleMechs given to the Pandora Planetary Guard," Deschanes said. She had her comm in her hand, one hand over the microphone.

Nobu looked at her and blinked. They were in his office at the Palace of the Gods, desperately trying to find out exactly what had happened at Vandmaal. "Says who? Is that him?"

"No, it's Benchley. He says the MechWarriors just left. Took their 'Mechs and left."

Nobu gestured for the phone. Deschanes rose and handed it to him. "Benchley!"

"My lord—"

"Under no circumstances are you to let those BattleMechs go, Colonel. Those pilots swore oaths."

"Sir, I can't—"

"I don't want to hear 'can't,' Benchley."

"Sir, they're *gone*." When Nobu didn't immediately speak, Benchley pressed on. It was more backbone than Nobu could remember the old man showing in years. "Those Malthus scumbags, they just walked out of the briefing. They got a message, all of them at once, like it was some comedy show. Just looked at each other and stood up and left in a group. By the time we realized what was happening, they were already in their 'Mechs."

Nobu swallowed. It was Keeling, Deschanes was right. No one else could get the whole group to act as one. He controlled his anger—and the flight of terror that slid beneath it—and took a deep breath. "What do you have left, Colonel?"

"Sir, with A Company out of contact, the Malthus 'Mechs were most of B and C Companies. I've got about two lances of 'Mechs left. And almost all the regular battalions." Benchley stopped and took a breath, as if saying that many words at once was foreign to him. "The Guard is strong, sir. We don't need criminals."

"The 'criminals,' as you put it, have all the BattleMechs," Nobu said, and ended the call. He tossed the comm back to Deschanes and spun about in his chair. The view out the window was quiet, but Nobu's mind was anything but.

"Sir—"

"Get Keeling. Get him here if you can, but I want to talk to him ASAP."

"I will," Deschanes said. "We should also check on the Taffies. If the Gray Death Legion got Jurasco, they could be coming this way. We're going to need everything we can to stop them."

"Why don't we *know*?" Nobu spat. "Two billion people on this planet. All of them have comms and the globalnet. All of them have cameras on their comms. How can no one have seen anything?" He spun around, putting a thumb over his shoulder. "I can see six flights leaving Deliverance any given minute. Some of them fly that way. No one can look out a window?"

"The Taffies," Deschanes pressed.

"I'll do that," Nobu said. He touched the button that raised a flatscreen video comm out of his desktop. Deschanes retreated across the room to her own calls. Nobu entered the combination for the duty desk at the new TAF command center. A moment later, a young man in TAF battledress appeared. If Nobu recalled the epaulet scheme, he was a leutnant.

"My lord baron," the leutnant said. "How may I help you, sir?"

"I need to speak with Kommandant Hakima," Nobu said. "Securely."

"Of course, my lord. I'll have her contact you as soon as she's able."

Nobu blinked. "Now. I need to speak with her *now*."

"I regret that is not possible, my lord," the leutnant said. "She is away from the command post."

"Away," Nobu repeated.

"I'm told she expects to return momentarily."

"Return," Nobu repeated. "The kommandant is aware there is a battle going on near Vandmaal? That the criminals who attacked us all—attacked *you*, Leutnant—are still out there? I need to be able to reach the kommandant at any time!"

"I'm sure the kommandant is fully aware of her duties, my lord." He paused. "She can reach you at this code when she returns?"

Nobu smashed the *disconnect* button with the heel of his fist.

"Good day, Kommandant Hakima," Lieutenant Guyon said as she slid the window down. "Won't you step into my office?" She touched a control and the spaceport van's side door, opposite the seat where Zee sat, slid open. A blast of cold air slid in, but Zee already had chills.

"Cute," Hakima said. "Just give me whatever you came to give me. Next time leave it with the gate guard."

The kommandant looked tired to Zee's eyes. *She should be.* Even if she hadn't been bent, overseeing a military force reeling from a decapitation strike would take far more hours than any one human had to give.

"It's voice," Guyon said apologetically. "The courier back there has to tell you. Be warmer for all of us if you step in." Guyon shrugged. "You know how intelligence people are."

Hakima stared at her. "You're joking."

"We don't bite, Kommandant," Staff Sergeant Gleason said. "Let's get this over with."

Hakima looked at each of them, then rolled her eyes and climbed into the seat. The door slid shut behind her. Hakima pushed back the hood of her parka, sighed, and glanced at all three women in sequence. "Well?"

"By now the Gray Death Legion has defeated the Planetary Guard unit sent to apprehend it," Staff Sergeant Gleason said.

"If all is going to plan, Major Carlyle is marching toward the city at this very moment."

Hakima stared at her. "I was under the impression no intelligence had come back from Vandmaal."

Gleason smiled thinly. "No Taffy intelligence, no."

Hakima frowned, but Zee recognized her cue. "Kommandant, I don't think we've ever met, but you knew my boss. Hauptmann Candiz?"

"Candiz...the intelligence officer? Bredell's head spook?"

"I work—worked in his shop," Zee went on.

"You—" Hakima's eye widened. Her hand shot to the van's door handle, but the *snick* of the door lock engaging was as loud as a gunshot. "Let me out of here," she said coldly.

"You're in no danger, Kommandant," Staff Sergeant Gleason said. "We're on your military reservation, surrounded by your troops. We're not even armed. We're here to give the truth of what's happened and let you make the right decision."

"What right decision?" Hakima's hand jerked, testing the door handle, but it remained locked. Guyon had the good grace to look sheepish where she watched in the rearview mirror.

"Where your duty lies," Zee put in. Now that the event was on her, her nerves had settled down. Waiting was always the hardest part. "With Tamar. With your oath. And not with Baron Nobu."

"My oaths are intact," Hakima said.

"This goes faster if you don't waste time, ma'am." Zee shifted in her seat. "I know you went to the Palace and met with the baron. You weren't the first, and if the Legion hadn't landed and pushed everything into the fire, you likely wouldn't have been the last."

"I—what?"

"The baron," Zee said, as matter-of-factly as she could, "blackmailed you into acting in his favor after he had Leutnant-Colonel Bredell assassinated. The fact that you were away from HQ when the bomb went off confirms it well enough for any board of inquiry." Which was nonsense; there was zero evidence that wasn't circumstantial. But Hakima didn't need to know that.

And besides, Zee was sure. It felt right.

"If you're accusing me of being involved—"

"We're confident you didn't know about the bomb, Kommandant," Staff Sergeant Gleason put in. "But you were the right person to step in after the fact."

"I didn't *step in* to anything. I was next in the chain of command!"

"Which is why the baron needed you," Zee said.

Hakima's face had gone pale, then florid red, and now pale again. "What are you talking about?"

"All the private rooms at the Briar Club are wired for full HV, Kommandant," Zee said, again as matter-of-factly as she could. "What you do in your off-hours this many light years away from your wife is up to you. Certainly there is nothing in TAG regulations about what consenting adults do."

Hakima froze.

"I haven't seen the recording," Zee went on. She hadn't been completely sure there *was* a recording, but the record of events Bill Henderson had put together between that first stroke of luck in the Palace of the Gods video and the bombing was conclusive that Hakima had been at the Briar Club. "But I'm pretty sure no one's put a Lyran—or Tamar—officer up on a conduct unbecoming charge for off-hours activities unless it was non-consensual."

"He said he'd bury it," Hakima whispered. Her skin was the color of day-old yogurt now. "How did you—he said *no one would ever see it!*"

"The Legion is coming," Gleason said from the front seat. Like Zee, she'd taken a look at the evidence and agreed this was the most likely scenario. Now that Hakima had all but confessed, her belief had solidified into certainty. "You have a choice, Kommandant."

"A choice..." Hakima whispered. "What choice? Climb out of this van, tell them you're saboteurs, and have them light this box up?"

"Serve Tamar," Zee said. "With you and your battalion, the Legion has the authority to unseat the baron. I'll help you round up the other people Nobu is blackmailing. One of them will confess to being blackmailed. Put that with the evidence I'm sure the Legion will find, or I will find after the fact, and we'll put him away. You'll be a hero."

"A hero?" Hakima barked. "He'll release the recording."

"So what?" Gleason asked.

Hakima glared at her. "People will see—" She stopped. "Just because something is legal doesn't make it right. Not to everyone. Not to perception. Not even to yourself, sometimes, when you look back."

"The public loves redemption stories," Gleason said, beaming. "Besides, you're going to come out of this golden, Kommandant. You're going to be the hero who rescues Pandora from a usurper."

"But Nobu—"

"What happens after, happens after, ma'am," Zee said. "What matters right now is what the governor-general would expect of us. What we should be expecting of ourselves."

Hakima took a deep breath. "How would it work?"

"First," Staff Sergeant Gleason said, "you're going to tell me where that bastard Nobu has put the people he kidnapped at Camp Clay. Then you're going to go back inside and arrange for your battalion and whatever other force you deem necessary to go and meet the Legion outside the city."

"Camp Clay..."

"The mercenary cantonment outside the city," Gleason added.

"Oh. I don't know—I can find out."

"I need access to records," Zee said, "so that when you and Major Carlyle confront the baron, I have the evidence ready." She remembered the frustration she'd felt earlier, standing in Hester Parendoupolos' newsroom, feeling helpless. Now she could see a way to stop what was happening—ever so tenuous, but so very *real*.

"Okay," Hakima said. There was still very little color in her face, but her voice gained confidence with every syllable. She looked at Guyon, who was still watching in the rearview mirror. "And you?"

Guyon shrugged. "I'm just the ride, Kommandant," she said, "but I think you're doing the right thing."

CHAPTER 15

Gleason gave Zee Khaled a quick hug. "You've got this. Stick to the plan."

Zee squeezed her back, but then frowned. "I don't like this, Mira." She glanced past Gleason to where Bill Henderson stood in his full battle rattle with the infantry from the Gray Death Legion who'd come into the city. The stealth Cavalry helicopter had already started spinning its blades.

"You'll be fine," Gleason told her.

"It's not me I'm worried about."

Gleason laughed. "I'll be fine, too. I've got your Sergeant Henderson to keep me safe." She patted Zee on the shoulder and turned away to duck low and shuffle beneath the spinning rotor blades. Zee retreated, holding a hand up to shade her face from the dust the helicopter kicked up, until it lifted up and away. She watched it until it disappeared behind a nearby building.

"Staff Sergeant."

Zee turned. Kommandant Hakima stood there, with two aides trailing at a discreet distance. She wore battledress and carried a combat vehicle crewman's helmet by the strap. She looked every inch the professional armor officer. Gone was the pale, shaken woman they'd spoken with just hours earlier.

"Ma'am," said Zee.

"Time to go, Staff Sergeant," Hakima said. "Your mercenaries have been spotted approaching the city."

Zee glanced back over her shoulder, but the helicopter was gone.

"Gonna be real fun if this doesn't work," Bel said.

Ronan rolled his eyes. He found her *Hatchetman* in his HUD, where it paced his *Marauder.* "Helpful," he told her.

"Just making conversation."

"Sure." He wiped his palms, one hand at a time, against the thighs of his combat suit. It was a useless gesture—the combat suit gloves covered his hands completely—but it made him feel marginally better. The march from Vandmaal had been quiet and quick; they'd essentially retraced the path the logistics section had taken when it had fled Camp Clay to join them. This time, however, the support elements were safely escorted by C Company.

"Anything from Gleason?" Bel asked.

"You know there's not," Ronan told her.

"Azarri and the others will be fine."

"I know they will," Ronan agreed. *They have to be*, he told himself, *or I will burn this whole city down for their pyre.* He couldn't, wouldn't, but it felt good to think it. It helped press down the gnawing agony of not knowing.

A chime on the nav screen told him they'd reached the next nav point in their sequence. The city was about twenty kilometers away, close enough that if the horizon had been flatter and less cluttered with trees, he'd have seen the buildings. He slowed the *Marauder* to a halt.

"Send the scouts out," he told Bel. "I want to know if we've got a welcoming committee. And let's get tied into the globalnet and get the news. If Gleason and Khaled succeeded, it should be quiet."

"And if they didn't?"

Ronan wrapped his hands around the *Marauder*'s gunnery controls. "Then it gets simpler."

Zee had never been in a tank before. She'd ridden APCs, but it turned out that was like comparing a shower to a rainstorm. Hakima commanded her battalion from the turret of a Manticore tank rather than a mobile headquarters vehicle. The Manticore's interior was cramped, hot, and noisy. She'd been put in the assistant driver's station, which she'd learned was kind of a backup station for everything. She was deep inside the Manticore, beneath the turret, sitting so reclined she was almost lying down, with screens above and around her and driving controls near her waist that she had been very patiently instructed never to touch.

Everything vibrated. The combat vehicle crewman's helmet she'd been given blanked out a lot of the dull noise, but she felt her bones vibrating. If she put her teeth together, they chattered uncomfortably. She didn't understand how anyone stood it. It had been barely an hour and she wanted to scream.

"Comfortable, Staff Sergeant?" Kommandant Hakima asked. Zee heard the sarcasm in her voice. If she twisted just right and looked over her head, Zee could just see the tips of Hakima's boots.

"Very, ma'am," Zee lied. "But I don't know how to read the screens." Which was true.

"We're deploying out of the city," Hakima said. "Your mercenaries are coming up from Vandmaal. I'm taking the whole Three-Seven to meet them. The other battalions will take emergency positions inside the city."

Zee had to admire those sentences; so full of fact, yet so devoid of context. "PPG?"

"We're not coordinating," was all Hakima said.

Okay. Zee looked at the tiny screens around her again, searching for meaning she could decipher or invent, but found nothing. It made her almost laugh, to be sitting—well, half-laying—here at the nerve center of the Taffy response, completely unsure what was going to happen.

She had the evidence; once inside the Taffy systems, it hadn't been that hard to find. That wasn't what she was unsure about. What concerned her was that it still required Hakima to risk exposure to the do the right thing. The thing was right, objectively right.

But we all act in our own best interests, Zee told herself.

"My lord!"

Nobu ignored the startled salute from the sentry outside the entrance to the Pandoran Planetary Guard command center beneath the Palace of the Gods. He swept through the doors almost too fast for them to open, Nessa Deschanes following close behind.

"Keeling is still not picking up," she hissed.

"Keep trying." Nobu ground his teeth, trying desperately to regain his control. Fate itself must be against him for so much to be turning against him so quickly. He burst through the final door to the central command area and stopped. "Benchley!"

"My lord?" Colonel Benchley, a slight man of advanced years who looked like he had shrunk inside his uniform every time Nobu saw him, raised himself up from where he'd been looking at something. "I wasn't expecting you!"

"What is happening?" Nobu said. He slid into the nearest seat that would let him see the main screens and the holotank. "I need an update, Colonel."

"Sir." Benchley made his way over and stopped in front of Nobu. "Indications are the mercenaries have defeated or evaded A Company. They've been spotted—corroborated reports, sir—outside the city." He stopped and swallowed. "I've got the whole Guard on alert, sir. In Colonel Jurasco's absence. He went south with the company, as you'll recall."

Nobu said nothing. His first reaction, profanity, wouldn't have been useful. He was getting himself under control. "Keep trying to reach the colonel," he said. "What is the status of the Taffy units?"

"Sir?"

"Have they deployed? What is Kommandant Hakima saying? She's not answering my calls."

Benchley looked confused. "I haven't spoken to the kommandant, my lord."

Nobu closed his eyes for a long second, then opened them and beckoned Nessa Deschanes close. She stepped in and leaned over so he could speak in her ear. "Get ahold of Hendries. I want to know the prisoners are secure."

Deschanes nodded.

"Colonel, I want you to contact Kommandant Hakima," Nobu said. "I want the PPG coordinated with any reaction the TAF deems appropriate. When our BattleMech elements return—" *Even if I have to fly to Red Devil and strangle Keeling with my own two hands.* "—we will want their support." He paused to take a breath, but Deschanes caught his eye. She held her comm near her ear, but shook her head. *"No answer,"* she mouthed.

Nobu licked his lips. He sat back in the uncomfortable chair and crossed his hands across his belly. When he spoke, it was just a single word.

"Shit."

"You can't be here," snarled one of the men on the floor with his hands held behind his head.

Sergeant Bill Henderson made sure his rifle was on safe, then slid it around on his back on its sling. He crouched low enough that his upper arm would be in the man's sightline. "See that?" he asked, slapping the Tamar emblem on his sleeve. "That means I can be anywhere I want."

"Traitor," the man muttered. "Offworld scum."

Bill climbed back to his feet. His hands brought his assault rifle back around to tactical carry. He glanced around the guardroom, making sure none of the captured PPG goons looked like they wanted to get froggy. Truth be told, he kind of wished they would. It would feel good to hit something. It had been so long since he felt like he could affect anything.

"Offworld scum with a rifle," he corrected the man. "And the legal authority to use it."

Gleason had been surprised when Hakima admitted the Legion prisoners were still at Camp Clay. It didn't surprise Henderson; nothing he'd seen of the Pandora Planetary Guard made him believe they had any great thinkers doing their planning, up to and including the baron.

The Cavalry had adopted a fake PPG transponder as it approached Camp Clay, but that hadn't been necessary. The Pandoran assault had smashed the radar station, and no mobile replacement had been set up. The Legion pilots had just flown in like they owned the place and set down on a rough-marked LZ near the main building entrance.

And the PPG captors had just come out, unarmed and smiling, to wave.

"I guess they use black helicopters, too," Gleason had said with an air of disbelief.

Disarming them had been child's play for Henderson and the Legion infantry team. He hadn't had any trouble slotting in with the Legionnaires, either. They'd all been trained in the same school. Henderson had been in a different battalion than Sergeant Major Sarris, the senior Legion non-com, but he recognized competence when he saw it.

They'd left him holding the guardroom and the guards, then went deeper into the building in search of their people. Henderson had let them; it was that or face the gnawing horror that he didn't know how his own squad in the Tamar battalions was faring. He couldn't contact them. His face was on wanted posters, along with Staff Sergeant Khaled.

The door to the interior slid open, revealing a black-armored Legion infantrywoman. She stepped into the room and to the side so a line of people in disheveled Legion battledress could shuffle furtively past and out the door. At the end of the procession came more black-clad infantry and then Staff Sergeant Gleason, who escorted a smaller man in a tightly wrapped dastār on his head. He was bruised and had a swollen lip, but still carried a defiant glint in his eye above his full beard.

"All accounted for, Staff Sergeant," Sergeant Major Sarris said.

"Bill?" Gleason looked at Henderson.

"All quiet here," Henderson said.

"Traitor," the man on the floor growled again. Henderson kicked him, half-hard, in the ribs.

"Mostly quiet," Henderson said, just before the kicked man's comm chirped for attention. He looked at Gleason and shrugged. "Okay, it was quiet until you got back in here."

Gleason smirked and, stepping past Henderson while careful not to get in line with his rifle barrel, knelt to work the man's comm out of his pocket. "Deliverance code," she said, looking at the caller. She gripped the man's face and twisted it until the comm could see it and open.

"Hendries," a woman's voice said. "Report status." Her voice was stern and cold, a tone Henderson had heard in his mother's voice when he and his brothers had misbehaved just a little too much as boys. The tone said she was right on the edge of exploding.

Hendries opened his mouth, but didn't speak as Henderson leaned down and put the barrel of his rifle against the man's cheek. Gleason grinned up at him, but pushed the barrel away. "Go ahead," she whispered to Hendries. She held the comm out to pick up his voice.

"Ma'am—" he grunted.

"I require status, Hendries," the woman said.

Hendries looked as best he could between Gleason, whom he could see, and the barrel mouth of Henderson's rifle, which he had to cross his eyes to see. Gleason nodded.

"Ma'am, we've been taken," Hendries said quickly. "Surprise attack from mercenary infantry in one of our helicopters. There was nothing we could do."

"What?"

Gleason pulled the comm back. "Who is this, please?"

"Who is this?"

"Staff Sergeant Gleason, Gray Death Legion."

"You've attacked a Pandora Planetary Guard facility," the woman said. "You will be arrested as pirates."

Gleason chuckled. "Good luck," she said, and closed the connection. She grunted as she stood out of her crouch. "Let's go."

"What about them?" Henderson asked, indicating the prisoners.

"Leave them," Gleason said from the doorway. "You can come back and arrest them later if you want. After."

"A-After what?" Hendries asked.

"After we take care of your boss," Henderson said, and followed Gleason out of the room, toward the helicopter.

Ronan stood in the chill air, smoothing the wrinkles of his combat suit, while the civilian tilt-rotor settled on its rough-terrain wheels. He felt like a weight had been lifted from his shoulders with the news from Gleason and Sarris, but the battle was far from won. This next part would be uncomfortable, but necessary. He'd never liked talking to the press, and the logo on the side of the bright-painted tilt-rotor made his hackles rise. He would get through it, though.

It was needful. And unpleasant.

The back ramp of the vehicle fell, and a gang of people clambered out. Ronan recognized two HV camera operators, a sound person, and the slight woman in semi-formal attire who must be Parendoupolos. He sniffed once, hard, pulling the cool air into his sinuses and lungs to prepare himself.

"Major Carlyle, I presume," the newswoman said when she was close enough. When he nodded, she smiled. "I am Hester Parendoupolos."

Ronan shook her hand cautiously. Her palm was small, and felt at once frail and strong. Thin-boned, but with muscles of carbon fiber. "My pleasure," he lied. He'd never missed the public affairs officers so much before in his life. They were endemic in the social-conscious LCAF, and he'd firmly quashed any mention of adding one to the Legion, but it was times like this when he reconsidered that decision.

Parendoupolos looked around past him at the Legion laager. B Company was up and on security duty, while A Company was deployed in parade order behind his *Marauder*. An infantry trooper directed the HV operators where to stand; Bel had already determined that would ensure the Legion grinning skull on the *Marauder*'s shin would be in the shot behind him. "You don't seem like fearsome killers," she observed.

"We would try to hide it if we were," Ronan said, his tone apologetically insincere.

Parendoupolos chuckled politely in that way that said *I recognize your attempt at levity, recognize that it failed, but acknowledge you made the effort nonetheless.* Behind her, one of the HV operators cleared his throat.

"Major Carlyle," Parendoupolos said, her entire demeanor shifting. "Please state your intention and the intentions of your mercenary battalion currently outside our capital city of Deliverance."

We've begun, Ronan realized. He straightened his back, forcing his face into the expression Bel had so carefully coached him on. "We are under contract to the Tamar Armed Forces," he said, clearly. "We are fulfilling that contract."

"Did your contract include assassinating your commanding officers, Leutnant-Colonel Bredell, and his staff?"

"Of course not," Ronan said. In his mind, he could see the scripted practice Bel and Tang Cai had put him through quickly hours before. He was to control his natural desire to scoff at the ridiculousness of the question. He tried very hard to do so.

"Then why does the Pandora Planetary Guard, and Baron Nobu's office, continue to claim that you did?" Parendoupolos asked the question matter-of-factly, careful to remove any trace of inflection from her voice. She could have been reading the weather report aloud. A boring weather report.

"Because the baron orchestrated the whole thing," Ronan said. He felt sweat welling at his neck, his armpits, and his forehead, but he ignored it. He knew his duty. "Because the baron is intent on removing Pandora from the Tamar Pact, and he's in league with mutinous elements of the TAF military and nefarious criminal actors here on Pandora to accomplish it. We, the Gray Death Legion, are convenient scapegoats." Ronan glanced past Parendoupolos at the cameras, conscious of the red indicator lights proving they were recording.

"A bold accusation," Parendoupolos said. "You have evidence of this?"

This was the most critical part, Bel had said. He had to answer this question perfectly. Not just the simple word, but the inflection. Certainty, without braggadocio. This would be broadcast across Pandora. It would be shown to his contract guarantor. It mattered.

"Yes," he said, with as much simplicity and certainty as he would have if asked if his father loved him.

"And can you share it with us?" Her back to the camera, Parendoupolos let the barest hint of a grin color her expression.

The timing was perfect. Just as it had been orchestrated. From behind him came the *thrum* of a helicopter. The HVs panned away to capture a stealth Cavalry helicopter headed their way, nose down, barely twenty meters above the ground.

"I'll let you speak with the prisoners we just liberated," Ronan said, raising his voice to make sure he was heard. "Prisoners taken in an illegal raid on our facility. Prisoners who were noncombatants." He made sure to look right at the HV lens for the last part: "The real evidence, though, Hester, is with the TAF armored battalions even now approaching us from Deliverance."

CHAPTER 16

PALACE OF THE GODS
DELIVERANCE
PANDORA
TAMAR PACT
7 MAY 3152

"I have Keeling," Deschanes said. She held out her comm.

Nobu took the comm and spun around in his chair. "Irwin," he hissed. "You *coward*. Give me back my BattleMechs."

"My lord baron, you lost," Keeling said. "I hope you have a plan to evade capture."

"I haven't lost anything," Nobu hissed. "With the 'Mechs, my people can crush these mercenaries. With them defeated, we can reshape the story. We always anticipated some challenge to the narrative. We're prepared for that. I can *handle* that." He lowered his voice. "But I can't deal with military defeat. I need those 'Mechs back."

"Those 'Mechs are already repainted in Red Devil colors," Keeling said. "Even if I released them, it's fifty-fifty you beat them or they beat you. Your—*my* 'Mechs—get beat up no matter who wins. Those aren't odds I care to play." He paused. "It was a good hand, Elam," he went on. "I wish it had played out." The line clicked closed.

Nobu stared at the comm for a long moment, then handed it back to Deschanes. He looked around, furtive, to see if anyone had been close enough to listen, but Benchley and the others had wisely retreated to give him space.

"My lord?" Benchley called. Nobu stood and spun to face him. "My lord, the Taffies are about to meet the mercenaries." He pointed to a colored map of the area outside Deliverance, showing a red mass of icons approaching a mass of blue ones.

"Do we have units in the area?"

Benchley spread his hands. "Kommandant Hakima is still refusing our communications."

Nobu ground his fingernails into his palms inside clenched fists. "So we have nothing?"

"Colonel Jurasco should have torn them up some, sir," Benchley said. "The Taffies can take them."

"If they even try," he heard Deschanes whisper.

She took the words out of his mouth.

Across the room, someone swore. "Are you seeing this?" someone else shouted. All around the room, people half-stood in shock, looking at their consoles. Nobu leaned enough to see one flatscreen. It showed Hester Parendoupolos talking with a tall blond man in gray battledress. A skull rode his chest pocket, with a larger example on the 'Mech behind him.

Nobu swallowed, then nodded at Deschanes to follow him out of the room.

"Step up here, Staff Sergeant," Kommandant Hakima said.

Zee looked up from where she was standing atop the Manticore's forward hull to where Hakima stood atop its turret, then took the proffered hand and climbed up. "You can just see them," Hakima said, pointing.

Zee turned and looked. The rolling fields in front of them gave way to forest about a kilometer away, a solid wall of trees cut only by the slice where the highway ran down toward Vandmaal. It took her a moment to locate the clutch of trees swaying against the breeze. Soon she was seeing flashes of angularity among the branches.

The Legion was coming.

Not that it was a surprise. At least a dozen helicopters, civilian and military, were up in the area. Zee had finally deciphered the screens around her seat enough to know this close to the city a network of military sensors tracked the Legion's every move.

"It'll be a shooting gallery," Hakima muttered. "Them coming out of the trees all piecemeal, with my tracks and guns lined up to meet them. The kind of engagement armor officers dream about every time they have to listen to some MechWarrior asshole talk about how high and mighty their 'Mechs are."

"But that's not what's going to happen," Zee said slowly, watching Hakima's face. The older, paler woman didn't look away for a minute, until she sighed and met Zee's gaze.

"But that's not what's going to happen," Hakima agreed. "Today, I'm going to do what I can to salvage my honor, and pray the governor-general is merciful."

Zee felt an involuntary stab of empathy for the woman. Hakima had faced and made incredible choices in the last few weeks. Some she regretted. Some she had to know she'd have cause to regret in the coming months. But Hakima looked at peace.

The empathy lasted a moment, and no longer. Hakima may not have had Bredell and the others' blood directly on her hands, but she was hardly untarnished.

"Radio," Hakima barked. One of her crew handed up a wireless headset.

"*Achtung*, all Tamar Armed Forces units within the sound of my voice," Hakima said. "I am declaring the Pandoran Planetary Guard an illegal armed force. They are to be disarmed, by force if necessary, until a full investigation can be completed into the allegations against the baron and the PPG in relation to the leutnant-colonel's death."

Around her, the heavy armored tracks of her battalion growled to life like angry junkyard dogs. On the flanks, tracks spun as the battalion split in half to open a gap in its ranks and reorient facing back toward the city.

"Major Carlyle," Hakima went on. She made a motion by her knee, and another headset came up. She handed it to Zee. "Come in, please."

"Carlyle," came the scratchy voice in Zee's headset. "Copy."

"Major, as the ranking TAF officer on-planet, I am activating the emergency codicils of your contract and placing your battalion under my command. You are to move with us to Deliverance to disarm the PPG and arrest the baron. You will provide such support as I direct. Is that understood?"

Zee looked up at the flock of helicopters, finding the white tilt-rotor bearing the insignia of Hester Parendoupolos' network. She knew there'd be an open radio connection there, an HV pointed out a window, if there wasn't one built into the tilt-rotor itself.

"Ma'am, the Legion always honors its contracts," Major Carlyle said. "We will join you shortly."

Hakima nodded, even though Carlyle couldn't see her, and peeled the headset off her head. A few stray hairs got caught in the headset, making her wince as she pulled them free. Zee removed hers as well.

"Let's get this done," Hakima said. She beckoned to the small hatch in the Manticore's forward hull Zee had climbed out of.

"You're doing the right thing," Zee said. She didn't step down. "I'm glad you are."

"I hope I will be tomorrow," Hakima said.

"He's gone," Bel said.

She stood outside her *Hatchetman*, in the courtyard of the Palace of the Gods, wearing battle rattle and carrying a submachine gun. She had always been too close with the infantry for Ronan's taste.

In his *Marauder*'s cockpit, he frowned. "Any idea where?"

"Would I be standing here if I knew?"

Ronan rolled his eyes and toggled a different frequency. "Tang?"

"Sir, we have the PPG HQ," Captain Cai reported. "My battlesuits got right in. The doors were open, and most of the Guards inside surrendered fast enough. A few holdouts, but nothing serious."

"Good work," Ronan said. He toggled. "Curtain?"

"Major," the boisterous big man said, "The main assembly area is deserted. It looks like the pigs who did not surrender have fled. I do not have an inventory yet, but the TAF sergeant here thinks she can get one for us. We can run them down soon enough."

"Good work," he repeated. "Stand by there."

"Roger."

Ronan toggled the channel closed and looked through the *Marauder*'s HUD, taking in the grandeur of the palace. Things didn't feel entirely real at the moment. Three days ago, he'd been a different person, he felt. So much had happened since then. And now he was standing here.

His comm chirped. "Any word, Major?" Kommandant Hakima asked.

"No sign of the baron, ma'am," he said. He gave her the brief version of what had been reported. "The deserters will have been seen leaving the city," he added. "We learned that doing counter-insurgency on Crimond. Someone always sees the tanks."

"I'm not worried." She paused. "I just had the oddest conversation."

"Ma'am?"

"The CEO of Red Devil Industries, Irwin Keeling, just called me. He offered the full facilities of the factory in 'our time of national need.'" There was a pause. "Do we need him?"

"Not right now," Ronan said, slowly. His mind was replaying some of the things the PPG colonel, Jurasco, had let slip since he'd been taken prisoner. Keeling was by no stretch of the imagination a saint.

"I thought not," Hakima said. "Staff Sergeant Khaled had some rather interesting things to say about Keeling."

"Ah," Ronan said. "I understand, ma'am. I think I've heard similar stories from some of my prisoners."

"Another day," Hakima said, tacitly ending the topic of conversation. "Today our priority is Nobu."

"Someone will know where he's gone," Ronan said. "We just have to find the right person to ask."

"I was going to ask Khaled," Hakima said. "But she's gone. Is she with you?"

Ronan frowned. "No, she's not."

Nobu tapped his fingers impatiently on the door handle as Deschanes brought the car to a coasting stop. The sun was already setting, casting deep shadows between the small craft hangars at the Deliverance spaceport, and the port lights were just spooling up to full brilliance. It was the perfect time to disappear.

"I never liked this part of the planning," he said.

"You'll be glad I insisted," Deschanes said. She opened her door and climbed out. Instead of opening his door, as Nobu had expected, she went immediately to the personnel door of the hangar and tapped in an access code. Nobu tugged the door open and climbed out himself. Deschanes disappeared into the dark interior.

Nobu stopped at the doorway, taking a last look at the evening sky. He'd never looked up at the stars and seen limits, but now he did. It was not a heartening experience. He sighed and turned away.

"Nessa," he said, as he stepped inside, but stopped as he nearly collided with her. Behind him, the door slid shut with a heavy metallic *thud*. "What are you doing?"

"Welcome, my lord baron," a woman's voice said from deeper inside the hangar. "You piece of shit." The lights came on.

"Temper, Staff Sergeant," Bill Henderson said. The barrel of his rifle never wavered from where it pointed at the assistant's forehead.

"Tsk," Zee said. "Guilty." She breathed in, and then out. "Where were you going?" she asked the assistant.

The assistant said nothing. She just held very still, glaring murder at Henderson. Behind her, the baron blinked and gobbled, clearly confused.

"Your escape plan wasn't hard to find, Baron," Zee added.

"Let us go," Nobu said, finding his voice. By the last syllable he had regained the haughtiness Zee had heard in every address of his she'd ever listened to.

"I think not," Zee told him. "You're under arrest."

Nobu scoffed. "You can't arrest me."

"Seems like we can do whatever we want," Henderson said. "Since we have the guns." Zee watched carefully, saw the twitch of Nobu's eyes toward the woman with him.

"I figured," Zee said. *She's the muscle.* "Lieutenant?"

"I've always wanted to do this," Port Lieutenant Guyon said from two meters or so to the baron's left. He flinched, not having seen her. The assistant's eyes flicked to the side, then back at Henderson. Her hands, raised beside her head, flexed toward fists. Guyon raised a dart gun and fired.

A dart gun was a simple weapon, what an earlier time would have called a taser. It fired a small metallic dart that trailed a wire; once it struck its target, the gun fed voltage into that target. The assistant jerked from the prick, then gasped and collapsed as the dart gun buzzed like an angry wasp. Nobu yelped and leaped back against the closed door.

Zee stepped close enough to check the assistant's pocket and sleeves; she pulled out two small lasers and a wicked-looking, needle-shaped knife and tossed them aside.

"Now do him," Henderson said.

Nobu, who had been watching Zee from behind wide eyes, flinched.

Guyon stepped around to stand near Zee. "I called your friends, like you asked," she said to Zee, "as soon as the door closed behind them." She jerked her chin deeper into the bay, toward where the intrasystem shuttle was parked. "I also pulled that thing's registered flight plan. Two days from now it's scheduled to visit a mining post on Hope's backside."

"The moon," Zee murmured. "I guess that's a good place to hide out until you could get a ride to the jump point."

"I am a noble of the Pact," Nobu said. "You may not arrest me. You don't have the authority."

"I have a gun," Henderson put in. "And you killed a lot of my friends."

"I—" Nobu said but stopped when Henderson tapped the rifle's receiver with a callused thumb.

"Some of us take our oaths seriously," Zee said, looking at Nobu. "I swore an oath to the Pact and the governor-general, same as you. You don't get to turn your back on that."

"The governor-general," Nobu sneered. "She turned her own coat to make this bandit kingdom," he said. "You don't think she's just doing what I was? Getting as much as she can, while she can? Look around you, soldier. We're surrounded by Clans and the Commonwealth. You think either of them are going to let some pissant little polity exist for too long?"

Zee regarded him, then held out her hand to Guyon. The port lieutenant slapped the dart gun into her palm. Zee took it, checked the charge, and leveled it at the baron.

"Wait—" he said. Zee fired. The baron whimpered and collapsed. His legs spasmed twice, and wetness appeared at his crotch as his bladder let go. That happened sometimes.

"I made my decision on Arcturus," Zee told his unconscious body. "I'm not going back on that."

EPILOGUE

DELIVERANCE SPACEPORT
PANDORA
TAMAR PACT
22 MAY 3152

"The council 'declines' to arraign Keeling," Bel said, stepping into the hangar. "Can you believe it?"

Ronan looked up from the map table. "Yes," he said. He'd learned a lot about Irwin Keeling in the last few weeks, especially about his supposed ties to the Malthus crime syndicate. His father, Gardner Carlyle, had waged a lifelong war against the Odessan branch of the Malthuses for as long as Ronan could remember, and each of those snakes was too oily for prosecution to stick. Even with what the magistrates were getting out of Benchley and Jurasco and the others, a lot of people on Zee Khaled's list were going to escape serious prosecution. Nobu's plan had been good enough for that.

"What are you looking at?" Bel asked, stepping closer.

"Tang is out chasing down that armor platoon of the PPG that's been giving us so much trouble," Ronan said. "I'm trying to decide if I need to send you and your company out to give him a hand."

"For one short platoon of medium tanks? I think he'd be offended."

"He might," Ronan allowed, "but I want to be done with all this." He straightened up and crossed his arms, looking past

Bel at the *Marauder* hulking in the background. "It's not what I thought," he said, more softly.

"What's not?"

"This," Ronan said, gesturing around the hangar. "The Legion. Being a mercenary."

"What'd you think it would be like?" Bel raised an eyebrow at him. "I never guessed you'd ever thought about it once."

"We both grew up with that," he said, waving at the *Marauder*. "You can't not think about it." He met her eyes, then shrugged. "You feel it just like I did. The romance—the mercenaries, beholden to no one, out in the Inner Sphere fighting the good fights that need fighting, standing up for the innocent and weak, doing what regular army units can't."

"Steal from the rich, give to the poor," Bel quipped.

"Get the girl," Ronan said.

"Boy," Bel corrected him.

"Whatever. But it's not any of that." He gestured down at the map table. "It's supply requisitions and accounting and personality issues like why Private Gomez can't stand to be in the same room as Corporal Bennett. It's wondering if I sent good people, people I'm responsible for, out to get hurt or killed fighting ridiculous century-old Vedette tanks, for all the dark gods' sakes."

"That was the job in the LCAF, too," Bel said softly.

"In the LCAF it was orders," Ronan said. "But not like this." He rubbed his close-shaven head. "I brought us here, Bel. To this planet, two months from the nearest JumpShip that could take us away. If this had gone the other way, our bones would've been cold in the ground before Mom and Dad could've even gotten rumors."

"But it didn't."

"But it could have."

"Oh, come on," Bel snapped. "Get over yourself. You could slip and break your neck in the shower tomorrow, too. A light could fall from the ceiling right now and kill you. All kinds of things *can* happen, and don't." She slapped his upper arm. "You could make the wrong decision and get us all killed. You could. But you *won't*. Or if you do, it'll be because there is no right decision, and we're all going to die anyway. We're soldiers. That's part of the deal."

"Easy for you to say," Ronan said. "You're not sitting in *that* every day, with his ghost looking over your shoulder."

Bel turned to look at the *Marauder* with him. "No, I'm not," she said. Then she turned her back on it and smiled an imp's grin. "But I never wanted to. Not that machine. Anyway, guess what I really came to tell you."

"What?"

"I just came from Buthra and his people."

"He's feeling okay?"

"Of course he is," Bel said. "You know him. Work is his best therapy. And he's been busy."

"Okay..."

"You remember the 'Mechs we took from the PPG at Vandmaal, right?"

"Of course," Ronan said. He'd had to stand his ground twice with Kommandant Hakima over those machines. They were legitimate salvage, spoils of war. There was no way he was giving those up. They were enough machines to bring the Legion almost to a full BattleMech battalion if he could find pilots for them.

"One of 'em was a *Shadow Hawk*," Bel said with a face-busting grin.

"Oh no..." Ronan said.

"Buthra got it working and refit. He's already painted *Boss Lady II* alongside the canopy." She sounded like a six-year-old on Christmas morning.

"Just like great grandma's 'Mech," Ronan moaned. "Bel—"

"Don't even say it," she snapped. "I'm keeping it. It's the same model as the one I had to give up on Arcturus. It's the machine I trained on, more or less. It's the right 'Mech for me."

"Fine," Ronan said, spreading his hands. "Fine." He looked up at the *Marauder* again. "I guess you have plenty of time to get used to it," he muttered. "We're here for six more months at least."

"And then what?"

"I don't know," Ronan admitted.

"The Taffies will offer us a new contract," Bel said with conviction. "They have to."

"They will," Ronan agreed. "But I don't know if I want to sign it."

"Why not?" She crossed her arms. "These are our people."

"Great grandpa used to talk about being the light against the darkness," Ronan said, looking again at the *Marauder*. "There's plenty of darkness here. Plenty of darkness everywhere. I guess we have to look for the place where we can shine the brightest."

"That's here," Bel said. "Anywhere else, we're small fish in a big pond. Here, we're one of the largest units under contract."

"Maybe," Ronan said. "We'll see."

"We'll see if Tang ever gets his job done," Bel said, pulling him back around to the map table. "Show me where he is. I've got a new 'Mech to break in."

"Is it even loaded?"

"Don't ask silly questions," Bel said, leaning over the table.

Ronan bent as well, twisting to look at the *Marauder* one last time. Then he pointed at a space on the map, showing his sister where her next chance to make a difference might be.

Behind them both, Grayson Death Carlyle's *Marauder* stood sentinel, looming beneath the bright lights with the darkness pooling behind it.

ARCHER
HEAVY—70 TONS

BATTLEMASTER
ASSAULT—85 TONS

BUSHWACKER
MEDIUM—55 TONS

GARGOYLE (MAN O' WAR)
ASSAULT—80 TONS

GRIFFIN
MEDIUM—55 TONS

ACS

LINEHOLDER
MEDIUM—55 TONS

MARAUDER
HEAVY—75 TONS

ONAGER
ASSAULT—90 TONS

SCARABUS
LIGHT—30 TONS

TALON
LIGHT—35 TONS

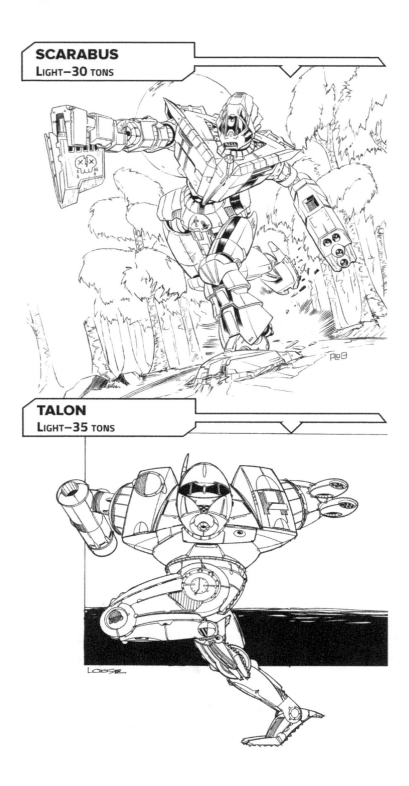

BATTLETECH GLOSSARY

AUTOCANNON
A rapid-fire, auto-loading weapon. Light autocannons range from 30 to 90 millimeter (mm), and heavy autocannons may be from 80 to 120mm or more. They fire high-speed streams of high-explosive, armor-piercing shells.

BATTLEMECH
BattleMechs are the most powerful war machines ever built. First developed by Terran scientists and engineers, these huge vehicles are faster, more mobile, better-armored and more heavily armed than any twentieth-century tank. Ten to twelve meters tall and equipped with particle projection cannons, lasers, rapid-fire autocannon and missiles, they pack enough firepower to flatten anything but another BattleMech. A small fusion reactor provides virtually unlimited power, and BattleMechs can be adapted to fight in environments ranging from sun-baked deserts to subzero arctic icefields.

DROPSHIPS
Because interstellar JumpShips must avoid entering the heart of a solar system, they must "dock" in space at a considerable distance from a system's inhabited worlds. DropShips were developed for interplanetary travel. As the name implies, a DropShip is attached to hardpoints on the JumpShip's drive core, later to be dropped from the parent vessel after in-system entry. Though incapable of FTL travel, DropShips are highly maneuverable, well-armed and sufficiently aerodynamic to take off from and land on a planetary surface. The journey from the jump point to the inhabited worlds of a system usually requires a normal-space journey of several days or weeks, depending on the type of star.

FLAMER
Flamethrowers are a small but time-honored anti-infantry weapon in vehicular arsenals. Whether fusion-based or fuel-based, flamers

spew fire in a tight beam that "splashes" against a target, igniting almost anything it touches.

GAUSS RIFLE

This weapon uses magnetic coils to accelerate a solid nickel-ferrous slug about the size of a football at an enemy target, inflicting massive damage through sheer kinetic impact at long range and with little heat. However, the accelerator coils and the slug's supersonic speed mean that while the Gauss rifle is smokeless and lacks the flash of an autocannon, it has a much more potent report that can shatter glass.

INDUSTRIALMECH

Also known as WorkMechs or UtilityMechs, they are large, bipedal or quadrupedal machines used for industrial purposes (hence the name). They are similar in shape to BattleMechs, which they predate, and feature many of the same technologies, but are built for non-combat tasks such as construction, farming, and policing.

JUMPSHIPS

Interstellar travel is accomplished via JumpShips, first developed in the twenty-second century. These somewhat ungainly vessels consist of a long, thin drive core and a sail resembling an enormous parasol, which can extend up to a kilometer in width. The ship is named for its ability to "jump" instantaneously across vast distances of space. After making its jump, the ship cannot travel until it has recharged by gathering up more solar energy.

The JumpShip's enormous sail is constructed from a special metal that absorbs vast quantities of electromagnetic energy from the nearest star. When it has soaked up enough energy, the sail transfers it to the drive core, which converts it into a space-twisting field. An instant later, the ship arrives at the next jump point, a distance of up to thirty light-years. This field is known as hyperspace, and its discovery opened to mankind the gateway to the stars.

JumpShips never land on planets. Interplanetary travel is carried out by DropShips, vessels that are attached to the JumpShip until arrival at the jump point.

LASER

An acronym for "Light Amplification through Stimulated Emission of Radiation." When used as a weapon, the laser damages the target by concentrating extreme heat onto a small area. BattleMech lasers are designated as small, medium or large. Lasers are also available as shoulder-fired weapons operating from a portable backpack power unit. Certain range-finders and targeting equipment also employ low-level lasers.

LRM

Abbreviation for "Long-Range Missile," an indirect-fire missile with a high-explosive warhead.

MACHINE GUN

A small autocannon intended for anti-personnel assaults. Typically non-armor-penetrating, machine guns are often best used against infantry, as they can spray a large area with relatively inexpensive fire.

PARTICLE PROJECTION CANNON (PPC)

One of the most powerful and long-range energy weapons on the battlefield, a PPC fires a stream of charged particles that outwardly functions as a bright blue laser, but also throws off enough static discharge to resemble a bolt of manmade lightning. The kinetic and heat impact of a PPC is enough to cause the vaporization of armor and structure alike, and most PPCs have the power to kill a pilot in his machine through an armor-penetrating headshot.

SRM

The abbreviation for "Short-Range Missile," a direct-trajectory missile with high-explosive or armor-piercing explosive warheads. They have a range of less than one kilometer and are only reliably accurate at ranges of less than 300 meters. They are more powerful, however, than LRMs.

SUCCESSOR LORDS

After the fall of the first Star League, the remaining members of the High Council each asserted his or her right to become First Lord. Their star empires became known as the Successor States and the rulers as Successor Lords. The Clan Invasion temporarily interrupted centuries of warfare known as the Succession Wars, which first began in 2786.

BATTLETECH ERAS

The *BattleTech* universe is a living, vibrant entity that grows each year as more sourcebooks and fiction are published. A dynamic universe, its setting and characters evolve over time within a highly detailed continuity framework, bringing everything to life in a way a static game universe cannot match.

To help quickly and easily convey the timeline of the universe—and to allow a player to easily "plug in" a given novel or sourcebook—we've divided *BattleTech* into eight major eras.

STAR LEAGUE
(Present–2780)
Ian Cameron, ruler of the Terran Hegemony, concludes decades of tireless effort with the creation of the Star League, a political and military alliance between all Great Houses and the Hegemony. Star League armed forces immediately launch the Reunification War, forcing the Periphery realms to join. For the next two centuries, humanity experiences a golden age across the thousand light-years of human-occupied space known as the Inner Sphere. It also sees the creation of the most powerful military in human history.

(This era also covers the centuries before the founding of the Star League in 2571, most notably the Age of War.)

SUCCESSION WARS
(2781–3049)
Every last member of First Lord Richard Cameron's family is killed during a coup launched by Stefan Amaris. Following the thirteen-year war to unseat him, the rulers of each of the five Great Houses disband the Star League. General Aleksandr Kerensky departs with eighty percent of the Star League Defense Force beyond known space and the Inner Sphere collapses into centuries of warfare known as the Succession Wars that will eventually result in a massive loss of technology across most worlds.

CLAN INVASION
(3050–3061)
A mysterious invading force strikes the coreward region of the Inner Sphere. The invaders, called the Clans, are descendants of Kerensky's SLDF troops, forged into a society dedicated to becoming the greatest fighting force in history. With vastly superior technology and warriors, the Clans conquer world after world. Eventually this outside threat will forge a new Star League, something hundreds of years of warfare failed to accomplish. In addition, the Clans will act as a catalyst for a technological renaissance.

CIVIL WAR
(3062–3067)
The Clan threat is eventually lessened with the complete destruction of a Clan. With that massive external threat apparently

neutralized, internal conflicts explode around the Inner Sphere. House Liao conquers its former Commonality, the St. Ives Compact; a rebellion of military units belonging to House Kurita sparks a war with their powerful border enemy, Clan Ghost Bear; the fabulously powerful Federated Commonwealth of House Steiner and House Davion collapses into five long years of bitter civil war.

JIHAD
(3067–3080)

Following the Federated Commonwealth Civil War, the leaders of the Great Houses meet and disband the new Star League, declaring it a sham. The pseudo-religious Word of Blake—a splinter group of ComStar, the protectors and controllers of interstellar communication—launch the Jihad: an interstellar war that pits every faction against each other and even against themselves, as weapons of mass destruction are used for the first time in centuries while new and frightening technologies are also unleashed.

DARK AGE
(3081–3150)

Under the guidance of Devlin Stone, the Republic of the Sphere is born at the heart of the Inner Sphere following the Jihad. One of the more extensive periods of peace begins to break out as the 32nd century dawns. The factions, to one degree or another, embrace disarmament, and the massive armies of the Succession Wars begin to fade. However, in 3132 eighty percent of interstellar communications collapses, throwing the universe into chaos. Wars erupt almost immediately, and the factions begin rebuilding their armies.

ILCLAN
(3151–present)

The once-invulnerable Republic of the Sphere lies in ruins, torn apart by the Great Houses and the Clans as they wage war against each other on a scale not seen in nearly a century. Mercenaries flourish once more, selling their might to the highest bidder. As Fortress Republic collapses, the Clans race toward Terra to claim their long-denied birthright and create a supreme authority that will fulfill the dream of Aleksandr Kerensky and rule the Inner Sphere by any means necessary: The ilClan.

CLAN HOMEWORLDS
(2786–present)

In 2784, General Aleksandr Kerensky launched Operation Exodus, and led most of the Star League Defense Force out of the Inner Sphere in a search for a new world, far away from the strife of the Great Houses. After more than two years and thousands of light years, they arrived at the Pentagon Worlds. Over the next two-and-a-half centuries, internal dissent and civil war led to the creation of a brutal new society—the Clans. And in 3049, they returned to the Inner Sphere with one goal—the complete conquest of the Great Houses.

LOOKING FOR MORE HARD HITTING BATTLETECH FICTION?

WE'LL GET YOU RIGHT BACK INTO THE BATTLE!

Catalyst Game Labs brings you the very best in *BattleTech* fiction, available at most ebook retailers, including Amazon, Apple Books, Kobo, Barnes & Noble, and more!

NOVELS

1. *Decision at Thunder Rift* by William H. Keith Jr.
2. *Mercenary's Star* by William H. Keith Jr.
3. *The Price of Glory* by William H. Keith, Jr.
4. *Warrior: En Garde* by Michael A. Stackpole
5. *Warrior: Riposte* by Michael A. Stackpole
6. *Warrior: Coupé* by Michael A. Stackpole
7. Wolves on the Border by Robert N. Charrette
8. *Heir to the Dragon* by Robert N. Charrette
9. *Lethal Heritage* (The Blood of Kerensky, Volume 1) by Michael A. Stackpole
10. *Blood Legacy* (The Blood of Kerensky, Volume 2) by Michael A. Stackpole
11. *Lost Destiny* (The Blood of Kerensky, Volume 3) by Michael A. Stackpole
12. *Way of the Clans* (Legend of the Jade Phoenix, Volume 1) by Robert Thurston
13. *Bloodname* (Legend of the Jade Phoenix, Volume 2) by Robert Thurston
14. *Falcon Guard* (Legend of the Jade Phoenix, Volume 3) by Robert Thurston
15. *Wolf Pack* by Robert N. Charrette
16. *Main Event* by James D. Long
17. *Natural Selection* by Michael A. Stackpole
18. *Assumption of Risk* by Michael A. Stackpole
19. *Blood of Heroes* by Andrew Keith
20. *Close Quarters* by Victor Milán
21. *Far Country* by Peter L. Rice
22. *D.R.T.* by James D. Long
23. *Tactics of Duty* by William H. Keith
24. *Bred for War* by Michael A. Stackpole
25. *I Am Jade Falcon* by Robert Thurston
26. *Highlander Gambit* by Blaine Lee Pardoe
27. *Hearts of Chaos* by Victor Milán
28. *Operation Excalibur* by William H. Keith
29. *Malicious Intent* by Michael A. Stackpole
30. *Black Dragon* by Victor Milán
31. *Impetus of War* by Blaine Lee Pardoe
32. *Double-Blind* by Loren L. Coleman
33. *Binding Force* by Loren L. Coleman
34. *Exodus Road* (Twilight of the Clans, Volume 1) by Blaine Lee Pardoe
35. *Grave Covenant* ((Twilight of the Clans, Volume 2) by Michael A. Stackpole

3. *Ghost Hour (Rogue Academy, Book 2)* by Jennifer Brozek
4. *Crimson Night (Rogue Academy, Book 3)* by Jennifer Brozek

OMNIBUSES

1. *The Gray Death Legion Trilogy* by William H. Keith, Jr.
2. *The Blood of Kerensky Trilogy* by Michael A. Stackpole
3. *The Legend of the Jade Phoenix Trilogy* by Robert Thurston

NOVELLAS/SHORT STORIES

1. *Lion's Roar* by Steven Mohan, Jr.
2. *Sniper* by Jason Schmetzer
3. *Eclipse* by Jason Schmetzer
4. *Hector* by Jason Schmetzer
5. *The Frost Advances (Operation Ice Storm, Part 1)* by Jason Schmetzer
6. *The Winds of Spring (Operation Ice Storm, Part 2)* by Jason Schmetzer
7. *Instrument of Destruction (Ghost Bear's Lament, Part 1)*
   by Steven Mohan, Jr.
8. *The Fading Call of Glory (Ghost Bear's Lament, Part 2)* by Steven Mohan, Jr.
9. *Vengeance* by Jason Schmetzer
10. *A Splinter of Hope* by Philip A. Lee
11. *The Anvil* by Blaine Lee Pardoe
12. *A Splinter of Hope/The Anvil* (omnibus)
13. *Not the Way the Smart Money Bets (Kell Hounds Ascendant #1)*
    by Michael A. Stackpole
14. *A Tiny Spot of Rebellion (Kell Hounds Ascendant #2)*
    by Michael A. Stackpole
15. *A Clever Bit of Fiction (Kell Hounds Ascendant #3)* by Michael A. Stackpole
16. *Break-Away (Proliferation Cycle #1)* by Ilsa J. Bick
17. *Prometheus Unbound (Proliferation Cycle #2)* by Herbert A. Beas II
18. *Nothing Ventured (Proliferation Cycle #3)* by Christoffer Trossen
19. *Fall Down Seven Times, Get Up Eight (Proliferation Cycle #4)* by Randall N. Bills
20. *A Dish Served Cold (Proliferation Cycle #5)*
    by Chris Hartford and Jason M. Hardy
21. *The Spider Dances (Proliferation Cycle #6)* by Jason Schmetzer
22. *Shell Games* by Jason Schmetzer
23. *Divided We Fall* by Blaine Lee Pardoe
24. *The Hunt for Jardine (Forgotten Worlds, Part One)* by Herbert A. Beas II
25. *Rock of the Republic* by Blaine Lee Pardoe
26. *Finding Jardine (Forgotten Worlds, Part Two)* by Herbert A. Beas II
27. *The Trickster (Proliferation Cycle #7)* by Blaine Lee Pardoe
28. *The Price of Duty* by Jason Schmetzer
29. *Elements of Treason: Duty* by Craig A. Reed, Jr.
30. *Mercenary's Honor* by Jason Schmetzer
31. *Elements of Treason: Opportunity* by Craig A. Reed, Jr.
32. *Lethal Lessons* by Daniel Isberner

ANTHOLOGIES

1. *The Corps (BattleCorps Anthology, Volume 1)* edited by Loren. L. Coleman
2. *First Strike (BattleCorps Anthology, Volume 2)* edited by Loren L. Coleman
3. *Weapons Free (BattleCorps Anthology, Volume 3)* edited by Jason Schmetzer
4. *Onslaught: Tales from the Clan Invasion* edited by Jason Schmetzer
5. *Edge of the Storm* by Jason Schmetzer
6. *Fire for Effect (BattleCorps Anthology, Volume 4)* edited by Jason Schmetzer
7. *Chaos Born (Chaos Irregulars, Book 1)* by Kevin Killiany
8. *Chaos Formed (Chaos Irregulars, Book 2)* by Kevin Killiany
9. *Counterattack (BattleCorps Anthology, Volume 5)* edited by Jason Schmetzer
10. *Front Lines (BattleCorps Anthology Volume 6)*
    edited by Jason Schmetzer and Philip A. Lee
11. *Legacy* edited by John Helfers and Philip A. Lee
12. *Kill Zone (BattleCorps Anthology Volume 7)* edited by Philip A. Lee
13. *Gray Markets (A BattleCorps Anthology)*,
    edited by Jason Schmetzer and Philip A. Lee
14. *Slack Tide (A BattleCorps Anthology)*,
    edited by Jason Schmetzer and Philip A. Lee
15. *The Battle of Tukayyid* edited by John Helfers
16. *The Mercenary Life* by Randall N. Bills
17. *The Proliferation Cycle* edited by John Helfers and Philip A. Lee
18. *No Greater Honor (The Complete Eridani Light Horse Chronicles)*
    edited by John Helfers and Philip A. Lee
19. *Marauder* by Lance Scarinci
20. *Fox Tales* by Bryan Young

MAGAZINES

1. *Shrapnel Issues #01–#15*

Made in the USA
Monee, IL
13 November 2024

69972654R00193